The Hook

Surfing to survive a shattered family, drugs, gangs
and the FBI

Kathleen Doler

Published by BookLocker.com, Inc., St. Petersburg, Florida.

Printed on acid-free paper.

The characters and events in this book are fictitious. Any similarity to real persons, living or dead, is coincidental and not intended by the author.

BookLocker.com, Inc.
2017

First Edition

To Brian,

husband, cheerleader and cattle prod.

I love you.

Chapter 1

I plunge headfirst into the roiling darkness. The wave's lip punches me down, and its roar fills my head. My eardrums pop. I rise up and then I'm spun, rotated horizontally. Or for all I know, I'm head down, twirling like a top. The sharp tug of the board's leash stretches my leg and hip. My throat and chest tighten; I need air. I force myself to resist thrashing... even though I feel it lurking, always at the edge of my thoughts in every hold-down, the terror of being buried alive. The wave has me in its maw. I remind myself: Don't fight, just fight the urge to struggle too hard.

I wait for the wave to expend its energy and release me.

*

Ten seconds, twenty five. The urge to breathe is all-consuming; every cell in my body screams for oxygen. I open my eyes to distract my brain. My eyes sting, but still I can see the blurry dark-green water and foamy milk rush around me. The leash is taut, but it's stopped dragging me. I pull wide with my hands and arms and instinctively right myself, head up, kicking and crawling toward the lighter green, toward the promise of air. Breaking the surface, I gasp, my mouth wide open, and gulp a breath. And then the coughing of a hold-down wracks me. Water rammed up my nose when the wave's lip took me down. My sinuses burn and drain down my face.

I've surfaced in a lull between sets and my leash didn't snap. My board floats behind me. I finally stop sputtering and wriggle aboard, then paddle to the edge of the impact zone, to safety.

I float there, panting. My body rocks in the passing swells. I swipe the back of my hand across my still dripping nose and mash my hands into the neoprene of my wetsuit, under my arms, trying to warm them.

I replay the drilling in my mind...riding out, speeding well ahead of the pitching curl. But the wave didn't peel off; instead it broke in one big section and drilled me from behind. I shrug. Life — just when you think you've made a clean getaway you get caught, caught from behind.

*

At the car, I fumble and twist, pulling cotton over clammy skin; my fingers are frozen claws. My keychain hits the floor when I drop it trying to shove the key into the ignition. On the second try, I get the key in the slot and then use both palms wedged together to turn it. I crank the heater; it rattles as it blasts, slowly warming air at my feet and hands.

From the parking lot, I watch one more set of waves rise outside the lineup and then roll through. My hair soaks the back of my hoodie. I huddle down in the Honda's torn bucket seat, a melting popsicle. I can't put it off any longer; I need to see Joe and find out what he knows about Shane.

Dammit, Shane. We used to surf, the two of us together. We'd escape, blanking our minds, and later our memories.

*

On the drive, I note the changes to Half Moon Bay, more chain restaurants, more traffic. I miss how it used to be, a community of ruddy complexions and calloused hands, fishing and farming. Now it's an outlying burb for Silicon Valley engineers, with their computers and their pallor, too many hours lit only by screens of code. Even the surf has gained some respect and notoriety. Local surf dogs discovered a break called "Mavericks" years ago. Two miles out from Pillar Point, it only breaks when giant winter swells roll across the Pacific and hit its treacherous underwater rock reef. Now, every winter it's the site of an invitational big-wave contest. Pro surfer Mark Foo died at Mavericks in 1994, which just increased its status and media coverage. And the annual contest has brought more tourists and transplants to town.

Yuppie rebuilds notwithstanding, the blocks closest to our family home are still more Pabst Blue Ribbon than Anchor Steam. The house's beige stucco is stained worse than ever, from years of fog and field dirt blowing down the coastline.

I pull into the driveway, behind Joe's primer gray pick-up, but before I unfold out of the car, I hesitate. It's been three years. Entering this house never gets easier, and talking to Joe is always stilted and awkward. I've brought him a carton of Marlboros, so that ought to get him to acknowledge me, though that might depend on which sport he's watching on TV.

I stumble up the uneven brick walkway and jab the doorbell. The musical "ding-dong" is answered by a cacophony of barking. Behind the door, Lady's and Sampson's toenails tap down the hall. Farther back in the house, I hear a gruff "Shush! Shuuuush!"

My father is shoved aside, as the dogs bounce out and circle my legs.

I step forward and he pulls me in close. He squeezes me to his barrel chest; his day-old beard scratches across my forehead. At nearly seventy, he's still solid; he has the inner strength of the athlete he once was, plus the brawn of thirty-five-years working as a welder and marine mechanic. He

7

smells of smokes and spearmint gum. I hand him the Marlboros.

"How was the drive?" He sticks the smokes under his arm.

"Not bad. I made tracks and did it in six and a half hours."

"Did you check the oil and water before you left?"

"Yeah Dad." I dig my fingernails into my palms. I'm thirty-five years old and a world traveler, not a hapless teenager.

We walk down the dark hall to the living room; my nose is assaulted with cigarette smoke and damp dog fur. HBO is broadcasting a fight — looks like bantam weight division. I know my boxing; I spent my whole childhood watching sports with my Dad, "quality time" with him. Not much communication, but I can talk sports with the boys in the newsroom.

Nothing's changed here. It's the same early seventies décor, high-low, brown-and-beige carpet, light-sucking chocolate brown sofas, mustard appliances. Why update it; it's just the dogs and Dad, traveling between the master bedroom and the recliner in front of the TV.

He drops into his chair, and the dogs sit expectantly at his feet. He pulls two dog cookies from his pants' pocket. Each dog sits and takes his or her reward gently from his fingertips. "Easy...good pups."

Lady, a stray bitch, was sleeping in the alley until Dad began feeding her. She was skin and bones, some kind of shepherd/collie mix. Now she's glossy and friendly, though easily startled. Sampson is a belligerent Jack Russell terrier. He's the brains in this duo, though his motives are suspect. He always has an angle — not surprisingly, he and Shane are uneasy in each other's company.

Dad stares at the sparring boxers. I wait him out.

"Shane looks bad," he finally says.

"How bad?" I stare at the side of his face, as he continues to watch the boxing.

"His arm's a mess and he's skinny and scraped up."

I gulp and then prod. "Did he say anything about how his arm was broken?"

"No...well, not exactly. He was ranting before the ambulance took him to the hospital, about someone twisting it...and about those drugs." Joe looks at his hands and shakes his head. "Goddamn it, Dana, when is he going to take responsibility for his life?"

I study the dog fur on the carpet and push my still dripping hair away from my face. "Have you visited him since he was admitted?"

"No."

He goes back to the TV and I sense that this is all the information I'll get. Even if he knows something else, he doesn't want to know it. Once, Shane was his blond wonder boy – Dad wanted everything for him and would give him anything. But decades of petty crime and drug addiction have left Joe drained of his emotions and his savings.

Part of me is yearning to see my brother, or the brother I used to know. Wild, dangerous, beautiful Shane: Images of him as a big-eared, buck-toothed boy, a gangly teenager and a broad-shouldered man flip through my brain. Tarzan, I've often thought of him as Tarzan, the half-wild ape-man. He lives half in this world and half somewhere less civilized. His crooked grin says, "I'm bad and you love it." His charisma is as undeniable as his character flaws.

I slouch, waiting. Will Joe ask me anything about my plans while I'm here, or perhaps something about my life in Los Angeles or my writing? It's a childish thought. Just because Joe doesn't want to deal with Shane's problems anymore doesn't mean that he'll take more of an interest in me or my life. When I'm away, living in L.A., I deal with his indifference quite well. But in this house the long-held childhood resentment bubbles up. I'm not his son and I have never been the center of his attention. I loathe my juvenile desire for recognition.

Fleeing, my usual strategy, is the best course of action. I never stay here when I come to town. This house can suffocate me faster than any wave. From the time I was old enough to form the thought, I remember telling myself, "I'll be okay when I get the hell out of here. I'll be happy then."

I pull myself out of the sofa's collapsed cushion. "I'll be at Dylan and Maria's. You can reach me at their house or on my cellphone. I'll check in when I know more about Shane's situation and his arm."

Joe brightens. "Ask Dylan how his fence is holding up, and say hello for me."

"Uh huh." I stiffen. Joe has always had plenty of time for my boyfriends, doing projects and enjoying chummy relationships with them, even well after I've departed the scene. And he always takes their side during the inevitable break-ups. They all think "he's a great guy" and don't understand the uneasiness between us. I don't let them in. I stuff my resentments and keep my inner dialogues to myself.

Oh hell, Mom, Shane's in trouble again. I'm back in town trying to find out the details of his latest mess. Dad can't cope; big surprise. I remember all your talks with Shane when he was a boy, your attempts to love him and straighten him out, the screaming and the hugs.

Shane's hurt, and Dad says he looks awful; I'm glad you can't see that. You were always so proud of your gorgeous son.

I don't have your touch with Shane, Mom. I don't know if he'll rebound this time. How do I make him see the positives in life? You couldn't teach him this…not as you struggled to hold on. You gave in to the darkness and let it swallow you. You shot yourself and wounded all of us, especially Shane.

Chapter 2

"Those drugs" are pot, coke, and now meth; and clearly Shane's been on a serious binge. Not all that unusual, except apparently this time he hit the pipe hard, ending up under Craig's house.

I turn inland and follow a twisty, pot-holed road up into the eucalyptus-covered hills. My car tires crush the trees' acorns, releasing more of their minty smell into the air. It's dusk and the sea mist is thickening — soon the fog blanket will be pulled over the chin of the coastline for the night. The remodeled contemporary leans off the hill, as if peering down to the shoreline below. When Craig purchased it twelve years ago, it was abandoned, except by the mice and bats, and it was sliding off the crumbly hillside. A fisherman had lost it to the bank. Even before the bankruptcy, the house had already suffered, as the fisherman medicated away his money troubles with double Old Fashions.

Craig, a draftsman for an architectural firm in San Francisco, was a carpenter in his starving younger years. Slowly, he's rehabbed the house. The six-year project cost him all of his disposable income, and his second wife. I'm pretty sure he always loved the house more.

He's in his driveway, cutting boards with a table saw. He looks exactly the same as the last time I saw him three years ago. And he's changed very little since we first became friends as teens. His hairline was already receding as an eighteen-year-old, and it's still creeping back. He's not bald; he just has a four-lane forehead. He has olive skin and kind, dark eyes and the slight build of the cross-country runner he once was.

He turns off the saw and removes his safety glasses. A grin spreads slowly across his gaunt, tan cheeks. I climb up the steep driveway toward him.

"Hey Dana." He squeezes my shoulder while pecking me on the cheek. "Welcome home."

Home. Not a warm and fuzzy word to me. I deflect. "The homeowner never rests, huh, Craig." He's used to it — his home-construction addiction is a constant source of needling from his friends.

"Let's go inside and get a beer."

I follow him up the stairs at the back of the garage, through the first level and up to the top living space. The redwood treehouse is a bachelor pad; there are few homey touches, just masculine leather sofas and a 1970s-era stereo tuner, topped with a CD player. It feeds audio to oak-paneled, hip-high speakers — the kind every man owns. A telescope on a tripod stands in the center of one of the room's nearly floor-to-ceiling windows facing the shore.

I walk to the scope and bend my face down, centering my right eye into the eyepiece. The break at the harbor comes into view. Mushy, thigh-high waves roll in, as the weekend warriors scramble to catch the last curls before dark. "Did you get out today?" I ask, while I'm watching a longboarder drive his yacht-sized board into the sand.

"Yeah, drove down the coast for an early session at Ward Creek. Clean waves and no kooks."

We're stalling, neither of us wants to start a conversation that always ends in frustration, when we can't reconcile why someone with so many natural gifts is such a natural disaster. Craig was Shane's first surfing buddy. They started riding waves at thirteen, pedaling their high-handled cruiser bikes to the breaks around town.

Craig hands me a frosty brown bottle. "I'm sure you want to hear how I found him."

"Please."

He begins, in his quiet monotone, to recount the incident. "I'd just fought the traffic back from work on Wednesday. When I pulled into the garage, and cut the engine, I heard thumping and yelling."

He went to the entrance of his crawl space where he stores surfboards, windsurfing gear and other constantly damp water toys; the hinge and padlock were smashed and the door ajar. "I wasn't sure what I should do…check it out or dial nine-one-one."

Then he says he thought he heard a familiar voice — it was alternately yelling and mumbling, and the thumping continued. "I still went back to the garage and got a section of galvanized pipe."

He tips the beer and takes a slug. "I threw open the door and Shane was sitting next to the board rack, rocking back and worth. He'd been hitting his forehead on the beam supporting the rack — that was the thumping."

I flinch. "What was he saying?"

"Something about his paddling arm. 'Don't fuck-up my arm, man. That's just not cool.' Then he screamed and said 'I'll get your stuff; I said I'd take care of it.'"

"I called his name and said 'Hey buddy, it's me, Craig. I'm coming in. Don't freak, man. Take it easy.'" But he says that as he walked toward him, Shane scooted backwards and started screaming unintelligibly.

"He was hugging his left arm to his torso. I could see that it was swollen up triple size, and it was dark purple." Craig rubs his hands down his jeans. "I couldn't deal with him by myself, Dana; you know how strong Shane is. So I called Joe.

We weren't sure if he was really high, or had an infection, or what. We thought he should go to Greenhouse."

"The psych hospital?"

"Yeah, but we called the paramedics and they said they were pretty sure his arm was fractured so they took him to Community Hospital."

"Where all the perpetually uninsured go." It's not a bad hospital; friends work there. But it's regularly swamped by the indigent and undocumented.

"The ER doc said Shane's arm was broken — badly, Dana — and that they'd do surgery. But first they needed to run a toxicology screen to see what recreational chemicals Shane had pumping through his system. They couldn't put him under when he was high on street drugs. They operated the next day. Joe phoned me, said it went fine."

"That's when he called me, too."

"The doc says if he takes care of his arm, it will heal to usable in about four weeks, assuming Shane doesn't re-injure it by doing something stupid." Craig's skeptical face says it all: Shane excels at stupid.

Normally, he would have checked himself out of the hospital by now and been back in close conversation with his pipe. But he's hooked up to a legal dope drip so he hasn't run, yet.

We lock eyes. "That's what you know, but what have you heard around town, Craig?"

Half Moon Bay is a very small town, especially the nucleus of long-time residents. Rumor is sport, entertainment, and trade in a place without a department store mall. If you have news, you'll trade it, for better gossip or something thirst-quenching, preferably on the rocks.

"Shane and I don't share much time anymore, Dana. And I avoid the human flotsam that floats in from The Hook. That's not my crowd anymore." Disgust colors his voice.

The rough Hook crowd is a band of surfers who've never left the life. They ride waves and get high; all else is subordinate to the pursuit of those two hedonistic activities. They have a hostile relationship with law enforcement and all other rule-makers.

"Can you ask around? I need to find out what I'm dealing with." I plead with my eyes.

Craig nods.

*

I step to the far side of the room and call the hospital. The receptionist connects me to Shane's room.

"Hell no!"

"Shane, it's Dana."

"Ms. Diane Sawyer of the Southland, greetings!" He's trying for cheery, but his voice is low and weak.

"How are you?"

"Just peachy, Sis. They have push-button drugs in hospitals now. Technology is a wonderful thing."

I wince. "Are you in a lot of pain?"

"Only when I fall asleep and haven't pushed the magic button for a couple of hours, but just a few clicks and it's all goooood."

I marvel at how a hospital will give a street junkie access to push-button painkillers like anyone else. "I want to come and see you this evening. What time are visiting hours?"

"We're open until eight forty five, Miss. I'm finishing up my chicken and green beans. I'll save my lime Jell-O to share with you."

He doesn't question my sudden appearance in Half Moon Bay — that would mean acknowledging that once again he needs my help. I tighten my lips but I don't call him on it. If I did, he'd just get belligerent and combative.

Next, I dial Dylan's house. Maria answers.

"Dylan and I had a bet on your land-speed record. Less than seven hours, am I right?"

I smile. "And no tickets, Maria. How's Marco?" Maria and Dylan's son is sixteen. Hispanic features and dark hair with blond streaks — he's already a lady killer, but not a surfer. Maria's made sure of that. Her son will travel beyond the fog-line to college no matter what she has to do. College wasn't an option for many in her family, who came to town from Central Mexico to work the artichoke and brussels-sprout fields.

"Oye, the way he eats Dana! A full meal and two hours later he's tilting my refrigerator. When should we expect you?"

I tell her that I'll get to her house sometime late this evening. I'm going over to see Shane. Later, Craig and I have plans to meet for dinner, along with Nick, a former colleague.

"Have you spoken to Shane? How does he sound?" The Latina sing-song quality to her voice fails to disguise her disapproval. Maria has little tolerance for self-indulgence.

"He's enjoying the ready access to pharmaceutical drugs." I'm feeding her disgust, unable to cover for him among my closest friends. We chat a little more — the loft will be open, whenever I arrive.

Craig is staring out the darkened window. His reflection shows his calm face and the beer cradled in the crook of his arm. He spins away from the glass, a smile spreading across his mouth. "When are we getting out windsurfing?"

I exhale hard. No doubt he's been formulating this plan since I walked up the driveway. I think of various excuses and settle on the obvious one. "I don't have any equipment with me."

"I have enough gear for both of us, Dana."

"It's been nearly a year since I windsurfed off Kanaha in Maui, Craig, and before that I hadn't taken a board out in four or five months." Los Angeles isn't a great windsurfing location. L.A. winds are weak; perhaps they've developed emphysema from the smog.

I want to sail, but I want to perform. It's my competitive streak, inherited from Joe, and evident since I was a girl in pig tails following Shane around. I'd skin my knees; then do it again before the last scabs had healed. I'd never quit. Three years younger, I still expected myself to be able to do anything Shane could do, in or out of the water.

"Always sandbagging, Dana. You know you want to go." Craig challenges me with his too-knowledgeable look.

The ocean and the beach constantly draw me; they are my playground and my true home. I learned to walk balancing in deep sand; it cushioned my falls when I stumbled, and my diaper plopped softly down into the dimpled white. As a kid, I always had sand stuck between my toes, and it got left behind in my shoes and sheets. My mother would be appalled when she'd find that I'd been sleeping in a fine layer of sand, but it felt normal, comforting to me.

"Okay. But don't expect much." I start down the stairs.

Craig quietly tails me. I can feel there's something else he wants to say. He slaps the door-opener button; the lift pulls it up panel by panel, revealing the lights of town and the harbor off in the misty darkness. "Shane's into a real bad scene this time. I can feel it."

I look into his face and see sadness and frustration. Shane's battles and inner demons injure those around him, but he's oblivious to the impact. I hug him hard. "I'll see you at Las Palmas."

I stride to my car; tense with anticipation and dread. I want to see Shane. And yet I know I'll hate what I see, and what I'll hear.

Chapter 3

The hospital looks like a Rubik's cube, without the primary colors. I check with the information desk and make my way to Shane's ward. Before I step into the room, I take a couple of deep breaths. I need to be calm; I need to douse the fury building inside me at having to parent him...One. More. Time.

He's slumped in the bed, the TV remote in his right hand. I look at his face and then quickly look down, hiding my reaction — his forehead is black and blue, with a knot the size of a half of a lime in the middle of it, and his cheeks are sunken and scabbed in a couple of places along his jawline. His once-thick blond hair is a thin, tangled mess and his scalp is visible in several odd patches on the side and top of his head. The drugs have taken their toll on more than just his brain; they've ravaged his hair and skin and eaten away at his once muscular physique.

His left arm is wrapped in a massive piece of foam and bandages that continues up to nearly his shoulder. He grabs a baseball cap off the bed and pulls it onto his head. Obviously, he's vain about the hair loss. "Hey, little sister," he slurs.

I lean over and hug him. He feels like a frail grandmother, not my muscled big brother.

"Where's my Jell-O?" I'm trying to joke, but Shane looks like the zombie meth addicts on the TV shows, hollow eyes and scabby skin.

"Ah, I guess they took it away. That's a high-demand menu item from the hospital Happy Meal."

"What's the doc say about your arm?" I stare at his purple fingers.

"Four weeks, man. But I should get a removable splint after a week. You should get the doc to show you the post-surgery X-ray — the plate and screws are pretty cool." He holds the arm up a little as he's speaking. Since he's had a plate installed, he says they won't put him in a traditional cast. Once the swelling has gone down, and the doctor is sure the bone is stabilized, he'll just have the nylon splint.

At least Shane won't be tempted to act like a dog with a bandage on its paw. When he broke his wrist skateboarding as a teenager, he removed the plaster cast himself after just three weeks because he wanted to go surfing.

"How long do they want you to stay in the hospital?" I sit on the edge of an orange plastic chair.

"A couple of days. I have an infection from the arm, so they're juicing me with antibiotics and some tasty painkillers." He rubs his jaw and adjusts his cap.

"Do you want me to bring you anything from home?"

"Naw. I got some reading material from the nurses. There are some cuties who are taking good care of me," he winks. Shane is an irresistible combination of vulnerability and bad boy. I have no doubt that he has an admirer on every shift.

"So, are you going to tell me how it was broken?" I tilt my head at the bandaged arm.

He shifts in the bed and silently sets his jaw. "No need to go into that."

"Well I guess I can just listen to the tribal drums around town and see what they have to say." I keep my voice neutral and raise my eyebrows. "Is that what you want, for me to get the story secondhand?"

His jaw just sets tighter. I can see he won't be spilling tonight. It's eight-forty and a rotund nurse in one of those ugly, flowered pajama tops sticks her head in the door. "Visiting hours will be over in five minutes."

I hug him again. This time he clings for an extra few seconds. When I pull back, his blue eyes are dark and pleading. "Will you come back tomorrow?"

His need is a raw open wound. I've always been his champion. We never had a supportive home life. Valerie tried to help Shane but she was fighting unspoken demons. Joe shaped us like a rapacious seagull, tearing away pieces. He cut us down to make us tougher. Shane and I are damaged, missing parts that were pecked away, leaving invisible scars.

"Of course. I'll be back in the evening." Wanting to end our chat on a lighter note, I tell him I surfed this afternoon and that Craig is taking me out windsurfing tomorrow.

He pushes himself up in the bed. "The wind has been consistent down south for the last three days; you should get a good session," he advises. Typical surfer, he's hospital bound but he's up on the weather conditions. He probably spent half the day checking reports on the Weather Channel.

I squeeze his good arm and slide out of the room.

In the car, my brain is swimming in unanswered questions. Who or what broke his arm? What did his tox screen show? And why doesn't he want me to go by his house? He looks like hell; I'm limp with helpless feelings of sorrow. I slump down and start the car, sensing that this time I may be heading for the eye of a shit-storm that dwarfs all of the previous Shane squalls.

Chapter 4

Nick opens the laminated treats list and starts naming the candidates: "Dueño, Cazadores, Heradura, Patron...what's your pleasure, er poison?"

I wedge a chip with a generous helping of red salsa on it into my mouth, while taking in the restaurant's never-updated décor – burnt orange walls, linoleum with a Mexican brick pattern and velvet paintings. A true Mexican dive, but with a crucial difference: Las Palmas has a tequila menu.

"Patron Silver," Craig and I say in unison.

I think of when I first met Nick, the day he walked into the "new economy" magazine in San Francisco; the new art director. We formed a bond while coming up with zany art to illustrate tedious technology stories. It didn't hurt that we had a common enemy, Publisher Sam Stilton.

Nick and Craig are easy in each other's company — their aesthetic professions provide a natural bridge. A short Latina waitress wrapped in a red apron appears. "What would you like?" We order shots of Patron, along with beer and food. I pop another chip into my mouth. The grease coats my tongue — I need the tequila thinner.

The waitress returns, and Nick distributes the shots and raises his for a toast. "To round two." He throws down his shot in one gulp. I can see that he's ready to fly, and after a long day and my disturbing visit to the hospital, I'm willing to be his wingman. My mind returns to Shane's ravaged face and mangy hair. I pound my shot, shiver involuntarily, and bite a lime.

Craig shoots his tequila. He skips the lime and takes a long pull on his beer.

Nick is already searching for our waitress. He signals her over and orders another round.

I turn toward him. The booth's red vinyl squeaks. "How's our buddy Sam?"

"The Pillar of Publishing? He misses you, Dana; he says so all the time." Nick smirks and rubs his dark goatee.

I snort. "Sam misses making me cow to his idiotic, autocratic whims."

"Tsk, tsk, such hostility Dana. Sam only wants you to be all you can be." Nick winks and sips his beer. One of Sam's not-so-endearing characteristics is his love of clichés. In meetings, Nick and I would tally the number of clichés Sam used. We'd look over at each other each time Sam spouted another one and nearly fall out of our chairs. In a typical meeting, Sam would punctuate his useless pap with no less than a dozen clichés — Sam would have said "a baker's dozen."

I left the magazine and joined the newspaper before Sam ruined my love of journalism. At its best, reporting is a straightforward meritocracy. You're judged by your boss, your peers and the public on the news you break and the stories you write. Everything else is just noise...as long as you stay away from the few Sams in the business.

The second round of shots arrives and we toss back the Mexican lighter fluid. My stomach is burning. I punish it for being a whiner with another salsa-loaded chip.

Craig and Nick begin discussing Nick's Barracuda — a vintage car requires nearly as much attention as a mistress. After the food comes, the talk turns to Shane. Though I've only been friends with Nick a few years, he's become steeped in Craig's and my constant struggle to keep Shane alive and liberated. I don't really want to talk about the situation; it might dull the buzz. Craig fills in the basic story for Nick.

Nick asks how long I'll be in town. "I have a week to spend on tropical storm Shane. Then I'm off to a conference."

"You're not tired of the travel?" He bites a lime.

I play with the soggy label on my beer bottle. "Oh, you know, it's the perfect way to avoid any sense of permanence." Craig mouth tightens into a line when I say this. But that's not all. I enjoy the journalistic jousting with top economists and business leaders, rooting out the real story. As in sports, most of the time I'm going up against the men...I do it in the lineup at surf breaks and I do it at work. I'm fine with that. It's not personal; it's not emotional; it's business. It's the antithesis of my dealings with Shane.

We finish sticky platters of enchiladas and rellenos, and we're fighting over the tortilla-chip dust in the bottom of the basket when the waitress comes by. Nick orders one more round of shots. I sigh and burp.

Nick bursts out laughing and hugs me. "Ah, behold our sophisticated businesswoman."

The final shot is smooth. Tequila has a funny way of going from harsh alcohol to a sipping liqueur after just a couple of ounces have passed your lips.

We're all buzzed, though the cheese and beans have helped to tame the effects of the cactus juice. We pay our bill and walk across the mini-mall to the java hut. We each order cappuccinos and stumble outside.

I'm in the moment. The alcohol has mostly released my brain from the day's worries, and I'm with my two favorite co-conspirators. Tonight, my hometown is a familiar old shoe; it hasn't yet begun to rub and blister me.

*

We decide to take the Barracuda to The Hook. We pile in, three across the big bench seat. The swell has dissipated

— the waves are small and disorganized. Moonlight illuminates the foam.

Nick looks across me to Craig. "Been on the water lately?"

He nods. "And Dana and I plan to sail Waddell tomorrow afternoon."

Then Nick asks, yet again, what my plan is for dealing with Shane.

"I'll spend the next week getting him out of the hospital and hopefully on the road to recovery. And I'll dig around to see if I can find out who broke his arm and why, and whether I can talk or buy him out of his latest mess." Just saying these words is sobering me up. I crush my now empty coffee cup.

"Where's he living?" Nick adjusts the car's heater fan.

"He was cagey about that. I'm sure it's some surfer rathole." I flash back on some of his previous flops: converted garages, crumbling concrete-block apartments, illegal mother-in-law units in houses no mother would set foot in.

It's one-thirty and time to end the evening. The Barracuda rumbles back to the mini-mall.

Dew covers the Honda. I pull out of the parking lot, as the wipers slap rivulets from the windshield. Dylan and Maria's house is up a private road two miles inland from the water. It used to be small dairy farm, though the only farm animals now in residence are three goats. Dylan loves his goats; Maria tolerates them. They're troublesome beasts that will eat anything they can tear into, but they keep the dry grass mowed.

I slowly pull up the gravel driveway, keeping the crunching to a minimum, and then pad up the stairs to the loft over the barn, my overstuffed duffle bag crushing my shoulder. I love this space and have threatened more than once to become a permanent resident. It's a large room with a big bubble skylight and wood floors. Under a window at the end of the peaked roof is a queen-size iron bed, covered in a crisp white duvet and draped with a blue and white quilt. The bedside lamp is on.

I brush my teeth and dive into bed. In my dreams, I'm the one hitting Shane, and he's screaming. I wake in a sweat, shocked at my violent subconscious, my hatred of his ceaseless chaos.

Chapter 5

Stumbling into the shower, I let nearly scalding water pour over me and in and out of my mouth, which is coated in a dry paste and emitting a foul odor of alcohol and fermented salsa. I brush my teeth, twice, and gingerly walk down the stairs and across the gravel to the kitchen door. Only one thing will help cure the results of my juvenile over-indulgence in Mexico's evilest export. Coffee.

I raid the freezer, locating fresh-ground Sumatran, and soon the coffee pot is making its soothing spitting and hissing noises. As I sit down at the breakfast nook with a big mug, Maria rushes into the kitchen. She wraps me in a quick, tight hug.

"Ah Dana, you let Nick and Craig talk you into some foolishness."

"Yeah, I never learn. I look bad, huh?" It's not a question; it's an admission of fact. "It's so great to see you."

Maria, a slight Hispanic woman who claims to be five feet one inch tall (only, in high-heeled boots), hasn't hardly aged in the eighteen years since she and Dylan married. Her hair is glossy black and pulled back in a short ponytail at her neck and her skin is the color of my lightly creamed coffee. She doesn't walk from point to point, she bounces. She looks like a high school freshman, not the mother of her own teenager.

She sits down at the table with me, and we start with the easier topics: Marco, his studies and his athletic feats: my job and latest travels; Dylan's law practice. But eventually, the conversation stalls. We've reached the point of discussing Shane, and Maria disapproves of everything Shane represents. Still, she understands the importance of family.

I fill her in on my visit with Shane and the limited information I've obtained from Joe and Craig about his psychotic break with reality and his mysterious broken arm.

"So what's next? Who might be able to help?"

"Well, I thought I'd call Joey to see what he's heard, and if he knows where Shane is living now." I explain to her that Shane was being evasive last night about his current address. Joey is another local aging surfer. He has a painting business, and he's been one of Shane's informal parents — people who've helped him out of numerous scrapes. In Joey's case, he's employed Shane as a painter off and on for two decades.

"I'll also call Terry and check in. He won't want anything to do with Shane's latest drama, but it would be rude to come to town after three years and not call. Right?"

"Right. He's your brother too."

I picture Terry: four inches shorter than Shane, with a stocky build, a growing paunch and limp, thinning brown hair. Terry resents Shane's physical gifts, and his unwillingness to play by society's rules. He resents me because Shane and I have always been close.

"Does Terry still own the insurance agency?" Maria sips her coffee.

"Yup. Dependable Terry; he and Shane couldn't be more different." Terry clocks in from nine to five, plays with his kids (a boy and a girl), pays his taxes, and goes to church. Shane works when he needs drug money and hasn't filed a ten-forty in a decade. Terry enjoys golf, a game with decorum and a natty dress code, and he coaches Little League; Shane likes being naked or at least shirtless, lives a life filled with confrontations and fights, rides big waves and sells pot to minors. Forget brotherhood and brotherly love, he and Shane don't speak the same language and might as well be different species.

Maria and I turn to the kitchen entrance as Dylan appears in the doorway. His thin dark hair is buzz cut and he's in his weekend attire — 501 jeans, surf T-shirt and white athletic socks. He slides in a surfing stance all the way across the hardwood floor to the coffee pot and nonchalantly pulls a mug from the cupboard. Maria and I giggle our appreciation of his entrance.

"Anyone need a refill?" He holds up the pot.

We reply in chorus: "Yes, please."

He fills the mugs and plops down next to Maria. He addresses her as if I'm not sitting right there. "How rough is our wayward houseguest this morning?"

"I'm cursing my so-called friends." I rub my pounding temples.

He looks at me, a slight smirk playing across his lips. Dylan and I go way back. We dated when I was in my early twenties. I was rebounding from another one of my infatuations with self-involved bastards. Dylan was the only truly nice man I knew at the time, so I chose him as my transition man. It was stupid and hurtful. Dylan fell for me and I crushed him. He has a kind heart; he's considerate; he's too nice.

People walk on Dylan, because they can sense his vulnerability. It would infuriate me, a reaction that I couldn't help aiming more at Dylan than his abusers. I couldn't stand his inability to see it coming and how instead of standing up for himself, he would often just ignore a slight as if it didn't happen. Now that I'm older, if not wiser, I recognize that his vulnerability isn't a character flaw, but me rejecting him for it is.

He met Maria at the local Farmers' Market. Maria's an ICU nurse, but she was doing a favor for one of her uncles and selling produce that Saturday. She's since said that she thought Dylan was just another slacker surfer in baggy shorts when she first met him. He's told me that she was haughty and unapproachable, but that just heightened his interest so he asked around. A few days later he tracked her down at the hospital. When he showed up there, he was wearing a gray flannel suit. They went to lunch, and have been together ever since.

I fill Dylan in on yesterday's activities and my plans for today. As always, he offers to help if Shane is in any kind of legal trouble. A public defender, Dylan specializes in defending society's youngest offenders, the ones that might actually have a chance at going straight instead of maturing into career criminals...ten-year-olds with sticky fingers, pre-teen pot dealers.

I thank him for offering to help. It's probably a given that legal scrapes will be part of this saga; I'll bring him in when that part unfolds. I'm extremely independent, but Shane's problems turn me into a user. I down the last of my coffee and it's bitter.

After breakfast, Dylan goes out to feed the goats and I climb up to the loft to call Joey and Terry. I try Terry first, because it's likely to be a short call.

Terry often goes to his insurance office on Sunday morning to do an hour or two of paperwork without interruption from the three underpaid women in the office who do all the real work, selling policies and sorting out claims. This, of course, doesn't stop Terry from constantly complaining about how he has to review their work, because well, they just don't have the business acumen he, a businessman and a twenty-year agent, has. I'm not sure if he really feels this way, or he just says these things to build himself up and irritate me.

He picks up on the third ring, "Hi, Dana." His voice has the dead tone he reserves for Joe, Shane and me.

"Hi, Terry. How are you?" I try for neutrality, if not enthusiasm.

"Fine. What's up?" No niceties here, Terry just wants to know if I require anything of him and if not he'd like to get back to his day and his purposeful amnesia about the family he came from. He only wants to focus on his current two families, his wife Jenna's East Coast blue-blood clan and his kids.

"I'm in town for a few days, and I just wanted to say hello."

"I know why you're here, and I can't imagine why you bother." His voice is clipped and hostile. "Joe called."

"Well, I'm not expecting you to get involved, Terry." I try to keep a neutral tone.

"Dana, you left when you were seventeen. You have a degree and you've established a professional life. You should stay gone. Shane's life is a cluster; it will always be a cluster." His harsh words deaden the conversation for a beat or two. I left right after one of Valerie's long stays on the couch. I'd graduated early from high school; college at U.C. San Diego didn't start until the following fall. But I made my way down there months before that, supporting myself by waitressing at a breakfast place and cleaning houses for extra cash.

"Terry, I just thought I'd check in, do that familial thing that other families actually enjoy." I shouldn't, but I can't help baiting him a little.

Silence and then a sigh. "Well, let's see, Lisa and Tom are doing well in school and Jenna just got another raise and is now in charge of all hourly personnel matters at The

Cove." Cypress Cove is the town's only fancy hotel and golf resort, where Jenna is a human-resources manager.

"Good for her. She's really ascending the ladder." Another subtle dig — Terry is proud of his wife, but her career threatens his fragile, head-of-household male ego.

"Business here has been outstanding, too. I may hire another office girl at the beginning of next year. How long will you be in town this time?" I hear him shuffling papers.

"A week. After that, I'm flying out to a conference in Switzerland." Terry hasn't traveled outside the U.S., so, score one more point for me. But I'm already tired of the verbal sparring. "Well, I'm staying with Dylan and Maria if you need to reach me and my cellphone isn't cooperating."

Terry clears his throat. "Yeah, sure. Well, call if you need anything."

He doesn't mean it. Did he suggest a get-together...over a beer or a glass of wine? No, even that's too much civility for Terry. I'm here about Shane and that instantly puts me on the opposing team. Terry's resentment boils up at any attention Shane gets from family members, friends or surf fans...attention Terry always craved and didn't receive.

*

As I stare at the phone, I mutter, "jerk." Terry's poisonous wrath hurts him...and sometimes me.

After one particularly bad fight between Valerie and Joe, she was a medicated zombie for two weeks. One day, she left sixteen-year-old Terry stranded after baseball practice for three hours. When he finally got home, thanks to a neighbor, he was raging. I foolishly tried to calm him. Instead, he wanted me to be as enraged as him. "You know she barely touched you as a baby, right?" He got in my face, demanding I respond.

"I know she had post-partem depression. Dad told me." I didn't want to talk about this. I remember physically shrinking, pulling back toward the bedroom door.

"She didn't just have depression. She didn't hold you, Dana. Your crib was in the fucking hall." He'd leaned in toward me, ranting.

"We lived in a tiny house." It was down by the harbor, near Joe's shop.

Then he'd begun yelling. "Don't defend her! She didn't want anything to do with you. She left you in the hall every night, and to comfort yourself you rocked the crib so hard — head down, your butt in the air — the bottom would fall out."

I remember shaking my head, not wanting to acknowledge his words. The crib was in the hall for four years. It broke every couple of nights, when I'd rock it until it hit the wall and finally someone, usually Joe, came to check on me. It's a piece of my early years I've never shared with anyone, not my closest friends, not even my therapist.

*

I look up Joey's number in my phone's contact list and dial. No sense wasting energy trying to parse Terry's bottomless well of hostility. I get Joey's voice mail. In less than a minute, the phone dances salsa, my latest ring tone.

"Dana, it's been a while. Nice to hear from you. I'm screening calls, hiding out from the ex-wife and pain-in-the-ass clients." He chuckles.

"How's business?" Joey has done well, working on large apartment and condo complexes on the San Francisco Bay side of the hill. After twenty years, he's cultivated a network of friends among the property managers; Joey says he's painted some of the buildings six or seven times.

"Business is solid. But you're calling about Shane, right?" He's participated in numerous Shane rescues.

I sigh and tighten my grip on the phone. "Yeah. What's the rumor mill saying?"

He's heard around town that Shane has pissed off a big-time drug dealer for some unknown reason. And that Shane may be working off his drug debts by dealing. "He hasn't done any work for me in months, Dana."

"Is the law onto him?" I hold my breath as I wait for his answer.

"I don't think so. Though from what I've heard, he'd be better off dealing with a drug bust than this dealer. This guy isn't doing a little business to feed his habit. He's running a big drug franchise, and he has an employee pool of thugs and runners."

I gulp. A franchise? "What's the dealer's name?"

Joey tries to talk me out of getting involved. "Dana, don't go there. Just help Shane get healed and leave him to sort this one out. This is a bad scene."

I process his comments, and answer as I'm sure he's expecting. "I can get the name from someone else."

We're both quiet for a bit. I respect Joey's advice, but Shane doesn't "sort things out," not without being pushed, not without help.

"I actually don't know it, Dana, but I'm pretty sure I can find out. Are you sure that's what you want?"

"Want? I don't *want* any of this. But I need to find out who has Shane on a leash."

He's quiet for a bit. "I'll try. Give me a day or so to get back to you."

I'm no closer to unraveling the twisted web of Shane's current problems, but I have more information. His involvement with a big-time drug dealer doesn't shock me, but it certainly isn't a welcome development.

I need to blast over to Craig's for our windsurfing date. I wriggle into a bikini and shorts, then grab a small duffel bag out of my larger bag for a towel, suntan lotion, and some money. Pulling my long blond ponytail through a baseball cap, I'm good to go. The throbbing in my skull is starting to ease, and my adrenaline is surging, as I anticipate the wind and waves.

Chapter 6

The ocean is already white-capping, and it's only one o'clock. The wind here usually doesn't peak until three o'clock or so. On a good day, it holds steady for about three hours before the fog seeps back in, the breeze gets holey and it dies off. Or, some days it's just holey all day. No matter, if you're life-long coastal dweller sometimes you'll go out anyway, just to get wet. Without the smell of salt water on your skin and in your hair you might as well be living in, well, Tucson. "Inland" is a word that makes surfers shudder.

We pull into the parking lot at Waddell Creek, crunching across dirt and gravel. Craig's van rocks as a gust hits us. It was once a bakery delivery truck, delivering the daily bread, but it serves a higher purpose now. Forget sport utility vehicle: this is a recreational assault vehicle. Its white paint has no gloss coat left on it. Dents line the front bumper, reminders of rough rides through the artichoke fields and on adventures in Baja. Inside, it's carpeted and customized, with board and sail racks, and a multitude of plastic bins for hardware and wetsuits. A cooler sits behind the middle console that separates the front pilot seats.

I twist around and pop it open. An assortment of beer nestles in the ice, along with a few bottles of water. Craig laughs. "Don't you trust me?"

"Just checking the safety gear."

We stare out at the beach, evaluating conditions. It's going to be a big day, and it hasn't even reached its full potential. Eight vans and trucks dot the lot so far — none of the regulars are rigging yet. If you do, you'll just have to rig down later. The wind is building.

Waddell Creek is world renowned and the site of an annual wave sailing contest. Thirty-knot winds and mast-high surf regularly blast this beach, and the currents are treacherous.

It's also part of the Red Triangle, a section of coast inhabited by a large population of elephant seals and sea lions...and the great white sharks who feed on them. One leg of the triangle runs from Stinson Beach out to the Farallon Islands, another goes down to Año Nuevo Island, which is just northwest of Waddell, and the triangle's base runs along the shore between Waddell and Stinson. Every year, a surfer, boogey boarder or diver gets chomped. Luckily, most survive. It's the neoprene — a shark usually realizes its mistake after taking a nibble. Apparently a human, in a bun of neoprene, doesn't taste like seal.

The excitement is already hitting my stomach, causing it to cramp slightly and twist. I haven't sailed a day like this in ages, and any big wind day is a rocket ride. I will be doing battle, fighting to hang onto and maneuver a board and sail that a gust could rip away from me at any moment. I'm already visualizing the toss I'm going to take, when I can't get unhooked from my harness fast enough and the sail throws me into the rig. It's called a harness yank; it hurts.

Craig hops out of the van, walks through the lot and down onto the sand. He wants to feel the full strength of the blow, away from any diminishing factors like the cliffs.

I moan an "ah shit" involuntarily. Since we pulled into the lot, the wind speed has kicked up at least another five miles per hour. When I look beyond the shore break, I don't see individual white caps any longer. I see heaping foam and gray seas. A blow this strong means I'll be using Craig's smallest sail and still be fighting to hang on.

When you've decided on the tiniest sail in your quiver, you might as well get to it. I roll out the carpet remnant that's part of any Waddell local's kit. It protects your boom and sail from the parking lot's gravel, which can tear holes into your gear. By the time Craig returns to the van, I've put the 3.3-square-meter sail on the mast, and I'm already down-hauling, putting a nice bend in the carbon-fiber mast.

Craig watches me heave on the downhaul line. "Ah, breaking out the moist towelette. Good choice."

I grunt my reply, as I pull the sail down tight. Craig helps me attach it to the board. Once you've rigged a sail in heavy wind you can never leave it unattended. In an instant, a gust can take it for a ride, tumbling and flying across the parking lot, smashing into cars and people. It's wildly dangerous and identifies you as a windsurfing dweeb, one who shouldn't be rigging at Waddell on any day, let alone a day like today.

Next, I muscle the whole rig onto my head, sail folded below, board on top, and begin marching down to the water's edge. My arm muscles strain; my head feels flattened. At last, I arrive near the water, where I pirouette to get it down to the sand. I pull the sail around so the mast edge is into the wind. Then like a dog burying a bone, I kick sand over the sail and board to hold them down. It isn't failsafe. I've seen a gust launch a rig even when it was set down in the best possible position.

I've gassed up the very temperamental race car; time to don my driving suit. Back at the van, I strip down to my bikini and start rolling on my wetsuit, pulling it up like a pair of uncooperative pantyhose. I also wriggle into a butt harness, strapping it down as tight as I can without cutting off circulation. The harness — a nylon girdle with straps and a bar with a hook — catches the surgical tubing that dangles from each side of the boom. With it, windsurfers use their body weight to control a sail, instead of just their arms. Without it, on a windy day like today, my arms and grip would wear out in a matter of minutes.

Meanwhile, Craig, who sails every week when the wind cooperates, has rigged his sail in half the time it took me.

He rolls up the carpet and stuffs it under the van. The sand is blasting across our bodies as we walk to the water. I can feel it catching in my hair and scratching across my face. The sound of the wind and the waves is one loud roar, punctuated by a clap of thunder when each swell first collapses. I feel it more than hear it. The air temperature is in the sixties, but my palms are sweating in my sailing gloves, and my mouth is sticky and dry.

Craig walks over to me. "Ready for some action?" To strangers, Craig never seems excited, but his lean body is taut, his posture erect. He's charged.

"Yeah." I'm focused on the water; no thoughts of my family, Shane or dealers can intrude.

"Follow me out, I'll show you how to weave through the sand bars."

Waddell is notorious for its underwater ridges of sand. Bury your fin in a bar and you'll be thrown before you even get out to the breaking surf.

Craig drops his board to the water and steps around its tail. He quickly pushes the sail up into the wind and at the same time steps lightly onto the board. He glides off. Pulling hard on the boom a couple of times, he stretches the sail and fills it full of air; the board accelerates, as he shoves his feet into his foot straps. With the sail trimmed, he hooks into his harness and leans back. He's hit his Ferrari's gas pedal — the board bucks up onto a plane and rockets away. I smile; he makes it look so damn easy.

He starts working his way through the sand bars, making several distinct turns. I try to memorize his route. Taking a couple of deep breaths, I push my sail and mast upright and hop onto the board. I pull back as the wind tries to tear the boom from my hands.

The board wobbles a bit, and then picks up speed. I step into the foot straps, push my hips forward and hook into the harness loop. I'm up on a plane and the board is slapping the water as it flies across the chop. I follow Craig's course through the sand bars. Dead ahead is the danger zone, right where the waves first break. That's when the exploding foam is at its most powerful. I'll need to maneuver around two incoming waves to reach the blue water beyond the surf-line.

I drop off into a reach, turning a little downwind to pick up speed and to move to the left of where the waves are initially pitching. I'm coming up on the first wave — jump or try to ride across the top? If I cross the wave's crest with full speed in this wind, I'll get airborne without even trying. Slow down too much and my board can stall, making it impossible for me to get past the next wave in the set before it breaks. Can I trust my rusty jumping skills?

I fly up the face, unhook from my harness, hop just a few feet over the top and land fairly balanced — good enough, I'm still on the board. I gasp and hook into my harness again. I see one more wave ahead of me, before the blue water. I race toward it; the fin is buzzing. I scream up the wave's face, and emboldened by my success on the last swell, I fly over the top, catching about five feet of air and landing well beyond the backside of the swell.

I thrive on the mental game of competing against my fears and challenging my physical and mental strength. I never feel more alive than when I'm scared out of my wits. Shane and I share this love of the edges. It really is mind over matter — often my body wants to stop but my mind pushes me to continue. It's what enables marathoners to race and climbers to summit.

Moreover, in each of my dangerous endeavors, I'm asking myself the nagging question: Am I good enough? Perhaps athletes like me are just insecure adult-children, constantly seeking affirmation. And I always push on to the next goal because the last one never satisfies my need for proving my self-worth. I also realize that I'm continually seeking Joe's approval, even though I'll never get it.

Shane is the same. Joe pushed him to do sports, but he was always too critical, focused on technique and performance. Shane sought Joe's approval, but he rarely got it without a lecture about how to be better, faster, more precise.

It's not smooth out here beyond the surf-line, far from it. There's an ocean swell to contend with, and wind-driven chop rips across the surface. I see Craig off in the distance. He's just jibed and is fully powered up, flying back toward the waves. We pass and he hoots at me.

I'm already about a half to three quarters of a mile offshore and I need to jibe. Hopefully I can do this delicate yet high-speed turn without getting bounced off the board. Sometimes starting a jibe down the face of an ocean swell can make it easier and more fun. I watch the swells, push the mast forward and drive down one that looks a little less choppy than the others. The board arcs around, and I let go with my back hand. The sail flips and I catch it as it snaps around, switch my feet and sheet in. It wasn't the smoothest jibe; the board stalled a bit at the end, but any jibe that doesn't end in a splash is a good one.

I peer off toward the surf line to see if I can spot Craig's sail. He's coming back out through the foam, racing for a wave. He pops off the top of the crest and launches a good ten feet up, floating like a puff of sea foam. Then he gently guides the board back to the water, lands softly and speeds toward the next wave. Soon he's over the last swell and back out into blue water. His hair still isn't wet. Today, the Zen Master is making it all look easy.

I'm flying along too, approaching the surf zone. I glance back out to the open ocean, judging whether I'm coming in during a lull or a set. A set is forming up just behind me; I point up into the wind to slow down and let the waves catch me. I let one swell go by, and another. The first swell is nearing the point in the reef where it will crest and break. I sheet in and step on the gas. I fly over the second swell in the set and near the backside of the first one.

Unhooking from my harness, I drop into the wave, just as the lip to my left begins to pitch. The power of the wave hooks into my fin and board. Now it's not just the wind dictating my course; the wave has its own power. It's only a four-foot face, but it feels as big as a building to me. I speed down it, carve a bottom turn and drive the board back toward the lip. It may not be a mountainous wave, but it's rolling nicely, peeling down the beach. I make two more trips down the face and back up to the lip. Time to run for it.

I turn down the face, glide to the bottom and sheet in. Craig can jibe at the end of a wave, going over the remaining swell before it breaks and turning back out to sea with a quick flip of his sail. Not me. I'm too rusty for that. I speed up and run out ahead. Now I have some room between me and the breakers. I turn downwind, railing the board up onto its edge and driving it around with my feet. This will be a hairpin turn, as tight as I can make it.

The sail snaps around and I catch it and tip-toe around to my new stance — the board has slowed almost to a stop as I've reversed course. I balance carefully, bending my knees to absorb the chop and to keep from getting tossed off the back. The board wallows and skids in the swirling foam. But the sail fills just quickly enough, the fin bites and the board starts picking up speed.

After the first couple of runs out and back, the day passes quickly. I sail competently, though my jibes are rusty and sometimes end in a large splash, as I cartwheel off the back of the board. One time, I fall back very hard and kick out with my feet, shoving the board away from me. It's instantly well out of reach. Fear immediately takes hold, I'm more than a half mile offshore and I'm swimming for my board. Worse, the big bastard with the big teeth could be watching from below. I swim at full speed, lifting my head every other stroke to keep an eye on the rig. After ten frenzied pulls, I grab for the board's tail and latch onto it. Panting, I quickly flip the sail and line it up for a water-start. While hanging in the water from the boom, the wind pulls me back onto my board. I don't want to spend any more time than absolutely necessary dangling in the deep like a fishing lure.

Mercifully, I sail the whole day without falling in the waves, the impact zone, where limbs and windsurfing hardware can splinter like kindling. Craig sails circles around me, but shouts encouragement as he screams past. When I step onto the sand at the end of the day, I'm exhausted, exhilarated and calm all at once. It's why I windsurf, ski, surf, mountain bike, etc., etc., etc. The speed and difficulty of these sports slows the world and my overactive gray matter. They force me to live in the moment, no past, and no future.

*

I'm a good athlete, at least according to friends who have spent time surfing or sailing with me. And I am a sea creature — it doesn't matter that I've moved to the big city, or that

I'm a career woman who travels the world. Saltwater runs in my veins. And like Joe and Shane, I have uncanny strength and tenacity, qualities that enable me to push beyond where others will go.

But I'm a self-admitted disaster at romantic relationships. I've been trying to work that out with a therapist, Janelle. I've lived with two men; I've married and divorced; and I've instigated at least three clean-sweeps in my life — quit a job, exited a relationship and moved all at once. Pure housecleaning, in a physical and metaphysical sense.

Janelle says we have instincts dating back to the cave-dweller days, fight or flight. "You're very accomplished at flight, Dana."

I'm the quintessential California girl — tall and thin, with sandy blonde hair and green-blue eyes. I'm aware that my look is the anointed ideal in this country. I didn't ask for this and I'm not proud of it; I had nothing to do with the gene poker that produced my physical appearance. My athleticism and my writing, I'd like those to be recognized, celebrated.

Yet according to Janelle, I seek out men who won't look beyond appearances because I don't trust relationships. It guarantees eventual failure. I agree, though I've paid her way too much of my disposable income to come to this more-than-obvious conclusion.

*

Craig understands my tortured side, how blond beauty sometimes just adds to my insecurities. But he's not above getting a kick out of my decorative skills at the beach. I've just stripped out of my wetsuit, down to my barely there string bikini, and I'm using the sun shower that he threw on the van's roof to heat up before we went sailing. It feels great to rinse the salt and sand off my skin and out of my hair.

There's no way to do this discreetly so I don't try. Meanwhile the surf rats around the parking lot are leering and Craig is enjoying the show.

"You're cruel, Dana." Craig is immune to my physical charms — that would be like being attracted to your kid sister.

"Let 'em squirm." I turn off the shower and wrap up in my towel. "Bartender, I think I've earned a beer."

"Coming right up, ma'am." He pulls a cold one from the cooler and we chink long-necks. The ice-cold beer foams when it mixes with the residual salt in my mouth.

I tiptoe barefoot in the gravel around to the passenger side of the van and start wriggling out of my bikini bottoms, while keeping the beach towel wrapped around my waist. In less than a minute, I've jumped into shorts, a T-shirt and sweatshirt, sliding warm cotton over damp skin, no underwear necessary. After decades of practice, I have parking lot changes down to speedy, skinless stripteases.

While I'm changing, a dark-haired, pony-tailed guy comes over and starts chatting with Craig. I walk around the van and Craig introduces me, using my full name, to "Todd," who's still in his wetsuit and windsurfing harness. His rubber suit is frayed at the cuffs and ankles, and globs of wetsuit glue hold a couple of seams together.

He rubs the salt-encrusted soul patch below his lower lip. "Sorry about Shane. I heard he's in the hospital."

I'm not the least bit surprised that Shane's troubles are surf gossip. But Todd says one thing that stops me cold and erases the peaceful calm I felt just seconds ago. "He's got to stop playing with Asian fire, man. Those dudes take their drug business very seriously."

Meth and Asian gangs. I slump back against the van.

I want to go into interview mode and start pelting him with questions, but I'm afraid that will only make him clam up.

Craig jumps in, his quiet monotone so nonthreatening. "Who's the dealer he's been working for?"

"Ice isn't my scene, but at The Hook I've heard talk." Todd turns away and looks out to sea.

He squints and gnaws the side of his lower lip. But he's not leaving. After years of interviewing people, it's obvious to me that Todd came to talk. We wait. Craig looks down and scuffs the gravel with his flip-flops.

After a long pause, Todd turns to me. "A guy named Ling runs the action."

"Ling? Huh. Is that Vietnamese or Cambodian?" I try for a nonchalant tone.

"No, Thai." Todd hooks his fingers into his harness.

Now, I push away from the van and step toward him. "If I want to find Ling, what's the best way?"

Before I even finish asking, Todd is already rocking back onto his heels and shaking his ponytail. "Can't help you with that, man."

Can't or won't? I've just met Todd — I can't read him. I try a big smile and some flattery. "Well, thanks for the information. Hey, was that you out there on the yellow board and the sail with the orange trim? You were taking some high-altitude flights." He deserves the compliments — his sailing was aggressive and fluid.

He mimes with his arms and body the motion of popping over a wave at top speed. "Swell's building. Could be some nice ramps by tomorrow."

I beam one of my best smiles, reach over and squeeze his forearm. "Does Ling have any other recruits among the surf crowd?"

He doesn't want to answer me, but I've connected to his core, his surf ego, where he really lives. He looks upwind. "I've seen Ling spending time with Anton."

The conversation is over. He clasps hands in a brothers' shake with Craig, nods to me and ambles back toward his old faded blue Toyota pickup. I stare after him.

I shuffle around the van and drag myself up to the passenger seat; my chest is tight and my arms now ache. Craig starts the engine. Our silence, as he pulls out of the parking lot, signals the dread we both feel. Anton and his crowd are the worst of the wild animals that inhabit The Hook. If the surf lore is accurate, Anton has done two stints in jail, one in Baja. One was for drug possession with intent to sell, and worse, stateside he did time for carrying an unregistered handgun. He is violent in and out of the water.

I close my eyes and rest my head against the window. The loud roar of the cargo area makes it hard to carry on a conversation without yelling, and I'm no longer in the mood to talk. How long until Anton catches up to Shane?

Chapter 7

Surfers are notoriously territorial. Sure they surf around, and some take regular surf safaris to obscure breaks around the globe. But most have a favorite break — a place they check daily for swells; a den of salt and sea where they go to just hang out, even if they're not getting wet.

The Hook peels off a point, and when it's big, it breaks on an outside reef. This is no gradual beach break; the outside wave produces a thick, powerful lip that can take you down for a long, deep pounding. It's the jousting arena for the most aggressive surfers in town. I pull into a back corner of the parking lot and scout the action.

A few surfers come through in their surf rides — dented, rusted small trucks and econo boxes — to check the waves and smoke a fatty. Some of them I recognize as long ago acquaintances, definitely not friends. In those instances, we do the half-nod thing, and look away, not interested in making a real connection. But Anton isn't among them.

Shane has been a regular at The Hook since his early teens. He's known there for his surfing prowess and his willingness to mix it up with anyone who shoulder-hops his wave. Shoulder-hopping is a cardinal sin in the surfing world; it occurs when a surfer drops into a wave well away from where it first pitches, on the shoulder, after another surfer has already taken the wave at or near the pitch point. To the uninitiated, it can seem like a somewhat arbitrary distinction, but not to surfers. Do it once, to one of the local surfers, he might let it go. Do it twice and you're likely to get a fist to the face and your leash cut, resulting in the whitewater rolling your board across the rocks that line the cliff edge, the "boneyard," where fiberglass goes to die a tortured death.

Anton's crowd considers The Hook their own personal clubhouse. Enter at your own risk. I've seen more than a few out-of-town surfers paddle in from a Hook session with fat lips and bloody noses, simply because they dared to vie for waves with one of the local surf animals. It's my least favorite aspect of the sport. Windsurfing, especially wave sailing, requires some jockeying for wave position, but overall it's a much more congenial liquid atmosphere. When Craig and I sailed at Waddell, I didn't see a single altercation — sadly, that would be a rare decaffeinated day at The Hook.

*

Shane tells me the infection in his arm is improving, slowly. At least the migration from street drugs to legal ones seems to be doing him some good. His color has improved a little, and he's eating the hospital food and whatever else he convinces visitors to smuggle in...burritos, pizza...in my case Thai food.

"Thanks for bringing this." He looks at me while stuffing a red-chili shrimp in his mouth.

We speak of waves and weather. But I get him to tell me where he's currently crashing. It's an address in the low-budget section of town, where Mexican farm-worker families and blue-collar types inhabit shabby beach shacks and run-down apartments. He calls it a "studio apartment," but one that's part of a house, not an apartment complex. No doubt it's an illegal add-on built by one of its amateur carpenter/owners. I plan to check it out, perhaps pick up some clues to his current jam, though I don't reveal that to him.

*

On my way to Shane's studio the next day, I run into Joey at a gas station. We huddle behind his ladder-topped truck to talk. "Word is Shane's been working for a Thai guy named Ling."

"Why is Ling beating on him?" I lean in close.

"I haven't heard. But I don't think Ling was the one who broke his arm. It was probably some of Ling's muscle. Ling's a pretty big operator — from what I hear he has a whole network of employees and protection."

I go into reporter mode, confirming more of what I think I already know. "Who's his local muscle?"

He pauses, and then sighs. "It's Anton and his gang of thugs, Dana."

It's time to tell Joey the gossip I'd gathered from Todd. Like any source, he becomes more at ease as I relay the information. Somehow it makes him less responsible for spilling information he probably shouldn't.

But Joey has more details on Anton's role in Ling's operation. "Anton and his fellow surf slugs provide the muscle to protect large shipments of meth around Ling's network, and they collect unpaid bills from pushers and users."

"What's Anton like these days? Will he talk to me?" I swallow the golf ball that's somehow become lodged in my throat. I hate this idea, but I don't know how else to find out what he and Ling want with Shane.

"That's a very bad idea, Dana." Joey's eyes darken.

"What else can I do? Shane still isn't talking and I'm running out of time. I can't leave town and hope Shane will work something out with this dealer. He doesn't do that." Days have passed, and I'm no closer to understanding Shane's current conflict or how I might diffuse or resolve the situation.

Joey looks up and exhales hard. "Let me try to talk to Anton."

Now I change sides and I'm the voice of fear and reason. "This isn't your mess, Joey. You have a business and a reputation to protect."

He uses humor to lighten the load. "Ah, Dana, the world would be incredibly boring without Shane to shake the roof off every now and again. I can't let you have all the fun."

We argue back and forth, but Joey won't be deterred. He says he knew Anton when he was just a loudmouth, skinny high-schooler learning surf etiquette from older heavies and getting knocked around for his fouls. They have history and respect. Joey says he'll be in touch.

I pull out of the gas station. The fog gloom that's shrouding the coast today mirrors my mood. I'm frustrated by my lack of progress, and I'm starting to get resentful of the energy I'm spending once again on Shane and his latest troubles. Over the years, I've bailed him out of jail, financed trips to rehab, loaned him money, paid off debts. Even when I'm not directly involved, I'm on the phone advising him, cajoling him, nagging him, trying to keep his life from turning turtle. It's exhausting and it's unfair, and yet I can't turn away. I've been trying to save him from himself since we were kids.

*

Shane's out in the driveway jumping his high-handled bike over three concrete blocks lined up together. He must be about ten years old — he's wound up, with hyperactive energy that needs a release. Mom comes out and asks him if he's started on his homework. He barely acknowledges her presence, which results in her screaming at him to "stop!" He finally does and just looks past her when she says he can play another fifteen minutes. As soon as she goes back into the house, he rides the bike out into the street again, races back and pops it up over the blocks. Mom's Volkswagen bug is on one side of the driveway.

A little while later, Dad arrives home from work. Just as he's getting out of his truck, Shane leaps the bike again and this time he skids on the landing and nearly runs into the driver-side door of Mom's bug, missing it by inches. As usual, Dad's first interaction with Shane today is screaming at him. He bellows as he's walking up toward the door, "Shane, goddamn it, ride the bike in the street and get those blocks out of here. Stay away from Mom's car!"

I'm sitting on the front step and he pats me on the head, as he walks to the front door.

Shane straddles his bike and catches his breath. His mouth is set, and it's almost like I can see the decision process going on inside his brain. Behave, or enjoy the adrenaline of another jump? A few seconds later, he's pumping the pedals down the driveway and out into the street. He makes a tight U-turn, and he flies up the driveway. But his body position is all wrong, and he's too close to the bug. He tries to leap the concrete block closest to the car and ticks the bike's tire against it as he goes over. The bike tilts, skids sideways, and I hear a crunch. I can't see the impact from where I'm sitting, so I run over to him and the car.

Shane's bike has left a six-inch dent in the left front fender of the bug, and has scratched off a soap-bar-sized chunk of paint. I inhale sharply when I see the damage. Shane is tangled up in the bike on the ground; his left knee is scraped and bleeding. Fear flashes across Shane's face when we hear the front door open. I quickly back up to the garage door.

Dad strides over to the bug. His face goes from dark to black with anger. In one motion, he yanks Shane up from the bike and smacks him hard across the face. "You did exactly what I told you not to do. You little shit." He starts dragging Shane toward the front door.

"It was an accident, Dad." Shane is pulling away and trying to drag his feet.

"It's not an accident when you don't listen, goddamn it!"

I slide down the garage door, and hold my knees to my chest. Joe slams the front door, but I can still hear yelling coming from inside. I cover my ears with my hands.

Later, I remember Shane sitting silently at the dinner table. His cheek is bright red, and he's rubbing his shoulder. The atmosphere at the table is violent and threatening; Joe is still fuming. My stomach is in a knot, but I'm afraid I'll get in trouble if I don't eat. I move the pot roast and mashed potatoes around on my plate. Terry keeps his head down too; he eats quickly and asks to be excused. Mom just stares and smokes; her dinner sits abandoned. Dad has grounded Shane for two weeks. No visits with his friends, no after-school activities.

The next day it's raining off and on, but Shane doesn't come home from the school bus. He hides out in a fort he and some friends built in a nearby Eucalyptus grove. When he tries to sneak in just after dark, Joe immediately takes him to his room and whips him with his belt. Mom has to intervene after too many hits. I go out on the front step and shiver, while I wait for the violence to stop. I'm seven and I don't understand why Shane has to push and push and push. I'm pretty sure even he doesn't understand why he does it.

*

I shove the memories aside, as I roll up to the address Shane gave me. It's a peeling wood-sided two-story house, dirty white with faded green-apple trim. The sloped yard is covered in knee-high, dry weeds, with a long, skinny driveway running along the left side of the property. The asphalt looks more like broken dirt clods than pavement. I opt for parking on the street.

As I'm stepping over the clods, a stout Mexican woman in skin-tight orange polyester pants and a loose floral top appears on the upstairs deck. She gives an inquiring half-smile that invites me to state my business.

"Is this Shane's house?"

She points around the left side of the house and walks back inside. I guess that's what counts as a crime watch in this neighborhood. Up the driveway, I see a door that appears to access the crawl-space of the house, except this door has the house numbers, 512, and the letter B on a diagonal in the middle of it in those cheap, gold peel-and-stick numbers and letters that you can buy at any hardware store. As I get closer, I see that the doorjamb has been forced at the lock, and the door is just pulled closed.

Now what? Do I enter?

I definitely don't want to call the police — no telling what drugs or drug paraphernalia may be inside. Do I bring someone over and further involve my friends in Shane's latest mess? Against my better judgment, I decide I'll go in. It's midday and there are people upstairs, and whoever broke the door is likely long gone.

I push the cheap, hollow-core door open and scan the inside. It's a human rathole. Contoured into the sloped space is a cubby-hole kitchen with a hot plate, microwave, small sink and one of those box-sized refrigerators. The dirt is covered with artificial-grass remnants that have been pieced together to cover the entire space. A TV is hung from a platform below an exposed beam; it faces a futon with some bedding and Mexican blankets jumbled up on it. Everything in the space has been tossed by someone who clearly meant to send a message. Smashed in the middle of the kitchen area are a CD player/stereo and about three dozen CDs, out of their jewel cases and broken into gleaming bits.

I glance to the back of the hovel. A surfboard is shoved up against a far corner, alongside the only window that lets in diffused light through its dust-coated glass. Embedded in the center of the board is a nine-inch hunting knife. I stand completely still and shiver unconsciously.

I quickly back out of the door, pulling it closed, and stare at the reflective gold numbers. I picture Shane as a fresh-faced teenager on the swim team, clean and shiny with pool water, and try to reconcile that youthful promise with this dirty squat. My mind jumps to logistics. Where's the bathroom? I stumble farther up the crumbled driveway and see a tilted staircase leading to the upstairs. Next to the door at the top of the stairway is a small bathroom window. Somehow the fact that Shane's "studio" has access to indoor plumbing makes me feel a tiny bit better — it's a ridiculous thought, given the damp crawl space living conditions and the threat of the knife.

Pulling out of my shocked stupor, I remember that I should bring Shane some clothes for when he gets out of the hospital. I don't want to re-enter the hovel, but I make myself do it. I try not to look around more than I have to; I came here to gather information, but I'm confronted with something I don't want to see. I grab some clothes and close the door.

Once I'm back slumped in the Honda, I can no longer contain the ache in the pit of my stomach. Tears stream down my face. I'm holding Shane's sweat shirt to my chest, as it heaves in and out. Questions run through my brain: How do you get to the point where this is what you're willing to accept for yourself?

This is a half-step, a very small half-step, from homelessness.

I stuff the key into the ignition and roll down the road, seeing nothing. I'm driving, but I have no destination. I just want to get away from this — I want the image of Shane in that hole purged from my brain. I want calm without crisis. As usual, I want to run away.

But I go to the market instead to pick up some supplies. There I can inhabit a place of normalcy, at least temporarily. The cart squeals as I roll up and down the aisles.

While waiting for my turn in one of the checkout lines, I see a former high-school boyfriend checking at the last turnstile. We dated for a whole two weeks during the fall of my junior year. He had a nice Mazda and he was a sloppy kisser. Now he's thirty pounds overweight, and since he's wearing a white shirt and tie under his apron I assume he's a manager or assistant manager. He's heavy, but he looks solid, with a neck the width of one of the hams in the meat counter, evidence he was once a high-school football star. I avert my eyes before he feels the stare. I can't remember his name, and I'm not in the mood for reminiscing.

I bag my own groceries, after the teenage clerk slides them across the scanner. She asks for my club card, but I'm not the club-card type. That requires buying groceries regularly and meals eaten at a table instead of over the kitchen sink or in front of my computer keyboard.

As I'm loading bags into the trunk of my car, I feel someone come up behind me. I turn around and look up into the dead eyes and twitchy sneer of Anton. He's standing over me, feet turned out, arms crossed. Despite the cold fog, he's wearing long red-and-black board shorts, flip-flops and a black sleeveless T-shirt. The crown portion of his shoulder-length greasy brown hair is pulled up in a top-knot ponytail, the rest hangs to just below his massive shoulders. His cheeks show the scars of teenage acne and are dark with a two-day beard.

"Welcome back, Dana." He snarls, his thin lips pulling back, displaying small yellowed teeth.

"Been following me, Anton?"

"Don't need to. I have eyes all over town." He spreads his long tatted arms wide.

I give a casual shrug. I refuse to show my mounting fear, since I'm sure that's the reaction he most enjoys.

"I heard you want to talk to me. I'm listening." He leans in, breathing heavily.

I want to back up. His stale breath and too-close bulk makes me curl in on myself. "Did you break Shane's arm?"

"You begin our conversation with this accusation, Dana? Tsk, tsk, very bad manners."

"As if you know what manners are, Anton."

His eyes darken and his jaw jumps, as he clenches and unclenches his teeth. Is he on his first gram of the day or third, I wonder.

"You're out of your league, Dana. Go back to the land of plastic people."

I just glare at him. His surprise visit hasn't given me time to figure out how to deal with him and help Shane. If I start by showing my willingness to deploy my wallet, my only real weapon, he'll just extort money from me and go right back to pounding Shane for whatever misstep he's made. I opt for acting tough by snarling like a scared little mutt.

"Still playing the schoolyard bully, huh Anton?"

The sarcasm goes by unacknowledged. "Shane knows the score. But it's embarrassing to have to play rough with the town wimp, who needs his little sister to stand up for him.

Your former surf star is a pathetic addict, Dana. Not worth the cost of a single rock."

My face reddens.

"He has to step up and answer for his mistake. We can be reasonable...or not."

I recover my tongue, and let it loose in its usual reckless fashion. "Who's 'we,' Anton? Who's pulling your choke-chain?"

He quickly steps into me; his chest is just inches from my face. "I can hurt you too, Dana. I'd enjoy that."

Panic hits and I'm up on my toes, ready to run. I catch quick movement to our left, and before I can see who or what is coming, Randy shoves Anton away from me; he stumbles nearly falling. It's weird how his name escaped me when I was observing him at the checkout counter, but it instantly jumps into my brain when he barrels in as my protector.

"Get out of my parking lot, Anton, or I'll have the cops remove you." The apron pulled around Randy's ample middle is inflating, expanding like a filling red balloon, as the adrenaline spikes his breathing and flushes his neck and face.

"Your parking lot, Randy?" Anton looks up and laughs at the sky. "The produce manager is launching a takeover. Whoa, look out!"

Randy huffs and stands his ground. A siren blares in the background and Anton twitches.

"I'll catch up with you later, Dana. I'm not in the mood to splatter a box boy today." Anton sneers at Randy, and turns on his heels, walking quickly toe-heel across the parking lot. I notice that another cretin was observing from a van during the parking-lot encounter. Anton jumps in and the driver guns the V8 and turns north into highway traffic.

Though shaken, Randy is standing a little taller, a little more proud than when he was scanning groceries. "Are you okay?"

"Yeah, Randy. Thanks for standing up for me."

"I assume that was about Shane."

"You've heard?" My breathing is fast and shallow.

"I heard he's in the hospital, and that his arm's broken. That's all. I know you wouldn't have anything to do with Anton unless Shane's involved."

Randy spins the grocery cart around, shakes his head and stares back toward the store. "Didn't think I still had that in me."

"You fooled me, Randy." My voice shakes, and I hug my arms to my body.

He looks back toward me. "How long are you in town for, Dana? You're still living in L.A., right?"

I haven't spoken to Randy in years, but it's the nature of small towns — through the grapevine he's heard the basics of my life.

"I'll be here through next weekend. Then it's back to Smogland."

Then he notices my tightly clutched arms. "Are you okay, Dana? I want to drive you home. You shouldn't go alone; I don't want Anton catching up to you again."

I want to tell him I'm fine, but I'm not. Anton's dead eyes and snarling lips come back to me. I can't speak, but I shake my head.

Randy steps over and gently touches my shoulder. He takes charge once again. "Drive around to the back of the store. I'll let you out the loading gate. Where are you headed?"

I tell him I'm going up to Dylan and Maria's. He's standing tall again. "Okay, I won't drive you but I'll follow you until I'm sure you're safe." I quickly reach out and hug him. He looks down at his shoes.

I close the trunk and throw myself into the car. Randy folds himself into the passenger seat. I grip the wheel to stop my fluttering hands. Glancing in the rearview mirror to make sure Anton hasn't magically returned, I see my blood-drained face.

At the loading gate, Randy hops out and gets into an older blue SUV. We convoy out of town, and start up the canyon. Uneven puffs of fog separate from the gray bank and move up the cut like wispy scouts, showing the fog wall the way into the canyon and hills. Just before we reach Dylan's driveway, I pull to the side of the narrow road and Randy follows.

I trot to his car door. "Thanks Randy. You are my knight."

A shy smile widens his mouth. "You take care, Dana. Scum like that can be hard to scrape off."

*

In the kitchen, Maria is banging on her computer. Music blares from Marco's room down the hall. I bring in the groceries and start putting things away.

Maria closes the laptop's lid and sighs. She spies the wine on the counter.

"I didn't buy a great meal, but I got the most important side dish." I put another bottle on the counter.

She stands and opens a nearby drawer, extracting a bottle opener. "Red or white?" She holds up two bottles.

"After this day, definitely red."

She cocks her head at me, a question without words.

"Later."

Marco shuffles into the kitchen. He has Dylan's lanky build, but with another three inches of height. With his caramel skin and shaggy hair, he looks like an international soccer star. Fortunately, he's too intent on his target, the refrigerator, to notice my fawning. He pulls the side-by-side open and grabs a coke. He eyes the chips and salsa I bought sitting on the counter.

"Are these fair game?" He's about to rip open the top of the bag.

Maria gets him to put the salsa and chips in bowls on the table, before he begins shoveling in earnest. Then she starts her nightly grilling about the state of his homework. A straight-A student, Marco indulges her unnecessary interrogation with good humor.

He responds by grilling his Mom about the state of his biggest concern: dinner. Maria slyly says "look in the fridge again." He jumps up and utters a "yeah," when he spies a large plate of fresh tamales hiding on the bottom shelf. Maria takes the plate from him and turns on the oven.

We hear Dylan pull up. Soon the family is munching chips, sipping beverages and chatting about Marco's upcoming soccer game, a North Coast division final. I relax for the first time today. Though I'm not part of this, I let the warmth of this close family seep in through my skin and help soothe my still tense core.

We're scraping dishes and loading the dishwasher when Dylan says he has some news for me. I know Maria doesn't really want to hear it, so we step into the den. Settling into overstuffed sofas, we put our feet on the coffee table and give our extended bellies the airspace they demand.

I'd called Dylan earlier, after my conversation with Joey about Ling. I'd asked him to find out how local law enforcement views Ling. Though prosecutors and public defenders work at cross purposes, they spend countless hours together. In a strange way, they're co-workers at the courthouse. "Spoke to Rose, an assistant DA, about Ling." He absently rubs his hand across his stomach. "Ling is ensuring job security for a federal investigation squad."

"Here, in Half Moon Bay?" I stutter. It's hard to believe that G-men are lurking in the artichoke fields. Dylan explains that a San Francisco-based squad is temporarily camped at an undisclosed location in town. But he says word around the courthouse is they've gathered little in the way of real evidence on Ling's operation. He keeps moving his labs.

"Are they aware of Shane's involvement?"

"Yes."

I deflate a little, despite the tamale-laden gut.

"Shane might be able to cooperate, cut a deal." There's no lift to Dylan's voice; he doesn't like this idea and he knows I won't either. The feds won't protect Shane, they'll just use him to get the convictions they seek, and when they're done he'll be back on the street with his addiction and a new, perhaps even more dangerous, supplier.

I tell Dylan about my day, and choke up once again when I describe Shane's crawl-space apartment. He hangs his head at my description, but he stiffens when I briefly describe my encounter with Anton.

"You're underestimating these shitheads." Dylan rarely swears, but he's frustrated with my phony nonchalance.

"You're right. But I have to find some way of negotiating with them. I'm hoping that perhaps I can clear some or all of Shane's drug tab and that will settle things with Ling."

Dylan's eyes are dark, his brow deeply furrowed. "When will Shane get out of the hospital?"

"I'm not sure. His doctor is waiting to get some new X-rays taken and to review the latest lab tests. At Community, he's in a long queue for any hospital services."

Dylan, clearly agitated, leans forward and snaps at me. "Why is this *your* problem, Dana? You can never fix his life."

"I can't just let him detonate without trying to put the pin back in. Joe has given up."

I almost say it, but don't: Valerie. How I fear Shane will take her escape route.

"You need your own life — an emotional investment that returns something."

I scoff.

But it hurts.

Chapter 8

I'm lounging in the loft the following day, listening to the bleating goats and trying to avoid facing the day. I wish I could stay burrowed in the down comforter and let the cyclone that is Shane's life blow through. What can I really do against the threats of Anton and his gang of miscreants? But I drag myself from the cocoon and head for the hot water.

As I'm stepping out of the shower, my cellphone rings.

"Mornin', Baby Sis."

"Hey, Shane, you're sounding good."

"Feelin' freedom in the air. They're releasing me today."

My stomach does a back flip. The last thing I need is Shane out of the hospital, looking to score recreational drugs to complement his cocktail of prescription meds. Despite his run-down appearance, Shane's life force is strong, or he would have expired long ago. His poor abused body has powers of recovery mere mortals lack.

My brain goes into overdrive, trying to come up with a plan to keep Shane in a controlled environment. Anton and Ling will hear within hours if he's out cruising his usual surfside haunts. They'll be back on him like flies on kelp.

"What time do they say they'll have you signed out?"

"Gotta wait for the doc to come by on his rounds and sign off. I get one last meal of yummy hospital gruel and a free wheelchair ride out the door around eleven or eleven thirty. Can you give me a ride home?"

He needs transportation, so that's my chance to kidnap him and stash him in a safe zone.

"I'll be there just after eleven. I have some fresh clothes for you in the car."

"Did you go by my humble abode?" Sad resignation in his quiet voice.

"Yeah. We'll talk when I see you."

We say our goodbyes. I need help. I can't pull off sibling abduction without an accomplice. I dial Dylan.

*

"Dylan, Shane's getting released, today. Are there any rehab facilities that might take him on short notice?" Panic makes me stammer.

"Not easy, Dana. But I do have an idea. I was mulling it last night. There's a place up in Daly City that's not too expensive and owes me a favor."

I exhale and say a prayer to the rehab angels, who try to repair human wreckage when everyone else thinks addicts are disposable. Dylan says he'll call the facility and see if they have space.

"What's it going to cost to get him in there, Dylan?"

"They're going to want to keep him for at least four weeks. And even though it's a county-sponsored facility, it's going to run $2,000 a week."

I rake my hands roughly through my dripping hair. "I have the first two weeks covered and I'll find the rest." He says he'll make the call and get back to me. It's my third day here and Shane is doing the only thing he does as well as he surfs: drain my bank account. But spending this money will be easy — it's getting Shane to agree to rehab that will require all the power and finesse of netting a shark.

I decide to sneak away from Maria and Dylan's house, while waiting for Dylan's call back. I can't face Maria's scowl when she finds out that I'm funding another treatment program for Shane. I grab a hotel laundry bag out of one of the pockets of my suitcase — professional road warriors always have laundry bags from multiple hotels stashed in their luggage. I pile Shane's change of clothes into the bag; grab my purse and cellphone and quietly tip-toe down the stairs and across the gravel.

I head back to Shane's hovel. I re-enter the damp-smelling dirt den and push down my revulsion. I find a small duffel bag and fill it with underwear and another couple of T-shirts. No toothpaste or cosmetics necessary. If he's admitted to rehab, they won't allow him to bring in any liquids or creams that could hide drugs or worse. Alcoholics will drink mouthwash or rubbing alcohol; druggies will swallow anything that might offer a buzz. I've seen Shane pick up roaches off the floor and smoke them. I finish quickly and scramble back out into the light. Next I drive to the Java Hut.

I get my go-go juice and a twenty-ouncer for Shane. He's signing the discharge papers as I arrive, including a promise to pay. Right; they might as well file that document as "uncollectible" before we leave. He finishes with the administrator and I hand him the clothes I brought for him. While he's dressing in the bathroom, an orderly comes with the wheelchair.

We begin the parade across the linoleum landscape. Shane collects a few "take cares" and "see you soons" from his healthcare groupies. He chats with the tall orderly driving his steel wheels. At the car, he folds himself carefully into the passenger seat.

"We're going over to Dylan's office." I'm not asking for his input; I'm stating the plan.

Shane stares suspiciously at the side of my face as I drive eyes-locked-straight-ahead, concentrating more than necessary on the light coastal traffic. "What's up?"

"You'll just have to wait and see."

He exhales hard and squirms in his seat. But he doesn't yank open the door and roll out of the moving car — one possible reaction. I'm not being overly dramatic. Shane once jumped out of a second-story window onto a flatbed truck to get away from a fellow druggie gone loony tunes who was about to carve his face with a broken crack pipe.

We drive in silence to Dylan's office, which is located at the back of a low-rise building filled with business suites. At first, Shane sits sullenly in the car refusing to get out. But he owes it to me to hear what Dylan and I have in mind. "And you just can't wait to get back to your underground palace, right?" I glower at him.

He doesn't want to have that discussion with me, so he gets out of the car and walks slowly to the office door. We enter Dylan's small reception area, stuffed with a metal desk, plastic chairs, and a humming copy machine. Dylan is in his glass-fronted office to the left. He's on the phone, but he waves us in, and we settle into square office chairs in front of his desk. Dylan winds up his call with "Thanks again for this. I'll get back to you soon." He replaces the receiver and walks around the desk. Shane and he embrace in a quick, back-slap man-hug, as Dylan scrutinizes the large foam cast and sling enveloping Shane's arm.

"Hey Shane, nice accessory."

"Yeah, like, it's just so fashion forward." Shane mimics the voice of a teenage Valley Girl. His comedic skills are intact even if his limbs aren't.

I decide to launch right into my pitch. No sense trying to fool a master manipulator. And I don't have time for niceties.

"We want to talk to you about taking some time at Forest Glen up in Daly City." Dylan looks at me – he's all for the direct approach.

"Ah, you do-gooders need a project, eh? Mission Shane."

I try to hold down my anger as my face immediately flushes. His reply is so Shane: He doesn't need help; we need a rescue mission. He's not in trouble; we're on a campaign to meddle. He's not an addict; we're sad automatons who can't handle life on the edge.

Before I can blow, Dylan jumps into the airspace. "Wouldn't it make sense to rest the arm and recover your balance? Where else do you need to be, Shane?" Dylan has lots of experience with the words of intervention.

Shane locks his jaw and stares out of the window beyond Dylan, out into the free world beyond the glass. He already has the posture of a trapped animal. He's shifting in his chair, tapping his foot, and there's both resignation and resistance in the set of his mouth.

"Rent's due, I gotta work" is his eventual comeback.

"And your landlord has eager replacement tenants lined up for your deluxe digs, right?" My voice gets louder and I jab at him. "Your 'job' resulted in the busted arm. Don't you think you need some temporary disability leave?"

Shane throws out other ridiculous objections and we parry back and forth with him. But it's clear that for now we're going to prevail. Dylan explains the program — four weeks, therapy group sessions twice a day, a private counseling session every other day. Patients do all the facility upkeep, including cooking, dishes, yard work, cleaning, laundry, etc. Shane's familiar with the drill; this is rehab Part III, or it is Part IV? I've lost count. No visitors allowed for the first couple of weeks.

Shane mumbles "yeah, yeah, yeah." I figure he's already planning his early checkout, read "escape."

Oh well, right now I need him contained and out of Anton's and Ling's reach. Dylan calls Forest Glen and tells them we'll be arriving in an hour.

Our ride to Daly City is quiet. Shane dials the radio into some nineties rock and slumps into his seat and fakes a nap, with his hoodie thrown over his face. I follow the directions that Dylan printed out for me. Soon we're pulling up the treed gravel drive to some low buildings with green-painted wood trim and putty-colored stucco. It's an institution dressed like a ranch-style home. It looks similar to the last one Shane attended, or was it the one before?

The registration process goes smoothly — if a checkbook's weight is related to its balance, mine has just gone on a crash diet and is feeling very trim. After a quick hug and some mumbled "I love yous," an administrator leads Shane away for a facilities tour and drug test. I give the treatment director the rundown on Shane's drug use, rehab history and broken arm. Then we get to the really fun part: our family history.

From a distance, I hear my deadened voice describe our turbulent and violent childhood, Shane's wild-child difficulties and his untreated bipolar illness, Joe's current detachment, and oh yeah Valerie's manic depression, drug use and suicide. That about covers it. No shock registers on the director's face. He's heard it all before and plenty more that probably makes our upbringing look like a sweet family TV drama.

*

I pull back into memories that are better left unexamined. Days when Shane misbehaved, Joe lost it and beat him with a belt until he was screaming and he needed antibiotic cream to treat the bleeding welts. Times when I didn't want to come home because Mom had been in one of her depressive phases and hadn't moved from the couch in five or six days. Shane

71

internalized all of that, and I ran. Who had the healthier reaction?

Our mother was fighting her demons from her late teens. But we were first affected by her post-partum depression. She eventually got better, but then as I was graduating from the toddler phase, Joe told us she'd gone away "for a rest." What does that mean to a four-year-old? Mommy needs a rest because you've been bad – that's what it means. We thought we'd been terrible kids and that's why she needed a retreat. She was gone for four weeks, and a nanny took care of us when Dad was at work. I loved the nanny, Rosey; she paid attention to me. I resented Valerie's return.

When she came back she was drugged and twenty-five pounds thinner. After that, Mom and Dad didn't scream at each other, but they didn't talk either. Even Shane behaved, for a while. In those days, no one thought about the impact on us kids. It was like we had some kind of immunity to the chaos that passed for our family life. Mom was treated; Dad worked long hours and stayed away. The adults thought we were unaware.

But we saw all of it, processed it and used it to create our understanding, or misunderstanding, of relationships and families. Shane's hyper behavior and later manic depression intensified his reaction. I grew to reject the idea of a peaceful home life — I'd never seen one. And what I saw — why would anyone opt to live like *that*?

*

But I'm not sharing these memories with the counselor. He's peering at me, in that intense, raised-eyebrows way all counselors do, absorbing my speech and evaluating my mental stability. We're all just one binge away from a breakdown, his look says.

I loathe this part of the care and feeding of Shane. I have my own familial scars, but I've managed to put myself through college, cultivate a career and lead a stable life, even if that life doesn't include a steady relationship. I'm not an addict, and I'm nobody's victim. I'm not your next patient, pal. I am not my brother. And although I've done time on the couch, I'll do it on my schedule. I'm not in a sharing mood today.

I cut the interview short, with excuses about a made-up appointment. A quick shake of his hand, and I'm out the door and accelerating out of the parking lot, throwing gravel as I go. Demons and doubts can't wrestle down a body in motion, and I'm always in motion.

*

Mom tried to outrun her demons, too. She left college before graduating to take an executive assistant job that involved travel. But Dad wooed her back. A year after her breakdown when I was four, she left us again. This time she ran to her parents' house in Oregon, after she and Dad had a particularly bad fight. Her longest escape was when I was in junior high. Without a word to any of us, she left two weeks before Christmas. Dad had been gone a lot right before that. He'd been working very long hours, and missing dinners with the family. We'd heard them fight. She called Dad after twenty-four hours, but she didn't come home. We didn't understand — was Mom sick again, or had our behavior or one of their battles caused her to leave? Shane and I spoke with her twice on the phone while she was away. But Terry refused.

She came back four days before Christmas. Obviously medicated, her speech was slow, and she was lethargic. But things were calm, and she and Dad made a big effort to celebrate the holidays and be outwardly loving toward each other. We didn't buy it.

*

It's late afternoon, a low sun drawing white shimmering streaks west to east across the water. No marine layer yet. I decide life will look a lot better if I just add water. So I speed to Craig's and raid his toy stash. I pull into Harborside beach with two hours of daylight left.

Within five minutes of parking, I'm paddling out in ankle-biter waves. They're mostly one- to two-foot rollers, but peeling nicely right to left. I punch through a wave to get outside the break, pulling my knees under me and pushing my head and board-nose through the wave's lip, buns up. I emerge out the other side of the water wall; my head soaked and my wetsuit flushed. I grin, start paddling again and shake the sea from my ears. Yep, life is definitely better when wet. I dance across the waves, working Craig's longboard with my feet to hook into and hold rides all the way to the sand. No brother, no family, no past...and at times no thoughts.

I ride in as the light starts to fade. With the heater blasting, I check my cell and replay two short messages from Dylan, asking me to call.

He picks up on the second ring. "Hey, Dana, how did the drop-off go?"

"He's contained...for now."

"Good. Can you get to my office in the next twenty minutes?"

"Sure. What's up?" I push my wet hair behind my ears.

"I'd like you to meet one of the feds who's been tracking Ling. He's been over here discussing another case with one of my partners, but he should be free for a chat in a bit, if you can get here soon."

"I just got out of the water at Harborside, and I'm salty, but I'll jam over there."

"How's the swell?" Dylan may be a successful attorney, but every surfer wants the latest wave report, whether he can ride that day or not.

"One to two, but peeling and glassy. Longboard friendly."

I weave through quitting-time traffic. When I arrive, the G-man is already sitting in one of the square chairs opposite Dylan's desk. I stiffen as I enter.

They both stand as I walk into the office. He's in his late thirties, but still hanging on to that college prep look, polo shirt with the little embroidered horse galloping across his noticeably pumped peck. He's paired the baby blue shirt with perfectly creased khakis. City dweller all the way — no dry cleaner in Half Moon Bay can deliver creases that sharp.

Dylan makes the introductions. "Dana McCarren, meet Agent Stokes." As I lean forward and shake his hand, my wet hair drips onto his forearm.

"Sorry about that. Haven't had enough time to drip dry."

Agent Stokes' mouth turns up into a slight smile, with a sneer behind it, and he wordlessly and deliberately wipes the salt water from his forearm. He rubs his hands together to dry them; he wouldn't want to wilt those creases by swiping his hand across those perfect pants.

As we all take our seats, I glance sidelong at him and take in his imposing presence. Seated he still makes Dylan and me look diminutive. His light brown hair is conservatively cut, short sideburns, clean neck. He has hazel eyes, a long straight nose and a ruddy complexion. I'm thinking East Coast upbringing, graduated a name college, varsity crew team.

Without any preliminary pleasantries, Agent Stokes starts the conversation/interrogation: "So Shane is your brother?"

"Can I plead the fifth?" I'm not a criminal, G-man. What's more, to use a bad cliché, I question authority. I'm a journalist; it comes with the territory.

Dylan jumps in before the nipping and snarling can begin in earnest. "Agent Stokes, Dana is a journalist and lives in Los Angeles; she's only just arrived in town to help her injured brother. She's trying to find out how he got hurt, and how we can best help him."

Stokes apologizes, with obvious insincerity. "Sorry, I go immediately into interview mode."

"Me too."

He doesn't smile at my snarky remark. Instead Stokes feeds me a short teaser of information, hoping I'll reciprocate. "Ling has been on our radar for roughly two years. We estimate he's currently operating seven meth labs in Half Moon Bay, Daly City, Brisbane and South San Francisco. He's a Thai citizen, with a legitimate green card." He sighs. "Don't ask."

He continues his report. "Prior to cooking meth, he smuggled it in from Thailand. Over there, it's called *yaa baa*. It's as common as pot, and cheaper in some cases. Ling hooked up with some of the American surf crowd because Thailand is on the global surf radar: warm water, friendly ladies, and cheap drugs." Clearly, Agent Stokes isn't much of a surf groupie. And his esteem for the surf crowd is sure to decline further when he meets Shane.

"We think Ling recruited some local surfers to smuggle for him, before he came to the States. Thai authorities tell us he had a couple of small labs in Koh Samui, plying locals and tourists. But the high risk and severe penalties in Thailand for getting caught drug smuggling limited his drug mule recruitment and thus his franchise expansion. So he got a relative to give him and two friends legitimate jobs in a Thai restaurant, or that's how it looked to immigration. And they're cooking in the U.S. alright, but they're not whipping up curries." Stokes grins, so proud of his clever little turn of phrase.

"So why haven't you busted him?" Blunt, that's how I roll.

"We've arrested a couple of his dealers, but he uses runners to get the drugs to them, so they don't know the locations of the labs. If they knew, they would have cut deals with us and pled out. He moves his labs frequently and he cleans up when he moves on. We've only heard from one landlord, who thought his rental smelled foul and got curious when the previous tenant, a Thai family, cut out a few square feet of the kitchen's vinyl floor and volunteered that the landlord should keep their deposit."

Stokes tilts his head at me. "The subfloor in that kitchen tested positive for meth, but we were unable to track the 'family' to a new address. In Daly City, residents keep their heads down. No one could accurately describe their former neighbors."

I continue to listen...while waiting for the pitch ...

"As Dylan probably told you, we've dedicated resources and a task force to gathering evidence against Ling and shutting him down. That's where Shane comes in."

Bingo. As yet, they have no case against Ling and no proof that Shane actually works for him. But he's already on their ballot for top *yaa baa* informant.

I could tell him upfront that there's not a chance in hell that Shane would ever snitch. But he'd just get mad and try harder to nail Shane. And I want the information flow, even if it's just an FBI trickle, to continue for as long as I can.

"Shane's in rehab. And he's not allowed visitors for the first couple of weeks. After that, only immediate family will be able to visit him while he finishes his four-week program."

Stokes' face darkens. He's visibly frustrated by this news, not just because his chosen informant is untouchable for four weeks, but even more ego-damaging I've managed to stash Shane out of his reach before he knew he was being released from the hospital.

I don't want to enrage Agent Stokes, so I ease out some fishing line. "Perhaps you can tell me what you can do for Shane, and when I get to visit him I'll relay your offer?"

But this statement still gets Agent Stokes hot under his Polo collar. "Shane is in serious trouble — he's up against at least four felony charges and Ling clearly isn't pleased with him either. He needs to get smart and figure out who can help him."

Right, Stokes, you're his guardian. You can set him up to get killed instead of just maimed. But I keep this opinion to myself. "How would you *help* him?"

Shane's just a tiny anchovy in this ocean; long-term witness protection won't be on the fish hook. And if they had a case to charge him with he'd be in county jail already.

"He wouldn't need to testify, only help us locate labs and gather evidence. He'd get a pass on any charges for trafficking, selling and possession." Stokes crosses his ankle over his knee...a relaxed deal-maker, offering a reasonable solution.

While I mull this over, Dylan jumps in. "Could you relocate him temporarily afterward to a drug treatment facility out of state? And would the government pick up the tab?" Dylan has lots of experience haggling for deals with law enforcement. He says it's like bartering in Mexico for souvenirs: Only amateurs accept the first price.

Stokes rubs his chin; it looks like a practiced gesture to convey not-so-serious contemplation. "It might be possible. I'll see what I can do."

"Well, Shane is unreachable for two weeks in any case." I look at Dylan when I say this and he tilts his head at Stokes.

"Actually, if we charge him or name him as a material witness, a judge would order his treatment facility to let us see him." Stokes sits up taller, the stiff-backed commander. He places his feet flat on the ground.

I tighten my grip on the chair arms. "And you'd get nothing. You push Shane, and he'll just clam up. If you wait, and it seems to me your case needs a lot of work anyway, he'll be down off the ice and perhaps more cooperative." I don't really believe that, but it buys time.

Quiet fills the room. It's a stalemate, for now.

Still, I want one more piece of data, Ling's full name. With it, I can do my own research on Ling's criminal history, both online and through my journalism contacts. "Why do you call him just Ling? Is that his first or last name?"

Agent Stokes mulls his reply. Law enforcement only wants to gather information, not share it. He decides to open up...a little. "Ling is a nickname. But it's the only one he ever uses. His full name is Noi Krungbakorn."

I've just checked Shane into another rehab program, Mom. Do you think he'll stay? Will this latest treatment plan get him to recognize that the drugs don't take him away from his problems, they compound them? It's exhausting being his keeper, patron, guidance counselor and surrogate parent. You refused to give up on Shane...you always said that he'd eventually grow up and find his path in life. But it hasn't happened. He obsesses, he swings, he flies, and he crashes.

I'm glad you can't see where your golden boy is living, Mom. It would crush you. And I'm trying to extricate him from the mess he's in, but the good guys are as shadowy and malevolent as the bad guys. And Shane still hasn't told me why the bad guys hurt him.

P.S. I want to run. There's a reason I can't form lasting attachments. Strings can strangle.

Chapter 9

After my encounter with Agent Stokes, I need time to process his information and to just be alone, the space I inhabit most easily. I tell Dylan that I have plans for dinner (I don't) and that I won't be back to the house until late.

In the darkness and mist, my car is a travel-capsule of warmth and protection. I drive south, with no destination in mind. Passing artichoke fields and eucalyptus groves, I feel the ocean's presence and rhythms, though I can't see it. About eight miles south of town, I pull into a small parking lot facing the ocean at the south end of a U-shaped cove and kill the engine. I watch the surge and retreat of the surf and feel its seismic shaking.

Before leaving town, I stopped at the local Chinese takeout. Opening a brown paper sack, I unpack a large carton of fragrant and still-steaming noodles and chicken and pour a small tub of red-pepper garlic sauce over the top. I hold the carton under my chin as I twirl chopsticks into the mix and slurp up mouthfuls. By the third spicy bite, my nose is already running, and I have to interrupt the feeding frenzy to gulp bottled water.

I replay the conversation with Stokes, reprocessing his disclosures and mulling over what he didn't say. He didn't say what role he thinks Shane has been playing in Ling's organization, even though he listed criminal charges Shane could face. Clearly, that was FBI bluster. He probably wasn't even aware of Shane's connection to Ling until Shane's broken arm became drug-den gossip.

After processing everything that was said, I'm hopeful that he doesn't yet have enough of a case to interfere in Shane's rehab.

Tomorrow's agenda is clear: Work the web to learn more about Ling and meth lab operation and production. And hunt down some more of Shane's friends to try to gather information on his work with Ling.

I have a plan, and I have heartburn. It's time to get back to the barn.

On the way, I swing by Craig's to drop off his surfboard. He hears me pull up to the house and meets me outside the garage to help me unload. He's barefoot, in jeans that threaten to slide off his slim hips. A tight T-shirt accentuates his lean torso and divided biceps.

"Hey, Dana, how was the swell?"

"Mostly two-foot rollers, but fun rides. The rest of my day was less enjoyable. " I tell him about convincing Shane to go to rehab, and I describe the meeting with Agent Stokes. Craig silently absorbs all the news.

"Shane is off on a four-week vacation at Club Forest Glen." At the edge of the driveway, I shake the sand out of one of the Honda's floor mats. "Have you seen where he's been living?"

"No. I've only seen Shane once or twice in the past eight or nine months, always at a break."

I sigh and try to describe his crawl-space burrow. My voice shakes. "He's living like the rats that inhabit the rocks at the harbor's breakwater."

Craig rocks forward and stares at his bare feet, while he slowly shakes his head. We stand in silence, listening to the foghorn's long low call and the breeze rattle the branches overhanging the house. Craig has done his share of Shane rescues — he knows there are no easy fixes, so he doesn't offer any pat answers.

*

Craig hasn't just rescued Shane. Long ago, he helped get me out of Half Moon Bay.

In high school, my scholastic abilities emerged, with the help of a math teacher who took an interest in me and wouldn't let me slack. He was relentless; he saw my potential and pushed. By junior year, I had been consistently delivering a four-point-zero grade average.

Craig had already graduated and then became distracted by surf and carpentry work. But he'd refocused and had re-entered school, attending a junior college, with plans to go on to university. "It's miserable getting back into study mode again, Dana. I've forgotten so much in such a short time. Don't get sidetracked."

Jim, the math teacher, coached me to sign up for a prep class for the standardized tests, and found funding from the school's college prep program. He also helped me apply to schools — I knew right away that I wanted to attend U.C. San Diego. It was as far away from Half Moon Bay as I could get within the U.C. system, and surrounded by surf breaks. I aced the tests and was accepted early.

Valerie and Joe not only didn't encourage me, they actively tried to dissuade me. They tried to talk me into attending a community college. At the time, I was just angry. I knew they didn't have the means to help finance my education, but they had to disparage my dream as well? My therapist has helped me understand that as college dropouts it was fear they were voicing. They worried I'd end up facing failure as they had.

I was done with their fears, as soon as I drove south. Craig helped me move. At college, I discovered a fascination with economics, which requires math skills and logic and encompasses political theory and international business. My ability to write came naturally. I'd even edited friends' term papers for extra money. With a scholarship, financial aid, student loans, waitress work at a campus eatery and my already evident force of will, I graduated in four years.

*

My web surfing the next day is tedious, but informative. First I comb The Herald's archives to see if Ling's real name appeared in any crime stories in the past five years. Even though I work in L.A., any big Bay Area drug busts would likely make the paper's news budget. No joy. So I drop a quick note to a former co-worker who's now with the San Francisco Chronicle. Can he get me a temporary password so I can comb their archives for free?

My email program sings the happy song as he pings me back. Yes, I can have access, and yes I owe a favor. Typical journalistic trading. With a few keystrokes, I'm into the archives and searching on Ling's full name and keywords "drugs" and "meth."

It seems that Ling was arrested two years ago for meth dealing and possession — the initial bust is just a five-inch filler piece. But a follow-up story from two weeks later is much more interesting. It says the charges were dropped due to a lack of evidence and improper search-and-seizure procedures, which triggered an internal investigation of the arresting officers. Apparently the cops slapped around and questioned a teen cousin of Ling's without an adult present. Definitely a no-no. They used the information they gathered from the harassed juvenile to find Ling and search his car. So the search was predicated on an illegal interrogation of a minor and worse, it turns out the drugs they'd said they found on the seat were actually found in the trunk. After the bust, residue was found in the trunk, but not on the seat. They'd lied about the drugs being in plain sight, thus they needed a warrant and never got one. To make matters worse, the Thai community used the case to make noise about police profiling of Asians for drug crimes and law enforcement roughing up minors.

Nothing motivates the men in blue more than a criminal who beats the system and rubs their faces in it. No wonder Ling's the target of a joint task force.

I turn my attention to finding out more about *yaa baa,* drug culture in Thailand and meth production in the States. *Yaa baa,* aka yaba and several other names, is not the same as the U.S. version of meth, I discover. It is manufactured in pill form, and the recipe typically includes methamphetamine and caffeine. Shane's meth is usually sold in small rocks or crystals, and I've heard it called by many street names: crystal, crank and sometimes ice.

Then there's the term speed, which I learn can refer to meth or amphetamine, but they're not the same. Amphetamine is methylated phenyl ethylamine. Methamphetamine starts out as the same chemical, but it is double methylated, instead of only methylated once. I sucked at high school chemistry, but apparently this double cooking intensifies the drug, causing it to have a much more powerful psychotropic effect on users' brains.

I move on to more reading about *yaa baa.* One story says that the *yaa baa* formula was originally created and used by the Nazis to keep their troops awake for days. But the drug, according to reports from the BBC and Asian news sources, is becoming increasingly popular throughout Asia. The BBC says the translation of *yaa baa* is "madness drug" or "crazy medicine." No wonder the FBI is so worried about Ling's operation. He's brought fast-food meth to America.

Pill-form meth is sure to gain a following. No doubt this is why Agent Stokes is so motivated to shut Ling down, and this investigation has probably been blessed from much higher up in the FBI food chain. It's a sexy case. If Stokes can take down Ling, he'll likely swim up the FBI fish ladder a few rungs.

I dig deeper to learn more about meth production. One of the most popular methods of cooking meth involves using ephedrine or pseudoephedrine, but the sale of that once over-the-counter drug has now been severely restricted in U.S. No worries, dealers keep coming up with new recipes. And increased meth demand has attracted smugglers and a variety of producers: Asian, Mexican and other gangs, anyone who thinks they can cook and sell an illicit, but highly profitable product.

Several news stories detail scary explosions. Dangerous chemicals figure into meth production, and runaway chemical reactions or poor ventilation causes sometimes result in lab explosions.

I do one more search, this time on the name "Ling," nosing around Thai language sites and sites that discuss Thai names. Turns out "Ling" is the Thai word for monkey, and it's often used by teachers to refer to naughty students. Most likely, Noi Krungbakorn, aka Ling, started out as an unruly grammar student, probably pursued prep studies in drug use and petty theft, and eventually graduated to violent felonies.

With bleary eyes and knotted shoulders, it's time to take a break from the machine. As I start shutting down web sessions, a new email comes in from my editor, Wylie.

"Dana, when are you returning to town? We need to touch base before the conference. Call me. W."

Wylie and I have a respectful relationship, but it certainly isn't close. With his slouched posture and paunch, it's clear Wylie isn't a fan of physical pursuits. The shoulder seams of his rumpled collared shirts hang to mid-deltoid, and his soft white forearms poke out of his rolled-up sleeves, straws emerging from wrinkled paper packaging. His spectator sport is politics and he edits the reporters who cover that blood sport, as well as economics, my long-time beat.

Originally from Iowa, the ocean holds no special allure for him. He abhors the shore and sand, how it sticks to one's feet, grinds into one's skin and on a windy day blows into the eyes. He lives in Los Angeles but doesn't visit its famous beaches — that's like living in the Rockies without ever going hiking.

I finish closing down all my web sessions, except one, and click to the conference website. Quickly scanning the speaker list and agenda, I see that all of the top world economists and multinational business leaders are still planning to attend the World Economic Forum, no cancellations or changes. With the newspaper business in transition as websites and bloggers encroach on traditional media, the travel budget shrinks every quarter. And since I'm one of the paper's reporters who travels regularly, I'm constantly under pressure to justify my globetrotting. I dial Wylie.

"Townsend."

"Hey, Wylie, it's Dana." I've called before the final countdown to the daily press run, so the eyelid-twitching stress hasn't hit just yet. But this late in the day, I won't have to sit through a long discussion, which suits me just fine.

"Dana, are you still up north?"

Silly question. I put in for a week off but when you work for someone whose idea of vacation time is a few days gardening and watching CNBC, you have to be patient.

"Yeah Wylie. I'm planning to drive back on Saturday. My flight out to Zurich is Sunday."

He already knows all this, but he'll like hearing again that I'm flying on a weekend, burning my personal time for the good of the paper.

"Any changes to the agenda?"

"I just checked the conference website and it's all the same as we've discussed." Before I registered for the conference, Wylie and I spoke at length about the conference issues, keynote speakers and possible story topics. I'm hoping to do a series of interviews on banking reform, a topic that's become a hot button within the European Union and in America. Policymakers from France, Germany and Belgium will be attending the conference, along with top corporate and banking economists from America.

Nonetheless, Wylie has me run through all this again. In addition to the series, which I'll report and write as the conference progresses, I'll file a ten-incher on Monday, reporting the details of the opening keynote. It will appear in Tuesday's paper. He rings off abruptly when he's interrupted by the managing editor about last-minute cuts to one of tomorrow's page-one stories.

Replaying the conversation, once again I'm reminded of the dichotomy that's my life. Part beach rat/extreme athlete, part career woman; these worlds don't mix. When I'm in Half Moon Bay, I feel like I no longer fit in the small sleepy town that is blissfully removed from global issues. In L.A. or around the world, I'm respected as a hardened journalist but it's a cloak that disguises my true core. I work on land, but I inhabit the sea.

I've spent two-thirds of the day indoors and bent around my laptop. I need to untwist.

I decide to cruise a few surf spots to see if I can run into any of Shane's surf brahs. I'd like to learn Shane's exact role in Ling's operation.

First stop, Ward Creek, a ways south of town. It's a break that's popular with locals, but not often frequented by tourists from the City. It sports a hidden cove, where surfers can smoke a fatty before or after a session.

The waves peel right at this break, but today they're mushy and closing out. Instead of collapsing bit by bit along a horizontal path, long sections are falling all in one piece. I see two rubber-wrapped desperados trying to work a few rides out of these little bumps. Just two or three turns and they pop out the backside.

I pick up my sandals and plod through the soft sand, then angle out to the water's edge and push north against a light breeze. After a short walk, I can start to see around a rocky peninsula into a U-shaped cut-out in the sandstone cliffs. Huddled there are three watermen. They're probably just passing the time, aided by some inhaled conversation-enhancer. A toke and a talk, that's how the surf crowd rolls.

As I get closer, I recognize one of the guys sitting in the sand: Andy, a former teenage surf star and juvenile delinquent. Over the years and decades, he and Shane spent time together in pursuit of waves and chemically altered reality. Andy liked to find the margins, too, until his body had other ideas. Four years ago, he was diagnosed with multiple sclerosis. But in Andy's case the MS pushed the reset button in his consciousness that his family could never find. Last time I was in town, we met up in the water. He said he now puts as much effort into obtaining and consuming organic produce — he's become a vegan — as he once expended trying to score illegal drugs.

I turn up toward the group and Andy recognizes me. He jogs over to me and lifts me off the sand in a hug.

"Dana, you're back from the Southland." Like Shane, Andy has one of those loud, naturally growly voices. Even outside, with the background crash of the surf, he's ear-splitting. Plus his hearing is shot from "surfer's ear" — a calcium build-up in his ear canals from too much cold rushing water.

"I'm here just for a week, Andy."

"Have you been windsurfing or surfing?"

"Craig and I sailed Waddle the other day and I surfed some little lumps yesterday in town. But I've been otherwise engaged most of the week." I make direct eye contact and watch his face fall.

"I heard about Shane. How's his arm? Is he still in the hospital?"

I fill Andy in on Shane's medical recovery and much-hoped for chemical recovery. But I stop short of naming his rehab facility. One slip of the lip, and Ling's goons will be casing the place.

"I wish Shane could get the beast off his back." He shakes his head. "He's been at it too long. He needs to respect the temple."

I sigh and prod him for information. "I need your help, Andy. What have you heard about his role with Ling?"

As with Joey, Andy tries to talk me out of getting involved. But it's way too late for that. Besides, he's seen how dogged I am. As teens, Shane used to try to ditch me to go surfing either alone or with his buddies. I was stubborn; I didn't get left behind often. After years as a journalist, I'm far worse now.

We plop down on a sand ledge at the edge of the wet sand, where the high tide cut the beach on its last advance. He stares out across the blue-on-blue horizon, the late afternoon shimmer on the water reflecting in his sunglasses. "Shane let a little bit slip the last time I ran into him."

With raised eyebrows, I silently ask.

"He was working off some drug debts. Shane doesn't really want to hang with heavies like Ling."

"What was he doing for Ling?"

"Running batches between labs and distributors...a delivery boy."

"Was he skimming? Is that why Ling had his goons pound him?"

"No way, Dana. Even high, Shane has more sense than that."

"What then?"

Andy tosses his blond-tipped curls and turns his hands up. I notice a slight trembling in his right arm. A hint of the challenges he'll face ahead. "I don't know anything specific, but word is it was something pretty big."

We sit in silence, listening to the squawk of a few seagulls passing low overhead. I thank Andy for his help and ask about his health struggle. He gives me an update on his med regime, vegan cooking and his family. "Dana, in some ways MS saved my life. I'd be where Shane is now, or worse, if it wasn't for the MS bitch-slapping me."

I jog back down the wet sand and across the ankle-deep mounds to the Honda.

*

"Shane's gone AWOL." Dylan is nearly yelling into the phone, which is almost as alarming as his news.

"That stupid SHIT!" My face flushes. Tight, shallow breaths fail to fill my lungs.

My temples begin to pulse. "How did you hear?"

Dylan lowers his voice a notch, but runs his words together. "An old client, Miguel, works on the maintenance crew at Forest Glen. He was fixing screens in the wing of rooms where Shane was assigned. He'd just called me yesterday to check in, and I'd asked him to buddy up to Shane, keep an eye out for me. He thinks Shane slipped away after the group session."

"How? The place is pretty isolated." But my inner voice scoffs. Shane, even with a busted arm, is as slippery as an eel. And, Forest Glen isn't a locked-down facility.

"Miguel doesn't know, but there are always cars and delivery vans coming and going."

Rage is making it hard for me to concentrate on the road. I spin the wheel and pull into a sandy turnout. My thoughts whirl. Where will he go? He knows he can't go back to his hovel. Drugs — they'll be his first priority.

"Where do your clients go to score?"

Dylan exhales hard. "Uh, let me think...the field by the Hook is an open-air drugstore. But Shane won't go there, that would be like walking into Anton's office. The 7-Eleven on the south end of town — some of my clients have been arrested there. And the alley behind the strip mall, the one where Las Palmas is located, sees some regular action."

I burn out of the sand and jolt back onto the pavement. "I'm going to check the 7-Eleven and the strip mall. And I swear if Anton hasn't killed him first I will. Ungrateful asshole."

"Call me if you find him. And try to calm down, Dana. You know a heated confrontation won't work with Shane."

"Yeah, whatever." I step hard on the gas.

I should just turn my car around and head for L.A. I lean forward and scream out loud: "GO TO HELL, SHANE!" I'm pushing my old sedan so hard that the steering wheel shimmies. I don't care. I want to hurt something. Pressure builds behind my eyes.

Entering the south end of town, I cross a double-yellow without hesitation and stomp even harder on the gas pedal to get around a semi that's hauling a loader on a flatbed. He hits his horn when I brake hard to squeeze into the tight gap between him and the car in front of him.

I weave around cars, rocking the Honda. The 7-Eleven parking lot is nearly empty, a minivan and painter's van. I roll through without stopping and merge back onto the highway. My left leg jumps up and down. Two miles farther north, I shoot a marginal gap in traffic to cross the highway into the strip-mall entrance. Circling around the perimeter of the parking lot, I search for the entrance to the delivery alley.

Turning into the narrow passageway, I sit up and lean forward. I see Shane. He's standing next to a slight Hispanic guy, who's wearing a stained green apron. At first Shane doesn't see me, but his companion does. His eyes widen, when I accelerate down the alley then yank the wheel to the right and brake hard, just short of pinning Shane against the stucco wall that backs one of the mall's businesses.

I stare through the windshield at Shane, breathing hard. He glares at me, frozen. Then he slowly moves his right hand up to his face and takes a deep hit off the joint pinched between his thumb and index fingers. His companion looks at me, and then looks at Shane's set jaw. He walks quickly over to a screen door. It slaps as he disappears inside.

Throwing the car door open, I roll out and march up to Shane. He eyes me and inhales another hit. The pungent smell wafts over to me. My shoulders are up around my ears.

"Should I be done with you, Shane? Everyone else is. Most of my friends think you're a lost cause and I should walk away. Are they right? I'm so sick of this. Say the word and I'm gone." My tone is dead. It accurately represents how I feel about my relationship with my addict brother. Even high, Shane sees that I'm fed up and truly ready to bug out.

93

"I can't do cages." He drops the roach and steps on it with his flip flop. Then looking to the west, toward the ocean, he shoves his right hand under his foam cast at the elbow.

"The Glen isn't a prison. You're here, aren't you?"

"Sitting and sharing my fuck-ups with fellow pipe-heads, that's going to help me? The ocean helps me. Movement helps me. I can't *feel* anything inside those walls." He clenches his jaw and rocks forward and back, toes to heels.

I read up on meth withdrawal when I was researching Ling. The good part: unlike heroin withdrawal it's relatively quick. Shane's body would have cleared the drug in twenty-four to forty-eight hours. But now he's dealing with anxiety, sleeplessness and intense cravings. Worst of all for Shane, he's numb. Several articles explained that meth use makes the levels of dopamine in addicts' brains go down, and long-term use reduces their dopamine receptors, which means there's less dopamine *and* less receptors to receive it. Dopamine is the brain's pleasure drug. No dopamine, no pleasure. And the longer an addict has been using meth the longer it takes for the brain's dopamine function to return to normal.

Shane's whole life has been the pursuit of pleasure. So knowing that he's feeling dead to the world opens me up just a little. My empathy well is shallow, but not dry. Not yet.

"It's not the walls, it's the meth, Shane. It's deadened your ability to feel. You need to give it time."

He looks away, but he's not running. His face is gray and haggard.

I change tactics. "You have a new fan club."

He cocks his head at me and knits his eyebrows.

"The FBI is investigating Ling. Someone blabbed and said you knew him. The feds want to sit down with you."

"Never...gonna...happen." He growls and draws the words out.

"They could arrest you, charge you with something, pressure you. But not while you're in rehab." Now he gives me his full attention, though skepticism pinches his face. "Let me get Dylan on the phone. He'll explain the legal ins and outs."

Dylan tells Shane that there are strict rules that prevent law enforcement from interfering with or withholding medical treatment, including rehab. He also explains that because of laws enacted back in the 1970s to encourage addicts to seek treatment, rehab patients have an expectation of privacy and law enforcement must satisfy several specific and restrictive requirements to interview or investigate a patient under treatment. Shane just listens, staring at the ground. All he says is "uh huh," and then he shoves the phone back at me.

Dylan asks me if he's been convinced. I turn away from Shane. "Maybe."

"He's not ranting. He'll go, Dana." Dylan has more experience in lassoing addicts than I do. He says he'll notify Forest Glen that Shane will be returning shortly.

I tuck the phone into my jeans' pocket and turn back to Shane. I wait.

He scuffs the squashed roach with his sandal. "You win."

I stifle a scoff and just turn up my hand toward the passenger door. I don't trust myself to speak. I want to scream at him and tell him that I hate this bullshit. I hate the drama, the fear, the financial drain, all of it. Most of all, I hate how dealing with this opens me up to the emotional minefield of our past.

Halfway back to the center, he starts jabbering. "You should have seen the look on the truck driver's face when he realized someone was in the back of his truck. Damn, I thought he might shit himself."

"I told him it was a hold-up...for jelly rolls." He bends forward and guffaws raucously, the stoned class cut-up. "Come on, Dana, a stowaway on a bread truck. You gotta admit it's a little funny."

I can feel him looking at the side of my stony face. Instead of reacting to his getaway story, I prep him for our arrival. "They'll drug test you again, and search you. Are you holding?"

He stops smiling. "No."

Only because he didn't have any money. "Who was the guy hanging with you?"

"Just a dishwasher at Las Palmas. He came out for a break just after the bread truck left. It makes deliveries at the mall."

We fall into silence. It lasts until we're once again rolling up the center's driveway.

"I know you're trying to help me, Dana. I just don't know if I want it."

"It?" Does he mean my help or life? This may be the most honest thing he's said since I came back to town.

I park and look at him, my lower lip quivers. "Just try."

Chapter 10

Back at the farm, I'm still so pissed that I'm using fuck as a verb, a noun and an adjective as Dylan and I go through the recapture of Shane. I stop myself and change subjects, sharing the basics of my web search on Ling. Dylan agrees with my analysis; the cops and feds want Ling bad because he made fools of them. And his convenient meth packaging could make a cheap new party drug. I also relate the information I learned from my chance meeting with Andy.

"A runner, huh? No wonder Stokes is so eager to recruit Shane. He's been to numerous labs and distributors."

I start cleaning up from dinner. But I don't just load the dishwasher; I straighten the contents of the refrigerator, wipe under all the countertop appliances and start scrubbing the sink. I've done this since I was a kid — cleaning brings order to disorder. And there was always plenty of filth and disorder in our family home. If I start cleaning, it's a sure sign that I'm furious and frustrated.

"I'm leaving tomorrow." My abrupt declaration causes Dylan to set down his wine glass, which was on its way to his lips. "I need to catch up to my life before I leave for Zurich."

His eyes widen and his brows rise. "You *should* go, Dana. Shane is contained again. And now he knows about the feds. It's on him what happens next."

"Should I check in with Stokes before I leave?" I just want to bolt, but I'll do what Dylan advises.

"You're not a witness or a potential informant; you're not obligated to him in any way. But if you want to keep tabs on his progress it might help to humor him."

He purses his lips. "Call him from the road. That way you can check in with him when you're already out of reach."

*

The Honda is humming along on cruise control at seventy-three miles per hour. I left Dylan and Maria's place at just after nine thirty, late enough to avoid battling with the nine-to-five road warriors making their way to work. I zoomed through Silicon Valley, and I'm well on my way to the Central Coast. Despite yesterday's drama with Shane and the long drive ahead, I'm initially cheery. I always feel buoyed when my hometown is in the rearview mirror.

When I'm about a hundred miles south of Half Moon Bay, I figure it's time to call Stokes. Deep blue skies over rolling hills dotted with oak trees decorate my open road — even an impending conversation with the G-man isn't dampening my mood.

He answers "Stokes," after three rings, in that authoritarian tone he loves.

"Agent Stokes, it's Dana McCarren."

He hesitates for ten seconds or so and recovers from what was obviously a memory lapse, though I'm sure he wouldn't cop to that.

"Hello, Dana. How's Shane?"

Is this a test? From our previous conversation, he's well aware that I'm not allowed to contact Shane, as part of the rules of rehab. But if I have, and he can get me to admit to it, perhaps the rules can be bent. Or could he have heard that Shane busted out of rehab and I brought him back? I doubt it. I play it cool.

"As you know, I can't contact him right now. I'm sure he's still in the process of coming off the meth. It isn't pretty, as you're undoubtedly aware. How's your case against Ling coming?"

I hear him shuffling papers in the background. "Well, Ms. McCarren, our investigation is progressing."

"What kind of progress?" I can't help asking. It's part of my reporter DNA to pop questions.

He clears his throat. "We're working on a few leads. All I can say is we're looking at Ling's money trail and his Thai connections here and in Koh Samui."

Though this statement includes no new info, it reminds me that I need to review some Koh Samui news sources. There might be more background on Ling I can gather from the island patter. I can't help baiting Stokes a little. "Well, he's been busted before, so I assume there's some previous research your team can tap."

His crisp reply is exactly what I expect. "I see you've done a little internet surfing, Dana. But news sources and local law enforcement do not have the expertise and reach of the FBI (eff.bee.eyah). We're developing our own information." Cops are always peeing on each other's shoes, marking territory.

"Well, I hope you won't mind if I call you to get an update every now and then? I'm on my way back to L.A., but obviously I still have an interest in Ling."

His voice rises and he nearly stutters. "You've left town?"

"Well, like most civilians I do need to work, Agent Stokes."

I remind him that he has my work contact information, should he feel in a sharing mood. I could disclose that I'm leaving the country on Sunday, but that would ruin the surprise when he calls or emails me and gets my "out-of-office" automatic reply.

He recovers enough to regain his dictatorial tone. "Once Shane is through with rehab, we will be interviewing him. Good day, Ms. McCarren." He clicks off immediately, without waiting for my reply.

After another hour and a few sing-alongs to eighties rock on the satellite radio, I'm nearing the Central Coast area, San Luis Obispo, which is just east from Morro Bay. Years ago, I made many surf camping trips to this section of coast and the beaches south of here in Gaviota and Santa Barbara. A cooler, camp stove, and a sleeping bag took care of sleeping and sustenance, but the food for the soul was the discovery of little-known breaks with hollow waves and just a couple of friends to share them. We'd stay on the road for as long as we could, until we'd emptied the gas tank, the cooler and our wallets.

The bullying of the eff-bee-eyah couldn't flatten my mood, but my body tightens as memories of one surf trip to this area flood in.

*

Shane and I met here in Central California for a few days, just after his first trip to rehab. He was almost thirty. Oddly, it was Terry's actions that set off the chain of events causing Shane to enter his first program.

Shane had been living with Joe. It was before he'd completely quit the pro tour, but he'd been pulling out of contests and losing sponsors. While away for several contests in a row, Shane had lost his apartment; his rent was weeks overdue for the third time. It wasn't long after Mom's death, and Joe thought they could help each other crawl out from under the black cloud of grief. On good days, they'd watch sports on TV, make dinners and do home repair projects. I wanted to believe they could pull together and console each other with companionship, if not communication.

Except Shane's grief "process" was built around numbing himself with pot, cocaine and alcohol. Shane was a swinging mess; one minute nearly catatonic, the next so high and hyper he couldn't talk, much less surf. And since he hadn't been winning on the tour, he was funding his street meds by dealing...out of Joe's house.

Terry came by one day to borrow some of Joe's tools and saw a parade of Shane's "customers" roll through. He confronted Shane, and a neighbor broke up the resulting screaming match that nearly came to blows. Terry went straight to Joe's shop and told him he needed to kick Shane out. "If he gets busted, you'll lose your house." Terry's grief made him mad at the world; he was overflowing with bitter rage.

Shane was broken. He'd found Mom, with a bullet hole in her chest and the slug embedded in the bedroom wall. Grotesquely, he'd arrived at the house soon enough after she'd pulled the trigger to believe he might revive her. He'd called 9-1-1 and carried her out to the driveway. Joe's best buddy in the neighborhood, Phil, happened to drive by. He'd tried to pitch in, but said Shane wouldn't let anyone else touch her. He was howling, as he spent fifteen minutes giving her CPR and rescue breaths until the ambulance arrived. The paramedics knew she was gone, but continued the compressions and put her on oxygen, while Shane screamed, begged them to hurry, to do more, to save her. The trauma would have been devastating for anyone...but Shane, who'd been unstable since his childhood and doing drugs since middle school, escaped into his addiction.

The day after the confrontation with Terry, Shane passed out in a cocaine blackout and Joe found him on the kitchen floor when he got home from work. Joe revived him and Shane convinced him he didn't need to go to the ER. I raced back to Half Moon Bay and we clung to each other. He admitted he'd snorted his entire for-sale supply of cocaine and hadn't slept in three days. "When I'm high, I fantasize about dying, Dana." I stayed with him for hours in his old room at Joe's; we confessed some of our heartbreak and guilt; we reminisced about some good times with Mom; we watched reruns of "Home Improvement." Joe checked on us, but mostly stayed away. His own grief was still so raw he couldn't process his son's overdose. Finally, Shane wept and through his tears said, "Help me, Dana. And tell Dad I'm sorry."

I found a treatment center in Brisbane and he went away for several weeks. I went back to work, but I couldn't stop moving, couldn't concentrate. I spoke to no one, held my sorrow in as it ate me. I barely got through the days. Nights were worse. I'd stay up until well past midnight, fall asleep in front of the TV and dream that Mom was whispering to Shane, pulling him into a cobalt pool with no bottom.

When he got out of the center, all his remaining sponsors had dropped him. We met up for a four-day surf trip and afterwards he started painting for Joey. He stayed away from the hard drugs for a year or so, but he was smoking pot on our camping trip and was drinking again before a month had passed.

Terry distanced himself further from Shane. Self-preservation. He loves Shane, even though he hates him. He couldn't face another loss.

I'd run away from Valerie; I swore I'd never abandon Shane. He keeps testing that resolve.

*

The odometer ticks ahead as I'm weaving in and out of traffic through Santa Barbara. I grab some coffee at a gas station and force the paralyzing memories from my mind. I'm good at it...good at not feeling. Shane feels too much, enough for both of us.

This was once a surf town, too, until the ultra-rich built their Montecito compounds. Santa Barbara is the dividing line to Southern California. It's beautiful, but it's phony and tainted, just like the City of Fallen Angels.

After six and a half hours on the road, I'm entering the L.A. area. The smog is already noticeable, yellowish air hanging in the valley hills. At Thousand Oaks, I divert from 101 to Highway 1 via 23. Might as well check the surf on my way back to my loft in Santa Monica. My salt soakings in Half Moon Bay have rekindled my ocean addiction. Since it's Friday, I'll be slammed by weekend getaway traffic, but I'm willing to take the hit to get some sea mist in my lungs instead of just exhaust and smog. And if there's any hint of surf, I'll come back this way tomorrow before leaving on my business trip.

Just north of Malibu, I pull into a small parking lot to view a break. There's a small swell coming in, but it's a lousy direction for this location. I roll down the highway another two miles and pull into another lot. There's a small point of protruding rocks, and just a little sand fills the inner corner facing south. The sets are slightly southerly and thus hitting just right for the underwater geography here. Three-footers are breaking at several places along the shore. Considering the gusty wind and rising tide, these are decent waves. At low tide, in the calm of morning, they could be downright playful.

I fight my way through the BMW-and-Mercedes-laden Malibu traffic and enter the northern section of Santa Monica. I live in a transitional neighborhood, where developers have mowed down some of the old beach shanties and rehabbed a few warehouses to put in condo and townhouse complexes. My building dates to the 1940s. It began life as a plumbing supply company, became a sewing sweat shop and eventually served as a scrap-metal storage facility. After that, it sat vacant, except for the rats, for over a decade, before an inspired developer chopped the 15,000-square-foot brick building, with its large square-pane industrial windows, into lofts with exposed pipes and cement floors.

Behind the building are a row of one-car garages — a necessity for someone like me who owns more water toys than furniture. Industrial steel doors provide entries to the lofts at the back of the building. I stumble through the pile of mail below the door's mail slot as I push my way in. A steel and cable staircase to the left provides access to the loft living space, which consists of one large room. A petition sets off the bedroom area and a large galley kitchen runs along the back wall. Flooding the loft with light, the condo's whole front wall is windows, rising from waist-high to the eleven-foot ceiling.

Modern and spare describes my decorating style, no pets, no house plants. I tried succulents, which are supposed to go long stints without water. But abject neglect apparently wasn't part of the care description. A couple of geometric-patterned rugs soften some of the cement floor; a low-slung sectional fills the living room space. Along the loft's end wall are bookshelves, filled with mementos from my travels, small sculptures, masks, shells and a few other dust collectors. Above the shelves hangs a five-foot-tall by six-foot-wide graphic painting that's dominated by cobalt blues and sea greens, with a top stripe of red bleeding to orange bleeding to yellow. It could be an ocean sunset, but its subject is open to interpretation.

The painting was a present from Nick. He loves pouring out his creativity, without constraints from a pesky editor like me, onto a large mural-like format. He painted it after I'd waxed lyrical one day about a recent sunset surf session.

Over by the bedroom petition is an empty steel desk and office chair facing out the windows. Clutter represents a connection to a location, activities and events. I live an uncommitted life.

I want to get back to work. Where I know what's expected of me. Where I know I can deliver. Where I can compartmentalize and shove Shane and my family into the attic of my mind.

After dinner, I sit at my desk and pound the keyboard for more than two hours, catching up to all my work emails from my "vacation" week. The inbox is filled with press releases, Wylie memos and notes from sources. Newsroom jokes and multiple sick and outrageous stories forwarded by my colleagues, former co-workers and friends add to the digital detritus. All journalists love the most twisted news they can find, and they love to share it, Siamese twins, oh yeah, sex change operations, tap the forward key, Lorena Bobbitt updates, yessiree.

*

A day till I fly, I have an opportunity for one more dousing. I'm up just before six, checking the local tide charts. I've been hitting dawn patrol since Shane and I were scrawny surf punks. I roll out the door, toss my wetsuit in the trunk and strap my tri-fin to the rack. A scrunchy secures my uncombed tangled hair in a loose knot at my neck; sunglasses cover my sleep-crusted eyes.

The coastal fog stayed out last night and the sky is going from gray to pale blue as I wend my way up Highway 1 toward Malibu. Without yesterday afternoon's breeze, small smooth waves are pushing foam across the rocks. As I'd hoped, the swell has held and maybe even kicked up a half-foot. I pull into the parking lot with just six other cars, while a four-footer peels to the beach, the biggest of a set of three nicely formed waves.

My toes curl, as I wade into the cold salt foam. After a spent wave passes, I glide onto my board and start paddling out. My skin chills as the water seeps through my rubber suit. My timing is good and I manage to hit a lull between sets and paddle out without having to punch through any waves. The four surfers already out are loosely clustered where the largest waves are pitching out for the longest rides. Decision time: Do I join the pack and jockey for rides or do I try a less reliable break, a little farther in, where I'll have less competition?

Landlubbers don't understand how surfing, especially at a popular break, can be a scrum, with a lot of posturing, pushing and shoving. After yesterday's inactivity, I'm feeling feisty. I'll join the boys club and see how it goes. I paddle hard, making a bee-line for the take-off zone. A lanky teenager with a shoulder-length blond mop and chin acne is after the first wave of the set too, stroking in from my right. But I'm ahead of him, and I show no hint of hesitation. His startled look makes it obvious he's just realized he's paddling against a girl. That revelation, along with my fixed stare and obvious resolve, causes him to slow just enough for me to get to the pitch-point first.

I pull up, check my angle to the wave, push back down on the nose of the board and give five hard strokes, pulling with enough force to cause my torso to snake back and forth across the top of my board. The board hooks into the green-blue swell and I jump to a low crouch. The curl pitches out behind me as I extend my legs and glide down to the trough, rock onto my heels and drive a hard bottom turn, extending my arms out just below my shoulders for balance. I suck the momentum of the turn up into my folding body, drive up the four-foot rounded face and punch the board off the lip and with a quick snap pull it around to drive it back down the wave face.

I ride out away from of the curl, cut a hard backside turn, looking over my left shoulder. I pull back to the pitching peak and pop a turn off the just-broken foam. After my turn, the wave throws a section at me, a six-foot piece of the wave breaking all at once in front of me. I drive down the face before the section hits me, gaining as much speed as I can. I run out ahead of the foam and carve a smooth bottom turn, without hitting it so hard that I slow my board speed. I glide around the section and regain the sweet spot on the smooth water in front of the curl. I play the wave with a few smooth up and down turns as I ride out again. But this wave has spent most of its energy and is slowing and shrinking. After one more cut back, I ride out and turn up the wave, gliding over the top and grabbing my board's rails to ease my drop onto the deck. I paddle hard to get back out to the lineup.

Just as I pull up and straddle my board, I watch four pelicans gliding silently north, ten yards outside of the waves, their wingtips nearly touching the water. The blue-green rippling sheet glistens, fully lit from the climbing sun, which pulled up over the Malibu Canyon hills sometime during my first ride. Traffic noise, muted by the sounds of the sea, drifts out to the break, along with the distant barking of a joyous mutt.

I drop another wave. It's a short ride, but still offers a natural slide to float across on my magic carpet. I rack up nearly a dozen rides, but the crowd is growing and it's getting harder to gain the prime take-off zone. One or two more waves and I'll leave the swell to the latecomers.

I drop one more face, and as I'm gliding to my bottom turn I feel a surfer take a very late drop behind me. A rider in the wave's pocket, closest to the curl, has the right of way. But a late drop like this is a way to rework the water rules — it's also a way to get pounded by going over the falls, tumbling over the front of your board and potentially tangling up with the rider in front. I'll pull out and concede the wave, but only after I've worked a turn or two. As I ride out a little, the surfer behind follows me out instead of staying in the pocket. I quickly glance over my left shoulder and see the grinning face of Wayne. I glide over the top of the swell and drop to my board, as Wayne does the same just inches off my shoulder. As soon as we drop to our boards, he springs across the water at me, grabbing my shoulders and rolling me off the board across the top of him into the water. When I come up spitting sea water and laughing, he wraps an arm around my submerged waist and plants a firm salty kiss on my lips.

Immediately, my body responds. I feel a delicious contraction through my soft center. "Howdy, Dana!" Wayne's slight cowboy cadence contradicts his surfer looks. He's an SLO-raised ranch boy, who left the valleys and livestock of the Central Coast more than a decade ago. His rural upbringing built a set of impressive shoulders, and his wetsuit stretches across his mounded chest. Six foot two, with shaggy brown curls and green eyes, he'd be too pretty without a nose that's slightly flattened and bent off-center, the result of a ranch accident. Plus, his crinkled eyes, ruddy sun-spotted complexion and ever-present stubble make him all mature male; he's no androgynous pretty-boy out of the fashion rags. Truth be told, I find him utterly irresistible, which is rare for a cynic like me. Fortunately for me, Wayne feels the same. Despite its proximity to Hollywood and Disneyland, Malibu still doesn't have an overpopulation of dedicated mermaids, and Wayne has a soft spot for water girls.

"Wayne, you wave snake."

He swirls the water with his hands. "You were paddling circles around those boys; I had to even the score for the poor sad twits."

Then he cuts the water with a backhand and splashes me in the face. Wayne is a goof in an adult's body. Despite a bachelor's degree in business, he works as a property manager and handyman to rich hippies, musicians and artists in Topanga and Malibu. Not long after graduating with honors from Cal State San Luis Obispo, he tried office-life in Century City as an assistant trader at an investment bank. He'd come to L.A. with his college sweetheart, an aspiring actress. Their relationship spanned all of his college years, and like many of his friends they got married a month after graduation. Unfortunately, just six months after the move to Hollyweird, she chose to advance her career by sleeping with a fifty-year-old, reality-TV producer. After that, he realized he wasn't the least bit interested in becoming a titan of finance. One day, he called in "well," went surfing and never went back.

He's even more disillusioned with love and relationships than I am, and he's a water rat, which makes him the ideal friend with benefits...and his perfect pecs and silly sense of humor certainly don't hurt. His green twinkling eyes lock on mine. "Are you done embarrassing these boys? Can I make you breakfast?"

The salt water conducts the electrical current running between us and food is far from my mind...or his. I look right at him. "I'm not hungry."

*

I barely pass through the door to his shingled canyon cottage when he pins me to the backside of it, kissing me hard and pressing the door closed with the weight of our bodies. Wrapping my arms around his shoulders, I push my hips against his. He pulls up one of my legs and pushes every inch of his body against mine. I groan involuntarily, as I slide my hands down his back, pulling his hips to mine.

He half carries half drags me to the bedroom and his low-slung futon. We stumble up against it, and as we're kissing we're tossing shorts and T-shirts. In seconds, we're naked. Flint and steel, our skin sparks as we rub against each other.

He pushes me down on to the mattress and is rubbing his face across my breasts and teasing my nipples with his tongue. My hands are tangled in his hair and pushing against his shoulders. He moves down my rib cage and all the way down my stomach until I gasp. My mind shuts down and my body quakes. With his hands under my hips, he drives me into a frenzy with his tongue. I pant and twitch, as I arch up into the warmth of his mouth. Taking his time, he explores all of me. He finally pulls up on his knees, grabs my thighs and drags me across the bed to him, pushing into me in one long, very slow thrust. I gasp as his heat fills me, and we begin moving together in a slow rhythm. I'm lost in his mouth and body as he rocks slowly, then faster.

He groans, but he's not through torturing me yet. He rolls me on top of him, and as I straddle him he pulls my hips forward and back. He pushes my legs down, and we slide against one another fully prone, before we roll back again.

He pulls from me and slides down the bed, once again tasting and teasing me with his insistent tongue and his probing fingers. I feel the tingling grow until I'm completely taken over by it. My body starts pulsing and I arch in four long spasms, pushing and rubbing myself against his mouth and fingers. As the waves are consuming me, he suddenly pulls his mouth away and enters me all at once in one firm push. I cling to him, lost in his body, as he cries out and spasms, taking me with him.

We lie there, his long-muscled body covering mine, panting and kissing. He kisses along my jaw-line and down my neck. I smell myself on his stubbly face. My body is still buzzing.

He rolls onto his back and pulls me under his arm to his chest, then grabs my right thigh and pulls it across him. I nuzzle against him, drifting in spent, suspended animation. No thoughts invade my relaxed mind and body. I realize I'd drifted off to sleep when I feel him edge out from under me and walk to the bathroom. Then I hear him in the kitchen, and I awaken fully to the whirring sounds of a blender. The noisemaker quiets and I watch him walk out of the small kitchen with two tall glasses of fruit smoothie, one in each hand. A boyish grin is lighting his face, and I start laughing hysterically when I realize that he's wearing a potholder on his manhood. "Nice look, why are you wearing that?"

"I needed a bumper...that boy just won't lie down when you're around." He waddles to the futon, squats down slowly and hands me a glass, as the potholder points at me. I take two gulps of icy smoothie and reach up and remove the quilted oven mitt. I take him in my mouth and swirl my cold tongue around him. He grabs the mitt and pulls away, waddling back to the kitchen. I whimper as he calls over his shoulder "We need food. Got to refuel the machine."

I climb from the bed and visit the bathroom, where I find an extra-large navy-blue T-shirt draped on one of the towel racks. As I pull it on, I stuff my nose into the fabric and take in its scent of sea salt and man. I pad to the kitchen, toward the delicious aroma of sautéing onions, eggs and toast. Wayne's pulled on boxer shorts — the oven mitt sits next to the stove. Giggling, I pick it up and stroke it, then hand it back to him. He slips his hand into it and carries the pan of eggs to the small kitchen table.

We demolish the meal. I steal the last bite of toast from his plate, so he drains the last of my smoothie. We chat about the surf. The future isn't part of our dialogue. We connect only when we happen to collide; we don't make plans. The spontaneity of our hook-ups is so much fun that we let lunar cycles, tides or other natural forces determine our next encounter.

Chapter 11

The afternoon train ride from Zurich to Davos is a blur of too-loud, excited tourists and shadowy snow-covered peaks, visible intermittently through low clouds and snow flurries.

Early the next day, I collect my press credentials and make my way to the press room. I'm still jet-lagged, but the stupor might also come from the conference center design — a high-rise cement hotel tower, surrounded by a two-story conference center, with three ballrooms and numerous meeting rooms. I could be in any city in the world, London, Singapore, Chicago. This press room is identical to hundreds of others, featuring phones, press kits and a snack buffet. I grab some of the kits and take a seat. Spin, spin and more spin. I tear through the packets, skimming two news releases and three statistical reports that might prove useful.

I'm just packing up to make my way to the keynote speech as Ian, a reporter from London and a longtime member of the press corps, strolls into the room.

"Hey Dana. Another delightful conference, right?"

Ian and I are friendly and not competitive, since our papers are worlds apart geographically and in readership. A seasoned journalist, he has the droll wit I so appreciate in some Brits. He's a road buddy from numerous past conferences, including previous World Economic Forums, which have been attracting the glitterati of business, politics and finance since the meetings began in the early 1970s. The not-for-profit forum, held each January, shapes the political and financial dialogue for the coming year.

"I wish this was a longer trip for me," he grumbles as we walk down the hall. "Bloody hell, I've been in London for three solid months and it's making me wretched. I'm desperately afraid I might start having a real life."

I titter. We both know we've chosen this lifestyle deliberately, and we're addicted to it. Journalists, musicians, sales pros and other business travelers use the road to avoid normal life, relationships and family ties.

When French President Nicolas Sarkozy launches into his keynote, it's clear that this year's World Economic Forum is going to be different, very different. After the banking meltdown that began in late 2008 and continued into 2009, bankers have had about as much street cred as loan sharks. During the crisis, the U.S. government scrambled to set up a $700-billion-dollar bailout fund, which banks used to shore up their balance sheets in the fall of 2008. Critics grumbled loudly, but went ballistic when some American banking executives paid themselves, and their top employees, nearly $20 billion dollars in year-end bonuses. President Obama took them to task in January of 2009.

"That is the height of irresponsibility," Obama said. "It is shameful." Bankers pulled in fat bonuses as middle-class Americans continue to suffer. Stock market losses are slamming their retirement and investment funds, and home depreciation is erasing the equity that was an essential piece of their planned retirement nest egg.

Now Sarkozy is joining Obama in attacking excessive bonuses and endorsing banking reform, including limits on the size of banks, curbs on rewards, and restrictions on riskier trading. The audience, filled with banking's elite, is shell-shocked. But I'm a journalist, akin to a grave digger. Controversy and bad news? I'm giddy with the scent of a possible page-one story. It could even go above the newspaper's fold — jackpot for any daily news reporter. And, with the nine-hour time difference between here and

California, I have plenty of time to get reaction to Sarkozy's speech into my article.

I quickly review the session schedule, trying to identify a banking executive who's likely to take issue with Sarkozy's speech and expound on his displeasure. After leaving the ballroom, I wander and hit pay dirt in the second conference room. Barclays' Investment Banking Chief Bob Diamond warns that more rules will drive banks out of financial hubs such as London and New York. He says that having "well-managed banks, willing to take risks...is essential if we want to have jobs and economic growth."

Banking titans have done such a good job managing their risk in the past couple of years, right? They said no to subprime loans, sure they did. And the investment banks that bought all those bonds backed by those crappy loans, which are now worth nothing, they were making smart, carefully considered bets, right? Still, the financial wizards have found their platform and in interviews and sessions they warn that regulatory crackdowns on banking could damage a fragile recovery.

Recovery. What recovery? Americans are losing their jobs and losing their homes to foreclosure in record numbers. Later in the day, I track down one of my favorite independent economists and he goes wild with pessimism, which as a hardened journalist makes me swoon. By early evening, I've finished all my reporting and I'm holed up in my hotel room with tea, cookies and a crumb-laden laptop. I've pounded out ten inches of copy, and an extra four if the paper has room for it on the jump page.

Usually the paper's copy editors write the headlines, but I've stuck a working head on the story: "Sarkozy Blasts Banking and Bonuses, Calls for New Regulations." Back in California, it's coming up on ten o'clock in the morning;

editors will be gathering shortly for the day's page-one meeting. I hit send and envision the "ding" as my story announces itself in Wylie's inbox.

I munch shortbread and scan my inbox. A message from Agent Stokes landed about an hour ago, and another one came in just after the first one. My shoulders tense, and still a little smirk spreads across my face. He must have received my automated response that says I'm traveling. Even thousands of miles away, I'm pretty sure I can spike Agent Stokes' blood pressure.

My inbox dings and I open and read Wylie's digital shorthand: "Story in queue...off to P-1. Stand by for update...roughly 40 minutes."

Even though Wylie and I aren't bosom buddies, he'll still back my story for page one. It's a solid, multisourced piece on a hot topic, and better yet it justifies the money the paper spent to send me here. Besides, I sent him a link to the conference website where he can download a crisp pic of photogenic Sarkozy. Free art always makes our editor-in-chief (and every other penny-pinching newspaper editor) do the happy dance in his swiveling desk chair.

Now that I've dropped the story, it's time for some exercise, followed by cocktail hour. This hotel doesn't have a gym; many European hotels haven't joined the fitness craze. I put on some running gear and an iPod and search for the tower's stairwell. With musical inspiration from Rihanna, Pink and Shakira, I pound up and down the stairwell. Midway through my makeshift Stairmaster workout, I scare a hotel maintenance worker who steps into the stairwell for a private cellphone conversation, but other than that I have the cement and steel all to myself.

While I'm cooling off, I dash to the ice machine. I raid the minibar for two Tanqueray travel minis and a bottle of tonic. Editor comments and questions sound much more enlightened and reasonable when accompanied by alcohol. By the time Wylie calls or emails, I'll be properly medicated for the inevitable story grinding.

With drink in hand, I get back to cleaning out the inbox, a task akin to trying to empty a sink when the water is constantly running. After draining off the top layer, I decide I've had enough gin to read the messages from Agent Stokes.

"Dana: RE: Progress report on Shane — what's his current status? Bureau has gathered additional information on Ling's labs. Operations moving full ahead. Shane needs to get on the right side, while option still open. Respond ASAP. Agent Stokes."

Ah, Stokes, he's so fond of orders. Me? Not so much. He's still stonewalling, as far as passing along any information, and I'm in the information-trading business. I swirl the tinkling cubes in my G&T and open his other email.

"Dana: RE: Travel. You are hindering a federal investigation with your evasive conduct. Need your location ASAP; and an answer to my other email. Special Agent Stokes."

Pushy, pushy. In my experience, intimidation rarely leads to cooperation, especially with snotty journalists who are used to being the ones asking the tough questions. But I can't mess with Stokes. It will steel his resolve to charge Shane with something. My stupid hubris evaporates and gives way to a tightening in my throat. I need to check in with Dylan and see if he's heard anything about the bureau's investigation of Ling.

I grab my cellphone and dial Dylan's cell. He picks up on the second ring.

"Dana, how's the conference?" He's waiting to visit a juvenile client at the jail's morning visiting hours. His business venue is a far cry from my luxury European hotel.

I describe the keynote and my possible page-one story. Then we get into Project Shane. "What's happening with the FBI investigation of Ling? Have you heard any new chatter around the jail and courthouse?"

He has news, and it's a new twist to this drug manufacturing and distribution saga. Word on the street is Ling's operation is feuding with a Mexican meth supplier. A couple of violent incidents have been linked to this rivalry. One cop says an all-out war between the two suppliers is brewing. ATF (the bureau of alcohol, tobacco and firearms) has joined forces with the FBI and local law enforcement. That's because a cache of weapons was found under a false floor in a van that was the subject of a high-speed police chase and crashed on the 101 freeway. The Mexican driver is in a coma in the hospital, so he's not talking. But other tattlers are feeding information to the feds.

"Dana, this makes Shane's situation even more difficult. It means Stokes is going to have a new set of allies in his campaign to put pressure on Shane to cooperate with the investigation. A judge in our little court is going to have a hard time resisting the pressure of two federal bureaus, and local law enforcement, if they campaign to interview Shane while he's in rehab."

I take a large swallow of my drink, while I smash the phone against my ear. "How long will it take for them to get the paperwork together to make their case to a judge, and who can I hire to argue against their motion?"

Dylan, bless him, doesn't hesitate for a second. In fact, he's already one step ahead of me. He says that Judge Goldberg will be the one to receive any motion they come up with, and he's already notified her bailiff (a courthouse comrade) that he'll be the one handling any rebuttal to the fed's motion, if and when one materializes.

I chew the corner of my thumb. A mixture of relief and anger passes through me. Shane has no idea how many guardian angels like Dylan have stepped up on his behalf over the years, at tremendous cost to their lives and livelihoods. His favor bank is so far in the hole he'll never be able to repay it. And Dylan won't let me pay him for his time — it's not even worth asking. My costs for Project Shane run into the thousands of dollars and thousands of hours, but I'm his sister. I grew up in the same toxic home. Dylan is simply my friend, but out of his incredible loyalty to me he's caught up in Shane's unending life drama.

All I can do is say thank you, which I do for probably the hundredth time. "Dana, stop. I get a sick charge from going up against agents like Stokes. If he files this motion, I'll enjoy the fight." As usual, he's trying to make me feel better...another one of his wonderful qualities, one I didn't appreciate when we dated years ago.

We hang up and I refresh my glass with more gin. A quick Google search and I find some background on Mexican meth production and smuggling. Apparently, when authorities in the U.S. made it much harder to get pseudoephedrine, a key ingredient in one recipe for making meth, a large number of the cottage industry meth labs went out of business. But that created an opportunity for the so-called industrial meth labs of Mexico. They've been stepping up their production and their smuggling.

Meanwhile, the feds are playing whack-a-mole. They smacked down meth production in the U.S. only to create an opening for a bigger, more-sophisticated producer to gain ground. One report I read estimates that Mexican meth smuggling has increased tenfold in just the past year. Big money, which means they'll be motivated to swat away a pesky interloper like Ling.

My gut's twisting and my drink sits abandoned.

"Story slated P-1. Editing. Revision to you in 5 or 10." Wylie isn't the most gifted of line editors, but he's fast. I try to relieve some tension by stretching on the floor while I await his edit.

My email dings, and I pop back into the desk chair and pull down the edited version of my story. As usual, he can't resist mucking with the top, at least a little. I read all the way through the edit, satisfied that he hasn't fucked up anything too badly. He's inserted a couple of questions — he wants me to add a little background on the economic meltdown and the related housing downturn.

I answer Wylie's questions, add the information he's seeking and shoot it back to the newsroom. While awaiting the all clear, I hop into the shower and try to rinse away some of the Shane tension and the stress of the day. Journalism on the go is fraught with anxiety. Will I get a story that justifies my expense budget? Will I miss a bigger story that other reporters nail? How many stories must I file to satisfy the paper's bean counters that my trip was worthwhile? And it's a balancing act — I need to meet with top conference attendees and sources to gather information for current and future stories, while still allotting enough time to write the articles I've promised to Wylie for this week.

Wylie's response appears as I'm toweling off.

"Got revisions. All clear. Copy desk will go through it too, but I'll handle any qs. Good work. Check in tomorrow morning. W."

Usually the paper requires every reporter with a story going onto the next day's page one be available for possible copy-desk questions. But traveling reporters, especially those in other times zones, get special consideration.

*

Out on the street, I'm happy to stroll and breathe the crisp air. The town has more of a corporate feel than other Alps ski towns, due to its history and the fact that it hosts many conferences and thus has a lot of flat-topped cement hotels. Beyond sports, Davos is a centuries-old sanatoria, where the severely ill, some with tuberculosis, came to recuperate and seek treatment. Today it's a major health center, with a hospital and three clinics, several of which specialize in treating children.

The streets glisten under the fresh dusting of snow that fell the day I arrived and again last night. Set in the high-alpine (more than 5,000 feet) and with roughly 11,000 people, it's a fairly large Swiss town, which is split in to two, Davos-Dorf and Davos-Platz. Since it's a ski resort, as well as a summer vacation spot, the town's nightlife is lively. A multitude of restaurants offer varied cuisine to hungry visitors, and several night spots provide drinking and dancing into the late evening for those who didn't sufficiently destroy their legs on the slopes.

But I'm in no mood to socialize. I find a corner in a quiet bar with the arched doorways and massive thick plastered walls common in older Alps buildings. I order just soup and bread. Dylan's update has killed my appetite. Stokes is a hunter, with a license to stalk people. And he's used to capturing his prey.

Chapter 12

Two days pass in a flurry of session discussions on trade and finance issues, one-on-one interviews and early evening G&T-fueled writing frenzies. I stuff my Shane worries and crank out three stories in forty-eight hours, one that gets banked for Sunday's world news round-up. I need my job, for my sanity and my salary, funds for sustenance and Shane missions.

According to Dylan, Stokes hasn't drafted his treatise for Judge Goldberg yet, in which he'll ask the judge to compel Shane to submit to an interview while in rehab. So I'm clear of work and the legal drama for the next day and a half. Mother Nature has been sprinkling fresh snow on the town and mountains off and on and the temperatures, even during the day, have been brisk. I'm tempted to hit the slopes — I've been skiing since I was a kid. Another high-octane sport, skiing is fly-paper for thrill-seekers like me.

Or I could try to get back to L.A. early. I'm uneasy about being so far away, as Dylan battles the FBI on Shane's behalf. I pony up the change fee and a few hours later I'm at 38,000 feet on my way back to California.

LAX is a blur, and I arrive at my loft in the early evening. The City of Angels is sunny and smoggy, typical L.A. weather. When I reach the loft, I boot my laptop, determined to stay away from any new work email and just send out my expense report. But after weeks of dealing with Shane and Stokes I decide I need some nuanced female perspective to balance out the blunt-force masculine approach to life. I tap out a message to my two favorite gal pals, Lauren and Deena, suggesting an early Sunday workout, followed by brunch.

Fellow workout fanatics, all of us regularly sneak away from our jobs at lunch to expend calories instead of consume them. We met when we were on lunch dates with our gym's treadmills and elliptical trainers. Lauren is an agent for screenwriters; the written word is more common ground for us. She introduced me to Deena, owner of a trendy hair salon frequented by some Hollywood starlets.

They get back to me and propose a run on the beach and strand, followed by brunch at Sea & Sand, a hotel that overlooks the Santa Monica pier.

*

I'm stiff and jet-lagged, but I'm looking forward to today's run and lunch date. Girlfriends have become as important to me as my male companions, probably even more important. But I didn't really have any until college. I grew up surrounded by men...Joe, Shane, male surf buddies. I wanted adventures like the boys; I didn't play with dolls; I didn't want to nurture. And I learned from the guys; be tough; be stoic. You can't get hurt if you don't let yourself feel.

Valerie died before we moved beyond the mother-daughter relationship to one of friends. It is one of the biggest losses in my life, though I didn't begin to realize this until recently. My freshman year of college, she came down to San Diego on my birthday, trying to re-establish a relationship. But by that time I'd been rejecting her for so long it had become a habit. Now I am often observant, and jealous, when I see women my age and their mothers enjoying various outings...plays, shopping, lunches. It is a gap in my life that will never be filled.

Mothers teach you as children, but some lessons you can't absorb until you're an adult...how relationships really work and how much work goes into keeping them going. I judged my mother; as a child I thought the cracks in her and my father's marriage were mostly her fault, the result of her swings and depression. But over time, I've come to understand that my father was an equal contributor to their marital woes. He has always had a volatile temper, and he was extremely critical of us as kids; he was constantly rating us and pushing us, especially in sports, but in other areas as well. He was critical of our looks, our speech, our friends, our hobbies. Instead of celebrating our accomplishments, he kept setting the bar higher. He did the same thing to Valerie, but it was toxic for her. She had more than enough self-doubt; she didn't need his running critique.

I understand this now, but I can never say this to her. I can't make it up to her. I ran...and then she died.

Grief and guilt are chronic diseases: sometimes they ease, but they never go away.

When I arrive at our parking-lot meeting point, Lauren is there in her Lexus sedan, which is running while she talks on her phone. Her words are muffled, but by the scowl on her face it's not a conversation she's enjoying. I park next to her, and she waves to me through the window. Deena pulls up and parks on the other side of me. We jump out and hug. The day is fog-free and still. It's a little crisp — perfect running weather.

Lauren emerges from her car, shaking her head: "Whiny prick. You sold an option on your novella to a studio. You took the money and you signed the contract, which included the studio's right to modify the story! And you don't want to deal with rewrites? Seriously delusional. Hi, ladies!" Lauren's features are refined, with an aquiline nose, delicate pointed chin and startling light blue eyes. Five foot eleven in flats, her thick dark hair is cut in an edgy bob, courtesy of Deena. She jogs over and hugs each of us.

"I *need* to run after that start to my Sunday. Actually I need to box!" Deena and Lauren immediately engage in some playful sparring; both women regularly attend kick-boxing classes at the club. They've tried to recruit me, but I've resisted thus far. With my family history, fighting, even if it's feigned, turns me off, although I haven't confided this to either of them.

Easing into some slow jogging, we discuss today's mileage goal. I suggest eight miles.

Deena groans, "I didn't wear the double holster required for that."

We all giggle. By holster she means jog bra or in her case a bra on top of a bra. Deena's ample Ds need to be strapped down securely. Her Sicilian heritage is obvious. She's petite and curvy, with almond skin and dark shoulder-length wavy hair, artfully streaked with flickering rust tones.

We settle on six miles and boost our pace from a slow shuffle to a jog, as Deena gives us an update on the celebrity sightings at her salon for this week...and their bad hair days. Negotiating bikes, strollers, roller-bladders and walkers, we pick up the pace. We're all serious runners; we've been pounding pavement and trails for decades.

About a mile and a half into the run, I feel my body settle into a rhythm. My breathing is even, my gait fluid. I sense that today is going to be one of those blessed good running days, the ones all runners covet. Some days I feel like a jackhammer — every movement is jerky and labored. I rasp, and I only finish the run because I'm determined to put in the miles. But other days I glide instead of pound, and my mind shuts off as I stride out. It's the nirvana of endurance sports.

About a mile from the finish, the chatter begins again, and we discuss the real reason we're running: brunch! Sea & Sand's prices are L.A. trendy — read wallet-lightening. But one free glass of champagne is complimentary with each brunch order. It's smart; few customers will stop at just one. At a quarter mile out, we hit our final gear and challenge each other all the way to the parking lot. I stretch out and match Lauren's long legs stride for stride.

Lauren and Deena stretch and do a few yoga postures on the grass to loosen up after our run. But I opt for my standard post-run cooldown, plunging into Mother Ocean for a short swim part way out the pier.

Puny little rollers push kelp-strewn foam up the beach. I squeeze the goggles into my eye sockets with the base of my hands and dive in, immediately stroking away from shore. Without a wetsuit, my skin prickles from the cold. Just a short ten minutes out and ten minutes back will satisfy my aquatic urge.

As I reach my turnaround, I lift my head and tread water. The sea is calm with no wind chop and no swell. I turn back toward the beach and see Deena and Lauren walking down to the water's edge, carrying their shoes. I'm just about to put my head down and stroke back, when I hear a huff of expelled breath behind my right shoulder. With just the top of his head, round eyes and whiskered snout exposed, a harbor seal observes me from six feet away. His gray spotted fur shimmers in the sunlight. He stares at me for about ten seconds, tilts his nose up ever so slightly and silently slides back under the surface.

Encounters like this fuel my love of the ocean. Though my face is submerged, I'm smiling most of the swim back.

I jog out of the water toward my friends, but before reaching them I bend at the waist and flip my hair back and forth over the top of my head a couple of times to knock the water from my soggy mop.

"Good doggie, shake," teases Lauren. I chase her up the beach threatening to pull her into a wet embrace and drag her to the water.

*

Champagne bubbles in our glasses. Deena sips and asks about my business trip. I give them a quick synopsis of the tone of the event and the types of stories I filed.

Deena's not really interested in the news out of the conference and goes straight for the important facts: "Any cute guys at this thing, Dana?" Deena is divorced, but in a steady relationship with a contractor she met online. Lauren is on husband number two, a corporate attorney who dotes on her. Deena's interest in the conference man-scape isn't for her; it's for me. She's been on a mission get me back into serious dating.

I don't take the bait and throw her off the topic by going back to the dire economic news that came out of the conference.

She brings the conversation right back to men. "Do you ever hear from Kyle anymore? I saw him on television two weeks ago."

*

Shortly after I landed my first full reporting job at a weekly business newspaper, I met Kyle Gordon, my ex-husband. I've told Deena and Lauren the story. He was a pro volleyball player, and we met when I was surfing one day at Manhattan Beach. He was, and is, a gorgeous but self-centered lout and a horrible playboy — and I knew it.

"Why did you marry him?" I remember Deena asking. I didn't have a good answer, probably because I was working so much that I was feeling disconnected from the world. I was also estranged from my family. Valerie had died a few months earlier, leaving me reeling with guilt and feeling more unmoored than ever. My family had gone from damaged to blown to bits. Shane was just out of his first rehab and Terry had a new baby. Joe and I rarely spoke. Needless to say, none of them attended the wedding.

Kyle didn't love me; he loved my arm-piece qualities. He's one of those people who can turn on the charm and make you feel like you're the center of the universe...until he finds another center. We had a small beach wedding. One of his friends officiated; he had a mail-order minister's certificate. Our honeymoon was in Puerto Vallarta, because Kyle was scheduled to play in a tournament in Northern California at the end of the week. A quickie wedding and honeymoon for what's supposed to be a lifelong commitment? Not an auspicious start. The day after we got back to L.A. I started feeling caged.

He wanted me to play wife at our condo, while he traveled and strayed. Within a year and a half, one of the women volleyball players on the tour took me aside at a tournament. "He's not just cheating; he's hitting any slender groupie in a thong." She didn't sugar-coat it, and I didn't need that. I knew he was roaming, and I knew it was a good reason to leave...and blame him. I filed the papers and moved out while he was on the road. We'd shared nothing more than a bed, so we didn't even hire attorneys.

Beach volleyball has now become a sexy spectator sport with tour sponsors and media coverage, and Kyle has leveraged his photogenic looks and status as a former pro into a role as a TV commentator for the big tournaments. He charms the camera, and I'm sure he still charms female fans at every opportunity.

*

"Deena, stop. My track record with relationships is horrible, as you well know. And, no, I haven't heard from Kyle in years. Nor would I want to."

Deena won't be side-tracked. "So when is the last time you had a real date, Dana?" She's always blunt, and she's a close enough friend to feel comfortable calling me out.

I've told them before about my loose hookups with Wayne — how he's great fun, but not relationship material. Now that we're each on our third glass of champagne, I can't resist giving them a recap of my last encounter with him up in the canyon.

After I spill the tale, including a few R-rated details, Lauren is laughing and fanning herself with her napkin. "Oh Dana, who needs a live-in man, the snoring and smelly socks, when you have *that*!" she pants.

Deena still isn't letting go of her mission to push me toward dates that might result in a more lasting connection than a bedroom romp. "But Wayne's commitment-phobic, right?"

"His ex-wife crushed his heart, and he's never recovered. So yeah, he keeps everyone at arm's length."

It's interesting. I don't feel sorry for myself, with my cultivated allergy to relationships. But I sense some searching and a hint of sadness in Wayne. He's grown accustomed to be being alone, but that doesn't mean it's a natural or happy state for him.

The conversation moves on to the difficulties of men and women co-habiting. "It's hilarious that we humans make dogs and cats live under the same roof, and the fur often flies." They both nod when I make this comment.

"Let's face it, they have as much business being roommates as men and women do." Lauren adds that she loves her husband, but she'd like to take a flame-thrower to the ancient sports equipment, broken tools and miscellaneous crap he's hording in their garage.

"And what about the clothes they hold on to for decades!" Deena says her beau still owns too-short, Lycra running shorts from the 1980s — that are not only too short but too tight as well. "They're disgusting. If we get a place together, several boxes of his clothes and sports memorabilia will mysteriously disappear in the moving process."

We weave our way out of the dining room and say our goodbyes. Deena promises to arrange the next gabfest, though I warn them that I'll be traveling again soon. I'm happy that the conversation didn't touch on my trip up north. They've heard bits and pieces about my family and my brother, but I haven't shared the grittiest facts. Drugs and rehab regularly fuel the Hollywood narrative, and some sordid stories seem to actually boost a method actor's profile. Still, federal investigations and drug violence go well beyond the usual bad behavior that gets reported in the entertainment tabloids.

Shopping, errands and a sunset bike ride fill the rest of my Sunday. But my mellow mood instantly evaporates when I log on at the end of the day and see an email marked "urgent" from Dylan. I open it, and my fingers curl on the keyboard. He's heard through the gossip pipeline that Stokes is going to file a motion with Judge Goldberg on Monday asking that Shane submit to an interview while in rehab. He wants to talk strategy with me first thing tomorrow.

Once again I'm taking advantage of a friend in order to help Shane. I grind my teeth.

And can Dylan successfully outwit Stokes?

Chapter 13

The newsroom is quiet. A few other early risers are tapping away at their keyboards, but the hum of the big open space, with low cube walls, where thirty-five people work at any one time, is decidedly muted this early in the day. By deadline, the key tapping will be frantic, accompanied by occasional calls across the room for line counts, story status updates and art specs.

I've already sent a text to Dylan's phone, asking him to call me as soon as he's begun his business day. I have no idea what we can say to fight the feds' efforts to interview Shane, but I'm praying we can come up with a decent argument.

My cellphone rings at just after seven thirty, and while I answer Dylan's call I pop into the closest conference room for some privacy.

"Hey, Dylan, thanks for starting your day with this."

"Monday, Monday, Dana. Welcome back from your trip across the pond. Did you ski?"

"No, I flew back to L.A. on Saturday." I give him a quick summary of yesterday's run and brunch, and then we dive into the muck. One of the things he wants to include in his response to Agent Stokes' motion is Shane's drug use and rehab history. He believes it's important to show that Shane really needs this stint in rehab to work. I understand his strategy, but I wonder if this history might hurt our cause. We need to be careful not to portray rehab as such a common thing for him that this latest stay shouldn't be taken seriously. But I give him the information he's seeking — this is Shane's fourth rehab visit. I've paid for every single one.

I ask what other ammunition we have to fight this motion. He says that he's pretty sure Stokes has yet to tie Shane directly to Ling's operation. He still doesn't have anyone saying Shane was an employee; so for now Shane is just a victim of Ling's violence. And a victim, especially an ill one, shouldn't be treated like a criminal. Still, Stokes may try to portray him as a very important material witness.

Lastly, he gives me the best piece of info he's gathered. He was chatting with Judge Goldberg's clerk two days ago, and she let it slip that the judge's grandson is fighting meth addiction and has been to treatment a couple of times. This could make her more respectful of the treatment process and more understanding and sympathetic to our side.

Or it could go the other way. She could be fed up with the treatment merry-go-round and believe that letting Agent Stokes interview Shane won't be a game-changer for his recovery. Dylan will play up the need for Shane's counselors to follow a proven protocol for his treatment, including isolating him so he can focus on his recovery.

Shane has been medicating with street drugs since he was a pre-teen. It's a cliché, but he started with pot and worked his way up to more powerful substances. Memories flash through my brain of a teenage Shane playing with his food at the dinner table — so high he'd giggle as he chased his peas around his plate with his fork. He'd arrive home just as the food hit the table, his eyes red and watery. Surfing and salt water always provided a good excuse for the irritated eyes.

Terry and I always knew when he was high, even if Joe and Valerie were oblivious. I was already protecting Shane so I wouldn't say anything. Terry's motive was to keep the peace. If Shane was stoned, the evening would be calmer. After dinner, Shane would slink off to his room with a handful of cookies and sleep it off. And if Valerie was stable that week, the evening might even resemble the tranquil settings Terry experienced at his friends' homes.

By high school graduation, Shane had already graduated to hard drugs to cocaine, mushrooms, and ecstasy, whatever he could score.

Dylan says he'll begin writing his rebuttal motion this morning, and he'll send me a copy to review when he has it together. Once Stokes officially files his motion, he'll make some tweaks to his draft to address any arguments that we haven't anticipated.

I remind myself that we're only buying Shane a couple of extra weeks. The treatment isolation period is one month, and Shane has been in rehab for two weeks. Once the month is up, Stokes will be able to interview him, follow him, pressure him.

What then? Why does Ling want to hurt him? I still haven't answered this question. I'm under no illusion that the answer will help me solve Shane's problems. It probably won't make one iota of difference. But I hate working in the dark, stumbling after a story when I'm unable to unearth the facts.

I get back to my desk and continue the endless task of clearing my digital inbox. Unless some economic news breaks today, I won't be on deadline this afternoon. Much of my beat is driven by monthly and quarterly releases of economic data. But today the data pipe will be empty. I'll regroup and do some research on a couple of information nuggets that I picked up at the conference that might lead to stories.

I begin making a few sourcing calls. It may be early on the West Coast, but the Wall Streeters have been up and fully caffeinated for hours. Fortunately for me, it's a hum-drum day on the markets too, so the Masters of the Universe are in a chatty mood. Looks like at least one of my story leads will pan out: Two midtier southern banks are in trouble from bad commercial real estate loans for new housing developments that stalled when the real estate boom busted. These local lenders are seeking to be adopted by a top-tier banking parent. Within an hour, I have several sources confirming the talks and one think-tank source commenting on banking consolidation. I don't feel like racing to get this article into today's news hole, which is small due to low Monday advertising. I'll wait and deliver it for tomorrow's paper.

Overall, it was pretty easy to report this article, but I had to do some educating of one of the sources I'll quote anonymously. He told me some things and then said "this is off the record." Obviously, he's a press virgin. Anyone who talks to the media needs to understand, we're *never* off the record. What would be the point of that? If I'm calling you, I'm working. I don't do this for fun. That means any information I gather I'm looking to use. I might agree to keep your name out of the story if you say "not for attribution" *before* we start talking. But if you don't want me to use something at all don't give it to me.

I bang out ten inches. It's not a sizzler, but it's solid. And when I plug in some stats I expect to receive early tomorrow, it will be ready to toss into the queue.

*

As predicted, Stokes filed his motion today to Judge Goldberg, and Dylan, via his courthouse contacts, already has a copy. He emails saying Stokes' motion is pretty pedestrian and doesn't offer any novel arguments to compel the judge to bypass rehab privacy and protection rules and let him interview Shane. Dylan has attached his finished rebuttal motion for my review.

I read each motion carefully. Fortunately they're short for legal filings. I believe Dylan's argument is more convincing, but that could just be my inherent bias. Stokes' motion is as stiff and pompous as his in-person demeanor.

I send a two-word answer back to Dylan: "File it." He said earlier that Judge Goldberg tends to be very decisive in these matters. He expects her ruling by Thursday, Friday at the latest.

It's approaching one o'clock and the tension in the newsroom is starting to be palpable. Time to escape for an hour. I take a walk and return to my desk with a take-out salad just before the final page reviews begin. Since I'm not on the story budget for today, I'll help proof headlines, cutlines and stories just before the pages are sent down to our press. I email Wylie about my story for tomorrow's budget. He pings me back saying it could lead the inside business page. Excellent, I'll get prominent placement for a piece I've basically already finished.

*

The next day, it feels like I never left the building. I'm in early and polishing my bank acquisition story. I'm in the zone and writing well.

Wylie and I have a one-on-one scheduled for midmorning, after the page one meeting. And there's an all-hands editorial meeting after deadline today at four o'clock. It was announced after I left yesterday, and it has everyone buzzing. New policies? New direction? More layoffs? Speculation among the professional gossips, i.e. all reporters and editors, is rampant.

My meeting with Wylie goes well for the most part. He's pleased with my coverage from Davos. And it's always good to meet with your editor when you've just handed in a story that's likely to be an exclusive for the paper. One new directive gets placed on the table: Management wants more "contributed editorial," read free filler stories. And Wylie expects me to recruit business leaders to write op-eds that we can run on Monday on inner business-news pages, our least-valuable real estate. I don't love the idea of recruiting fluff pieces, but I can at least improve the content by helping to shape some more newsworthy ideas for columns.

The newsroom buzzes with tension today, even more than usual, due to a P-1 story that required a total rewrite. Plus, everyone is more jacked up than normal because of the upcoming late-afternoon, all-hands editorial meeting. I decide to slip out for an hour or so to evade the stress fest. I hop over to the fitness club for a quick spin on the stationary bike and an abbreviated weights routine. I'm back by three thirty, after most of the pages have shipped.

At the appointed hour, we're all gathered in the newsroom, waiting for the publisher and editor-in-chief to enlighten us. Just after four, they arrive, accompanied by our union rep, Bob. Well that's an easy tell; clearly we're facing another "reduction in force," as they so politely put it. And this layoff will be large enough that the union is involved and advance notice is being provided. We're being informed that the ax is falling, but we won't know which editors or reporters are getting chopped for another four to six weeks. We'll spend the next month guessing whether we have jobs or not. The newsroom will be positively toxic.

I tune back in to hear Bob describe the "package." If you get cut, here's what you can expect in severance: two week's pay for anyone with less than three years with the company. Another two-week's pay for those with three to ten years paddling this sinking ship, and a maximum of six weeks' pay for anyone who has put in more than a decade. So if I'm cut loose I'll collect a month's salary, plus unemployment benefits. In this economy, finding another journalism job in four weeks is a fantasy, and everyone in this room is aware of this unhappy fact.

They finish their presentation and start taking questions from a hostile group that's well-practiced in barbed questions. Bag it, listening to this won't enlighten me or save my job. I slip from the back of the room, through a door that leads to a hallway and a back exit. Before you can say "strategic workforce realignment," I'm looking for parking at Venice Beach. On a side street, I use a towel to change back into my still sweaty gym clothes and some running shoes. In no time, I have a nice rhythm going, as I jog the strand and enjoy the spectacle of musclemen, tramps and crystal-gazers that frequent this strip of L.A. concrete and sand.

I'm not immune to fretting over my livelihood or future, but soaking up others' angst isn't going to help me. I need to strategize my own work realignment, with a clear head. And I do some of my best mental masticating while running. Bizarrely, part of me is already starting to see this potential layoff as an opportunity — one of the advantages of being rootless is that change doesn't throw me as much as it does the perpetual planners.

The week drags on, with the usual newsroom stress, plus rampant bitching and speculation over the coming layoff. By Friday, I'm counting down the hours until I can escape the noxious environment. Then good news hits, from Dylan. Judge Goldberg denied Stokes' motion to interview Shane during his rehab isolation period.

"But Dana, this means we've only gained a little over a week. Once Shane is beyond the isolation period, Goldberg has ruled that he has to speak with the FBI as a material witness."

"I understand, Dylan. But we'll get to him first, right, and get him to spill about his connection with Ling and why someone bashed his arm."

"You're coming back up?"

Well, I didn't realize I was until this moment, but I have to find a way. It's horrible timing, with the impending layoff I should be trying to stay under the radar and not take more time off. Unless I actually want a lot of time off.

"I have an idea about how to swing that, Dylan. But yeah, I'm definitely coming up. I'll be there on the first day that I can talk to Shane."

He promises to forward the full motion by Goldberg so I can see it. As usual, he offers to put me up in the barn.

I get back to the pages and focus on finding any gotchas everyone else might have missed. Once the corrected pages are sent, I send a brief note to the only trustworthy human-resources person in our corporate bureaucracy, Sandy. I ask her if she has time for a short meeting before she escapes for the weekend. She's a sixty-three-year-old executive assistant turned HR functionary. The divorced mother of three grown sons, she's just riding the desk until she can retire. If she can help me, she will.

Her single-sentence reply: "Come down at four thirty."

When I arrive at the HR department, Sandy is at her desk, and she waves me toward the small conference room in a corner off the HR bullpen. I realize as I step in the room that this is the space often used for exit interviews of fired and laid-off employees. These walls are permeated with anguish and anger. Sandy slips in, wearing her corporate uniform, a conservative knee-length gabardine skirt and a patterned blazer over a fluffy blouse. With her gray head of curls, she looks every bit the corporate functionary, until she opens her mouth.

"TGIFF, thank god it's fucking Friday, eh, Dana?"

Sandy has a potty mouth like a reporter; she can even make her sons blush. I ask her how her boys are doing and she gives me the rundown on jobs, wives and her two young grandsons. "Boys, boys, boys, Dana, it's my lot in life that I get divorced twenty-five years ago and I'm STILL steeped in goddamn testosterone." She rolls her eyes. "Okay, enough about the family. What do you need?"

I explain that I want to make sure I understand the company's policy on personal leaves of absence. How do I request one? Are they really up to six weeks? What are the restrictions?

She says that there are federal and state programs for family leave, with up to six weeks off, but to qualify you have to be a new parent or caring for a sick parent or child. I ask whether the programs apply to caring for a sibling. No go. Once again, the system is set up to support the traditional family, but not the rest of us who've eschewed that path. But she gives me some good news: our publishing company actually has a pretty liberal policy of its own on personal leave. I can take up to four weeks at half pay, *if* I use the remainder of my vacation time (just four days) first and get my supervisor to sign off.

If I'm on approved leave, can the company cut it off and start my severance during that time? "No way, Dana. Any employee rights lawyer could take the company to court for discrimination if we did something that reckless."

Now I need Sandy to level with me. She's a no-bullshit gal, so I just come right out and ask the difficult question. "Are the cuts likely to hit my group?"

She looks directly into my eyes, through her stylish Prada glasses. "Very likely."

I thank her. She reaches across the table and squeezes my hand. Her job is a tough one that I don't envy. It will be a big loss for the employees when she retires...or gets cut in the layoffs. She reminds me that all HR forms can be filed online. But first I need to recruit Wylie …

Chapter 14

I throw on some jeans and a nubby sweater and blast out of the loft on my cruiser bike. It's a foggy morning, but the cloud cover is warm.

Sal's Diner is a landmark for the blue-collar crowd that once worked in this previously industrial neighborhood. But it's become a hang-out for surfers too. Big, hearty concoctions and reasonable prices have enabled it to court a new generation of loyal regulars. Work boots have given way to flip-flops. Its Formica tables and steel chairs are so old they're retro cool again. It's the kind of place where if you can't order within the first five seconds of the waitress' "What'll you have?" she'll give you a brusque "Hold on" circle around to another table and come back. Niceties aren't part of the fare. Only if you've been coming regularly for years do you rate a "Nice to see you, what'll you have?"

Every table except one is filled with the usual mix of older retired couples — men in plaid shirts and John Deere caps, ladies in floral blouses and polyester pants. Loose-limbed surfers wearing T-shirts and baggy shorts and sporting long tangled locks and soul patches sit at a table in the corner. Two of them are acquaintances — guys I've shared swells with here or up in Malibu. Their names come to me: Weed and Skyler. Surfers love nicknames. Weed's real name is Reed, but since he inhabits the kelp and tokes up before nearly every surf session everyone calls him Weed. I catch Skyler's eye and nod a hello.

I call a truce with my burrito about three quarters of the way through. Time to make a plan for the day. The evening is booked — another gym friend, Rayan, a studio musician, is

141

throwing a birthday party for himself at his house in Laurel Canyon.

Curb hopping my bike like a preteen, I make my way back to the loft through the breaking fog. It's turning into a warm spring day, with no breeze, ideal conditions for stand-up paddling. Invented by the ancient Hawaiians, who used big wood-plank paddleboards for transportation, fishing and fun, today's stand-up enthusiasts paddle flat water and also take their boards into the waves. On flat days, I enjoy the simplicity of just stroking through glassy water.

Movement is my salvation. If I'm moving, physically pushing myself, I can outrun emotions and memories that might flatten me. And I'm constantly reassuring myself that I'm not Valerie, all those days she spent on the couch; I associate rest, especially lying down or napping, with depression.

I spend two hours paddling through the channels at Burton Chace Park in Marina del Rey, viewing power launches, sailboats, houseboats and other floating structures, and communing with ducks and one blue heron that views me suspiciously but decides if he stands stock-still I can't see him. The day warms to the mid-seventies; it's one of those early spring days that make East Coasters so jealous of Southern California life. I certainly can't complain. Today, I've walked on sparkling water, gotten some sun and eaten California's true cuisine, cheap Mexican food.

*

Like many gay friends, Rayan, a studio musician, has a talent for parties that mix people from a variety of gene pools, the hip music crowd, the gym rats, his family and other friends. They're always casual, inviting and fun. Arriving in the fashionably late range, I find Rayan and wish him happy birthday with a kiss on the cheek and a box of his favorite truffles.

"Dana, you are a very bad influence; you're skinny and you feed others chocolate." Rayan leans toward stocky, and at only five foot eight he has to work out to keep his waist size from dwarfing his pant length.

I laugh and hug him again. He introduces me to Brett, whom I suspect is his latest friend with benefits. He's all smiles and enthusiasm — clearly they're still in the bubbly early romance phase.

I say hello to some of Rayan's other friends, whom I've met at the gym and at previous parties. One of them guides me to the bar, set up just outside the patio doors. Tonight's confection is a grapefruit juice cocktail: silver tequila, citrus liqueur, red grapefruit juice, a splash of club soda and a small slice of grapefruit. Served in a tumbler with a sugar rim to cut the tart of the juice, it is dangerously good.

The party revs up when Rayan starts jamming with some friends. The music and dancing go to midnight. Maudlin thoughts about Shane and my impending unemployment drive me back to the bar too many times. When the music stops, I'm melted into the living-room sectional, sipping drink number who-knows-what. Rayan convinces me to stay the night. He's such the consummate host that I don't feel too weird accepting.

*

When I pad into the kitchen, I hear "Morning Sunshine." Rayan is slumped over the island. He pours me a cup of coffee and holds up the cream. I nod and he doctors our cups. We sip and make our way to the couch. Party remnants dot the horizontal surfaces of the room: tumblers, crumpled napkins, some smudged wine glasses. The hardwood floors feature a few sticky spots and some crumbs, but the house seems to have come through the maelstrom without any lasting injuries.

After we start on the second cup, we're able to converse in graveled voices. Rayan asks about my family — he knows about my troubled northern roots. I give him the short version of Shane's latest drama. But after some prodding I describe his injury, rehab and dangerous liaisons. I tell him that I'll be going north again in a week, when Shane's therapy-imposed isolation is lifted.

Rayan isn't interested in Shane's mysterious injury or in handicapping the effectiveness of his latest rehab. He cuts directly to the impact on me. "How many more rescue missions do you have in you, Dana?" Even though it's a question I've asked myself too many times, it's jarring hearing it spoken so plainly by one of my good friends.

I stare into the distance. "A few more, apparently, Rayan. I'm not ready to give up on him, even though Joe and Terry have walked away."

"But you can't let him take you down, Dana. That serves no one."

I look away. Down from what? Sadly, Shane's dramas actually fill my detached existence. He connects me to an emotional side of life that I otherwise avoid. He is my brother, my friend, my only real relationship and my child all rolled into one dysfunctional package. Yep, I'm co-dependent. What of it? To me that's a psychobabble word that describes any person who's not so self-involved as to avoid acknowledging anyone else's problems.

There are no ah-ha's coming from this dialogue. But I appreciate Rayan's concern and upfront honesty. Fortunately, the somewhat awkward silence that follows his comments is broken up by Brett shuffling into the room in a terry robe and fuzzy slippers and declaring, "Tequila should have its own specific warning label. I feel like twitching, nearly dead road kill."

"Eww!" We both squeal and laugh as Brett drops like a rag doll onto the cushion next to Rayan, who pats his hand. The conversation moves to a review of last night's jam. It's a much more appropriate discussion for hung-over party animals.

*

Early Monday, I'm back in the newsroom, scanning the wires and mentally composing the outline for my discussion with Wylie. First thing today, before any doubts could stop me, I emailed him, asking for an early meeting.

I figure he's already been notified about layoffs for his group of reporters. He'll protect Lou, the senior member of the economics staff. And he'll have to keep Sally, our very junior Columbia School of Journalism intern. It's a contract, and if the paper wants the continued benefits of this alliance — nearly free slave labor — it can't lay off coeds. Besides, it would save no money. That leaves me and Russell. He's a competent reporter, and more importantly he sucks up to all the right people in the newsroom and the executive wing. Plus he's a family man, laying him off comes with major guilt. Logic predicts, and Sandy as much as confirmed, that in our editorial group I'm the one that will get it in the neck.

The only question is, will Wylie help me extend my actual end date by approving my personal-leave request? And will he sell the leave approval to his managers, the executive editor and editor-in-chief?

*

We face each other in the small conference room. Wylie's brow is knit with deep furrows; his eyes look tired and his rumpled shirt looks even more slept-in than usual. He doesn't know what this conversation will cover, but his news instincts tell him it's related to the layoff, and he's girding for a very uncomfortable discussion. I decide to start with the story of Shane, which confounds Wylie because he was probably expecting me to sell him on saving my job. As I'm explaining Shane's latest mess, my trip up north a few weeks ago and my need to return to Half Moon Bay, I actually start tearing up. Even I'm not sure if I'm acting or truly getting emotional, but it's certainly out of character for my work persona. When I get to the part where I describe my request for personal leave and my research into the company's policy on this leave, he's already nodding slightly.

I completely level with him on how my accrued time off, personal leave (if approved), and severance would give me the ability to deal with Project Shane and get a better start on the potentially long process of landing another paycheck. His consternation with my emotional tale gives way to his tactical nature, as he grasps how this whole plan amounts to a way he can do the company's bidding and lay off another long-time staff member, but at the same time use the paper's own drafted policies to ease his guilt and help me. Before I've even finished my pitch, he's in.

"Dana, I can't imagine a more appropriate use of the personal leave policy than the work you're doing on behalf of your brother. I will support your application."

He sits back in his chair; his arms are on the table and he rolls over his hands, palms up. "The paper is going downhill, Dana. They're not providing us with the resources to do the kind of journalism we were once known for. I fear for the future." That's as negative as a politically astute manager like

Wylie is ever going to get, but in this awkward way he's trying to apologize for firing me. We end the meeting shortly after discussing how I'll electronically file my leave request.

With my plan of escape in motion, I look ahead and try to keep the woe-is-me thoughts from taking me down. Besides, stability is an illusion. I've done all the right things, good grades, college, pursuing my career, making savvy job changes, and look at me: I'm rootless, relationship-less and out of a job. I have some funds, but my current situation is no more "stable" than Shane's.

The week passes in routine economic reports, banal short stories and on Thursday, an email from Sandy. "Your leave has been approved. Don't be a stranger." That's as warm and fuzzy as she can get with the corporate network police lurking. It's a good thing the plan worked, because I've already begun packing. This time, the length of my stay is yet to be determined so I've begun stuffing the car with clothes, plus gear for running, camping, surfing and diving, and a few other of life's necessity...a go-cup, my iPod, my computer.

On Friday afternoon, I'm trying to beat the weekend traffic north, having escaped the newsroom at just after three. I won't be returning — I know it and Wylie knows it — so I have no one to impress by staying to the closing bell. And we've decided to keep my personal leave quiet, a request from the upper managers who don't want others to get any ideas. There's no goodbye wishes or farewell party. It's a cold parting; I just slip away.

I won't kill myself trying to get to Half Moon Bay tonight. Instead, I've made a reservation for a yurt at a campground near San Luis Obispo. I'm hoping for a Saturday morning surf session; the weather reports and tides look favorable. I slog north on 101, working my way through pockets of traffic that continue all the way to Santa Barbara.

I try to keep my mind empty and just drive. But frustration and self-doubt seep in. My only close relationship (besides Shane), my job, is gone. I rub the back of my neck, as I process some of the hurt of being let go when I've worked so hard. But then I take some deep breaths and sit up straighter, refusing to give in to my job angst. I'll flip the switch and put this behind me. I'll move on, as I always do.

Reaching the campground after hours, I pay my overnight fee and circle through the eucalyptus and pines to my yurt. It's a cozy little octagon, with an outside BBQ and picnic table. Inside there's a single bed on one side and bunk beds on the other side. A small table sits in the yurt's center, and a bare overhead bulb illuminates it. I switch on the small wall heater to take off some of the damp chill. The campground is probably an eighth of a mile from the coast, so you can smell it but you can't see it.

Soon I'm snuggled into my nylon-covered cocoon, with my headlamp lighting my latest novel, a spy story set along the Mediterranean coastline.

*

I roll out of the campground early, and by seven I've duck-dived though the lineup out to a point break that I haven't surfed in ten years. The waves are small and mushy three-footers, but the sets are reliable enough to provide regular but short rides. A drippy fog enshrouds the coast, coloring it in shades of gray light. A couple of sea lions cruise by, swimming and rolling through the outside green-gray swells. Two late-teen boys and a middle-aged longboarder vie with me for rides, but it's a relaxed vibe and we trade off waves.

After a parking-lot shower from a gallon milk jug I filled with hot water from the camp showers, I'm cruising north again. I drive with my knees while inhaling two breakfast sandwiches in rapid succession. Still chewing, I dial Dylan's office number.

"Hey, Dylan, it's Dana, your too-frequent house guest."

"Hi, Dana. I got your email. Where are you?"

"Just north of Atascadero. I should arrive in Half Moon Bay by early afternoon, as long as I don't hit any Bay Area traffic knots."

Dylan's tone is tight and direct. "Not a minute too soon. Tomorrow Shane is allowed his first visitors. Fortunately for us, Agent Stokes is out of town until Tuesday. Initially, you should talk with him solo Dana. He can disclose information to you about Ling that I may not want to hear. As a member of the court, I could be compelled to reveal those facts if they pose an imminent danger to others."

Acid reflux is my stomach's reaction to that last comment. Shane's world of hidden threats awaits me. I ask him about visiting hours.

"One to four on Sundays. I've notified his counselor and sponsor that you'll probably be coming at one."

"Thanks Dylan. What's your schedule tonight? I could use some coaching on what information you think I should try to extract from Shane."

"I have a jail visit this afternoon, but I should get back to the farm by six thirty. Maria is working swing shift and Marco's out of town at a soccer tournament, so we'll have plenty of opportunity to gnash our teeth over Shane — without Maria's evil eye."

"Maria has every right to despise Shane and how he's lived his life so far. I don't defend him, I just rescue him. It's a sick familial compulsion."

"Still, it'll be easier to talk on our own. Let yourself into the loft and house whenever you arrive."

I reach the southern end of Half Moon Bay by early afternoon, and stop into The Hook to check the surf. The stereo is pounding out some Pearl Jam and I'm focused on an incoming set, when my passenger door swings wide open and Anton drops heavily into the seat next to me. He starts doing some seated head banging to the beat of the music, as I coldly stare at his jerking body, controlling my fear and channeling it into disgust.

"Dana, back again from La La Land? Shane must need his butt wiped."

I just stare blankly at Anton's profile, keeping calm.

"You can't fix Shane's problems this time, Dana. He's gonna have to be a man and make things right all on his own. And once he's out of rehab, we will find him." The sneer on his face — half smile, half leer — makes me want slap him. Instead, I chuckle, which has the desired effect of confusing him.

"Anton, your school-yard bully routine got old way back in junior high. And you're just one bully in Shane's growing fan club."

I see his mental gears moving behind his knit Neanderthal brow, as his brain, which didn't develop much beyond puberty, tries to work out what I might be telling him.

Finally, I make it clear enough for even this caveman to understand. "The feds are way scarier than you are, Anton. And they have more resources. And guess what, they've been watching me too, so you can hang out if you want and I'll introduce you."

As expected, this last comment, though pure fiction, gets his attention. His spine straightens, and he glances into the side mirror to see what's behind the Honda. He recovers his composure quickly and makes another threat.

"If Shane sings to the cops, he'll never ride another wave, Dana."

"With or without Shane, the feds have plans for you and your buddies, Anton. They have a nice zoo prepped for you, populated with other animals that bully and bite."

He leans over and growls into my right ear. I recoil and turn my head away and ease my hand up to the door handle, ready to throw it open and spring out.

"Shane can make it right. But it's a limited-time offer."

I stare ahead and try to keep my voice from shaking. "You want to be a little more specific?"

"He knows what's what. You just tell him he's got a week." With that, he pops out the door and slams it so hard the car rocks. I watch him in the rearview mirror stride to an oversize pickup that throws dirt as he accelerates out of the lot.

I start my car and burn out the other end of the lot, leaning forward in my seat and glancing in the mirrors every few seconds. Was tipping Anton and Ling to the scrutiny of the feds wise or foolish? I went with my gut, hoping it would make them more cautious. But it could make matters worse.

When I get to the farm, it becomes apparent that Dylan has been withholding some new information that will rattle me even more than my interaction with Anton. He says the battle between Ling's meth operation and the Mexican gang running meth in the Bay Area is intensifying. A meth lab was recently firebombed — authorities at first thought it was an accidental explosion, but an investigation by fire marshals turned up evidence of an incendiary device. Shane's on the wrong side of a drug kingpin, in the middle of a gang war, and a person of interest for the feds. The news just gets better and better.

Dylan rarely advises running from problems, yet now he says Shane needs to disappear. But he can't give this advice to Shane directly...too tricky for an officer of the court. Only I can do it, and I'll have to fund it. I'm praying Shane has some thoughts on a clever hidey hole.

Chapter 15

Two surfers are working the break, which offers up three-foot peaks coming in regular sets. Good enough for a morning baptism in my Northern California house of worship. Visiting hours at the rehab center don't begin until after lunch and I might as well take advantage of my new jobless status. Castle Cove is just three miles south of town. It's named for a 1920s mansion that once overlooked the beach, but its cliff-side perch on the fickle sandstone was claimed by a powerful winter storm a generation ago.

I wriggle into my wetsuit, booties, gloves and a hooded vest for extra protection from the liquid freezer burn. When I punch through the first wave, my cheeks feel like they've been pin pricked two dozen times. I paddle rapidly, trying to generate some heat and reach the take-off zone in time for an incoming set. One surfer is behind me, paddling back out after a decent ride. The other surfer drops the first wave of the set. I concentrate on the swells coming behind it, and paddle out and slightly right, positioning myself for the third wave in the set. It's too small to call my entry a drop; it's more like hopping onto a rolling log. But it rolls long enough for four or five turns and a couple of cutbacks, before I glide up and over what's left of the mushy crest.

When I get back out to the lineup, I see that my fellow riders are two clean-cut twenty-something young men, who have long lean bodies yet to be filled out by beer and manhood. Even their rubber suits seem to hang on these two. We exchange banal pleasantries about the mediocre surf and the numbing water. The surf might be less than adrenaline pumping, but with just three of us out we enjoy a consistent session of paddle, drop, twist and turn, repeat.

I stay until I have the break to myself, except for a couple of floating gulls. I can't remember the last time that I rode waves until I was sated and tired, instead of on a timetable set by work or other adult commitments. The surfing has soothed and rejuvenated me. I drive slowly back through town, thinking about Shane.

It's no wonder he can't communicate, regulate his emotions, or deal with conflict. When we were kids, our parents either didn't speak or screamed at each other, and us. And they both believed wholeheartedly in corporal punishment — Joe's weapon of choice was an old, well-used brown belt. Valerie, she should have been into the martial arts. She had a lightning-fast backhand, which she could deploy while holding a menthol light in her other hand. Later she'd be crying and blaming us for making her "lose it."

She loved Shane, but she saw herself in him. Joe didn't understand her or Shane. And his boot-camp approach to molding Shane just made him rebel.

A breeze shakes the trees that line the road to Forest Glen. I make my way to the reception desk. An attendant searches my purse, pats me down and escorts me to the visiting area, a lounge and patio at the back of the building. Shane will be brought to me.

He shuffles in, wearing loose, saggy Levi's, a surf T-shirt and flip-flops. His arm is now in a flexible nylon and elastic brace, with Velcro tightening straps. His startling light blue eyes are clear, his shaggy hair is filling in and it's clean. He's even put on a couple of pounds; his cheeks are no longer sunken to his molars. I stand and hug him gently on the side of his body away from his still-healing arm. We take a small table in the far corner of the patio.

We start by discussing neutral topics — surfing and windsurfing. But I have little patience for chit-chat today. I go to the blunt approach, my natural style.

"Shane, I need to know what kind of trouble you're in. Not because I'm meddling, but because we need a plan. This is bigger than just you pissing off some neighborhood drug dealer. As I told you before, the feds want you. They have a whole special task force working in town. The local cops have been bullied aside."

"Fucking G-men." Neither one of us has much respect for any bureaucratic authority. I work to expose their flaws, and Shane breaks their rules just for the fun of it.

"As I'm sure you can figure out, you're in a very precarious position. Ling's probably aware of the investigation and he knows you know too much. Plus you've already pissed him off. But I don't trust the feds to protect you if you talk to them. They'll just use you and leave you to fend for yourself. But if we can throw them a bone to work with — and get you the hell away from here while the shit flies — maybe they'll take care of neutralizing Ling."

"You and Dylan have been scheming."

"Of course." I see no reason to be anything but honest. This time Shane is going to have to participate in saving himself. We can't do it for him. It's like the twelve-step program. The addict has to take responsibility for his actions and for his decisions. I can point the way, but he has to take the steps.

Shane studies the stains on the table. "Some of my memory of what happened is gone. I have pieces, but not an hour-by-hour or even day-by-day account of those couple of days."

I chew on his statement. Interacting with Shane, processing anything he says, is difficult. It's like listening to a cheating lover tell you something — once you've figured out the depth of his betrayal and how many times he must have lied to you to cover up all the clandestine meetings, how can you believe a single utterance that comes out of his mouth?

"Let's start with you describing to me what you did for Ling. I've heard you drove deliveries from *yaa baa* factories to dealers."

I look at his face and I can read the conflict going on in his brain. He doesn't want to admit to his job as a courier. I'm not sure if he doesn't want to involve me, or he just doesn't want to concede his role in the meth operation.

"By the way, Anton has been tailing me. He wants me to let you know that he's watching me and looking for you. He thinks he can scare you into coming back to Ling."

His face darkens with anger. "Fucking piece of headless meat." Shane's descriptive powers have always been finely honed.

At first he just stares at me. Then, looking down again at the tabletop, he rolls his eyes. "I don't remember the factory locations, and Ling moves them frequently anyway. The dealers move around too...I rarely delivered to the same place twice."

We're making progress. He's admitted to the job he did, but what did he do to get Ling so enraged? I wait out his silence as he slumps down further; his neck is resting on the back of his plastic chair. Review, admit and apologize, it's part of the addict's journey to recovery. It hasn't been Shane's forte, which may be one reason why his numerous recoveries have been short-lived. And the McCarren family tradition has always been to bury the past and deny its impact on our lives. I do it too, only I run instead of medicate.

Now I'm going to advocate running, but first I need to know everything he's running from.

"It's poison, man, pure poison." At first, I think this is just a comment about meth in general. But looking at his trembling fingers, it dawns on me that he's trying to tell me something much more alarming. I guess and lead him on.

"Ling's meth was poison?"

His anger causes him to whip his head back and forth. "The stupid fuck let some new guys from Koh Samui run one of the labs. He trusts those homies, but some of them are just ignorant peasants. They got stoned, stayed up all night and cooked a bad batch. I wasn't supposed to find out."

The story pours out of him in a rush of words, peppered with expletives. He'd delivered a rush order, the first of that "rat-poison" batch, late one evening down in East Palo Alto to a dealer he'd serviced many times before. By morning, one of this dealer's customers, a sixteen-year-old, was in the hospital in a coma and three of his friends were sick.

Fortunately, Shane hadn't sampled this batch. He says he'd been trying to slow down his consumption and still had enough stash that he'd already been given as part of his pay for his delivery service.

But the dealer got suspicious. After all, this is his product and his livelihood. Sickened customers impact sales. And the information flow among even the most stoned addicts is surprisingly efficient, so if word got out about him selling tainted product he'd lose business. He took the suspect pills to a lab geek, who tested a bunch of them. The pills shouldn't be lethal, but the batch was extremely uneven. And some pills had high amounts of heavy metals in them. That's likely what took down the kid in the coma. The dealer should have spoken only to Ling, but he was so furious that he lured Shane to a meeting and made the call to Ling in front of him, while his muscle bounced Shane around a bit for sport.

"Did they break your arm?"

"No, that came later."

He stalls in the storytelling. He's involving me in criminal activity, and not misdemeanors, felonies. Despite all the years of dealing with Shane's troubles, I've never been in this deep before. I haven't been an accomplice or put in the position of harboring a felon.

"I dumped it, man." Shane traces the scratches on the table with a shaking hand.

"Dumped the meth? How? Where? Does Ling know?" My mind is racing. No wonder Ling and Anton are intent on punishing Shane. And keeping him from the feds is likely their biggest priority, because any information about tainted meth would surely put a new urgency on the feds' investigation of Ling's operations.

Shane explains that after the dealer ripped Ling up and down, Shane was ordered to meet up with Anton and give him the rest of the bad batch. Shane suggested that he could just bury it somewhere, since it wasn't saleable product...or so he thought. But when he spoke to Ling, it became clear that he had no intention of dumping the toxic meth. He just wanted to move it to another market, further away from his operation, perhaps to a contact in Southern California.

"Dana, you probably think I have no conscience whatsoever, but I would never knowingly sell poison or help that dirt-bag sell it. Sure, meth is a horrible drug. Don't I know that. But tainted meth? That Thai punk is a worm."

"So you dumped it?"

"Yep, buried and gone, especially after the last rain. Took it to a place away from streams and Mother Ocean. Covered it up good."

"Then what happened?"

"Well, even high I knew I was gonna pay, one way or the other. Anyway, I had an itch that needed scratching. I smoked a load, and a couple more, before I drove back to town from Palo Alto. Got back just before the early commute, whatever day that was. I just wanted to crash, but Anton, the goon, was waiting for me. He was already in my den when I got there."

I'm thinking "how can you call a crawl-space hovel with a dirt floor a den," but I don't want to interrupt the story. Still, he processes the look on my face.

"Yeah, okay, it's no luxury loft, but I had a few things to make life comfortable. Anton and one of his meathead helpers just started randomly smashing stuff, before he'd even asked me where the batch was. When he did ask, I said I'd stored it somewhere safe. If I'd told him it was all gone...well, let's just say I didn't want the reward he would have handed out for that bit of news. But Anton figured he could beat the information out of me. He and the other meat started taking turns pounding me. I wasn't really lucid at that time. I was tripping pretty hard, so I started screaming...and, well, I can get pretty loud."

A slight grin spreads across his face and over to mine. He was always in trouble as a kid for being too loud.

"But this time it was a good thing. My upstairs neighbor came out on the deck and screamed at the goons. She speaks mostly Spanglish, but she can say "police" pretty darn clearly. So Anton told me he'd find me later, and he and the other meat split. I did, too, cause I was in no shape to have a heart-to-heart with the local boys in blue."

"Was your arm broken already?"

"Yeah, I think so. But I was really high. Sis, I was binging pretty hard. I couldn't get that kid in the coma out of my brain. I kept hitting the pipe till I couldn't think."

"How did you end up at Craig's house?"

"I don't remember. I probably had the good sense to go there to hide. Once you do enough meth, psychosis sets in. I knew that, but I've learned more about it here at rehab. It's ugly, little sis. I just lost touch with reality and didn't really regain it until they were treating me at the hospital and bringing me down from the meth."

"Did you keep any of the bad *yaa baa* batch?"

"Yeah, I did. I put a little baggy aside. I figured I might need it for leverage."

"Where?"

"It's taped to the inside of the hubcap of my Corolla. Right back tire, I think. Why?"

"Well Agent Stokes might leave you alone if he can get his hands on some of this tainted product. Ling is the only producer of *yaa baa* pills in the area, right?"

"Yeah. He produces *yaa baa* and crystal. The Mexicans are big into meth, but their product is all rock."

I mull the idea of giving Stokes the pills. I'll have to discuss it with Dylan; that's assuming the pills are still under the hubcap. And oh yeah, I need to find Shane's car.

"Where's Sea Flea?" That's the name Shane gave his Corolla years ago. It's a rust bucket that smells of swampy salt water and mildew. Faded T-shirts serve as seat covers. Its rear bumper is a PVC pipe, painted silver, which Shane thinks is hilarious.

"It's down the hill from Craig's, in the neighborhood that's to the west on the flats. I don't remember the exact location. But if you just drive a couple of those twisty streets you'll find it. I parked it under some big, overhanging eucalyptus trees. What will the feds do with the poison *yaa baa*?"

"I don't know. I need to ask Dylan what he thinks about this idea of providing evidence to an FBI investigation. Even though it's evidence that's not coming directly from Ling there still might be some benefit."

We sit in silence for a bit. I want to ask him how he is, but I'm still so angry with him that part of me wants him to be suffering. And I've heard him spew the twelve steps before — I've heard it all before. Can I listen to an addict's apologies, regrets, excuses and revelations one more time? If he sucks me in, it will hurt that much more when he slips again. They say relapse is part of recovery. Oh really? And what does a relapse do for the family members? Is a relapse supposed to be a revelatory part of *our* journey? What are the take-away lessons for us? We're supposed to set boundaries with our addicted family member. When it comes to a relapse, which boundary are we supposed to use? Which one makes them save themselves and which one aids their slide back into the abyss?

Shane senses my uneasiness, my doubt. We are connected that way. He feels it when I'm peering into him.

He stares off into the woods. "I'm trying, Dana. For the first time in a long time, I actually want to be clean. I don't want to be a part of Ling's evil. When I'm using, all I care about is the next hit. But I don't want to be his droid anymore. I'm learning to live here at the re-habitat. I'm not sure what I am now, where I fit, but I know I don't want to be that."

Despite my resolve, a small crack opens in the wall I've put up. I want to believe. He shocks me even more when he actually asks about my life.

"How long before you roll back into Smogland? Do you have any business trips scheduled?"

I chuckle. We are equals in a way now — we're both unemployed vagrants. "I've been laid off, Shane. My time is my own, until the cash reserves run out."

Anger flashes across his face, his eyes pull together and a vertical furrow forms between his eyebrows. "What? You've won awards for that rag! How can they do that?"

I explain the turmoil that's rewriting the newspaper business. I don't go into details about my leave of absence and severance package. Perversely, for once it feels good to see him worried about me.

I bring the discussion back to him. I explain to him that Dylan and I think he should disappear for a while once he's out of rehab. We don't want Agent Stokes or Ling trying to play him. I ask him where he might have friends who can be relied upon to keep quiet. In my mind, I'm thinking "Are there any friends who still care what happens to you?"

He shifts back and forth a few times in his chair. "I don't want Ling or the FBI to run me out of my town, Dana."

"You need to stay out of this war. The feds want Ling bad. If you stay in town, this guy, Stokes, he'll find a way to charge you with something." I look at the side of Shane's face as he rubs his knuckles. He wants to fight this collapsing net.

We're quiet for a minute or two. Finally, he pulls up in his chair. "I hate it, but I know you're right. Anton will hunt me just for fun. And now I gotta deal with a tight-ass fed too? Maybe I can get to Kauai or the South Pacific. My surf brothers there will help me, and they never talk to outsiders."

My mind churns on how to get him to Kauai or beyond without making it easy for the FBI to track him. He can't fly; the feds will be able to trace him with their computers. But not too long ago he used to help deliver sailboats that had been sold and needed to be moved up and down the coast of California. Private sailboats don't require crew lists, and they don't file paperwork with the IRS. So there's likely no paper trail of him doing this work, nothing to tip off the feds. And rich folks often have their boats sailed from San Francisco or

Southern California to Hawaii, so they can use them to cruise the islands without having to do a Pacific crossing.

Since Shane's brain is no longer drug-fogged, he'll pick up quickly on my thought stream. "Do you still have sailboat delivery connections?"

A sly smirk spreads across his mouth. We bounce around various boat seller and skipper names and departure locations on the West Coast. He has a little less than two weeks to find a ride to Hawaii. He writes down some names for me. Craig has friends among the yachting crowd and might be able to arrange something, using his office phone. I'm so paranoid about Stokes' wiretapping abilities that I don't want to possibly ruin the plan by making any calls from my cellphone or Dylan and Maria's phone. And Dylan can't get involved with hiding a witness the FBI wants to interview.

As I drive away from Forest Glen, I'm not cheery, but I'm feeling like a roadmap is emerging for Shane. I have steps and a plan, just like rehab. It's a start. And I have Shane's cooperation, which is huge. Plus, seeing him clean is inspiring, even though I've been optimistic and later shattered so many times before.

First step, call Craig. I give him the surf report, and move right into my real reason for calling. Craig and I have been friends too long for me to try to sell him on any mission involving Shane. He listens intently, and a short silence ensues. I'm asking a lot. But the three of us have been entwined our whole lives, since our kiddie surf years, and I'm pretty sure the thread still isn't broken.

In his quiet monotone, he says "Yeah, I'll make some calls. Give me the list." I inhale, realizing I've been holding my breath while he chewed on my request. I read him the five names, some of which have phone numbers. Others are just names of yacht delivery services. He says he knows three of them pretty well, and the other two are acquaintances. I caution him to only use his office phone for the calls, perhaps at the end of the day when he has more privacy.

He asks me if I now know what happened with Shane. "Some of it, but the less you know the better. With the feds chasing this, you don't want to know anything that you could be questioned about."

"How is he, Dana...really?"

"I don't want to sound overly optimistic, Craig, but he said some positive things he hasn't said before. All the drugs are out of him."

We leave it, and then the guilt washes over me. I'm a user. Addicts use their family and friends to finance their next fix, and family members use their friends to help their addicted loved one. Acid rises in my throat, but I choke it down because I need the help.

It's late afternoon, and I decide to call Dylan to see if it makes sense for me to come to his office, where we can talk in complete client-attorney privacy. He picks up immediately and tells me to come on over. But first I need to find Shane's car. I drive into the area Shane described and start cruising up and down the streets, with their chipped curbs and old sedans. Sea Flea fits right in here. I'm hopeful it will still be here.

I turn a corner and see a grove of six drooping eucalyptus trees. They lean over, cocooning the Toyota. Fortunately, the streets are quiet. I glance around and slip out of my Honda, moving up Sea Flea's right side. I have a screwdriver, and I've put on gloves that I keep in the car for emergencies. In just a few seconds, I pop the hubcap and examine a baggy taped under it with duct tape. Through the cellophane, I can see a half a dozen small pills. I don't want this stuff in my possession. I quickly replace the baggie and slap the hubcap back into place. I figure it will be fine here for a while, among all the other dented rides with faded paint and cracked vinyl. No one in this neighborhood will report an abandoned car; they all have their own dead rides.

Slumped down, I drive quickly out of the neighborhood to Dylan's cramped office. He's partially hidden behind a desk that's stacked with ten-inch piles of legal folders. His tie is loose, and he's reading a file that's at least an inch thick.

"Dana, take a seat. Let me just finish this arrest report."

"Take your time."

He reads through three pages, and scans back through a few. Exhaling, he closes the file and then places it on top of the pile closest to him.

"Sixteen and this is his fourth arrest. This kid is using juvenile detention like a community college. But he'll soon graduate...to prison." He states this last bit flatly, but his sadness is still apparent. "What did Shane say?"

I recap my visit and what I've learned. When I get to the part about the tainted *yaa baa*, the kid in the coma and Shane's destruction of the tainted drugs Dylan sits up straighter and leans forward.

"Hold on." He picks up his phone, dials a number from memory and asks for Nurse Shannon. After a few questions about a teenage overdose victim, and a few pleasantries with the nurse, he hangs up.

"As you could probably tell, that was Palo Alto General. I have a good contact there. The kid who ingested the *yaa baa*...he died."

We sit in stunned silence. "Whuh-what will that do to Stokes' investigation?"

"Make it bigger, which he'll love." Dylan's forehead accordions with furrows. "But Stokes hasn't made the connection yet. The nurse says no feds have shown an interest in this O.D. The hospital sent out the tox screen from the autopsy to get a full report, but it hasn't come back yet."

"No media has paid attention because it's East Palo Alto." Dylan bobs his head at my statement. To some, a meth addict dying is news to be cheered, not questioned. "This is getting scarier."

"Oh, yeah." Dylan's face is noticeably paler. "Let's set that aside for a moment. How is Shane doing in rehab? Is he lucid?"

I give him a full report on Shane's treatment and his progress. "He seems calm, Dylan. It actually seems like he wants to stay clean. Given all that's come before, that sounds naïve, but the episode with this kid shook him."

I share with him my talk with Shane about slipping away. But I don't mention the possible escape route or destination. Even as his attorney, Dylan can't participate in hiding a witness from the FBI.

Lastly, I tell him about the toxic *yaa baa* that Shane stashed.

"Shane kept some as a possible insurance policy. He told me where to find it, and I made sure it was there just before I came to your office."

He stares over my head. I can see the legal gears spinning behind his unfocused eyes. What does this piece of evidence mean and how can it be best used?

Dylan starts thinking out loud. "It's a gamble, turning this over to Stokes. He could use it to force Shane to give a deposition, or even charge him as an accessory to a murder or manslaughter. On the other hand, it will give him fuel to intensify his investigation of Ling, bringing him more agents and visibility, something Stokes craves."

He sits still and mulls options. "Or we could start by telling Agent Stokes about the death of this kid. If the tox report shows that tainted *yaa baa* killed the kid, Stokes doesn't really need Shane's stashed pills to request more resources for his investigation. Ling is the only *yaa baa* producer in the area."

"I'll do whatever you say, Dylan. I just don't want that stuff in my possession."

"Me either. I can't withhold evidence that might be material in a federal investigation that includes a homicide."

"We can leave it where it is. Shane's car won't draw attention for quite a while in that neighborhood. Maybe we'll never need it." Maybe.

Chapter 16

The next day, while I'm getting depressed perusing journalism job sites from my temporary home in the barn loft, I hear from Craig. He gets to the point quickly. He says he's found a ride for Shane to Hawaii. A recently refurbished and sold sailboat needs to be delivered to the islands, so a skipper is sailing it down, with a planned departure a couple of days after Shane is released from rehab. Two catches: The boat is leaving from the Olympic Peninsula in Washington State, and the skipper is an ex-con.

"What was his offense, Craig? Is he a user?"

"He did time for manslaughter. He killed a mother and child in a DUI accident years ago. His employer says he's been working the twelve steps every day since he was released from prison eight years ago. And in addition to delivering boats, he's a group leader at a rehab house."

"The trip could be one long meeting for Shane and a ride to the islands. It sounds perfect."

"But we have to get him to Port Townsend."

I don't relish the idea of a long road trip with Shane, but I'll do it to make this plan work. Like all surfers, Shane made his first pilgrimage to Hawaii, surfing's Mecca, just after high school. He went back later as sponsored pro, surfing the big contests on Oahu and living on Kauai. But he tired of the rules and the slick packaged tour. He walked away to just surf for the purity of the sport. That gave him status with the local Hawaiians, many of whom see surfing as a spiritual pursuit, not commerce. He lived on Kauai for two years. But eventually he drifted back to Half Moon Bay, after reconnecting with a former girlfriend. She drew him back to

California and subsequently broke his heart. His downward slide steepened after that.

I spend the week leading up to the trip surfing and hiding from Agent Stokes. I make one very quick visit to Shane's hobbit hole, collecting clothes and gear. And I contact his landlord and cancel his lease, forfeiting his deposit for the back rent Shane owes, though this sticks in my throat. How can he have a damage deposit on a dirt-floor crawl-space? I cough up his rent for the month, until I can move the rest of his stuff.

I stage trip supplies in the loft: Shane's duffel bag and one for me, camping equipment, surf gear for both of us, plenty of CDs, a cooler, food and snacks. Just in case Anton has been trying to track me, I've stayed away from the rehab center since the visit when Shane confessed the story of the poison *yaa baa*. Shane and I have had a few short phone exchanges — he knows the plan. I've also spoken with his counselors. They say he's as ready as he'll ever be for the world. Unlike some treatment centers, this one doesn't believe in long retreats. At some point, an addict has to face what's out there in the big screwed-up world and deal with it. Rehab gets you cleaned up, but the real work begins when you re-enter real life.

I've been lying low and helping Dylan with some farm projects, fence repair, a shed rebuild, and goat care and feeding. The hard labor has been good for my head and body – no deadlines, office politics or calls from public-relations gnats. Tomorrow the journey up the coast begins.

That evening Craig insists on treating me to dinner out. He calls me an "unemployed slacker" though he means it affectionately. This is the first time I've been officially unemployed since I was a pre-teen working as a part-time motel maid.

I get back to the barnyard early. Dylan and I have a brief chat in the kitchen.

"Stokes called twice today. Fortunately, I was in court all day so I was able to avoid him."

"Does he know anything more, or is he just courting you?"

"He's just scratching around. I've checked with my fed watchers and they say his investigation is stalled. That makes our boy Stokes very restless and unhappy, so he wants to share that uneasiness with anyone he can intimidate." Dylan is well-versed in the psychology of law-enforcement lifers, having sparred with them on a daily basis for the past two decades.

"What will you do once you've dropped Shane off wherever? It might be better if you stayed out of town for a while, too."

I've certainly thought this myself, but I'm not sure what my next step should be. An adventure is always appealing, and no one loves to run away more than me. But I feel the need to stretch my leave-of-absence funds by living on the cheap. With the journalism job market in turmoil, it may take some time for me to find the next benefactor for my byline.

"I don't know what I'll do. I'll mull it over once I take care of Shane." He gives me that parental look that says "what else is new?"

I'm having a hard enough time dealing with the dramas of my brother's life to get into analyzing my own rootless world. I change the subject.

"When will you call Stokes?"

"I left him a voice mail tonight. I said I have nothing more to share with him, and I won't have anything to say until Shane is out of rehab...after I've had an opportunity to consult with him. Once Shane has disappeared — and I don't want to have any involvement in those plans — I'll tell Stokes that I'm not working with Shane and I don't know where he is. Later, I'll disclose the *yaa baa*-related death. Two separate conversations."

"Will he ask about me?"

"More than likely, especially if I can't produce Shane. But you're not a witness to anything. You're just a family member of a possible witness. He has no legal standing with you. Nonetheless, being out of his reach would be wise. Stokes is nothing if not persistent."

We hug and say our goodnights. I promise to call after Shane has shipped out.

Soon I'm rolling around in the bed, trying to shut down my brain and get some sleep. Even though I've shunned emotional commitments in my life, I've led a planned existence in the past few years, with steady work, consistent business travel and a fairly regular home routine. No more. I'm actually being encouraged to go rogue. So much for being a responsible adult.

I drift off for what feels like a few moments, and then I jump to the buzzing of my travel alarm. It's four thirty, and I've slept nearly six hours, even though it feels like I just dosed off.

In the pre-dawn, there are almost no cars on Highway 1, so I don't have to worry about anyone tailing me. It's still well before sunrise when I roll into the gravel lot at the center. I call the nurses' desk, as pre-arranged, to let them know I'm ready to collect Shane.

While I slug coffee, the side door by the building's corner opens and Shane pushes through it. A linebacker-sized black male attendant in scrubs fist bumps with Shane and gives him a wide smile and a peace sign. Shane lifts just his eyes and thanks the man again. Slinging a small duffel onto his shoulder, he turns and lopes, flip-flops slapping, to the car. Once his seat belt clicks, I hand him his coffee.

He snorts its steam and takes a sip. "High test, thanks, little sis. The "re-habit" had its pluses, but real java wasn't one of them."

"You're welcome."

For the next two hours, we push across San Francisco to the East Bay, eventually turning north on Highway 5. Once we hit this interstate artery, I set the cruise control to seventy-three and relax my shoulders. We are well beyond Stokes' or Ling's sphere of influence now.

Our conversation thus far has been just pre-dawn mumbling about traffic and our route. After a quick bathroom break at a truck stop, Shane asks for more details about the captain he'll crew for on the sailboat delivery. I tell him everything, including Garrett's DUI history and his status as a group leader. When I deliver this information, Shane doesn't make any snarky remarks or even roll his eyes, his usual histrionics. He just absorbs it. I keep talking. The boat they'll be delivering is a five-year-old, 46-foot trans-Pacific veteran named Claudia, and she's been sold to a retiring real estate broker who intends to cruise her down to the South Pacific. She's been equipped with all the latest high-tech navigation and safety electronics. Her inboard has been re-built and she's been fitted with a new autopilot system, lots of new hardware and a couple of crisp sails.

"Has she been taken out for some heavy-weather testing since the refits?"

"Captain Garrett says he's been making Claudia put out."

By early afternoon, we're nearing the Oregon border and we're hungry again. Shane has offered to drive a couple of times, but I'm happy to chauffer. I ask him to get out the maps and figure out where we can camp for the night. I'm willing to forgo some forward progress to take a detour out to the coast, *if* there's a reasonably direct route and the possibility of waves.

"Is your arm in good enough shape to paddle?"

"Hell yes. It needs salt water healing!"

He saw the boards on top of the car when I picked him up, but until now we've both been so focused on getting away from Ling and Co. that we didn't discuss the possible fun component of the trip. He leans through the seats and pulls the weather-band radio from his duffle (I found it unbroken at his squat and packed it for him). Every surfer owns one for weather and buoy reports, and most also have a computer, tablet or smart phone with a couple of preset weather and wave sites at the ready to provide data and forecasts.

The radio calls out the coastal forecast and starts going through the buoy reports, as Shane searches through a park directory I picked up from AAA for Oregon. Cape Blanco, the western-most point in Oregon, has rustic cabins in a campground overlooking the beach. Equally enticing, there's a historic lighthouse at the park with a second-order Fresnel lens. This makes us giddy, and we almost don't need waves. Shane and I both have a thing for lighthouses with gorgeous Fresnel lenses.

"Did you know that centuries ago families marked the entrances to harbors for their sailors with wood or coal fires?" Shane holds the directory open at the Cape Blanco page. "Then later they used oil lamps."

"What does it say about the lens at Cape Blanco?"

He reads me the entry, starting with the Fresnel history: "In 1822, French physicist Augustin Jean Fresnel introduced his new lens design that revolutionized lighthouse lights. It resembles a giant beehive, with a complex system of multifaceted glass prisms that refract, concentrate and magnify light. Each lens focuses a light source into a single beam and produces an individual light pattern." Shane and I have seen a number of them. First-order lenses are over twice my height, up to twelve feet tall; second-order lenses are smaller, at about six feet tall.

Many Fresnel lenses have been replaced with automated light beacons, but some are still standing guard. The book says Cape Blanco is Oregon's southernmost lighthouse. Shane reads: "It was fitted with a first-order Fresnel lens in 1870 and retrofitted with a second-order Fresnel lens in 1936, which is still in place."

We swing west over to Highway 101 to get to Cape Blanco. We can't resist. The buoy reports promise a small but consistent swell of three to four feet — and there's a lighthouse.

Talk of surfing keeps us away from more difficult discussions: family, rehab, Ling and the FBI. By late afternoon, we pull up to the park kiosk and a ranger who's just about to quit for the day sets us up with a cabin rental for the evening. The cabins and campsites are in a wooded canopy on the cliffs above the beach.

Instead of going directly to our cabin, we drive to the beach overlook first. Surf comes first, rest and food are secondary. Three- to four-foot swells in steady sets are ending their journey across the Pacific onto this wide windswept beach, littered with whole trees of driftwood. Shane is literally bouncing in his bucket seat in anticipation.

At our cabin, we throw gear inside and don wetsuits, booties, hoods and gloves. By the time I lock the cabin door and hide the key under a nearby rock, Shane is already jogging down the cliff path to the beach with his board under his good arm. It's a bit of an unruly storm swell, but the sets are decent and there's a sand bar just a bit farther north of us that's generating the best pitch. We'll enter south of that area and paddle diagonally to the take-off zone.

Even with only one good arm, Shane is out through the broken waves in minutes. His body's muscle memory is inscribed with thousands of waves. He doesn't think; he just glides over the water, his hands sculling through the liquid with the power of pulling a rope. I'm strong, but I don't have nearly his stroke and feel for the water.

Before I can make it through the white water, Shane has already lined up his first wave and pops effortlessly to his feet, his board locking into the face as if it's riding on a rail. Ahead of him, the wave jacks up even higher and begins pitching out, so he presses through his ankles and feet and accelerates the board forward, then tucks and lets the small curl envelope him in a perfect three-second tube ride. I hoot and laugh, shaking my head from side to side. All the drugs, petty crime, hovel-life...it's all completely irrelevant when Shane's in the water. He's at home, if only I could keep him off of terra firma where all his demons lurk.

He rides out that first wave, with a couple of smashing off-the-lip turns, pops over the curl's top and immediately paddles north to seek out the next swell. I reach the smooth water beyond the foam as he cackles and drops his next wave. This one is much smaller and soon he soars over its top and paddles up directly behind me. Grabbing my leash, he growls, yanks me back and paddles right past. I feign anger, but I'm just happy to see him healthy and loving the moment. I've had a couple of weeks of surf sessions awaiting his release; meanwhile, he's been cooped up in rehab.

We surf until dusk. I catch about half as many waves as Shane, but my shoulders and neck still ache when we walk through the foam and onto the soft sand. My fingers and toes are numb and my cheeks are stinging. Shane is shivering, so as we make our way up the beach toward the cliff he starts jogging circles around me like a small dog. At one point he stops, bends toward a large piece of driftwood, sniffs and imitates a dog lifting its leg, taking a long pee and kicking sand over the marked wood. This is the Shane I keep trying to restore, my loveable goofy brother. He can dissolve me with one of his inventive pranks.

We slam some trail mix before rinsing off the salt at the campground showers. Then we barbeque in the spreading dark. The waves pound the beach, a dull continuous roar. I ply Shane with ginger beer instead of real brews, and he doesn't offer one snide comment. This is news. Has he really gained an acceptance of his life as an addict?

Soon we're climbing into sleeping bags, spread out on the cabin's cots.

"Dana...thanks for all of this." The quiet, low voice comes out of the creaking darkness.

This too is completely out of character for the old Shane. The old Shane would never acknowledge that he needed help, and he wouldn't say "thanks" when he received it. Before I can reply, I hear him start to snuffle and snore.

Does he get it now, Mom? Is he really ready to change? Despite all his troubles in school, his hyperactive behavior, his flying in the face of every authority, you always told everyone that he had potential. By high school, you were his only cheerleader. Joe was done. But you said Shane would grow into a man, find his way. Then you truncated your path, so what value can I put on your words, your heady predictions?

He needs to face his addictions and build a stable path that will improve his life. But to do that, he has to believe that his life won't parallel yours.

Your legacy, Mom?
We're constantly looking at ourselves, looking for you...looking for crazy.

Chapter 17

I trot across the sand to reach the foam and my freezing-cold wake-up call. Five thirty, the light is still weak. As I'm making my way to the water's edge, Shane catches and rips a wave. He doesn't seem to be favoring his arm at all. And all his years of experience reading a swell's direction enables him to hone in on the take-off zone without any wasted paddling.

The waves have grown since last night. Sets are jacking up four to five feet, and yesterday's wind-driven chop has eased. Gulls circle in the early light, sweeping down to munch unlucky critters stranded by last night's high tide.

After an hour, Shane and I have each danced across a dozen or so smooth, rolling curls. We are utterly frozen, but loving a swell made just for two. Only one other person has come across the beach, and no one has joined us for the water ride. We surf and laugh, paddle and splash. It's like we're teens again.

In Shane's company, I'm more daring. I take a couple of late drops, paddling into waves after they've already started to pitch. Feeling gutsy, I take one more big drop and...nothing but black water. I've pushed it too far and a five-foot wave drills me. I tumble down, get sucked back up the curl and smashed over and down again. Pushed and pulled, I'm a chew-toy being shaken by a dog. The whitewater explodes, churns and holds me down — the wave's roar hammers in my ears. At last, it releases me and I'm able stop spinning and kick to the surface. It's not my worst hold-down, but it's enough to leave me gasping and disoriented. Shane sees the whole wipeout, as he paddles back out from a ride he took to the beach. He strokes hard and reaches me just after I've surfaced, but before I've gotten back onto my board.

"Damn, that was the definition of over-the-falls, sis."

I cough. My sinuses burn with salt water.

I pull my board to me, sink it, and exhaustedly climb on. We turn and paddle out to the take-off spot together. Shane can see that I'm stunned, so he holds back before going after another wave. I shoo him off. "I'm fine. Go."

After a short rest, I stroke into a smaller swell. Two more uneventful drops and acceptable rides reassure me, and I start to block out the pounding I took.

After two solid hours, I can't feel my feet anymore and I catch a last wave and ride in. Shane promises to follow me shortly. We'll drive through to reach Port Townsend by evening.

I jog back to the campground and quickly rinse and change. Shane arrives and in a flash he's rinsed, dressed and packed. He's even loaded our boards and stowed the soggy wetsuits in the plastic tub in the trunk. All this while he's toting a big cup of oatmeal and slamming down throat-fulls of cereal in between trips from the cabin to the car.

We drive over to the lighthouse and sweet-talk our way into the tower before normal visiting hours. The local docent, an older gentleman, is perfect as a light keeper. He looks like the gray-haired, bearded fisherman depicted on the frozen fish-sticks package. His says his son surfs and he'd been using some powerful binoculars to watch us. We wax on about how much we adore Fresnel lenses and that seals the deal. He gives us a short tour, lets us lovingly circle and admire the multifaceted lens, and sends us on our way with a pamphlet he wrote about Oregon lights. We try to tip him, but he won't have it. I stuff some cash in the donation box.

For the first hour driving, we review the day's surf session and discuss the lighthouse and the keeper who charmed us.

"It's criminal that more money hasn't been spent preserving those lights." Shane turns to me.

"Yeah, states and communities seem to find money for roads and sidewalks, but not for living history. But at least some towns raise funds from light lovers like us to keep them going."

"If I ever make any money, I'm going to help save a lighthouse."

Shane's comment, to make a bad pun, illuminates a new awareness in him of things of importance beyond a moment's thrill-seeking or the next bong hit. It's been decades coming, but this awareness is still something that gives me hope.

An hour or two later, as the highway mile markers fly by, we get into a discussion that's less encouraging. It starts when Shane criticizes Craig's dedication to his job, and how he's pulled away from his old cronies in the Half Moon Bay surf crowd.

"He has a career he's proud of, Shane, and you should be happy for him, not critical."

"I am, but he doesn't need to ditch his buds. He shines us on for parties and beach gatherings." He crosses his arms.

"You mean when everyone is high, binge drinking, talking shit and fighting? Why would he want to participate in that juvenile scene? He's a grown man, and he's moved on."

Shane falls silent. I've had this talk with him before, about paddling out of the tide of bad influences. I can't resist one more comment.

"When you've moved on, you'll feel the same way Craig does. You'll remember the good stuff from your younger years, but you won't feel the need to keep trying to repeat it.

Craig still surfs; he just does it while pursuing other goals too. And he doesn't need to justify those goals to that group of perpetual tweens who haven't established adult lives."

"Tweens!" He giggles, snorts and giggles some more. "You should say that to Anton. I'd pay money for you to call him a tween to his face and watch it turn purple." He rocks forward, bending at the waist and pulling down his seatbelt.

We ease into silence for a while. The counseling session is over, and he didn't refute my statements about his future. It's a small victory.

*

Port Townsend was established in the mid-1800s as a commercial shipping hub serving the Northwest. It features a large collection of Victorian homes leftover from its heyday. The Victorian ladies sit on the northeast end of the Olympic Peninsula, overlooking the Puget Sound and facing east toward Whidbey Island. The town is southeast of the Strait of Juan de Fuca, a nearly 100-mile natural channel between Vancouver Island and the Olympic Peninsula. It's used by mariners big and small to sail out to the Pacific Ocean. The international boundary between the United States and Canada runs down the center of the Strait. Fur trader Charles William Barkley named the strait back in 1787 for a Greek navigator who sailed with the Spanish in the 1500s. A ferry connects Port Townsend to Whidbey Island, which has ferries going to other islands in the sound and over to the mainland, north of Seattle.

Our destination is a budget-conscious bed-and-breakfast housed in a smaller white and blue Victorian, with peeling shutters. It's flanked by a couple of guest cottages. We toss our gear into cottage number three. It has a living area that includes a navy sofa-bed and a kitchenette, a small bedroom, and a cramped bathroom with a stand-up shower and peeling sailboat wallpaper. Nautical decorations abound, reminding us we're on a waterway. The 1950s-era gas wall heater hisses and pings as we crank it up to take the damp chill out of the clapboard structure. There's no view from our cottage, but just a short walk down a hill takes us to the edge of the commercial waterfront. We stretch our cramped legs after the all-day drive-a-thon.

As we walk, Shane calls Captain Garrett from my pre-paid cellphone and leaves him a voice mail. Tomorrow they'll take the boat out, putting her through a checkout sail while they take measure of each other's sailing skills, ability to communicate and annoying habits.

The town is a combination of craft shops, restaurants and a few dive bars from Port Townsend's days as a commercial port. There are still a number of hard-drinking establishments without windows, which prevents anyone getting tossed through them during a bar fight. We're hungry, so we find a pub, with windows, that offers fried seafood, burgers and other bar fare. As we're seated at a heavy wooden table with a water view, Captain Garrett rings Shane back.

It's a short, all-business conversation. Garrett says Shane should be at dock J at ten tomorrow morning. They'll complete a dockside checkout of the boat together, which should take about an hour and a half or two hours, depending on what they find. Garrett says he's done his own check, and he's already sailed her a few times. But he wants Shane to make an inspection with him, since they'll be doing an ocean crossing in just a two-person team. After that, Captain Garrett says they'll go out for an all-day sail, working through all her sails and systems. If all goes well tomorrow, he says they'll sail again the next day, Claudia's final check ride. He's invited me along for that sail.

"He sounds like he knows his shit. He's already checked the equipment once, and yet he wants to do another check with me. And I'm glad we'll do two days of sailing together."

"He's checking you out, as well as Claudia."

"That's cool. I'd do the same." Shane slugs some ice tea. Even though alcohol hasn't been a problem for him, his rehab counselors convinced him that with his brain chemistry he needs to steer clear of all addictive substances. Besides, Captain Garrett is a recovering alcoholic, so Claudia will be a dry boat.

We finish our meal with small talk about sailing. I'm exhausted from the surfing and the long driving day, and by nine we're back in the cabin and sacked out.

When Shane leaves the next day to meet Captain Garrett, I break out my running shoes and decide to make a foot tour of some of the town's historic streets. I set a steady pace and run through the Victorians and their working-class neighbors. A light fog is lifting from the peninsula as I run, pulling out and drawing back in, but slowly retreating from the land till the next evening when it will mysteriously reappear, emerging from wherever it hides during daylight hours. After a little over an hour, I've weaved through most of the nicer neighborhoods, and I return to the cottage for a shower and a late breakfast.

I need to spend some quality time with my computer. I want to see if Dylan has sent any updates on Agent Stokes or the drug gangsters. Did Shane and I get away clean? Is anyone pressing Dylan for information about Shane?

First, I open an email that came through last night from Dylan. He says he's still dodging Stokes. He's been in court for several days with a juvenile trial, so his assistant has informed Stokes he'll have to wait until Dylan can get back to him. He hasn't heard anything from the surf crowd about

Ling's or Anton's pursuit of Shane. No one has messed with Shane's car; Dylan did a drive-by. Sea Flea is still gathering leaves and acorns — its hubcaps are intact.

I quickly cull the junk mail and unearth a keeper. It's a note from one of my former co-workers, Dale, about a possible job in San Francisco. It's a new online business magazine, but one that takes a wider editorial view of the world beyond Silicon Valley. It includes a business politics and economics section. Interesting. My former co-worker says the job hasn't been advertised yet – his contact, the editor, is just getting budgetary approval for the position.

Fear and freedom wrestle in my psyche. When I was first cut loose from the paper, the fear of no paycheck and no journalistic identity ruled my sleepless nights. I was pissed and angst-ridden. Now instead of being excited to hear about a job, it actually brings me down a little. Thoughts of freedom, exploring and traveling, are now outnumbering my waves of anxiety.

I'm reviewing some bills and making some online payments for my abandoned L.A. loft, when my disposable cell rings. I let it ring four times, trying to decide whether to take the call. No one besides Dylan is supposed to have this number.

I give in. "Hello?"

"Hey, beautiful. What's shaking?"

"Hi, Wayne. This is a surprise." Hmm, Wayne almost never calls, and he's never called me when I'm out of town.

Wayne explains that he's up in Northern California for some "business." He's vague on the details. He once met Dylan, when he and Maria visited me in the Southland, so he contacted him to find out if I was up north and to get a number for me. All of this is a bit out of character for Wayne. He doesn't plan. He doesn't take business trips.

"Dylan said you're out of town?"

"Yeah. It's a long story. I'm up north. But I'll be coming back down to Northern California in a couple of days."

"When do you have to be back at work?"

"I don't. That's another long story. But the short version is I got laid off. I'm on personal leave until that runs out and then there's a severance package."

"I'm so sorry, Dana. I know you liked the job, but that's the brutal corporate world, right?" He doesn't offer up much sympathy — he feels every desk job is soul-stealing. I don't agree. I actually love the intellectual challenge of chasing and writing stories.

"How long are you going to be around the Bay Area?"

"I need to be here for a couple of days. But I'm taking a break from the Southland too. I scheduled some guys to fill in for me with my handyman clientele. I'm footloose for a week to ten days after I finish up with my tasks here." Our conversation is full of holes — neither one of us is sharing the details. That's okay; one of the many reasons I like Wayne is he's capable of deeper conversations, but he doesn't always have to have them.

Still, as he says this, I can't help but think "when are you not footloose?" But I'm currently unemployed and he still has work; who am I to judge?

"I'm thinking of a surf and sun safari while I'm still on the paper's payroll. Since you're currently on sabbatical, want to make a plan?" After the words come out, I can't believe I just said this.

His answer is immediate. "Definitely!" I love that answer, and the idea of hooking up with Wayne gives me a nice warm rush all over.

We discuss possible options. Having just spent days in the car, another road trip isn't very appealing. So we have to make our way to a place equipped with water toys, if we don't want to tote them. Wayne suggests La Ventana in Baja, north of Cabo. I can try to score some flights on miles. And Wayne says he will look into an inexpensive cabana so we can cook our own food and make our own tequila Slurpees. Surfing and diving would keep us entertained, and fishing would keep us fed.

Still, Wayne and I haven't spent more than about four hours together. We've always clicked in bed, but traveling, cooking and co-habiting for a week or more? Would it work? Can I lie next to him for multiple nights without panicking? My job angst has eased up a bit for now and an adventure has landed in my lap; I squelch the doubts and take the leap.

"Okay, let's do this. Can you see what kind of casita you can find, and we'll finalize plans when I get back to Half Moon Bay?"

"You're on! Call me when you're nearing SF. Then you can tell me about your mystery trip."

"Hmm," I mumble. "We'll talk soon."

We click off. I need to store his number in the phone's directory, so I pull up the address book function. But instead of keying in his name with the entry, I type in "Oven Mitt." That leaves me giggling off and on for a good half hour.

Shane returns to the cabin just as the light fades and the water is turning from blue to gray. He's tired, but pumped at the same time. And he's starving, so we stride down to town, as he sings Claudia's praises.

"This boat has every sweet navigational toy, Dana! Garrett says her new owner put at least fifty thousand dollars into new electronics and sails after he purchased her. He went with all the name brands, Lowrance electronics, Harken hardware and everything is either new or in perfect condition. And her cabin is equipped for oceangoing, not too fancy, plenty of stowage, everything can be locked down for heavy weather."

"Okay, she's nicely dressed, but how does she sail?"

His face lights up. "All I can say is she may be my best ride, ever. She's not a downwind sled; she carves the water on all points of sail. We took it to her today. Had her doing nine knots in some heavy chop. She just blasted her way. She's no prissy princess, no shudders, no heavy rolling."

We've reached a Vietnamese restaurant that looks like a match for our budget, plastic tablecloths, vinyl-covered chairs and linoleum floors. We choose a booth and order.

"So Claudia is dreamy; what about Captain Garrett? First, what's he look like?"

"Medium-brown, wavy head of hair, mid-forties and so thin he looks almost unhealthy. As first, I was worried. I mean, I've seen fatter stick figures. But you look closer and he's all stringy muscle and every ligament stands out in his arms and neck; they almost look like ropes. And he's like Craig; he's so quiet that you worry you'll have to carry both sides of the conversation just to have one. But he speaks up when he wants action, and he's very direct, easy to follow. Later in the day, I asked him a few things about his sailing experience and his counseling job, and he talked. You just gotta do the asking."

He goes on to describe the route they sailed through the islands and all the sail changes they practiced. "Garrett takes nothing for granted, even though she's a newer and re-dressed boat. He had me pull every single sail and he knows exactly how to trim and drive them. It was hard work, Dana, but it made me get a feel for her moves. I want to go to sea with this guy in this boat. He's got skills."

Shane says they tested all the electronics and annoyed a handful of sailors within range with all their radio and position checks. "So be it. We need to make sure she can walk and talk."

"Is he still up for me joining you guys tomorrow? If he wants more checkout time with just you, I'm fine with that." I say this, but it's not really true. I'm dying to get on the water.

"Hey, it's cool. Last thing he said to me was that he's hoping you'll come tomorrow. He welcomes more eyes on the boat; different sailors see different stuff."

"Great. But I don't want to interfere with any test sailing or checks you guys want to do."

"Garrett says he's feeling pretty on top of it. He's provisioning the boat first thing in the morning. He even asked if there was any particular chow or munchies I'd like. But I told him I eat like a goat, mowing down pretty much anything in my path."

Although Shane's done plenty of boat deliveries up and down the West Coast, as far north as here in San Juan Islands and south into Baja, he's never sailed the trans-Pacific route to Hawaii before. He has the sailing skills; he just hasn't had the ride. Funny that rehab, crime, and being on the lam is presenting new adventure opportunities. But I keep my thoughts to myself. Though I'm skeptical about Shane's latest recovery, I like seeing him light up with joy and anticipation at something other than a chemical high.

He nabs the last spring roll with his chop sticks, and gives me the eyebrows-up dog-begging look.

"Yeah, yeah, finish it."

He stuffs the whole thing into his mouth.

"Nice table manners."

He just chews, with rounded chipmunk cheeks.

The fog is pulling in and out, draping the eucalyptus trees in gray cotton as we walk back to our cabin. I marvel at how much I enjoy my brother's company when he's healthy and not raging against the world in some chemical-induced schizoid trip.

*

By ten, we're at the dock, and we catch up to Garrett as he's loading supplies into a wheel-barrow at his aged SUV. Shane introduces us. Garrett's slight appearance is counter-balanced with a firm, calloused handshake. We each make several trips down the dock to Claudia, toting food, motor oil, well-worn foul-weather gear, and more. I'm happy to run the loads up and down the dock, but I leave the stowing duties to the sailors. If the weather turns rough, they need to know exactly where everything is cached.

After Garrett gives me a quick tour of Claudia, we don layers of fleece and foul-weather jackets. We motor out of the harbor into a freshening breeze and clearing skies. Once we're past the harbor entrance's marker buoys, Shane tugs the sheet, raising the mainsail. Garrett cuts the inboard motor. Shane unfurls the jib, trims it with a winch and cleans up all the lines. I just perch in the cockpit near Captain Garrett and use my decorative skills. After a couple of days in the car, I'm loving the fresh breeze and the chill on my cheeks. Claudia hooks into the wind and cuts through the small white caps, vocalizing her efforts with groans and line squeaks.

"Is she ready for the Pacific?"

Garrett gives a quick nod. "Yes, I believe she is. I don't believe in test sailing for days and days. You can do that and still have an equipment failure on the second day out."

"Do you trust the mechanics who did the engine work and the techs who installed the new electronics?" I try to get a little more of a conversation going, as Claudia goes to weather, riding up on her side and rocking into the waves.

"Sure. They've worked on other boats I've delivered, and they're pretty good. Shane and I tried nearly every setting and feature of the nav system yesterday. We've tested and retested the radio and all the signaling gear."

Garrett doesn't take much care with his personal appearance; his hair is shaggy, his clothes are tattered, and his cap has sweat and salt stains running over the top of each other. His sailing gear, however, presents a different picture — it's top notch and in excellent condition. No salt stains; I'm certain that after each sailing day it gets rinsed before he does.

Shane has danced, bent-kneed up to the rocking bow, where he squats checking a safety rail that seems slightly out of alignment with the others. He pulls a ratchet from his squall jacket pocket and tightens the rails footing bolts.

I state the obvious, "He's out to earn a few attaboys."

Garrett just grins slightly and keeps quiet.

"Thanks for giving him the opportunity. You're taking a leap of faith."

"We all need a hand up once in a while. Others have pulled me from some dark places, when I wasn't much of an odds maker. I earn my sobriety by paying it forward."

"I hear you work part-time as a peer counselor?"

"Seeing others struggle and sometimes backslide shows me daily the blessings of staying clean. In a way, it's selfish. Sure, I might be helping other addicts, but I'm really helping myself. This is a sneaky disease. As soon as you think you're above it, you think you're cured, that hubris will open you up, talk you into that first slip...a beer, a snort, a bowl, whatever. I'm not above anything; I'm recovering every single day. So is Shane. He probably still thinks recovery has a finish line. It doesn't. Once he learns that, his odds of staying clean improve."

This is lot of talking for Garrett. But he's opened up a bit and I'm grateful.

Still, I haven't told Garrett about Ling, Anton and the rest of Shane's troubles. When I spoke with him from California, all I said was I wanted to get my brother, who's just out of rehab, on the ocean, away from bad influences, and over to Kauai for a fresh start. No sense complicating his part of the mission. But from what I know of Garrett's past, Shane's full story wouldn't throw him. He's been down in the slime himself, and he's worked with too many addicts to be easily shocked.

The wind freshens and soon we're more engaged in sailing than conversation. Though the white caps are standing up a bit, Claudia's bow cuts the chop with authority. We pass the far end of Whidbey Island, and beat up toward San Juan Island and the town of Friday Harbor. With Shane out to demonstrate his skills, I do little more than trim the occasional line and hand out drinks.

When we sail between the southern end of San Juan Island and Lopez Island we come upon a pod of Orcas that Garrett says are regulars in the area. Their three- to four-foot black dorsal fins are unmistakable. They're moving north at a leisurely pace. As the apex predator of these waters, they go where they want, on whatever schedule they want. Later, we spot a group of sea lions. They, too, seem unhurried, which with Orcas in the area surprises me.

"Our Orcas are fish eaters. They don't hunt mammals."

"And the sea lions trust their palettes won't change?"

Garrett turns slightly to starboard. "Yeah, not sure I'd be as trusting." We spot a boiling in the water ahead to Claudia's starboard side. "Looks like they're bubbling."

A group of sea lions will dive down under a school of fish and blow bubbles, herding and confusing them and pushing them tighter together and up to the surface. Then they'll take turns diving through the school and picking off snacks as they go. When we near a group of six of them, they spy-hop and bark like guard dogs.

The rest of the day passes with creature encounters, some hard sailing and some cruising. Claudia shows her stuff. Garrett wants to swap out one battery that doesn't seem to be holding a full charge. Other than that, she's ready for the passage to Hawaii.

Shane is focused and performs as well as Claudia. Even I'd hire him, based on the skill and energy he demonstrated today.

We get back to J dock at a little after five. Once the boat is tied in for the night, we sit in the cockpit watching the light fade and discuss departure times for tomorrow. Garrett says there's no reason to leave super-early and burn diesel waiting for the wind to come up. They set a ten-thirty rendezvous. I'll come down to see them off, then start the long slog back to Northern California.

"Sleep ten to twelve hours tonight if you can, Shane. It's the best sleep you'll get in a good long while."

Shane steps to the dock. "Do you need us to do anything tonight?"

"Nope. We're good." With that, Garrett starts up the pier, swinging the seventy-pound battery like it's a plastic flashlight.

Shane and I circle town in search of one more budget feeding station. By nine, it's lights out. I lie in the dark. Tomorrow Shane will be off on his adventure, his escape is imminent...and I'll still be spinning. No job, no plan. I tell myself that Baja is just an unexpected diversion...and yet. Could I finally open myself to more?

Chapter 18

"I owe you big, little sister, for all that you've done."
I've just stumbled into the kitchenette, but he's obviously
been up for a while; his gear is packed and waiting by the
cabin door.

The old Shane was always so separated from his
emotions by drugs, and so focused on the next score, that
others' efforts and struggles went completely unnoticed. Out
of the chemical haze, for the first time in years, a new more-
empathetic Shane is emerging. I suppose it's a natural
evolution for him, but it's jarring for me. At first, I'm not sure
what to say, and we remain suspended in silence. This causes
Shane to go further, descending into demeaning himself for
his past actions and past cluelessness.

"I've been a burden on you...and Joe too. Just your
typical dumbass drug addict. But I want you to know that I
see it now. Seriously, it's one of the hardest aspects of
recovery, to really make yourself see all the crap you pulled,
all the people you hurt...and to admit to all of it." He's bent in
his chair, starring at the coffee mug encircled in his hands.

"I'm not making excuses, Dana, but I was broken by
Mom's death. You know what I saw...and even before that I
was hanging with her more than the rest of you. I watched as
she became more and more depressed and paranoid, just goin'
down. I couldn't stop it. Her depression was pulling her into
the fucking swirling drain." Even as a kid, Shane was better
with her than the rest of us. He'd be the one who would try to
get Mom off the couch with some crazy antic, practical joke,
flowers.

I wait; we've spoken very little about Mom's death. All
of us, Shane — Terry, Joe and me — have buried our feelings

deep. Her bouts of depression drove me away, and after her death we all descended into punishing guilt. Her swings also kept her from holding on to a job, which she needed for her self-esteem. She'd get hired as an office assistant, and get fired after taking too many sick days. For a while she worked as a clerk in the city planning office. She loved that job, but had a breakdown at her desk one day and never went back. She tried real estate, but couldn't take the pressure.

"Man, it all went dark for her. She couldn't find any good to spark her days. She'd tried the real estate gig, but she just wasn't a saleswoman. That failure stomped her. And it happened at a time when she was already spiraling down."

He sticks his chin out and looks at me hard. "But I'm not her, Dana. Yeah, I admit it, I swing. And I've fucked myself up on drugs. But I love the carnival ride of life, and *I am not getting off.*"

My eyes fill, and I don't trust myself to speak. Instead I pull myself out of the chair and step over to hug him hard around the shoulders. His body is starting to feel solid again, like the old Shane. Rebuilding fueled from the inside out? We both sniff, as we choke back the emotions that could pour out. Neither one of us needs a meltdown before our strenuous travels.

"I have something for you," I call over my shoulder as I trot back into the bedroom. I rifle through my duffle bag and come back to the dinette with a small nylon stuff sack. I push it across the table to him.

"I can't take anything more from you, Dana."

"You need a stake. And I need you to have this, so I know that you have enough to get started, wherever."

He stares at me and slowly unties the sack and pulls out the contents. There's a throw-away cellphone in a blister pack that's pre-loaded with $100 of short- and long-distance calling and a nylon wallet with a Rip Curl logo on it. In the billfold is $800, and stashed in two of the picture pockets are lists of important names and phone numbers that I've printed and laminated. His eyes widen and his chin drops as he examines the contents of the wallet. He slumps and rocks slightly.

"I want to refuse this, but I need it and you won't let me turn it down anyway. But I swear, Dana, I *will* pay you back. I have to prove to you, and myself, that I can be something other than a blood-sucking parasite." He looks up, his eyes glassy and his cheeks and nose burning red. I say nothing. With all the broken promises of the past hanging in the air, the proof will have to be in the doing.

So instead I surprise him. "Jog with me. It will be a good way to expend some energy before the sea claims you."

Shane's never been one for land-based exercise, but today he's game. He throws on a T-shirt, loud-printed board shorts and an old pair of thrift store running shoes. We wind through the misty neighborhoods above the strait. The slap of our feet is the only noise on this quiet dawn. We chat intermittently about the town and its historic homes. Shane is winded after a mile, but he refuses to give in to it. We push through a slow three miles before returning to the inn.

At ten twenty, we're at the dock. Clearly, Garrett has beaten us here by at least an hour. The sail covers are off, all of his gear is stowed, and he's sitting in the cockpit, listening to the weather radio's latest update.

When the broadcast finishes and the buoy reports begin, he shuts it off. "No new concerns. Seas four to five, moderate winds, and no lows in our area."

"Sail on, sail on, sailor," Shane hums. That gets a rare grin out of Captain Garrett.

We haul Shane's gear aboard, a big duffel, a sleeping bag and a backpack. He's sailing into the future mostly unfettered, at least by material possessions. He stows his gear and hops onto the dock to give me a farewell hug. As he does, he urgently whispers in my ear, "Stay out of it. Ling will go down. Forces are moving against him." I freeze, stunned.

He stares hard at me and pulls away abruptly, steps over the life lines and into the cockpit. I look at him quizzically. What did he hear while he was in rehab? But I can't ask at this time, in this place. Not with Garrett ready to sail, delivering Shane to a safer place and leaving no tracks. Life is full of moments when you just have to let the future unfold and forget about trying to steer a course.

Garrett starts Claudia's diesel engine. She chugs to life and they motor out of the harbor and into the strait. I jog down to the harbor entrance breakwater and watch Claudia go by with her bow rocking. By the time they've pulled out into the waterway, Shane has raised the mainsail and Claudia is cutting through the chop. I sigh and stroll back to the Honda.

Traffic is light and in no time I'm well down 101 and headed for the Oregon border. Drizzle coats the windshield. With no schedule for this trip, I can take three days to get back or I can crush the accelerator and get back tomorrow. It's this freedom from any commitments or restrictions that has thus far kept me from checking in with Wayne. I've always been someone who loves to go rogue. Checking in just isn't in my DNA. It doesn't make me feel connected, it makes me feel trapped.

I've logged nearly one hundred and fifty miles before I pull in to a truck-stop for a bathroom break. It's time to get back on the radar, at least with Wayne.

As I'm pulling back onto the highway, he picks up. "Hi, gorgeous!"

A grin spreads across my face. "Hey, Wayne, what's shaking?"

"Oh-oh, Mexico," he sings.

I giggle and shout, "Tequila!"

"That too! Hey, I have great news on a Baja surf camp. We can get an ocean-view cabana from an old surf bud, Jerry, for sixty dollars a night, including linens, water, ice, and use of a panga for fishing. We'll need to rent a Jeep in Cabo and drive up. On our way out of town, we can buy a cheap cooler and fill it with provisions for our stay."

"Sounds great. When do you want to go?"

"Waiting on you, mystery woman. I've taken care of my business here, and I'm ready to be your devoted cabana boy."

So much for a leisurely ride back to California. As he's describing this enticing plan I've pushed the Honda up to eighty miles per hour. "What about boards? Do we pay up to get them on our flight or can we find rides in La Ventana?"

"Jerry assures me that he has a selection of boards for us to choose from. I have a collapsible fishing rod, and we can score tanks and weights at a dive camp nearby."

Wow, clearly Wayne has previously hidden organizational skills.

"So, the only question is where are you, and when can we book our flights?"

"I'm in Oregon." In fact, I'm just near the junction with Interstate 5. I intentionally called before this junction, in case our plans spurred me to lead-foot it back to the Bay Area. That decision is in the rearview; I'm pushing the Honda to its limit, above which its rattles go from loud to downright frightening.

"I don't want to drive through, but I can find a motor lodge for late tonight when I need a break. I can be back by midday tomorrow."

"Excellent! What about flights? Do you want me to start hunting for deals?"

"No, I have my computer with me, and I'll look for flights when I get to a motel tonight. I have frequent-flyer miles to burn, so let me see what I can finagle."

Wayne tries to insist on paying his way, but I shut him down. "Listen, cabana boy, you're just going to have to let me be your patron, or matron, on this one. After all the business travel, I'm holding miles on every single airline. Let's burn let 'em and save our cash for tequila and fish tacos."

He grumbles a bit longer, but finally concedes to the wisdom of my plan. "When are you going to tell me about this mystery trip?"

"You can torture the information out of me in Mexico."

"Baby, you can bank on that!" I can feel his wicked grin through the phone connection.

"And tit for tat, I want to hear what you've been doing in the Bay Area."

"Share and share alike," he promises.

I lock on to a Latin station and spend the next half hour doing salsa shimmies, readying my moves for Baja. During seat-dancing breaks, I visualize Shane and Garrett heading out to sea. For many, the idea of a loved one on a long open-water passage might be cause for some trepidation. The ocean is vast and unforgiving of the unprepared and inexperienced. But Garrett and Shane are neither of those things. Each is more in his element on the water than on a city street. And Shane faces more fearsome human threats in the Bay Area than he does from the briny deep.

After rehab, the ten- or twelve-day crossing should recharge Shane's spirit and rejuvenate his still-healing body. And with Garrett's quiet guidance, maybe Shane will learn how to live as a former addict, not to deny its hold on him, but to choose a fully present life every day.

Mid-Oregon, Eugene, and the traffic has thickened. As the afternoon passes, I weave around minivans clogging the left lane and semis in the right. Near dusk, I'm outside of Ashland and decide to stop for the night. On the south side of town, I find a stucco motel that has notions of B&B grandeur, but it's really just a motor inn. Looks like a winner, especially when I spy "Free Wi-Fi" advertised on a sandwich board sign on the sidewalk.

A woman in her mid-sixties with long wavy gray hair, a loose linen blouse and crystal jewelry checks me in to number nine, in the room-row furthest from the street. I sweet-talk her from seventy-four dollars down to sixty-five, which is still above my per-diem for a solo night sans business expense account. But tonight I don't want to hunt outside of town for camping. And I want a computer connection and in-room shower. Besides, she says the burrito joint next door, Señor Gringo, will build you a custom gut-bomb.

After navigating the availability of award travel on three different sites, I have tickets for Wayne and me for two days out. Before I hit "book travel" I have a moment's hesitation, but I click through anyway. I need a vacation from my unemployment and a break from Project Shane. Hiding out in Mexico for ten days sounds like an ideal plan.

I close the laptop and snuggle down into the covers.

*

Blowing by mile markers, I'm back in the Golden State. I make a quick call to Wayne and give him my ETA on reaching the Bay Area. I also make sure that he received the itinerary for the Cabo flights I booked last night.

Next, I check in with Dylan to find out if Agent Stokes has any clue about Shane's departure, or if he's hunting for Shane or me.

"Dana, you wild woman. Nice to hear your voice."

"Hey, Dylan, how are the juvenile offenders, er, I mean your clients?"

"Up to the usual tricks...graffiti, breaking and entering, shoplifting, taking drugs, and underage drinking. Oh, and I left out stealing cars. Let's see, I think those might have been some of your hidden talents back in the day?"

"Hold on a minute, I have no artistic skills; I never tagged!" I say with mock outrage.

"Did you get on the water while you were on the road?"

"Yeah, got some sweet waves. But I'm stomping the accelerator on the way home — surfing alone isn't that fun, you know?"

He immediately catches on. "Ah-ha." Message understood; the package has shipped out to parts unknown. We agree to catch up this evening at the farm. "Drive safely."

Right. I dial in some easy listening hoping it will tame my aggressive driving. It doesn't work. Traffic is light and the truckers are leaving plenty of hopscotch room.

My mind drifts to the Cabo plan and Wayne. He seems to actually see me as a whole person, not just a surfer, a journalist, or an arm-piece. But instead of soothing me, the fact that he actually "sees" me has me a little on edge. And he may intuitively understand my personality, but I haven't provided many details about my broken family and the impact it had on me. I had two parents, but I raised myself, and though I have a type of confidence, it's really just self-reliance.

I'm not rooted. I don't trust relationships. I don't trust the notion of the happy family. Joe and Valerie used to tell us that the upheavals in our household were normal, or even fun, and that other calmer families were faking it or were "pretentious." It was a way to control us. When we were young, we didn't know any better, but as we grew older and started spending time with our friends' families, we began noticing the differences.

For me, it was a slow realization. I'd been lied to — madness isn't part of every family. But I didn't find that reassuring. No, I got scared, because I realized that I didn't t know how a stable family or a stable relationship works...or how I'd ever fit into one.

And yet...I've felt a change recently. My heart is starting to open to the idea of taking a chance on fully connecting with a partner. I haven't been actively seeking a relationship yet, but inside I've been mulling it. I guffaw at my own pathetic justifications for my inaction. I also realize that Wayne has been pursuing the same path of commitment avoidance. He's the good-looking guy who's too nice to be a heartbreaker, but any savvy female with an ounce of intuition understands that after a casual meeting, dinner or even a hook-up he just isn't going to call, ever. I laugh that we're the perfect pair, total equals in commitment-phobia. Mexico should be interesting. Which one of us will panic and bolt first?

I arrive in the Bay Area at mid-afternoon. I'd love to clear my head in the waves, but as I drive toward Dylan and Maria's I get a good look at a few surf spots. The sea is gray and flat. Oh well, I need computer time anyway and to sort through some gear and clothing for Mexico.

I dig through the inbox and find another message from Dale. He says the new senior editor/reporter position has been approved by management and the editor, Drew, is ready to start reviewing resumes. He's sent Drew's contact information, and says I should send a resume to him today. He adds that he's already mentioned me to Drew, and that I should say that he referred me in my cover letter.

Fond memories of the days when Dale and I were cube neighbors bubble up. His snarky humor brought levity to the weekly grind at a magazine we both felt left us unchallenged and devoid of creative opportunities. We've stayed friends — I'm still on his email distribution list for sick-and-twisted oddity news — a hobby he still has even after his mild taming vis-a-vis marriage and kids. Many years and multiple job jumps later he's become executive editor at a major newspaper, which makes him a reference of note.

Fortunately, during my last week at the paper I had time to polish my resume and have Sandy bless it. She's reviewed hundreds of boring career summaries, and she's attuned to the key words that make a candidate look experienced and yet on-trend. I bang out a cover letter and send it to Drew, highlighting my awards, and I delve briefly into my knowledge of economics. I also name-drop, mentioning my extensive contact list of top economists from around the globe. After some nip and tuck, I'm convinced it will at least get read and might be buoyant enough to float up to the upper layer of the undoubtedly large resume pile.

I sort my Mexico gear into two piles: dive/surf gear and beach clothing. The latter pile won't even fill a roll-aboard bag: bikinis, shorts, tees and a sarong. Done. Bag number two is a heavy sucker, full of all the essentials: wetsuit, buoyancy compensator, regulator/computer, fins, mask, booties, flip-flops and running shoes.

Less than forty-eight hours to departure, I need to call Wayne. "I'm packed!"

"Right on, baby. Me too!"

"Do we need any camp gear that I can beg or borrow?"

"I have it covered. And I'm working on deals for a Jeep."

I make a spur-of-the-moment decision: "Do you want to come to dinner tonight?" If I'm going to step up this casual connection to travel buddies, it would be nice for him to become better acquainted with Dylan and Maria. And as I wait for his reply, I decide I'll add Craig to the guest list.

"I'd love that! What time and give me directions?"

"Let's say seven o'clock." I give him directions on how to find the farm. I okay the dinner plan with Dylan and Maria. And I text Craig. His reply back comes in just ten minutes: "Feed me? Hell yes!"

I make a flash trip to the market to buy the ingredients for lasagna. It comes together quickly, with only a limited number of tomato and pesto stains on the walls and me. My wet hair from a quick shower is still dripping onto my cotton shift dress when Wayne arrives. He lifts me off the floor, and plants a warm kiss on my lips. Maria catches herself, as her mouth falls open.

I re-introduce him to Dylan and Maria. He starts to win them over immediately, with his self-deprecating resume description: "I'm a failed investment banker, turned handyman/landscaper. Now I help others invest in plant therapy."

Craig arrives and the conversation turns to surfing and surf spots in Mexico. As Maria and I get dinner on the table, she comments, "Oye, dios mio, Dana! I'd forgotten about him from that time we met in L.A. That's a hot one. I feel like I've been eating habañero salsa!" She fans herself with a paper napkin.

Chapter 19

The party goes well into the evening as we decimate dinner, all the wine, and move on to some sipping tequila. Everyone is charmed by Wayne. He's easy-going, devoid of artifice and an engaging conversationalist on topics from sports to business to current events.

As Maria and I finish washing pots and stuffing the dishwasher, she giggles: "Wayne is a charmer. Mexico could be the start of something good if you give in to it."

I sigh. "Let's not put any expectations on the trip, Maria, please. He's been a casual lover for a long time, and neither one of us has messed with that successful formula."

"Claro." But she can't help whispering, "If I'm right I will be crowing, Dana."

We laugh and hug.

The next day, my head feels too big for my neck to hold aloft, but I'm too excited about Baja to let it slow me down. I repack my bags, making sure all my scuba gear is as protected as possible from the inevitable abuse of the baggage maulers. As I'm finishing, my cellphone rings. The number isn't one I recognize.

Guessing this might be a business-related call, I answer, "This is Dana."

"Hi, Dana, this is Drew at World Business Report."

I immediately sit up straighter in my chair.

"Hi, Drew. Nice to hear from you." I congratulate myself for being professional, for pushing the hangover cloud out of my brain.

He quickly moves past the social pleasantries. "I'm eager to fill this position, Dana, so before you left town I thought we could connect on the phone and evaluate how this job might match up to your skillset."

He launches into describing the beat coverage of the position he's filling, his travel expectations for the journalist who takes the job, and the workload he feels is appropriate to this senior reporting post. All of it matches up nearly perfectly with what I've been doing at the newspaper for the past few years. The only difference is that this job is all about feeding the demand for online news, which is clearly the future of journalism but has been a rough business to monetize, as the industry transitions from selling print to selling webpage impressions and web advertising.

But, Drew tells me that World Business isn't just building a new, online news operation; it has a technology division capable of marrying its news feeds with various corporate content distribution systems. It's already landed some Wall Street clients. Drew says they'll expand by selling the news service to accounting firms, multinational corporations, and others who need up-to-the-minute economic news and analysis. The more I hear, the more I'm convinced this startup has a chance at gaining a following before it burns through its seed capital and wilts without establishing roots.

"Have I convinced you?"

"I like what I'm hearing, Drew. But I'm a journalist; I need the facts confirmed by multiple sources."

His reply is direct. "I would expect nothing less."

He asks me to describe my work for the newspaper...beat areas I most enjoyed, typical workload, review cycle, deadline demands and travel budget. He steps in with questions when he wants more detail. "When can we meet?"

"I'm eager to meet with you as soon as I return. Perhaps the day after?"

He's not thrilled at having to wait, but I sweeten the deal by giving him Wylie's number and two other references, former co-workers and editors. This appeases him a little, but he tells me he'll be interviewing other candidates this week.

I lobby a little on my behalf, "I understand. But I think I have exactly the skillset you're seeking, and I'll just have to believe that my body of work and top references will convince you to hold off on a decision until we can meet."

This bit of uncharacteristic salesmanship seems to appease him. He sets up an in-person interview with me for the day after I return from Baja. Mission accomplished...I think. Part of me wants to land the next job and settle back in to the security of my work routine. And yet I'm looking forward to Baja more than I'm comfortable admitting, even to myself...possibly a different kind of security?

Nonetheless, after we hang up, I do a little jig around the loft.

*

Our flight to Baja goes smoothly and we make a supply stop on the outskirts of Cabo at a store we dub K-Mex, because it's half groceries and half an amazing array of dry goods, including tires, plumbing parts, hardware and more. We pull up to the surf camp just as the sun is dipping to the horizon, causing both the sea and desert to shimmer.

I meet Jerry and he hands us frosty Mexican beers and escorts us to an adobe casita set on a dune, with a stunning ocean view and unobstructed access to the water. The rustic blue casita has a thatched patio and bright orange shutters. Inside, the front room combines a small kitchen with built-in bench sofas in one corner and a small rough-hewn wooden dining table. The bedroom has a queen bed and an attached half bath. Out a side door is an outdoor walk-in shower. The only other camp guests are in a cabin on the other side of the main office/house, so we have complete privacy.

Jerry gives us a rundown on the casita lights and propane fridge, camp generator, and camp schedule, which is to say no schedule. After he leaves, we unload the jeep, and then grab beers and drop into the canvas directors' chairs on the patio to watch the last of the daylight fade to black. We are quiet, but it's a comfortable silence, with neither of us needing to fill the air with words. Instead, Wayne briefly disappears inside and comes back with an iPod plugged into an external speaker. He selects a playlist of Spanish guitar music, which floats across the background thumps and rush of the shore break.

I speak first. "I'm staying. I'll sell my loft. I'll do whatever it takes. Sell trinkets, make lousy hockey-puck tortillas and sour salsa, clean fish or scrub casitas, whatever."

Wayne smiles, widely. "This exceeds my hopeful expectations."

I look into his eyes, "Thank you."

He comes over, bends down and kisses me...a long, firm, commanding kiss. Pulling me to my feet, he leads me to the bedroom. The bed doesn't creak or knock too much; we give it a thorough shakedown. Wayne covers me with his massive chest and shoulders, and we rock to the pounding surf. Before long, I'm twitching and rubbing hard into him. I gasp and cry out; he slows his rhythm and shudders. Spent, we tangle up in each other under the damp twisted sheets.

"Lovely start to the adventure, surfer girl!"

"Beer me, cabana boy."

"Yes, ma'am."

He hops out of bed and is back in a flash with two beers. I hear him starting the barbeque. I wrap up in a sarong and help organize the meal. After we clean up, Wayne breaks out a squat bottle of tequila, one of four we bought on the way here. We procured two at K-Mex, and we stopped at a local liquor store and found two other bottles that the shopkeeper assured us are "muy bueno." They're from obscure distilleries; brands that we haven't seen on shelves in the U.S. He opens one of the mystery bottles and pours us each a tall shot. "To surf, sand, fish and...fuh-un!"

I giggle and dribble a little tequila on my fingers as I lift my shot. I switch hands and lick my fingers. "One go, or are we sipping?"

"Definitely sipping. We have a week ahead of us."

At dawn, I wake suddenly, listening to Wayne snuffle into his pillow. I slip out of the casita's front door into the weak early light; the water is the silver pink of a prom dress. Sandpipers skitter in and out of the rolling foam, sucking up tidbits from beneath the sand. Up beyond the last casita, I see an old man surf-fishing. He's squat and barrel-chested, well shorter than I am, and he wears a stained woven poncho and stiff grubby jeans tucked into rubber waders. It's in the mid-seventies, but he moves like he's chilled.

I pad up the damp, compacted sand at the water's edge, just as he reels in a seven-inch perch.

"Buenos dias!"

His shy smile displays a gold front tooth and a missing eye-tooth. He bends stiffly and deposits the fish in a tall plastic paint bucket at his knees. As I approach, I can see that it holds four perch, including the one he just pulled from his hook. It flaps and twitches atop the pile of unmoving schoolmates.

"Desayuno?"

"Si."

The casita is still quiet when I return, so I close the door to the bedroom and start assembling breakfast. But first I get the coffee pot singing revelry. The aroma entices Wayne out of bed, and he shows up at the kitchen counter wearing my sarong low on his hips. There's nothing sexier than a man wearing a skirt, sporting morning stubble and tousled hair. He wraps his arms around my waist and nuzzles my neck.

"You cook?"

"I stir and heat. Don't overstate the facts."

"Good enough. But you make strong coffee, right?"

"Oh yeah. Don't submerge any plastic utensils. They'll melt."

While devouring everything I put in front of him, Wayne details his proposed agenda for our first day. Apparently, last night when he and Jerry were gabbing and catching up on old times, and I was checking the beach, they loosely planned a surf safari for today to a point break ten kilometers north. On the way back, we'll stop at a camp where Jerry says we can arrange to rent a panga (a colorful wooden Mexican dory), captain and scuba tanks for tomorrow. After that, Wayne promises lunch and hammock time. He says Jerry filled him in on a couple of good surf-fishing spots we can try at some point, today, tomorrow, or the "manana" after. Beyond that, he says, "to be announced."

Wayne hunts down Jerry and they load Jerry's pickup with ancient longboards and a cooler. We rumble north, bouncing our kidneys off of our other innards, until Jerry pulls into a small circular parking area at a deserted point that rounds into a cove with a pebble beach. Small waves push into the cove; the rolling rocks make a soft purr. Though they're only about two feet, the waves have staying power and keep curling for a good ten or more seconds. Best of all, there's no one here. Our only audience: seagulls, pelicans and a few speckled harbor seals sunning themselves on the rocks.

We don shorty wetsuits and grab a collection of boards that are so well-loved that they have dents on their decks where a multitude of feet have spent time driving the boards across the water. Their fiberglass has yellowed and they sport dark spots like ripe bruised pears where they've sustained water damage to their foam cores.

After a short paddle, we're catching wave after wave, sometimes trading off; other times it's a group ride and we amuse ourselves by cutting around each other and striking silly poses. Wayne wins style awards with his antics, including pulling off a coffin ride, laid out on his back, arms crossed. I bust a few disco shimmies and hip hop moves up and down my board. But Jerry one-ups both of us on the next ride, doing a nearly perfect imitation of a harbor seal by riding on his rather large beer belly, with both his head and legs lifted and his hands flapping at his sides like flippers.

When the breeze kicks up and starts running bumpy white caps over our waves, it's time to catch the last of the rides and roll back to camp. As planned, we stop into the neighboring fishing camp and talk to the owner about renting a panga, tanks and a boat captain for some scuba diving. Wayne uses his junior-high Spanish to negotiate the cost, and Jerry helps out with some translating. After a little haggling, it's all set. We have a boat, tanks and a driver for tomorrow morning.

The rest of the day passes quickly with beach combing, fishing and a leisurely siesta with not much sleep and a lot of sex. While I'm still drowsing in bed, Wayne prepares a happy-hour feast with ceviche from our day's catch and margaritas. He rounds up Jerry and his fishing guide, Miguel. Jerry collects his only other guests, a young couple from Oregon on a month-long Baja road trip. The party turns into a full fiesta and potluck.

*

At just after sunrise, we're out the cabin door. We want to dive before any breeze kicks up, which would make for a rougher boat ride and potentially reduce the underwater visibility. The camp owner, Milo, introduces us to Juan, our boat captain for the day. He looks like a direct descendant of the Mayan people who once ruled Central America. Standing just five foot three or four, he's well shorter than I am, but with a barrel chest. His sharp cheekbones and hooked nose make way to a wide smile that rarely leaves his face. His English is way better than our Spanish, which is a pleasant and helpful surprise. As he drives an ATV down the beach, we discuss dive sites. We load our yellow and blue panga with tanks that we've already strapped to our buoyancy compensation (BC) jackets and topped with regulators, then toss in a second set of tanks and the rest of our gear.

Milo meets us at the water's edge while we're wriggling into our wetsuits. After a short wait for a wave that pushes well up the beach, we strain to shove the metal bottomed dory out into the small surf. Once the boat is deep enough for the prop to spin in water and not sand, Milo waves goodbye and retreats up the beach, as the rest of us throw ourselves into the boat. Juan navigates beyond the surf-line and in no time we're skimming across the water to the hum of the well-worn outboard that lost all of its logo paint long ago.

The panga cuts through the glassy water, and we motor around a point and across the next cove. On the far side, Juan says a rock reef, with spires coming up, runs perpendicular to shore, dropping from twenty-five to seventy feet before it peters out into rubble. Without local knowledge, you'd never find it because none of it is visible from the surface. A plankton layer makes the top ten feet of water a milky green. But Juan seems confident that conditions will be much different below. We plan to drop on the far side of the reef, kick along its contours until it runs out at seventy feet, swim around and come back along the closer side, where we'll be protected from any current that's running in the prevailing north-to-south direction.

Once we've geared up, Wayne takes one side of the panga, toward the bow, and I perch on the rail on the opposite side, near the stern. We give each other a quick okay signal and simultaneously roll backward into the water. Instead of dropping immediately to the reef, we meet as planned behind the boat so we can drop together. In these milky conditions, if we don't descend together we may not find each other underwater and the dive might have to be aborted before it's ever begun. Wayne takes his reg out of his mouth and asks, "Ready for some bottom time?" I give him the thumbs down.

At twenty feet we level off. The plankton has thinned and visibility has improved significantly. Below us we can see the reef's craggy top. We kick ahead, finning over the top of the rocks to the far side and then dropping almost to the sand at thirty-five feet.

I kick alongside Wayne's right side, and he reaches out and grabs my hand. It is unexpected and a little surprising. He wants to be my protector, and I have to acknowledge that, for once, it feels good. I smile into my regulator and match my fin kicks to his.

Diving is an escape into a three-dimensional liquid world. Once I trim my BC, I feel like I'm flying through the water, weightless and agile, despite the heavy tank strapped to my back. And the rhythmic breathing through the regulator can have the psychological Zen effect of a short meditation or yoga session. I'm exhilarated and relaxed at the same time. Some divers are hooked from the first splash. I certainly was.

The reef is covered in white and orange hydrocorals, as well as an abundance of greenish-blue anemones, purple and red starfish, and black spiny urchins. Snapper hang over the crags, along with a few small schools of perch and other smaller bait fish. Once we reach a depth of about fifty feet, I let go of Wayne's hand and move just ahead to peer under an overhang in the wall. I giggle a little and pull back. I wave Wayne over and point under the overhang. A quizzical look moves across his face, but instead of giving him a specific hand signal for lobster or crab, I just point insistently under the ledge. He tilts down and sticks his head and shoulders under the protruding rock. An instant later, in an abrupt jerk, he waves his arms hard forward and he snaps back out from under the rocks, blowing a large exhale of bubbles.

He turns, and he's clearly laughing while he wags his finger at me. I pull my reg from my mouth and give him a big toothy grin. Backed into a hole cut in the rocks under the ledge are two three- to four-foot wolf eels wrapped around each other with just their heads and fore bodies sticking out. These prehistoric-looking gray eels have black spots, protruding lower jaws and scary buck teeth. They eat mostly urchins, mussels and clams, but they look like they'd enjoy a finger or two. I wouldn't want to tempt them.

We continue out and down to roughly seventy feet, where the wall dissolves into boulders. As we round the rocks and start making our way back along the other side of the wall, a spotted eagle ray with a four-foot wingspan flies by, with a couple of reef fish tailing him. Midway back along the top of the wall, we see a cabezon, a camouflaged green and brownish sculpin with bulging eyes, a wide head, spiny dorsal fins that are poisonous, and fanned pectoral fins. They lie on the top of rocks, sometimes guarding eggs. A few more kicks and Wayne signals that he's low on air. I still have more than half a tank, but I'm starting to shake so I'm happy to surface. We rise to fifteen feet for a three-minute safety stop in the murk to blow off some of the nitrogen gas we've loaded. We surface less than ten feet from Juan. He hooks a small metal ladder on the back of the dory, and after tying off our gear to the side of the panga we climb aboard.

Once we haul our gear in, Juan hands us towels and pours cups of hot black tea from a Thermos. The sun is glaring on the water and the air temperature has risen to the high-seventies. I quickly recover from the cold and ask Juan about the next dive site.

Our second dive, off a point just south of the fish camp, is just as diverse as the first one, with the added highlight of two five-foot blue sharks that pass us and swim on. Our ride back up onto the beach provides the adrenalin rush of the day. Juan instructs us to wrap our hands tightly into running lines secured on the inside of the panga's rails. He turns to shore and guns the engine just outside the surf-line, and we fly toward land. At the last possible moment, he pops up the motor and we hold tight to keep from getting thrown out by the deceleration, as the metal boat bottom slams into and skids across the wet sand. Wayne howls like a desert coyote, loving this wild exit ride.

*

For the next several days, we fall into a rhythm of physical hedonism: sex, water sports, beach walks and occasional naps. I even slow down enough to get horizontal in the middle of the day without equating it to depression and Valerie. We avoid any deep conversations — instead we chat about surfing and diving; we talk about our Southern California haunts; we socialize with Jerry and the rest of the camp staff; and we numb our brains by exhausting ourselves with over-activity and tequila tranquilizers. Still, we're growing more connected by the hour. Despite my inherent reserve, I'm starting to feel like Wayne is not just a lover and companion, but more like an appendage. When we're sleeping, we always have contact...a foot, an arm draped across a hip, his hand between my thighs. I wake when he leaves the bed; I drift off again when he returns.

I'm afraid to say anything...afraid I could ruin it. And several times I notice Wayne catching himself before he says something too intimate that he fears might startle me. He views me like a half-tamed horse, one minute eating out of his hand but likely to bite, kick and bolt in the very next instant.

One evening toward the end of the week, when we're alone on the casita's patio at dusk and our tongues are lubed with shots and beers, Wayne decides to move beyond the invisible barrier and share details of his Northern California mission. His tone instantly snaps me back to sobriety. By revealing himself, even a little, he's pushing us forward, regardless of our fears.

"I've been working at a goal, Dana, one that I haven't spoken of to anyone yet. I wanted to be sure that it would actually pan out before I said anything."

"A career move?" That's what I'm hoping, thought the silly teenage girl still residing inside me instantly fears a competitive relationship. We've been playing house for less than a week and we've made no declarations of any intimate feelings, much less promises of a future beyond Baja. Still, the bond I feel to him, though certainly far from set, has already formed enough in these past few days that it will pull away a piece of me if it's severed.

"Yes, though it seems laughable for a handyman to be talking about his career path."

"We both know you have other abilities, Wayne, besides repairing screens and sprinklers. And hey, I'm unemployed right now so I might soon be seeking a handyman apprenticeship."

"Not a chance. You'll get another job before your leave of absence runs out."

"So, stop stalling. What's the news? What have you been working toward?"

"Okay, I'll just blurt it. I've been attending nursing school, believe it or not."

I jump out of my camp chair and run over to where he's sitting on the patio's rock wall. I push in between his legs, wrap my arms around his shoulders and kiss him. "That's a great move! Wow, and how long have you been keeping this under wraps?"

"Over two years."

I pull back and stare at him. "Damn. I guess I shouldn't assume I know what's going on with you. Clearly, you can keep a secret."

"It's not like that. At first, I was afraid I'd screw it up. And even though I finished my undergraduate schooling with a minor in biology, going back to school is tough. I didn't want to talk about it and then have to admit to people that I didn't finish. As it became more real, it seemed like talking about it could jinx it. And it's not like you were around enough for even monthly progress reports. You've been a phantom, Dana."

He's right. "But I'm right here, right now, and I want to know more." I kiss him again, and settle onto the wall next to him.

He explains how he'd always thought about medicine, even when he was studying finance. But his parents pushed him to move into the business world. He'd tried to mold himself into a numbers lover, until he realized finance wasn't just dull, it was smothering. After his divorce, he got out. The handyman gig fell into his lap; it was easy and he could surf every swell.

"I was healing from the divorce and the career flameout, Dana. And I got complacent. I had to figure out what I really wanted to do. This time I didn't want to pursue someone else's idea of a life; I wanted to build my own." His lifelong fitness and love of anatomy and health helped him recognize his interest in healing, and he had the biology credits to get him beyond the nursing prerequisites.

"My handyman schedule, if you can call it that, allowed me to adjust my commitments to accommodate the classes and training I needed. I still had to take the slow road in order to finish it while working, but I'm finally there."

"When do you graduate?"

"Ah, well, that was last week."

I stare at him and for a moment my jaw drops open. I turn and trot into the kitchen, retrieving tequila and two shot glasses. "Congratulations!" We clink our shots. "This is your graduation celebration! I'm honored to participate."

"Dana, this has been more than a graduation party. Don't you think we can maybe admit at least that much now?" He looks directly at me.

I return his gaze and then turn out to the dark ocean, and the horizon, where just a hint of orange-yellow light still lingers. When I turn back, his face is uncertain and questioning, eyebrows raised but jaw set. "Yes, it's more. I don't know what it is, but it's more than that for me," I state quietly.

He slams his shot and pulls me back between his legs. Holding my face between his hands, he says, "Dana, I've been deliriously happy these past few days. Haven't you seen that? I've been trying to play it cool, but I'm on the fishhook flopping around. I'm caught."

He kisses my mouth, nose and cheeks. Then he wraps me tightly to him and nuzzles his nose into my neck and hair.

His announcements about the nursing and us, though wonderful, leave me feeling off-balance. I move the conversation to where I'm comfortable, asking him about the new career. "Have you had any interviews?"

"Yes, I've actually had a couple. It turns out that being a newly minted nurse, though of a certain maturity (he winks), isn't necessarily a drawback. Health workers are in high demand, especially at inner-city hospitals. When we get back, I'll go for a second interview at a hospital in South San Francisco."

"That's fantastic!" I move back onto the wall next to him, but he holds onto my right hand and absently rubs it against his thigh.

"Yeah, they get a rough crowd coming through sometimes, so they like male nurses and orderlies with some brawn. The head nurse, a plain-spoken gal in her mid-fifties, spent more time sizing up my muscles than my resume."

I grab his bicep and gently squeeze. "Did she drool a little?"

"Next, I'll get grilled by the hiring committee, which is made up of doctors, lead nurses and a human-resources manager. If they hire me, I'll start at the bottom of the heap, but the pay isn't bad. Plus I can live in Half Moon Bay or Pacifica and the commute would be bearable. I've already seen some rentals in Pacifica. I might be getting ahead of myself, but I wanted to see what my budget would get me."

"And your hours won't be nine-to-five so you won't be traveling the roads with the office commute crowd. Plus, the flexible schedule will enable you to surf."

"Yeah, I admit that when I was figuring out what to do next I knew I couldn't go back to the stagnant office environment. Last fall, I did a six-week internship at an ER down in L.A., and I loved the variety and the quick pace. In one shift, we saw four sick kids and a bunch of sick adults, a heart attack, a gunshot wound, and three broken bones. When I thought about how I used to move numbers around a spreadsheet it seemed ridiculous. Nursing has real value, and it fits my need to be on the move."

"I'm really happy for you, Wayne. When will you tell your family?"

"When I have a job. I'm sure they'd be happier if I was returning to finance, but at least now they won't be embarrassed to tell their friends what I'm doing for a living. Still, my dad will have to get his head around the idea of his son as a male nurse."

"Let's get Jerry and Miguel and celebrate your graduation."

*

Jerry's in, and Miguel graciously agrees to be our designated jeep driver. At a small seafood restaurant south of camp, Jerry introduces us to nearly every other diner. By ten o'clock I've lost count of the shots. But early on I signal the waitress to skip my glass. She just waves the bottle over it and I fake like I'm sipping fire water.

The next morning, Wayne is nursing a serious hangover. His eyes are bloodshot and he's shuffling from couch to coffee pot. Savoring the second-to-last day of our Baja beach escape, I take a run on the sand and across the bluffs. Reality is about to reel us back in, but I want to make the most of our last full day here.

When I return to the casita, I see Wayne body-surfing in the foot-high, mushy shore break directly out in front of the camp. Salt water as soothing salve — he's administering his cure.

While he's playing in the waves, Jerry comes by.

"A Dylan called for you on the resort phone? He says it's important. And he's going to call back in ten minutes." Worry pinches Jerry's face.

We walk quickly to the camp office, and he steps outside to give me privacy when the phone rings.

"Dana, I'm sorry to call but you need to know what's going on." Dylan's words are clipped, his voice tight.

He's told Agent Stokes about the poison *yaa baa* and the death at the hospital in Palo Alto — he had no choice, since Stokes was pressuring one of his clients, who's a *yaa baa* user. Dylan didn't want his client, who's facing multiple charges already, to open himself up to any more scrutiny by trading sketchy gossip about Ling and the *yaa baa* death. Stokes then tried to contact Shane at rehab and discovered he'd checked out. That set off a shitstorm of calls, with Dylan telling Stokes that he was unaware of Shane's departure from rehab and has no idea where he's gone. When Stokes asked about me, Dylan told him I'd taken a short vacation, but should return in a week or so.

"Stokes is frying mad, Dana. He flat out stated that he'll use all his resources to find you and Shane. I hope the feds won't meet you at SFO, but it's possible." He didn't want to text me; he didn't want a written record of this warning.

"Maybe I can leave early, get ahead of Stokes efforts to track me?" My voice quakes.

"It might help. I'm just not sure what Stokes will do." I thank him for the warning and quickly hang up the phone.

I thank Jerry, and jog back to the casita. The feds can certainly track my credit cards and find my flight itinerary to Cabo and back. But I'm still fairly confident that I covered my tracks well on my trips to and from Port Townsend — I didn't use my credit cards the entire way, not for gas, food or any of our camping or hotels. Shane and I used a burner, throw-away cellphone. And there's no record of Shane's transportation to Hawaii; Garrett assured me of it.

Since I'm just Shane's sister, I doubt Stokes will go to the trouble of getting the necessary approvals to work with Mexican law enforcement and track me down here or at the Cabo airport when I'm getting ready to fly back. But he could easily meet our flight in San Francisco. And if he does that means Wayne will be involved, which I'm determined to avoid. It makes me nauseous to think Shane's latest screw-up, and my involvement in it, could harm Wayne's plans.

I start a little pity party in my mind, playing out a scenario where Wayne walks away from the "us" that's just begun to be a tantalizing possibility because of this mess with Shane and his involvement with this drug lord. Or...I can end it. I can do what I've done so many times before. I quickly go from heartsick to shutting down. I can walk away, decouple, before I'm responsible to Wayne for anything. I've bolted from would-be relationships many times before; I'm a pro at the emotional demolition derby.

If I change my flight and leave today, without Wayne, there's no chance he'll get caught up in any net Stokes is setting for me. I can take the Jeep, and Jerry can get Wayne to the airport tomorrow. I'll borrow Jerry's phone again to see if I can get on a flight this evening, thus avoiding sending any more location data on me out onto the airwaves.

When Wayne comes in from the outdoor shower, I'm already halfway packed. My dive gear is slammed into its still-open gear bag, and my roll-aboard is filling up. Wayne stops, dripping, in the bedroom doorway. He stares for a good ten seconds, the shock visible on his face, before he speaks.

"Dana, what the hell? Why are you packing?"

It's obvious that I'm not just getting a jump on preparing for tomorrow's planned departure. He can identify a bolt when he sees one.

"Something has come up, and I need to get back today. I'm going to try to get on a flight tonight. But you should come back as planned tomorrow." The dead tone and finality in my voice says there's no room for discussion on this plan.

"And you actually think I'll agree to that...with no explanation?" Stifled rage edges into his voice. I look up and give him my best "whatever" look. I blank all emotion from my face and body language. I need to convince him that I'm putting the brakes on us, and that I'm just another flighty female, into fun but not looking for a future. If he believes that, he won't care and he won't get tangled up in the collapsing mess that's waiting for me in California.

No deal. He strides over to me and grabs my hand; he pulls me out into the front of the casita and onto the couch. He wraps his arms around me. "We're not leaving this couch until you explain what's going on. I will not let you shut me out, Dana. Whatever it is, you can tell me. I will not let you run. Not now, not ever."

Unable to remain stoic and detached, my breath catches and tears run down my face. Wayne pulls me tighter to him. And even better than that, he waits, patiently, for me to open up. This is not about him. Few men can take their agenda, their need for control, out of an emotional crisis. I well up more, as I realize Wayne has this quality.

I pause to regain my composure, turn sideways on the couch and begin, "Do you remember the few stories I've told you about my brother, Shane? About the drugs, his chaotic life, and his trouble keeping a job or a place to live?"

"Yes, I remember most of that. He was once a pro surfer, right?"

"Briefly. But he screwed that up, with drugs and irresponsible behavior. He's had issues since he was a child. And he's fallen further and further from a stable life over the past few years." As always, when I start relating information about Shane, it's difficult to figure out where to begin and which stories are worth including for the listener to understand the latest Shane drama. I summarize how he's fallen into legal and financial holes in the past, and how I usually end up being the one to rescue him, because our father has nothing left to give and Shane has no relationship with our brother Terry. "And you've met Dylan and Maria. Dylan has done more than any friend should ever be asked to do. He's used his legal skills and gone to court on Shane's behalf. Without him, Shane would have been sent to prison long ago."

I recap the call from Joe and my trip north. I shudder and start crying again, tears dripping down my face and onto the couch, when I describe what Shane looked like in the hospital, his busted arm, bruised face and his hair falling out in clumps. Wayne just holds my hand and listens. I explain how Dylan and I got Shane into rehab. And I divulge that he's mixed up with a major drug dealer. I give him only the information that will allow him to follow the story — for his own good I hold back details about Ling and the poison *yaa baa*.

Finally, I get to the information Wayne must understand — the potential mess he could get sucked into simply by being with me in Mexico. "An FBI agent named Stokes is looking for Shane. Stokes has a team that he's running and they've been investigating this drug lord for months. They want to take down his whole network."

I explain that as yet Stokes doesn't have enough evidence to charge Shane with anything, but he wants to pressure Shane into being an informant. But before he could do that, Shane left rehab and disappeared. "That's where I come in."

"And you were bolting because you're worried Stokes will come after you here, or meet us at SFO, and I'll get pulled into this mess." Wayne quickly calculates the outcome of the Shane drama and where he fits into it.

"Dylan thinks it's a possibility, and I do too. I spoke to him on the camp phone while you were bodysurfing. I don't think Stokes can get permission quickly enough to work with Mexican law enforcement and come after me here. But he can easily find out my return flight schedule and have agents meet the plane in San Francisco."

I plead with my eyes. "You can't get mixed up in this, Wayne. Any hospital you apply to will do a background check on you. You can't be having chats with FBI agents. You need to let me go today, so we're not on the same plane."

Wayne gets up and paces in front of me. He doesn't like these statements; they don't fit with his paternal nature. But he sees the logic of my plan. Still, he's weighing other options.

"What if you call Stokes and promise him you'll come in once you're back?"

"I don't trust him, Wayne, and he doesn't trust me. He's unlikely to let me control the timing of my interview. The guy's a real prick."

"Well, let's both fly back tonight, before he can track us. We can call the airline and find out if the last flight is full. If it's not, we can fly standby. We'll put our names on the list at the last second. He can't move that fast."

It's a decent option — it certainly makes my road trip back to Cabo easier, since I'm unfamiliar with the Baja roads and Wayne's driven them. But Wayne's still taking a risk traveling with me, even on a pushed-up schedule.

I look down at my fists, ready to punch at this possibly tightening cage. "I don't want you to be exposed to Stokes' potential snare, Wayne. You've worked too hard for this new start."

He stops pacing and stares hard at me. "And all of that won't mean a thing if you're not a part of it, Dana." He pulls me up off the couch and I wrap my arms around his waist, and lay my cheek against his chest. So there is an "us" forming — I can hardly let myself believe it. And the timing is spectacularly bad, which is so typical for me.

"We go this afternoon, *if* we can find out about a flight tonight with open seats that we can standby on. But you can't sit with me, just in case. We get on the plane separately, and we get off separately."

"Okay, Nancy Drew." He smiles for the first time since he walked in from the shower.

I'm a little relieved, but my body vibrates. Without another word, we ram gear into our bags.

Chapter 20

When we arrive in San Francisco, immigration and customs are busy but not overwhelmed, and we retrieve our luggage and get through in twenty minutes. My hands are shaking as I hand my passport to the immigration officer, but he doesn't notice and asks me no questions. He just grunts a gruff "Welcome back" and slides the passport back to me. Wayne says his immigration officer was chatty but not inquisitive.

Soon we're twisting and turning up and over Highway 92 to Half Moon Bay. The cab, which costs a paycheck even with Wayne negotiating a flat rate, drops us at Wayne's friend's house. We'd arranged a ride from a shuttle service for tomorrow's arrival, but it's worth it to be back early and to have successfully avoided a possible welcoming committee from the FBI. My Honda is waiting on the street – it looks sad and soggy, dripping in fog slime, with clouded windows. After a week in Baja, we shiver while saying goodbye.

"Will you call Stokes tomorrow?"

"First I'll ask Dylan the best way to handle it. But yes, I will. It's always better to have things unfold on my timing, not his. Besides he's a fed — he hates that."

"Don't poke at the snarling guard dog, Dana. His masters make the rules."

I nod solemnly. Stokes already dislikes me; I'd be a fool to antagonize him further.

Then I realize that with the breaking Stokes drama, I forgot to tell Wayne about my job interview. I give him a quick summary of the possible job at World Business.

"That's fantastic news, Dana." He pulls me close and wraps his arms around my waist.

"I had my heart set on working for Jerry. But yeah, this job could be a good next step...as long as I don't end up wearing some steel bracelets."

"Don't even say that in jest. Call me tomorrow and fill me in on your chat with Stokes?"

"Will do. And when's your follow-up interview at the hospital?"

"Three days out at ten in the morning. Tomorrow I'll get together with a friend of a friend — a doctor with privileges at the hospital. She's promised to give me all the behind-the-scenes dirt on the ER."

We kiss and cling. I need to get going. Yet in just a week I've become accustomed to having Wayne at my side. It's unsettling for me to feel this way. I have been autonomous for a very long time.

We pull apart. He squeezes my hand and walks me over to my car.

"Dana, you've protected me from all the details of Shane's situation. But secrets make for distance; there's a cost. At some point, I'd like you to tell me the whole story."

"I will, soon. I've dealt with Shane's legal scrapes before, and even though this one is much more twisted than past episodes, Dylan will help me find a way through it." I sound way more confident than I am.

I slump in my seat and drive. I've been acting in control since we made the escape plan, but the strain is hitting my gut, which is so twisted it's collapsing me in the middle. My breathing is ragged; my spine feels folded. I pull up to the house and just sit there. I'm finally somewhat safe, and I'm utterly exhausted.

The porch light at the back door comes on, and Dylan walks out to the car. I hop out, and we hug in the driveway. I thank him for the warning and fill him in on how we decided to come home a day early, just in case Stokes was planning an airport surprise party for me. "You will have to talk to him, Dana."

"Tomorrow can we talk about it and strategize? I'm sorry I woke you."

"I was still up — well, if falling asleep in front of the TV counts as up." His hair is tousled and he's in his torn, smashed slippers. "Let's go through some potential questions and answers tomorrow at breakfast. Maria will be leaving early for a shift, and Marco will be off to school."

He peers at me. "Are you okay? You look a little wrecked."

"I'm spent, Dylan. I just need sleep, and I need to feel like I have some idea how to handle this interview." My eyes search his face and my hands fidget at my sides. I've lost my bravado; I left it in Mexico.

"You've done nothing wrong, Dana. Stokes hasn't charged Shane with any offense, and he still hasn't subpoenaed him, so anything you did for him wasn't illegal in any way. Get some sleep, and we'll go through all of it tomorrow." He helps me haul my bags up to the loft. We hug one more time, and I hear him shuffle across the gravel back to the house.

*

Before I go down to the kitchen, I turn on my phone. It doesn't matter now if Stokes finds out I'm back. I intend to pay him a visit today before he even considers tracking me. A text from Wayne pops up. "Hate waking without u next to me. xxx W." Tremors flutter through my stomach. I'm giddy, yet embarrassed at my mooning.

But that doesn't stop me from texting back. "Miss u too. Call later."

Dylan escorts Marco out to his light truck, discussing afternoon soccer practice and dinner time. When he returns, he pours orange juice into tall glasses and launches right into our strategy discussion. "Stokes will first try to pressure you for Shane's location. He'll claim that you're hiding a key witness to a homicide, and you could be forced by the courts to cooperate."

I've just taken a sip of juice, and I swallow hard. My throat tightens.

"But that's just bluster, Dana. Shane clearly isn't with you, he's somewhere else. You're not hiding him. He's not under subpoena, at least not yet, so you're not obligated to tell Stokes anything." He looks intently into my eyes.

"And Stokes doesn't seem to have any information tying Shane to the bad *yaa baa* that killed the addict in Palo Alto; otherwise he'd have a subpoena already. I've spoken to a few local cops, and they say Ling's associates don't talk, ever. Nearly all of them are Thai nationals and the idea that they could cut a deal for protection is absurd to them. A gangster like Ling would cut them down without hesitation if he sniffs out any slight disloyalty, much less betrayal."

My hands are sweating in my lap. "Should I just refuse to talk to him?"

"I don't think so. He'll think you're hiding something. Try to get him to ask you something in a way that you can answer directly, without lying."

I mull this over. Technically, I don't know where Shane is now. I've had no contact with him since he left Port Townsend for Hawaii. But like most avid surfers, he has surf buddies in Tahiti and Fiji too. And he has enough money to keep moving across the Pacific if he decides to go on. Garrett has extensive contacts in the sailing community; if Shane performed well on the crossing he could have set him up with another crewing job. Although I didn't discuss this with Shane or Garrett (because I knew it would be best if I was completely out of the loop), it was an unspoken option.

Dylan adds, "You've been interviewing people for your entire career, Dana. Flatter Stokes. Make him believe you want to help him, and get him to do the talking. Flirt if you have to. You can work it when you want to, Dana; I've seen it. Frame the questions that you want to answer, and keep the conversation away from the ones you don't want to address."

"Should I drop in on him?"

"Yes. Making an appointment will just give him time to come up with more questions. I'll call over there, and find out if he's in the office today. If he is, you should go over there and just ask to see him. He'll be surprised, but I'm pretty sure he'll take the meeting. He won't want to let you get away or pass up an opportunity to speak with you."

"I don't want you to go with me. I don't want you involved."

"That's fine. The interview will go better if you march in there demonstrating that you have nothing to hide and that you're being fully cooperative."

"Any other tips?"

"Keep that sassy mouth of yours in control. Pissing Stokes off will only cause him to work harder to pressure you and find Shane. It's better to be a damsel in distress than a warrior princess. Stokes is a macho guy; he'll want to protect the damsel."

"But warrior princess suits me better."

He exhales hard. "I'll go call Stokes' office. Hang here for a moment."

I need to eat something, but my stomach is knotted again. I grab a small yogurt from the fridge, and mindlessly spoon it into my mouth. Dylan pads back into the room.

"He's in the office all day. Go there just before lunch, say eleven thirty. If he's in a meeting, he'll pull out of it for you. And remember, Dana: If it gets to be too much, cut the interview off and call me."

Dylan drives off to court, and I go back to the loft to shower and dress. What does one wear to an FBI interview? Something innocent looking. I put on an embroidered, cream-colored blouse, fitted navy pencil skirt and wedge sandals. I pull my usually out-of-control hair into a ponytail. I survey the overall effect in the mirror...girlish and nonthreatening. Perfect.

Despite driving slowly for once, I arrive at the feds' office building too soon and wait in my car, fussing with my hair, smoothing my skirt and getting even more nervous. At eleven twenty six, I walk up to the FBI reception area and ask for Agent Stokes. The young man working at the front desk asks me if he's expecting me.

"No, but he wants to speak with me. Just give him my name."

I walk away from him, feeling his eyes follow me, and drop into one of the reception area chairs. He picks up the phone and presses a couple of buttons. The bureau doesn't provide its visitors with magazines; I stare at the wanted poster on the wall. I can't help imagining Shane's face in one of the photo squares.

No more than two minutes has gone by, when Stokes pushes through a side door and into the lobby. He tries to appear impassive, but his slightly lifted eyebrows give away his curiosity. "Ms. McCarren? Thanks for coming in." We shake hands. "Would you come this way?"

He waves his badge at the door, and it clicks open. He leads me down an antiseptic corridor, with white walls and dark mottled gray industrial carpet. We pass a couple of small conference rooms and an open office space, filled with five-foot cubes and a few agents. We turn right into an area with small personal offices that have windows facing into the corridor. Stokes' office holds a metal desk that's mostly clear, except for a computer monitor and phone, but a credenza behind his chair is piled high with two-inch thick legal-size file folders. Dark wood bookshelves line one wall, stuffed mostly with penal code volumes.

"So, I assume Dylan let you know that I need to speak with you?"

"Yes." Right away, I begin my efforts to disarm him. "I want to help you, Agent Stokes, but I doubt I have any information that could be at all useful."

"Really, Dana? You know your brother was involved with this drug supplier, Ling. We need to speak with Shane. And I believe you know how to contact him."

"Agent Stokes, Shane is a junkie, and he's mentally unstable. You've seen his record and you've undoubtedly asked around about him. I've spent my entire adult life trying to help him, but he has flunked rehab repeatedly. He can't seem to pull the hook. Have you visited his squat?"

Initially, he doesn't answer. I'm sure he didn't have a warrant when he tossed Shane's dirt den. I wait him out.

"Yes, we've gone by his apartment. He left rehab, and we need to interview him. He is a potential witness to a number of crimes."

"Apartment? Wouldn't you say that's an overstatement? His squalid hovel is no apartment. And what did you find there?"

"I'm not at liberty to share with you any information that we've gathered as part of this investigation." Typical FBI: He's trying to force me to spill, but not offering to disclose anything in return.

"Well I was there before you, and someone else tossed the place before I got there. Since you've been there, you've seen that. The knife in the surfboard was a nice touch, don't you think? Anyway, since you've visited and come up empty, it's clear he has no evidence for you."

"I need to hear that from him. He may have insights that may not seem important to him, but will help us tie up some loose ends."

Loose ends? I catch myself as I almost scoff at this comment. I quickly remind myself — Dylan said no snarky behavior. But it's a laughable statement. Stokes has a lot more than loose ends in his investigation or he wouldn't need Shane, a junkie witness. At this point, I decide the best strategy is to play stupid, act needy and ask for help.

"Well, with all your resources, I'm confident you'll find him, and I'm counting on it. And when you do, I hope you'll give me the opportunity to grill Mr. Responsible. I paid for that rehab; and he left early and left me with a large phone bill and other charges as well." I roll my eyes and act angry and indignant.

"You don't know where he is?"

"No, I don't. But if he's honed one skill in his sad life it's disappearing when he owes money. Shane hasn't paid this month's rent on that horrifying squat. I'll be covering that, too, and I'm not rich, Agent Stokes. In fact, I'm unemployed." I look down and wring my hands in my lap, playing the sympathy card. I shake my ponytail for added effect. I might get an Oscar for this performance.

I feel him staring at me. Am I getting to him?

Before he can ask me another question I probably don't want to answer, I pour it on a little more. "Do you have any idea what rehab costs? And this is his fourth visit that I've covered, Agent Stokes. Frankly, I'm worried about him, but with my current situation I'd be hard-pressed to fund any more treatment or other Shane expenses."

I lock eyes with him and give him a droopy eyed, pathetic look. Then I decide to point him toward another target. "Ling has hired some local muscle for his operation, a couple of tough surfers from the Hook crowd. They were scary characters long before they got involved in this drug operation."

"We've heard about a number of them. Who are you referring to?"

"Anton Krause. He was a bully in school and he's a bully in the water at The Hook. Now he's one of Ling's enforcers. He enjoys being feared, and he's even threatened me. You're not the only one who thinks I can produce Shane, Agent Stokes."

"We've heard about Anton. When did he threaten you?"

I can see that the female-in-need-of-protection routine is working. I pile it on.

"When I first came to town, when Shane was in the hospital, and again later."

"You should have told me this before. We've been watching Ling's operations, but we haven't had a specific watch on Anton."

"I've been out of town, so he hasn't confronted me recently. But if he hears that I'm now back I'll probably get another visit from him."

Stokes chews on this information. He can't ignore a citizen reporting a threat, and I'm appealing to his male protective nature.

I provide a little more incentive. "Anton hates cops, and he's a convicted felon. He might still be on probation. He hates the mainstream, and only respects those who defy authority and live on the edge."

Stokes takes this all in, his square jaw set. "I'm aware of Anton's record. We just haven't seen enough of him around the labs to think he was a more important player in the operation. Usually, Ling only trusts Thai nationals with key positions. What makes you think Anton has a significant role in Ling's operation?"

"The gossips in the surf crowd say he's a big man in Ling's network. And when he confronted me he made it seem like he has Ling's ear."

"Well, we are making progress in our investigation of Ling. We've reduced his ability to supply his network by causing him to move his labs regularly. And we've gathered a lot of surveillance footage of him and his distributors. We'll get some of our surveillance guys to tail Anton too."

Just as Stokes finishes talking, his phone rings. He holds up a finger and picks up the receiver. "Stokes."

He listens for thirty seconds, puts down the receiver and abruptly stands up. "Something urgent has come up. I need to go." I stand and he immediately starts herding me out the door and down the hall. "You've given me some things to think about. Thank you for coming in."

He isn't really feeling the need to be polite; he just needs to get rid of me as quickly as possible. As we get to the exit door to the lobby, I see numerous other agents rushing out of offices, huddling and making some kind of hurried plan. I'm just happy the interview has been cut short.

I walk out to my car. I've just settled into the seat, when I see three unmarked dark sedans, with removable hood lights flashing and sirens blaring, come tearing out of the back of the parking lot. Stokes is visible in the third car. Hmm, perhaps Dylan will have heard what's going down? Or with this much law enforcement involved, whatever is happening will likely end up on the local TV news. Nothing ever happens in Half Moon Bay, and so the incident, whatever it is, will definitely be newsworthy.

Chapter 21

With Stokes off my back for now, I need to prep for my job interview tomorrow. And I want to connect with Wayne.

Once I'm settled in at the barn, I dial his cell. I get his voice mail, so I figure he's meeting with the ER doctor. I leave him a short message, telling him I've met with Stokes and more importantly I haven't been detained.

A quick Google search turns up no reports on the unfolding FBI drama. Next I settle in and start some research on World Business Report and its editor, Drew Upton. I find a few articles that confirm the company's funding and discuss the technology they've built to marry their news feeds to corporate networks. For a nascent operation, they seem to have garnered a fair amount of press. I can't decide if this is good or bad. It sets high expectations, which they'll be hammered for if they fail to meet them, and yet it builds brand awareness and buzz.

Drew's background is also easy to unearth. He has an impressive pedigree, including an Ivy League education and stints at several big media companies, where he rose through the ranks quickly. I dig deeper and find an old article that discusses his abrupt departure from the Chicago Daily. It's a sourced story, and the details are unconfirmed. But it suggests that he was fired, or "pushed out" (the polite term for fired), from the paper after a dispute over editorial ethics with the associate publisher, who also happens to be the publisher's son. Interesting.

Journalistic ethics aren't upheld by a legal system or governing body. They're upheld by tough editors, who sometimes have to say no to the business side of the publication, when pursuing an advertising opportunity compromises the paper's editorial integrity. But saying no to the person who signs your paychecks can get you fired. Clearly Drew knew this, and he did it anyway. That's a plus in my estimation.

Time for a break. Sitting on the bench outside the barn, I visit with the goats and mow down a sandwich. The goats bleat at me, eyeing my meal. But they give up and go back to sticking their head and necks through the fence, snagging every green shoot they can nail. When I hear my phone ring, I bound back up the loft stairs, reaching it just before it goes to voice mail.

"Ah, he-hello?"

"Dana, are you okay?"

Wayne hears me gasp once more as I catch my breath. "Yeah, I just ran up the loft stairs to get the phone. Where are you?"

"I'm back at Darrell's house. I met with the doc, but our conversation was cut short when she was called into the hospital. Apparently a drug gang had a shootout on the freeway, and a couple of gang members and three innocent commuters were shot."

Ah-ha, I didn't even have to wait for the local news to find out what pulled Stokes away from our interview. I explain to Wayne how my talk with Stokes got cut short, probably for the same reason.

"This drug lord isn't just running drugs and roughing up junkies, he's shooting people? Damn, Dana, this is scary. Is Stokes satisfied with the information you gave him? Do you think he'll subpoena you or Shane?"

"I can't say, but by the end of our conversation he was being a little less threatening. If his hands are full with this shootout that's a positive development for me, although I feel awful for those innocent people just driving along on the freeway."

"I do too. But this shooting makes me even more worried about you. Shane has been messing with some very dangerous and ruthless people. They're violent, and they're taking it well beyond broken bones, Dana. It looks like they'll do anything to protect what they have."

I already knew this, but I can't admit it because I haven't told Wayne any details about Ling, Anton or the poison *yaa baa*. I try to soothe him with Stokes' report of progress in his investigation. "Stokes seems confident that they're getting closer to busting Ling." Okay, it's a bit of an embellishment, but Stokes does seem sure that their pressure is impacting Ling's operation.

"I'll keep a low profile for the next few days, Wayne. I'll stay away from public places. And once I've gone for the job interview, I need to get back to L.A. and check on the loft and collect my mail. Meanwhile, you need to stop worrying about me. What did the doc say about the ER?"

"She says it's a good facility. It's inner city, so it's very busy; and the staff sees all types of patients. I consider that a plus. Management is stable, and they invest in their people and equipment. They even get a rotation of UC San Francisco med students coming through each semester to do internships, which is great for a hospital in a tough area."

"That's great, Wayne. You just need to convince them that they need a hunky male nurse who looks fabulous in scrubs."

He snickers, and the tension of the discussion about Ling eases a little.

"What's your plan for the rest of the afternoon? Do you need to spend more time researching the job?"

"I've done most of what I need to do. What are you thinking?"

"Darrell says there's a funky bar down in Pescadero that sounds fun. We could take my truck and keep your car off the road. Along the way, you could point out some of the local surf breaks for me."

*

We cruise down Highway 1 as I play surf guide. We stop in at three or four places, where I describe the swell directions that bring the best waves to each spot, whether there are underwater obstacles (rocks, pinnacles) to avoid, where the wave sets typically gather and the best places to paddle out. At one stop we hike across some grassy sand dunes to a rocky beach with tide pools. They're filled with urchins, hermit crabs, tiny fish and anemones. Two oyster catchers — black seabirds with bright orange feet — are snacking at the pools. They call to each other and take flight. Birds that make a permanent pairing...I could learn something from them.

By five, we're warming bar stools at the Flying Fish in Pescadero. Just as our beers come, the TV over the bar starts broadcasting the local five-o'clock news. The drug gang shoot-out on the highway leads the broadcast. The news channel shows some pre-recorded footage from the location of the shootout, the mangled cars, police vehicles, tow trucks and traffic. Then the feed goes live to a reporter at the hospital where Wayne may soon be employed. We temporarily abandon our beers and focus on the broadcast; the bartender turns around to watch.

A pert Asian reporter summarizes recent clashes between Asian drug gangs and Mexican drug suppliers. She says that this incident appears to be more of the same, but this time innocent bystanders were caught in the crossfire. Two adults and one toddler were hit by bullets in what witnesses describe as a hail of automatic weapon fire on the freeway and a three-car crash. The adults are in serious, but stable, condition. The toddler is still in surgery — no word yet as to whether he'll pull through. The reporter says the FBI has been able to interview the adult victims, but the press is still waiting for a statement from the feds. Two of the Asian gang members are in surgery; one of them is badly hurt. They have yet to be identified by law enforcement.

The reporter starts to introduce another pre-recorded witness statement, and halts mid-sentence as she hears through her earpiece that the head of the FBI drug gang task force, Agent Kevin Stokes, is about to begin his press briefing. She taps down the hospital hall with the cameraman following her. Stokes is standing behind five clustered microphones.

He holds up his hands to quiet the crowd. "Ladies and gentlemen, this will be a very brief statement, and we won't be taking any questions at this time. At roughly noon today, two cars began an altercation on the northbound lanes of Highway 101, north of San Francisco airport." He recaps everything we've already heard from the reporter, putting it all in that detached, clinical language that only law officers use. After a report on the shootout, the car crashes and the victims, he provides the only small nuggets of value in his media briefing.

"We are familiar with these gangs. We have been investigating them for some time. They are violent and ruthless predators, who have no respect for our laws, and they are supplying our community with methamphetamine and other drugs. Our investigation has resulted in the closure of more than a half a dozen meth labs and interruption in the supply and distribution of this highly addictive drug. It is an ongoing international criminal probe involving multiple countries, which we believe will result in the arrest and prosecution of criminal participants up and down the supply chain. We encourage anyone with information that may be important to our investigation to contact us via the FBI hotline, which will be displayed on this screen. Thank you."

He steps back from the microphones and, surrounded by other thick-necked agents, hustles down the hall toward the exit. Several reporters try calling out questions about the nationality of the gangs, the status of any arrests, and the identity of the two wounded gang members, but Stokes just strides out the double doors.

The bartender turns down the volume as the broadcast moves to a report about another car crash. Wayne and I stare at the varnished bar. I take a gulp of beer and look over at Wayne. He's staring into his glass, lost in thought. We need to talk about this, but we can't take any chance at being overheard. I rest my hand on his forearm, and he looks up at me. "Let's finish these beers and start back?" He waves the bartender over so he can pay him.

In the car, Wayne says, "Stokes is an imposing looking guy, but his speech was content-free."

"That's the way he operates...all take and no give."

A look of frustration moves across Wayne's face. "If you dissect what he said, it sounds like their task force is nowhere near ready to make high-level arrests."

"But this gang war will get him more money and resources. And he made it sound like they've made a big dent in the drug supply, when really their heat on Ling's operation has just spread labs to more locations."

"You really don't like the guy, do you?"

"It's his autocratic approach. FBI agents always want to use people, like Shane, and toss them away. And he'll bend the law to get what he wants. I believe we need law officers, I just wish the profession didn't always attract lugs like Stokes."

"But you also have trouble with authority."

"Well yeah, true."

"But forget all that. This whole situation with Ling's gang and the Mexicans is getting more and more dicey, Dana. You need to stay out of sight. In fact, you should leave the area."

"I can't argue with you. But I have that interview with World Business tomorrow. And they may want me to do more interviewing after that. It's a good opportunity, and journalism jobs are hard to come by."

Wayne keeps the truck at sixty-five miles per hour. "Will you at least stay out of sight as much as you can?"

I lean over and kiss his cheek. "Yes, Mom."

*

I arrive at World Business Report's offices, a new concrete-and-glass eight-story tower in the southernmost portion of the South of Market neighborhood of San Francisco, right on time at eleven o'clock. It's an area of the city that's undergone a big transformation in the past decade, from dilapidated warehouses to office buildings designed to appeal to trendy technology companies. Drew, wearing a sport coat and striped tie with his cuffed khakis, is short and a little round, with a double chin and dark, curly, salt-and-pepper hair. He brings me up to his office and explains that he has a series of interviews planned for me. First, I'll meet with him and his news editor together. Later, I'll chat with their vice president of technology. My ears perk up at this part of the schedule; I figure it speaks volumes about my shot at the job. Why would you waste this guy's time on just another job candidate?

The news editor, Jason, joins us immediately. He's a tall, painfully thin man with a silver mane of hair and rimless glasses. His shabby corduroy pants and well-worn button-down shirt scream "newsroom lifer." I like him immediately. For the next hour, we discuss the state of the world economy, my reporting from Davos, and the economic coverage needs of World Business.

My discussion with the technology chief, Tom, a late thirties- or forty-something man of Chinese heritage, lasts just a quarter hour. He makes no attempt to interview me; in fact he's obviously impatient with this interruption of his development duties and thus distracted the entire time. Drew collects me from Tom's office, and he and I walk to a deli around the corner from the tower. Over lunch, he says they have two paying corporate clients already, and he boasts that two others "are about to sign up."

"What's your burn rate, and how many months do you have at the current rate?" I ask. Burn rate is how much money the operation is burning over what's coming in.

Drew doesn't flinch. "I'd ask the same thing. We have enough funding for eighteen months, and that's without increasing our monthly revenue."

That's a decent cushion, and what the hell, given my current jobless status and the state of the news business, I can't be too picky.

On the way back to the office, he tries to gather a little information on my personal life. I provide a little color, revealing that I'm a surfer and I live in a flat in Santa Monica. I add that I'm a "free-range animal." He doesn't push for more details and walks me to a small conference room. Next, he says he'll send in the HR manager.

Nancy clicks into the room. She's clearly an HR manager because her make-up is perfect and she's wearing a conservative business suit and heels. She asks a few questions, confirming the dates of my employment at my last two jobs, the titles I held, and my responsibilities. After that, she dives into a lengthy description of a web news organization, and the high stress associated with sourcing content for multiple news feeds. I humor her and let her give me her serious little speech.

When she's done, I reassure her, "Nancy, I'm a lifer in the news business. Sure, the web is changing the business, but at the paper we had rolling deadlines for various pages. I live for deadline stress."

"Well, good. The information I just provided may have seemed unnecessary, but job candidates need to understand the pace of our company."

I nod. "Are there any other questions I can answer for you?"

"No, I think we're good. I'll go speak with Drew, and we'll be right back."

In no time, they're stepping into the room. Drew gets right to the point: "Dana, we're prepared to offer you the position of senior economics editor. And we'd like you to start in three weeks. We've already prepared a short offer letter."

At that, he pushes the one-page document across the table to me. I read it quickly and hold back the smile that wants to spring off my face. Not only am I getting a job, I'm getting a raise! From Mexico surf rat, and potential FBI person-of-interest, to gainfully employed in just over a week. And the benefits are generous, including three weeks of vacation per year. I only need to nail down one point, which came up briefly at lunch.

"As we outlined earlier, you're okay with me mostly telecommuting?"

Drew assures me that this job will involve travel and reporting from the road, so he's not going to demand I keep regular office hours. "You'll need to come in for meetings, but it's going to be a fluid schedule. You can take the offer letter home to mull it over."

I take a pen out of Nancy's manicured fingers and sign the contract.

*

Well before rush hour, I'm bouncing in the Honda on my way back to the coast, giddy at my new press credentials. I know I'm qualified and have skills, but I'm also extremely lucky to have landed a new journalism position before collecting my first unemployment check. And a job represents normalcy to me; it's the first step to getting back my life and moving past this latest chapter of the Shane saga. And if Wayne lands the ER job …?

On my way back to the loft, I stop in at a convenience store on the edge of town. After all that talking and trying to come off as sharp, witty and professional, I'm exhilarated but spent and terribly thirsty. I nab a juice from one of the coolers at the back of the store and am paying at the register when I see a jacked-up pick-up truck pull up, right behind my Honda, blocking it in. Anton drops out of the cab on the passenger side, and another tatted-up cretin with shoulder-length stringy brown hair and bug-eye sunglasses steps around the front from the driver's side. The middle-aged Korean store clerk immediately looks terrified — he's obviously seen these guys or others of their ilk before. I yell at him, "Call 9-1-1, NOW! I scan the store for a back exit, but it's too late. Anton is striding toward me. He grabs me roughly by the elbow and starts shoving me toward the glass door, which his sneering driver is holding open.

"We're going off to meet Ling. No more friendly chats with me, Dana, you missed your chance." I pull my arms in tight and drag my feet, as terror grips me.

Chapter 22

My gut tells me that this time I'm going to get hurt, either here or probably much worse wherever they're taking me. I figure better to make a scene here. I never wear heels, but today for my interview I did. I put them to use for the only thing they're good for, other than sore feet. As we near the truck, I stomp hard with my pointy heel on the ball of Anton's left foot, breaking the heel. When he grunts and loosens his grip on me, I spin away from him.

But he doesn't let go all the way, so I spin down to the ground, pull free and start crawling away from him, in between my car and the truck-bed. I can hear the driver running around the other side of the truck toward me. But instead of reaching down and pulling me up, he kicks me hard in the ribs and growls, "Bad move, bitch. We're going to make you suffer for that one." Anton has recovered. He leans down and punches the side of my face as I futilely try to crab crawl backwards, under the Honda's bumper. I'm stunned for a moment, but as the driver reaches down to pull me away from the back of the car, I recover enough to kick at his hands and face so he's unable to get a grip on my ankles. Anton comes around the front of the Honda and is behind his driver.

While I'm kicking furiously and screaming "NO!" I hear a car bounce through the parking lot entrance, tires squealing. Anton's driver immediately drops to the ground and rolls under the truck bed, but Anton is out in the open. Time seems to stop as the sound of gunfire fills my head. It comes in two separate bursts from the car, and I hear bullets ping off the truck and hit the ground. I hear single shots to my right as Anton's driver returns fire from under the truck. But the car doesn't stop; it doesn't even slow down. It just accelerates by us and bounces back out the parking lot entrance and races away.

I've lost all ability to think like a human; I'm just an animal trying to avoid being prey. I see Anton lying face up on the asphalt, bleeding. His mouth is open and he's gasping; his eyes are wide and rolling. There's blood seeping out from his side, and some spurting from his left thigh. The sight momentarily stops me, because I've never seen blood spurt. Then I notice that there's blood on my left hand. I'm confused because I'm not that close to Anton.

Sirens, increasing in volume, fill my brain. Three police squad cars pull to the edge of the lot in a line and make a barrier. From behind the cars, one of the officers screams out, "Drop your weapon, NOW!"

Anton's driver yells, "Don't shoot, don't shoot." I hear something skid across the asphalt.

A different voice yells to me. "Ma'am, stay down."

"Okay, I'm unarmed. They were trying to take me."

"Just stay down."

The next few minutes are a blur. Peering from under the truck, I see two officers, with their guns drawn, rush up to the driver, who's laying face-down on the asphalt with his arms and legs spread. One keeps a gun drawn on him, as the other one yanks his arms behind his back and cuffs him. He sits on the guy's back and pushes his face into the pavement. "Stay still and don't move." The scene seems to be moving in slow motion like a film, one I can't comprehend I'm in.

The third officer, who's covering all of this from a safe position behind one of the patrol cars, calls out to me again. "Ma'am, don't move; he's coming over to you." His voice pulls my addled brain back to real time.

The officer crouches low and creeps around the front of the Honda, near Anton's head. I turn my gaze again to Anton.

His eyes are fixed, staring into the sky. The officer scuttles over to him, still in a crouch with his gun drawn, and checks his pulse on his neck. He calls out to the other two. "I think this one is dead."

He turns to me. I'm still on my hands and knees, and I'm starting to shake all over. But before he comes over he checks Anton for a gun and finds an automatic pistol stuffed in the back of his pants behind his T-shirt. The attack happened so fast, he couldn't reach for his gun. The officer tosses the gun out in the open.

"Are you hurt?" He scuttles up to me.

"I don't know." I sit back on my butt and lean against the fender. I look more closely at my left hand and arm. There's blood dripping down my hand to the pavement. And my suit jacket is torn at the shoulder. I reach up with my right hand and touch the tear; my right hand comes back bloody and I notice a burning on my left shoulder. "I might be shot." I'm dumbfounded. I stare at the blood spots on the pavement, my blood. My right leg starts to jump up and down uncontrollably and bile rises in my throat.

First, he pats me down, and makes sure I don't have any weapons. After that, he bends close and examines my shoulder. Reaching across his chest, he presses the button on his shoulder-mounted radio transmitter. "Patrol 21. We need an ambulance at the QuickShop at the corner of Seabird and Highway 1. Shooting victim down. And we need the coroner's van. One deceased, multiple gunshot wounds." The dispatcher acknowledges the call. The officer yells over his shoulder to the patrolman back at the police cruisers. "All clear, I'm bringing the victim out."

"Okay, let's get you back to the patrol cars and away from all this." He reaches under my armpit to help me up and I yelp, loudly. "The driver kicked me, and I think he may have broken my ribs." Leaning into him, we shuffle quickly to one of the cruisers.

Once we're around the far side, he opens a door and helps me into the back seat. He grabs a first-aid kit from the trunk, drops it on the ground and pulls out a package containing a large gauze pad. He rips it open and hands a pad to me. "Press this firmly against your shoulder." I whimper, as I do as instructed.

"Can you tell me what happened? Do you know these two guys?"

"The dead one is Anton Krause, a local thug. I've never seen the other one before."

"The store clerk called 9-1-1. He said they were abducting you." His eyebrows raise.

"I'm not sure. It all happened so fast. They definitely wanted to threaten me, and they pulled me from the store." I'm not lying, not exactly; I just don't want to make this more dramatic and newsworthy. Even in shock, I realize I need Agent Stokes; I don't want to become the news story. And I don't want to harm his investigation of Ling by saying too much.

"Krause has threatened me before. Agent Kevin Stokes of the FBI knows about it. They've been watching Krause, and others that he works with, as part of a drug gang investigation. Can you call him?"

*

The ER doc, a slight Indian man, says the bullet just grazed my shoulder and it only needs disinfecting and stitches. He examines my face. It's bruised, swollen and likely to swell more, but he assures me my eye is fine and no facial bones are broken. He orders X-rays to check my ribs and internal organs. An orderly wheels me to the X-ray room, and I yelp as they move me from the gurney to the table. The pain takes my breath away with each turn I make for the X-ray technician. The doc can't give me any pain medication until he determines whether I have any internal damage that might require surgery. But my X-rays come through the hospital's network quickly and he discusses the images with me as he's viewing them.

"Your two lowest right ribs are bruised and one has a hairline crack. It will heal on its own. I'm more concerned with your left kidney, which is swollen. We need to check your urine for blood, which I expect we'll see. We'll watch it to make sure it's still operating. We can give you some pain medicine now. A physician's assistant will clean and stitch your arm. You'll need to stay here overnight."

He reaches down and squeezes my right hand. "You'll be okay. We're going to take good care of you." I need the reassurance. The shock of the attack, the shooting and my injuries are overwhelming my brain and body. I keep replaying the scene in my head; every loud noise I hear sounds like gunfire and I jump repeatedly as I hear exam room doors open and close. I see Anton's face in death and the blood pooling under him.

A young Hispanic nurse gives me two Vicodin and an antibiotic tablet. She helps me undress and bags my clothes. I pee in a bed pan and she collects a sample of my dark, possibly bloody urine for the lab analysis — I'm shaking too badly to pee in a cup. The physician's assistant, another India immigrant, comes into the room. Her ebony, kohl-lined eyes have dark circles, and a wavy black ponytail splits the middle of her back. She efficiently sets up a tray next to my left shoulder with instruments, gauze and suture. "Hi, I'm Radja." She warns me of the needle stick as she numbs my shoulder.

I'm generally not squeamish, so I eyeball the damage as she cleans it. The tear in my skin is close to the top of my shoulder and it's about three-quarters of an inch wide and nearly three inches long. The bullet tore through most of the skin, but the muscle isn't visible. She asks me if the Vicodin is helping with my other pain, as she waits for the numbing agent to kick in before she starts to stitch my shoulder.

"It's easing a little. I just don't want anyone to move me again until I can't feel it." She assures me that she won't let that happen. She prods my shoulder lightly and asks if I can feel anything. I shake my head and she starts sewing.

Later, when I'm fully dazed from the drugs, they move me upstairs to a private room. I think I've lucked out, but the orderly says that law enforcement has requested I be isolated. I sense Stokes' hand in this. "Are there officers here?"

The orderly is quiet, as he tucks me into my bed. Clearly, he isn't sure if I'm a criminal or a victim. He makes up his mind. "There's an officer seated at your door. We couldn't move you up here until he arrived. And another officer, Stokes, is waiting to speak with you."

"I'll see Stokes whenever you're ready to let him in." But before that happens, the shift nurse comes in and introduces himself, Byron. He's a slight twenty-something young man who looks about seventeen. He has multiple small hoop earrings in each ear and his dyed spikey blond hair gives him a new-age crown of thorns. He takes my vitals, checks the monitors and scribbles onto my chart. At last, he stops moving and looks intently at me. "So you're ready to speak with your visitor? If you're not up to it, we will make him wait."

My tongue rolls around some syllables and finally assembles them into words. "Thanks for that, but I need to talk to him. Please tell him to come in."

Byron tilts his head toward the remote on my bed "You have your call-button; if it gets to be too much, buzz me." He strides out of the room. I hear some mumbling in the corridor and Agent Stokes fills the narrow hall into my room. For once, he actually looks circumspect, and he enters the room slowly, his head down. When he reaches my bedside, his first words are full of empathy and regret, which makes them startling coming from him. "Dana, I am so sorry for this. How are you feeling?"

"Like I've been run over by a speed boat. But the doc says the damage won't require any more treatment, other than the stitches I've already received and some rest. I'm sure they've informed you of my condition."

He dips his head. "Can you tell me exactly what happened?" For once, he doesn't try to demand a report, he asks politely. I run through everything, including that I asked the local police to call him. His surprise at this detail is obvious. He asks if I saw the car the shooters were driving. "A Nissan Maxima, black with blacked-out windows. I didn't see the license plate." I got a glimpse of the driver, but all I can say about him is that he was Hispanic, with short hair and wearing dark glasses.

"I need your help." I slur and rub the back of my hand across my mouth.

"Whatever we can do."

"I've heard there's an officer outside my room. I assume that's for my protection, not because you're trying to keep me here?"

"Yes, he's here to keep you safe."

"Can you keep my name and face out of the papers and off TV? I don't want to become the story. I'm just a victim in this drug war, Agent Stokes. And I don't want to rub my escape in Ling's face and give him a reason to make another run at me."

Unlike TV journalists, I've never wanted to be the story. I see my role in the traditional mold of print journalists: objective observer. More importantly, I don't want Shane to hear about this incident and come back to town seeking revenge. Nor do I want my new employers to wonder how a business reporter ends up in the middle of a drug war.

"I've told everyone involved in the investigation to keep your name confidential. Once you're able, you should leave town for a while."

Perhaps he's truly concerned for my safety after this violent attack, but even in my drugged state I work out that he probably doesn't need Shane or me anymore. Ling's operation is under attack. Anton is dead, and he has the truck driver. He's not Thai, and I bet he's cut some kind of deal with the feds and is already feeding them intel. But I don't mention this. I'm happy to benefit from the new, kinder Stokes, and his protection.

Stokes says they've towed my car to a crime-processing area, but they should be done with it tomorrow. And he asks, again politely, if I'll repeat my statement to another agent, one of his underlings, who will write up the incident report.

"Sure. Can we do it sooner rather than later? I'm likely to crash soon from the pain pills they gave me."

"He's right outside. If you're okay with it I'll ask him in, and we'll go through it one more time. I'd like to stay and hear it all again." I nod.

He goes and gets the other agent, who's carrying a notepad and tape recorder. I go through the whole story again, stating it nearly word-for-word the same way as I did the first time. It's a talent I've developed as a reporter — I can replay quotes and statements from interviews in my head and regurgitate them.

The junior agent leaves, and Stokes says, "Dana, I'm very sorry about this attack. We are going to apprehend Ling and these Mexican gang members. They've given us too many leads, and this outrageous violence is going to rain down a huge amount of law enforcement on them. Will you consider my suggestion and leave town?"

"Yes. I need to go home for a while anyway. I'm hoping to be released from the hospital tomorrow."

"Well, while you're in town we will have a team watching you. If you call me tomorrow, and the car is finished being processed, I'll have some agents deliver it to you."

"Thank you. Is my Honda injured too?"

"Is has two bullet holes in the right bumper, but the car is mechanically sound."

I stare at him, stunned and speechless. My aged Honda took a bullet for me, actually it took two. It may have saved my life. I'm keeping that car. Every day it will remind me of second chances. Before I can choke them back, tears stream down my face. It's the first time I've cried since the attack, but it won't be the last. Stokes reaches out and squeezes my right hand. "You've been through a lot, and it's going to take time to process it all. Have you called anyone yet?"

"Not yet. I wouldn't let the nurses do it because I didn't want them to scare my friend and put him in a panic."

"Always taking care of others, Dana. What about you? A piece of advice...if there's a man in the picture, don't be so tough. He's going to want to take care of you, and you should let him. It's what men want to do. We need to be the knight, even if you usually don't need it."

Wow, Stokes does have a heart inside that Kevlar-vested exterior. He has me write out names of potential visitors for my guard. He gently squeezes my hand again and walks out of the room.

I rub my face and take a couple of deep breaths. I grab my cellphone and dial Wayne.

He answers on the second ring, "Hi, gorgeous."

"Hi, baby, are you at Darrell's?"

"Yeah. You sound funny. What's up?"

I tear up again, so I hesitate. I decide I'll just tell him where I am and leave the details vague until he gets here. "I'm in Community Hospital. I've been hurt, but I'm going to be absolutely fine. They just want to keep me here overnight to run some tests."

"Whuh-what, when? What happened?"

"I'd rather tell you when I see you. I'm fine, really. But can you come?"

Wayne is very intuitive, and he instinctively knows there's something big I'm not saying. "I'm on my way now."

"Okay. Thanks, babe. See you soon." I consider calling Dylan, but decide I'll wait until after I see Wayne. I wonder if Maria is working today, and if she'll get word that I'm here? Since she's in the ICU, she may be very busy and isolated from the rest of the hospital. I could mention something to Byron, but I'm drifting from the pain medication.

I'm in a drugged half-sleep when Wayne arrives. He gets grilled and patted down by the officer at my door, despite being on the list of potential visitors. He kisses the unbruised side of my face. His whole body is tense and his brows are knit tight.

I start by once again reassuring him. "I'm going to be fine. I might look like a prize fighter, but the doc promises me it will all heal."

"I read your chart before you woke up. They're watching that kidney. How is the pain in your side and your shoulder?"

Wayne sounds like the nurse he's become. "Well if you read my chart, you know they've given me Vicodin. And the numbing stuff they injected into my shoulder before they stitched it hasn't worn off yet. I'm doing okay. Better since you're here." I attempt to smile, with the un-swollen side of my face.

"If you grab my sippy cup off the tray for me, I'll tell you the whole story." He hands me the cup, and helps me raise the bed up. I gasp, as my body bends and my ribs move. Once more, I run through the whole story, from the time I entered the convenience store to the ER. At the end, I stammer when I say again, "I'll be fine," not because I don't believe it but because Anton is dead and I'm here among the living. I start to cry again. Meanwhile, Wayne's eyes get darker and darker, and his lips form a grim line. He's living through the attack with me. He's outraged.

Next, I describe my visit from Stokes. "He was really apologetic and kind, Wayne. It's a little hard to reconcile, considering how he behaved before. And he suggested I get out of town as soon as I'm released from the hospital."

"Well, we sure as hell don't need his blessing for that, after what a spectacularly bad job he and his team did tracking Anton." Wayne spits these words.

"After your interview, can we head for L.A.?"

"Who cares about my interview? We need to get you out of town as soon as you can travel."

"But they won't let me out of here until after doctors' rounds tomorrow at the earliest. And your interview is early. There's no reason for you to blow it off, Wayne. Please?" He's still stiff, defiant, but I see he's at least considering my plan.

"You saw the security I have; I'm safe here, Wayne." He cocks his head slightly, acknowledging my words and logic, even though his emotions are still raging too hard for him to verbally agree. Just then, Maria comes charging into the room.

"Dana, my god. I just heard the whole story from one of the nurses. Ah, chica, I was so scared when I first heard you were here. I came as soon as I could get a break from my rounds. But you're going to be just fine. How is the pain?" She immediately goes into nursing mode, too, and I turn and look at Wayne.

"It's fine." Thankfully, she's already heard most of the story and doesn't ask me to recap it.

"Byron is one of our best nurses, Dana. You are in very good hands."

"And as if you and Byron aren't enough, I have another nurse too." I tilt my head at Wayne. "He's just graduated from nursing school, Maria, and tomorrow he's going for a second interview for an ER nursing job at Mercy Hospital."

She turns to Wayne, and as always Maria doesn't hold back. "You didn't mention this before Mexico? You're as bad as Dana at sharing information."

Then, she looks him up and down. "You're perfect for the ER."

"He wants to cancel or reschedule the interview because of me and my injuries, Maria, but that's completely unnecessary because I'm here, with you and my guard dog in the hall though midday tomorrow at least. You have to help me convince him to go to the interview. It's bad enough that this happened, but if he lets it screw up his chances at his first nursing job, I'll be really pissed."

Again, I can always count on Maria's candor. "Wayne, Mercy is a good hospital. This job is a great first step. As much as I hate to admit it, Dana is right. She's in good hands here, and you know how she is. If you hover too much she will just punish you for it."

Wayne can't help but chuckle at this last line; he relaxes just a little. Maria says she has to get back to the ICU, but will check in again with me at the end of her shift. The trauma, pain and drugs have all taken their toll, and I can't hold my eyes open any longer. I give in to sleep. When I wake up it's dark outside, and I desperately need to pee. The pain in my ribs and kidney area alternates between just awful and excruciating. Wayne immediately notices my set jaw, and he calls Byron for me. After I swallow the pills, Wayne helps me to the bathroom. I pee, and my urine seems a normal yellow color, though Bryon asks me to collect a sample for the lab. My face, however, is very swollen and already turning shades of black and blue.

Once I'm settled back in the bed, I notice a large bunch of yellow roses on a rolling table at the head of my bed. I kiss Wayne and thank him. On my tray are surfing and diving magazines, though I can't imagine that the hospital stocks these in its gift shop. I ask where he got them, but Wayne says "Your posse is pretty awesome, Dana," and he explains that Maria called Dylan, and he called Craig, who delivered the magazines while I was asleep. He also says that Maria came by again. She said that Dylan wants to talk to me, and when I'm feeling up to it I should call him. And he says Maria gave him great advice on what to say and not say at his interview tomorrow.

"She's really knowledgeable, Dana. ICU is one of the toughest nursing jobs in the hospital, and she's a lead in the department here."

"And she doesn't take any crap."

"Obviously. Are you hungry? You missed the meals on wheels, but Byron assures me he can get you a tray."

"I'm not hungry, but I'm very thirsty. And my face is pulsing from the swelling."

"I'm on it." He disappears, and comes back with an ice pack. Byron shows up shortly after that with a chocolate milkshake to "numb the inside as well as the outside...Wayne's idea. He's going to make a great nurse."

"Wow, you already have quite the fan club, babe!" I slurp the milkshake and insist that Wayne share some it with me. Once it's drained, I call Dylan.

He asks how I'm feeling, then fills me in. "I've called Stokes, and Craig and I will take care of the Honda. Stokes will deliver it to Craig's house tomorrow, and Craig will store it out of sight in his garage until you're well enough to retrieve it. Or we can just get rid of it?"

"No, absolutely not!" It's irrational, but the Honda has become more than a car to me. It's passed through a metaphysical plane too...between one life and the next. It's my touchstone, and it's staying with me for as long as I can keep it running. Dylan also called Joe and Terry, and they're going to come and visit me in the morning. He knew that I would need more time before I would want to deal with my family, which is usually more draining than reassuring.

"Do you want to hear about what's happened since the shootout?"

I huff. "I am a reporter, Dylan."

He says Stokes is being much more open with him now too. The driver, who is on probation, is feeding Stokes intelligence on Ling's operation. Stokes says he's going back to jail no matter what, it's just a matter of for how long. He's trading information to try to get the best deal he can.

"That means he'll plead out, Dana. You won't ever have to testify in court against him." This is a huge relief for me. Dylan says that there's so much heat on Ling from law enforcement and the rival Mexican gang that Stokes believes I'm no longer a high priority. In fact, the driver says that it was actually Anton's idea to try to grab me and bring me as a trophy to Ling.

Nonetheless, Dylan agrees with Stokes that I should leave town as soon as I'm released from the hospital.

"Wayne is all over that, Dylan." Wayne can hear both sides of the conversation and looks at me when I say this.

"I'll keep you informed, Dana. I really do think Stokes is now going after Ling with every resource. Get away from here and heal. Let Wayne take care of you." I end the call. Much to my embarrassment, I tear up again. Wayne squeezes my hand and kisses it.

"You didn't know I could be such a baby, right?"

"Dana, don't beat yourself up. You're going to be processing all of this for a while." I don't admit it, but I can't get the shootout and Anton's dead eyes out of my head. Even with all the painkillers and the sleep, I'm still jumpy.

Visiting hours are officially over, but Maria pulled some strings and Wayne has permission from the staff and my guard to stay with me in my room overnight. They've brought in a roll-away bed for him. He helps me get up again, and we squeeze into the bathroom and brush our teeth together, which feels very intimate.

I awake a couple of times in the middle of the night to intense dreams that replay parts of the attack. Wayne holds my hand after I awake suddenly one time, yelling and shaking. Once I crash again, I make it through to morning without any more nightmares. By six thirty, Wayne needs to get going so he can get back to Darrell's to change and drive to his interview. He's still hesitant to leave me, but he realizes I'll be like a feral cat, all claws, if he doesn't go. At last, it dawns on me that I haven't told him about my interview...or I should say my new job.

I quickly give him the details and throw down the challenge, "So you have to get this job, because I don't want a long-distance relationship and I don't date slackers."

"Wow, that's fantastic, Dana! Congratulations. And yep, I'm determined to land this job." He looks at his watch and jumps up. "And I have to go!" He kisses me and runs out the door, promising over his shoulder that he'll call as soon as he's finished. I ring the nurse and ask if I can shower — Maria says she'll bring me fresh clothes later today. In the bathroom mirror, I examine the bruises that have bloomed on my ribs and stomach. My ribs hurt every time I move, but my kidney seems to be functioning normally. I also examine my battered face. My cheekbone is bluish green, under my eye is black and my cheek is swollen as if I have a large wad of chaw tucked alongside my teeth.

I'm back in bed, icing the side of my face while I read the surfing magazine, when Joe knocks and peers around the entry hall's corner. "Dana, can we come in?"

"Yeah, Dad."

He walks slowly over to the bed, taking in my face and my bandaged shoulder. Terry is two steps behind him. Joe leans down and kisses the top of my head. Terry comes to the far side of the bed and squeezes my hand.

"Hell of a thing." Joe often starts sentences in the middle. "Dylan told us what happened. And the shooting has been on the news."

"But they kept my name out of it, right?"

"Yes. They said law enforcement is protecting your identity. And your guard made us sign in, and he patted us down."

"Yeah, everyone who comes to see me gets the free law-enforcement massage."

"How are you feeling? Dylan said you were shot." He looks confused as he says "shot." I'm sure it's a word he never expected would come out of his mouth in relation to his daughter. Terry just looks like he'd like to be anywhere else; his face is flush, and when he takes his hand away from mine I notice it's shaking. He stuffs it in his pants pocket.

"I'm okay. My shoulder was grazed and only needed stitches."

Terry joins the conversation, but he chimes in by spitting out an accusation. "You wouldn't be here if it wasn't for Shane's latest mess." He's right, but I can't heal from this ordeal by getting angry with my damaged brother. And I won't embrace Terry's anger because it comes from deep-seated childhood jealously and resentment. It's not righteous; it's petty. And right now I just need us to be a family, flawed though we are, and support one another.

"Please don't. Yesterday was one of the most shocking days of my life, and for once I need our family to pull together, not apart. Okay?" Terry looks sheepish and studies his shoes.

Joe reaches out and pats my forearm. Then he whispers. "Shane is gone?" I just nod.

I don't want to say anything more, so I change the subject. "Okay, this is an odd addition to yesterday's events: I have a new job, in San Francisco." I talk about World Business, how the news service works and what my new job will entail. Joe asks when I will move back up north, and I say that they want me to start in three weeks. I explain that

I'll head down to L.A. as soon as I get out of the hospital. I mention Wayne, but don't go into details. After that, we all fall into an uncomfortable silence. The three of us are family, but we aren't friends. Thankfully, the shift nurse, Ruth, a matronly woman with a head of dark curls and oversize glasses, arrives and announces she needs to change the bandage on my shoulder. Joe kisses my head again, Terry waves and they're gone.

After Ruth cleans and repackages my shoulder, which is tight and feels as though I've been filleted by a butcher, the ward doctor arrives. She reviews my last set of lab tests, my chart, asks detailed questions about my urination and closely examines my face. She's all business, and I feel like I'm a package of steak being examined for freshness and appropriate color. I'm given a passing rating, certainly not USDA prime. My kidney is functioning, but she wants me to avoid salty foods and alcohol. She examines my bruised torso, and her eyes widen at its rainbow of colors. She assures me that this is part of the healing. Every prod releases a shot of pain, though I try not to react. She looks at Ruth, not me, and says I can be released. But hospitals love their paperwork and another hour goes by before the patient liaison (read: money collector), comes and begins going over all my insurance forms.

Patience is not one of my virtues, especially when it comes to overly complicated bureaucracy. Thank god Maria drops by during this process, bringing me a fresh set of clothes. She helps me sort through the mound of exit forms, and the liaison finally signs my release order. Wayne texts: "Finished with interviews. Have you been cleared to leave?"

I want to ask him how the interviews went, but I feel like a cornered animal. I'm in a near frenzy to get away from the well-meaning but annoying watchers. The job discussion will have to wait. "Yes!!! Please get me the hell out of here." No more than twenty seconds go by and the phone pings. "On my way, Babe, escape is imminent. Xxx W."

I dress, which isn't a straightforward process when you have a cracked rib and a shoulder that doesn't move well. And I spend a little time at the bathroom mirror, putting on make-up that Maria has brought me. When I'm done, from a distance, my face is less startling — but close up it's about as effective as someone putting a thin layer of paint over a bad wall stain.

Wayne arrives, but there's one more snag to my discharge — my bodyguard needs to notify Stokes, and like a secret service agent he has a very forceful opinion about how we should exit the hospital. He arranges for us to use the service elevator to the basement, where there's a bay door for deliveries. He sends Wayne ahead to bring the car to the service bay, and another agent will be there as well, with a car to tail us. He puts me on the phone with Stokes. "Dana, I'm glad you're well enough to leave the hospital. What are your plans?"

"You probably think I never listen, but we're leaving town as fast as we can collect my stuff from Dylan's house. My friend Wayne is driving me in his truck and we're off to L.A."

"Good. As I said before, I believe Ling is no longer focused on you, but out of an abundance of caution I'd like my men to escort you as far as Gilroy, okay? I've also spoken to Dylan and warned him that agents will check his home before you arrive."

"I'm happy to have your help." I mean it. Just talking about Ling has made me shudder involuntarily.

"And when you arrive in L.A., please call me. I've already taken the precaution of having agents in L.A. check the exterior of your house. They assure me that it's secure."

I'm not sure I believe his agents just checked the "exterior" of my condo, but at this point I don't really care. I'm a privacy freak, but I don't have anything to hide...other than Shane. And there's nothing at the barn loft or my Santa Monica flat that would lead them to him. Having the FBI expend the effort to make sure that Wayne and I aren't walking into a trap or ambush is reassuring and frightening at the same time.

"I will call from L.A. Thank you for everything you're doing."

"Be well."

Larry, my bodyguard who looks like a former wrestler, average height but all bunched up muscle, is waiting with an orderly who's leaning on a wheel chair. I notice that Larry's lightweight blazer has a distinctive bump under his left arm. He's no talker and simply asks, "Ready?" I ease into the wheel chair's seat.

The ride though the hospital is a blur. I'm happy to be leaving, but I'm scared too. I've been trying to stuff my fears and flashbacks away, but the discussion of the security plans has brought it all rushing back. And once again I have the sensation of being the center of attention, with zero control. We make our way through the bowels of the hospital. Wayne is waiting at the loading dock, pacing and looking as jumpy as I am. The area is completely clear, except for him and the other agent and his unmarked navy sedan. Wayne helps me into the truck, and we're off to Dylan's. He packed before his interviews.

Larry joins the other agent in the sedan, which tails us at a discreet distance. When we arrive at the barn, I pack up my computer bag and Wayne puts the few clothes I've hung up into my roller bag with the rest of my things. Clearly, I won't be diving for a while, and I leave the open dive bag where it lies. Larry stands at the base of the loft stairs as we pack while his partner watches the approach to the house and loft from behind a large tree near the front of the lot. Instead of these precautions making us feel secure, we're on edge. Once we've driven across the hill to Highway 280, we start to calm down and breathe, but we barely speak.

The feds stick with the Stokes-approved plan and follow us to the edge of Gilroy, where they pull up alongside our car. Larry gives a quick wave as they accelerate to the next exit, cross over the freeway and circle back the other way. I turn and watch them reverse course, thanking them in my mind. Wayne reaches out, grabs my hand and kisses the back of it. We try to re-enter the nonviolent world — or, at least, the fantasy that such a place exists.

After a few more miles of humming tires puts distance between us and Ling's violent world, I break the silence. "What happened at the interview? Please tell me we have something to celebrate?"

He starts to give me the blow-by-blow...what time he arrived, who was in the group interview...but deliberate storytelling is for those who trust they have a lot of time. I've lost that faith. So I beg. "Please, Wayne, cut to the chase. I could use some good news."

"I start the week before you do." I bounce just a little in my seat despite the complaining ribs, and gingerly lean over and kiss his cheek and the side of his grinning mouth.

Mom, I'm still here. Someone tried to help me join you, but the Honda interfered. I made Shane safe, but it cost me.

Now your brave warrior is terrified. How much more am I supposed to do for him?

I have a chance to move forward in my own life. Shouldn't that be a priority too? There's a man, Mom, and he wants to be my partner and my guardian. He is sensitive and kind, and he doesn't try to control me. He loves me as I am. Who knew that combination was even possible?

Of course, I already tried to push him away, but he's stubborn and he wouldn't go. So even though I'm afraid of failure I'm fighting to control it. I'm trying to give in to this. I'm trying to let love come into my life.

Chapter 23

Wayne supplies all the details of his two-hour group interview. He finishes by saying, "I'm pretty sure they'd made up their mind about me before I got there. All I had to do was avoid screwing it up."

I want to ask about the money, but I don't want to pry. I don't care how much he makes; I just want him to be satisfied with the salary.

We arrive at my loft in the early evening, and the darkness makes us both jumpy. Mail is splayed across the entryway — it feels like I haven't been here in a lifetime, which in some ways is true. I've been to Zurich, Half Moon Bay, Port Townsend, Baja...and hell.

I should call Stokes as promised, but I really don't want to hear anything about the Ling investigation or get into any discussion that brings on more flashbacks. I text him instead: "Home in SM. All is fine. Will stay in touch, D."

*

Wayne heads up to Malibu to give notice to his landlady, Sarah, and his clients. I call Sandy at the Herald. Luckily I connect with her on the first try and I describe the new job. She's excited for me. "You're lucky you're not here. Since the layoffs, the atmosphere is pure poison, Dana. And another round of cuts is coming."

I've decided to rent the loft. Much as I like the clean-sweep approach to change — new job, new town, new man — I don't want to deal with selling the place right now and rents are so strong that I'm sure it will cash flow. Plus, startups are notoriously flaky; I need time to truly believe that World Business is a real media company, and not just a promising business plan.

I consider calling property management companies. But they'll want to tour the potential rental, and I'm not ready to deal with strangers yet. Instead, I decide to catch up with Rayan. I haven't seen him or spoken with him since his party.

"Dana, you gypsy, I've missed you. What's happening?"

The answer to that question is way too dramatic and complicated for a phone chat. But I do tell him about the new job, though I leave out the details of my short stint among the unemployed. Both Rayan and I have a love/hate relationship with Southern California; he's not at all surprised that I'll be moving back up north.

"Where will you live? Half Moon Bay?"

"No, I don't think so." Again, I don't want to share the Ling story and as I'm talking with him I realize that I don't want to live in my hometown...too much drama, both recent and past. "I'll probably look in Pacifica." I mention that I plan to rent the loft until I'm certain that the new job is a good fit and the company is stable.

"Hmm...I might be able to help with that." He says a music producer he's known for decades, C.J., needs a rental. He's working in L.A. for the next six months or so while he produces a new artist's first album. And he's finalizing another producing contract with a nineties rock band. My brain immediately envisions drug-fueled jam sessions at the loft, but before my imagination runs wild stereotyping anyone who works in the music business, Rayan anticipates my angst. "He's a 48-year-old vegan music nerd, Dana. And he's a happily married gay man and ridiculously tidy — I've seen his co-op in New York. Hotels are hideously expensive and good short-term rentals are extremely hard to find. This could be a perfect fit for both of you."

"It makes a lot of sense, Rayan. When will he be here?"

"He's actually in town for the next five days. Do you want to meet him?"

While we've been talking, I've been pacing around the loft. I stop in front of the mirror at the top of the entry stairs. My face is better today; the bruises are already fading from blue to a pale yellow. With just a little make-up, I should be presentable in another day or two.

"Why don't you come for dinner here the day after tomorrow? Bring C.J. and he can see the place. And you can meet my friend Wayne too."

"Terrific. Wayne, huh? Ooh, intriguing. Girlfriend, you've been holding out on me."

*

I start my packing process by just doing an inventory, room by room, of what I'll be taking with me. I desperately need to be outside, so I go out to the garage and start there. I've only been at it for four or five minutes when I hear the loud squeal of tires, as a car rockets down my street and makes a sharp turn at the corner. Suddenly I'm on the ground crab-crawling backward. I can't breathe, and I swear I hear gunshots. Anton's dead face appears in my mind. I mash the base of my palms into my eyes, trying to force the image away. Despite the fact that the man was a vicious animal, I'm still horrified by his senseless death. And for what? So one band of criminals can sell more drugs than its rival?

I stuff down my panic, and go back inside. To drown out any other traffic noise, I crank up the stereo. I'm nearly finished with my inventory when my cellphone rings. It's a number I don't recognize, but I dial back the stereo and answer it anyway.

"Dana? It's Shane. How long can we talk?" We'd discussed the possibility of law enforcement tracking my calls to try to locate him. His phone is a throw-away that he'll ditch when he's burned through its pre-loaded calling minutes. But it's still best to avoid suspicious numbers appearing on my call list.

"Wow, it's great to hear your voice. And we can talk a little. Things have changed a lot since you left." I detail the mounting drug war between Ling and the Mexicans and I mention that the FBI now has a Ling informant. I leave out any details about the shootout, my injuries and how they turned this individual into a snitch.

"I knew this was building when I left, Dana." Ah-ha. That's what he was hinting at just before he and Garrett sailed off.

"You're no longer the FBI's favorite person of interest, Shane."

"That's great news, sis." The conversation stalls a moment, as Shane weighs what he should and shouldn't say. "My travels were smooth." Good, that's nice and vague; clearly the crossing went well. "I'm working, and I'm clean. My brothers have come through for me."

"Fantastic, Shane!" I need this good news; I'm not going to let any skepticism invade my brain and impede my happiness. "Brothers" clearly means his surf family, which likely means he's still in Kauai. But I can't ask him any specific questions.

I chime in. "I've landed a new job." I quickly describe World Business, adding that I'll be moving back to Northern California.

He can't help getting in a dig at L.A., "Well done. I knew you'd land on your feet. And thank god you're leaving Smogland. But I wish you weren't moving up north quite so soon. Ling's turf battle with the Mexicans isn't going to end until one of them cripples the other's operation. These guys have no off switch, Dana."

Don't I know that. "I'll be working long hours, and I'll look for a rental in Pacifica so I won't be around Half Moon Bay much. We need to sign off. Take care, Shane."

"Love you, sis."

"Love you, too." I stare at the now-quiet phone. My plan worked. Shane is safe, and he says he's clean. He sounds clean. I may be banged up, but I have a small victory to celebrate.

I pull open the last closet in the loft that I haven't inventoried yet. It's a linen cabinet, but on the top shelf I see a plastic bin, one that I remember is filled with family photo albums. I've carted this bin from place to place, through apartments and condos, but I can't remember the last time I opened it. I usually stick it somewhere well out of sight, buried like my past. You'd think that the photos, which depict holiday gatherings, vacations and other events, would bring back the good times. And it's true; some of the photos can evoke happy times. But they can also make me recall long-buried traumas that are better left unexamined. I close the closet and walk away, unwilling to revisit my fraught family history while I'm still healing.

But that night at dinner, I open up to Wayne, explaining a little more about my family history and Shane's turbulent childhood. I want this man to know me, which is a huge step for me.

"It sounds cliché, Wayne, but Shane is self-medicating with the street drugs. He's emotionally unstable. Today they call it bipolar, but I prefer manic depressive, because it more accurately describes his extreme mood swings."

"Has he always been that way?"

"Yes. As a kid, he was beyond hyperactive. He would often do things, break something, yell, just to provoke a reaction. It was like he couldn't stop himself."

He waits for me to continue. "My parents tried to discipline him, but it just made him act out more. And they weren't equipped to cope with him. Joe wouldn't be around for the day-to-day struggles with Shane, but when it would escalate he'd step in and there would be a belt whipping, a couple of smacks, screaming. Shane would go from being ignored to being beaten. The unevenness of the reaction would have confused any child, but it was awful for Shane."

"How did your mom handle him?"

"She'd try to talk to him, try to make him want to behave, but sometimes she'd lose patience, and often she'd lose energy." I struggle as I try to describe her instability. So, I just blurt it: "Wayne, my mom was manic too."

He reaches across the table and grabs my hand. I look down at my empty plate. And finally I just want to have it out in the open. "And she didn't make it, Wayne. She killed herself. It was a long time ago."

"Oh, Dana, I'm so, so sorry." He holds my hand tighter, but his face goes slack; he pales.

"We were estranged at the time. After suffering her ups and downs as a kid, I reached a point where I just didn't want to deal with it anymore. Her death crippled me for a while, and it blasted the rest of us apart. Despite her demons, Valerie was the center of our family." My lips tremble; I twist the napkin in my lap. "Shane took it the worst. He was the one who found her, Wayne." I choke as I say this. "Drugs took over his life. He went to his first rehab not long after her death, but it only slowed down his addictive behavior for a short time."

"Joe gave up on Shane after that?"

"Exactly. He shut down. And Terry and Shane don't get along — they're opposites in every way. Terry has always resented Shane's physical gifts, and he resented that my parents spent so much time on Shane. He felt abandoned. He's still carrying those wounds."

"That leaves you...the only one who hasn't given up on Shane."

"Yeah, but I'm no saint, Wayne. Believe me. I've wanted to walk away so many times. And when I haven't heard from Shane in a while, I feel relieved and I don't call. I want to pretend that everything is okay, but it rarely is." I don't admit it, but I actually hide from his calls sometimes...then claim I've been out of town when I haven't been.

"But you've helped him many, many times, right?"

"Some of my close friends, Rayan included, would say too many times." I grow quiet. The reality: If we stay together, Shane's struggles will affect Wayne too.

He doesn't need it spelled out. He comes over and wraps his arms around me. "He's your brother, Dana. You won't give up, and I'd never ask that of you."

I'd like to accept that, but I know that Wayne, who's used to resolving problems, likely believes this Shane drama can be fixed, that his life can be righted permanently. He'll learn otherwise. How will he feel about dealing with the Shane chaos after the next four or five dramas...after a few calls at two in the morning and a couple of trips to jail? After Shane steals something from our house to buy a fix?

*

"Hi, gorgeous!" I hear traffic in the background, and the drum and hiss of waves collapsing and pushing water.

"Surfer boy, where are you? Are you salty? Make me jealous."

He's been up in the canyon packing. Now he says he's sitting at a break just south of Malibu. He's considering splashing, but isn't sure if he has enough time before our dinner party.

"You have time. Just be here by six. What's the swell doing?"

"Two to three, but consistent sets."

At five forty-five, he bounds up the stairs two at a time. He showers, and I pour him a glass of white wine to inspire his inner chef.

Rayan and C.J. arrive just after seven. While Wayne cooks, I give C.J. a tour of the loft. Rayan sits at the counter and chats with Wayne, keeping both of their wine glasses topped up.

C.J. raves about the loft and its proximity to the beach. He looks more like a natty literature professor than a musician — narrow hipster glasses, thick brush-cut gray hair, stylish slacks and pointy suede shoes. And it turns out he "adores modern design" as much as I do, so the furnishings make him feel right at home. By the time we're walking back in from the garage, he's asking me how long the place will be available and the monthly rent. He's warm and direct and I get a good feeling about him right away. When I name the monthly rent, a smile spreads across his face. "I shouldn't tell you this, Dana, but L.A. is such a bargain. You'd pay twice that much for a loft this nice in a good location in Manhattan."

Rayan overhears this comment and chimes in. "See, Dana, a lovely man and he's clearly a musician...no business sense at all."

*

277

The next day we clean and pack my loft, and the following day we hit the road again. After he wrote me a fat check the other night, I gave C.J. a key. I call him from the road and tell him he can move in anytime. I also leave Dylan a voice mail letting him know when we're likely to pull into the farm. And I finish my phone check-list, dialing Craig and arranging to retrieve the Honda from his garage. As a lifelong Californian, going just one week without my own vehicle is starting to make me twitch.

In the past couple of days, Wayne has been combing rental listings for Pacifica, and the other night I overheard him reconnecting with the rental agent that showed him a few places before we left. I also heard him practically whispering on another quick call. That kind of irked me. Okay, we haven't discussed our future living situation, but being secretive seems juvenile. Is he pulling back and having second thoughts?

Is Wayne really ready for a full-time girlfriend after years as a bachelor? Plus, I'm not your typical female — I'm terrible at relationship discussions and sharing emotions. I'm not going to be the mature one that starts an adult dialogue about our future.

Regularly feeding the truck's CD player, Wayne seems to be content to avoid any meaningful discussions. We spend a little time speculating about Stokes' investigation of Ling, but it's another topic fraught with anxiety. Instead we share surf stories of past trips up and down the Central California coast. We reminisce about beater cars, breakdowns and illegal camping jags to avoid camp fees so we could afford beer.

By dusk, we're working our way through Half Moon Bay and up to Craig's house. As usual, Craig sees us coming and just as we're pulling into the driveway he opens the garage door. There's a Honda parked in there, but it's way too pretty to be mine. My beat-up and shot-up "rice burner," as Shane refers to it, has had a full makeover: no dents, no bullet holes, shiny new paint in a silver/blue tone, and brand-new surf racks.

I hop out of the truck and run over to the car. Inside, the cracked bucket seats are covered with new Hawaiian-print seat covers. And as I open the passenger door I see new rubber floor mats. Hanging from the rearview mirror is a beaded mermaid.

I stammer, wide-eyed. "She's had a full facelift, Craig. This must have cost a fortune."

"Well, I took her to the beauty spa, but you can thank Stokes for covering her treatments. He wanted your ride to be repaired and disguised. He even had their motor pool mechanic tune it up." My jaw drops open. "You have new license plates, too, courtesy of the feds. Wayne and I went in together on the racks, seat covers and mats."

I look at Wayne, who's chuckling. "You couldn't stand it when I was whispering on the phone the other night. You should have seen your face."

I walk over to hug Craig. "Thanks for making this happen. I am really grateful, and obviously I had no idea." I step over to Wayne and lightly punch him in the shoulder. He laughs and quickly spins me into his arms.

"Has Stokes said anything about Ling and his investigation?"

"No. We've only communicated about the car. But Dylan probably knows more." Craig hands me the keys. "I don't want to be around when someone puts the first door ding in it, or when the wind throws a rock or a sail at it."

I walk over and lay across the hood, hugging the car. "She's tough, and she's my protector," I whisper.

*

After dinner at the farm, Dylan catches me up on Stokes and Ling. "Stokes' team is way too busy to care about you or Shane anymore. And Ling has been focused on getting revenge for Anton's shooting."

"What have you heard?"

"Well, this is common knowledge, because it's been all over the news. Apparently three of Ling's guys retaliated for the attack on Anton and carjacked one of the Mexican gang's vans. Several witnesses saw it go down. The van was later found out by the dump, torched. They haven't found the driver or the other guy who was in the van."

The table goes quiet for a bit. I hug my arms to my still-healing ribs. That could have been me, grabbed and disappeared.

Dylan's voice gets even tighter. "One of my sources in the local police says word on the street is that the Mexicans are bringing in some heavies from their headquarters in Michoacán. Ling may not realize the backing these local guys have from the drug lords who rule entire provinces down in Mexico. This war is going to get bloodier."

Chapter 24

Wayne plops down next to me on the loft bed. He hesitates and then starts the discussion we've been avoiding. "I don't want to pressure you, Dana, but we need to talk about where we're going to live, and if we want to get a place together."

I try to be mature. "We've moved really fast, Wayne, and it's been fantastic. I want this to work between us. But there's a lot going on right now. I'm still dealing with Shane's mess. And we both have new jobs. I'm afraid we'll go too fast and we won't take measured, fully thought-out steps."

Before I can say more, he starts laughing and rolling on the loft bed, and pretty soon he's just heaving. I stare at him. Here I am, trying to be mature, and he's in stitches. And it's starting to irritate me. He chokes back his giggles. "When has either of us ever taken 'measured steps,' Dana? We fling ourselves at life. We usually go with our gut, and our gut is rarely wrong. Now you want to take 'thought-out steps?' "

I lean over him and bite his lower lip. "I hate it when you're right."

"Get used to it, babe."

Now he looks at me earnestly. "I need to move faster than you. Once I start at the hospital, it's going to be full-on. You hate these kinds of emotional decisions; they paralyze you." How can he know me so well after just these few weeks? "So I'm going to meet with the rental agent today and try to find a place that would be great for both of us. And I'm going to rent it. I'm patient. I'll wait for my stray cat to decide it's not that scary to live inside the house, instead of just in the alley."

Later, after he's reassured me with his body as well as his words, Wayne leaves to meet with the rental agent. I need to call Joe, but as usual I'm stalling as much as I can. And besides, my nosey reporter nature is kicking in and I can't resist combing the web for some background on Michoacán drug cartels.

One kingpin, Jesus Lopez (what an ironic first name for a violent criminal), has an online presence as large as a Hollywood celebrity. His drug network reaches throughout Mexico and into the southwestern United States. Other Mexican drug gangs supply marijuana and cocaine, but Lopez trades in meth. His empire is vast, and he's built a web of affiliates who benefit from his political and distribution network as well as his iron fist. And he's wisely invested his drug profits to buy and dominate key businesses in Michoacán, including a shipping company and several medical clinics, another irony considering his group is believed to be responsible for killings, kidnappings, shootouts and explosions.

To the consternation of law enforcement, his shipping expertise has enabled him to effectively move his drugs and continually change his routes. Further, his medical clinics and his legitimate businesses make him both a scourge and a Robin Hood to the local community. Many locals have acted as law-enforcement spies for him, helping him stay steps ahead of any raids.

If Lopez comes to the aid of the local Mexican drug gang, the body count is definitely going up. I cut and paste a couple of articles into an email and send them to Dylan.

Then I finally call Joe. "Hi, Dad. How are you?"

"Dana?" Irritation rises up in my brain; does he have another daughter? I stomp down the childish peeve.

"Yeah, Dad. I'm back in the bay. How are you?"

"Just fine, girlie. No complaints. Are you with Wayne?" I mentioned Wayne when he visited me in the hospital. As usual, Joe is focused on any male connected with me. My temper starts rising again, and I struggle to contain it.

"Yeah, Dad. He's out looking for a place to live." I try again to get a conversation going. "What's new? How are the dogs?" Pets: always a good neutral topic.

"Fine, fine. Sampson was in frenzy the other night, though." I wait for him to elaborate, but he jumps topics. "Have you spoken with Terry?"

The abrupt change in subject throws me. "No, why?"

"Well, when Sampson was barking the other night, I came out here in the living room, must have been about three o'clock in the morning, and there was one of those Mercedes SUVs, those big fancy things, you know like Terry drives?"

"Yeah?"

"Well, it was parked in front of the house. And I'm pretty sure someone was in it."

"Did you call Terry's cellphone?"

"Well, er, no. I wasn't sure, and if I was wrong I didn't want to wake him. And, you know, Terry can get very excited." Excited? Ah, no. Irritable, rude and high-handed? Yes.

"What did you do?"

"I shushed Sampson and went back to bed. The car, truck, whatever, that big shiny thing was gone the next day."

I mull this. My Dad, even though he's presenting this account as uncertain, is very observant. If he thinks that it was Terry's Mercedes, it probably was.

"You haven't called Terry?"

"No. I figured he'd call if it was him." Right. Terry never calls Joe, unless he needs something or its Christmas.

Joe changes topics again, "Have you healed up, girlie?" I sigh to myself. He cares, he's just so emotionally crippled he has no tools to show it.

"Yeah, Dad. I'm all better." It's not really true — my flashbacks continue, my shoulder is sore and tight, and at times I still gasp from the sharp pain in my ribs — but that's not what he wants to hear.

"As usual, I'm up at Dylan's and I have my cellphone, if you need to reach me."

"Good, good. Take care of yourself, Dana." With that, he's gone. I wonder if I'll ever have a satisfying conversation with my Dad and what that might feel like.

And what about Terry? Should I call him and ask why he was lurking outside Joe's house the other night? Can I handle having two conversations with family in the same morning? I stall; I'll do it later.

I need to arrange with Shane's landlord to move his stuff out of the crawl space. Craig has agreed to store his belongings until Shane can collect them. As I'm making this call, my brain sorts through a few memories of moving Shane.

I've probably done it ten times, and poor Craig has been part of the moving crew at least five or six times. Dylan has helped out on numerous moves, too, and now Wayne will join the club. I wince when I think of this. But this move will be smoother that others, because we won't be waiting for Shane to show up. One time, we waited nearly two hours for him. When he arrived he was so high that Craig took his apartment keys from him and sent him away. Craig, Dylan and I moved his stuff to Joey's garage, where Shane camped out for the next four months. I can't remember where he went after Joey kicked him out; after so many evictions they've begun to run together.

I need to make one more call...to Stokes. I want to thank him for my car's makeover and check in.

He answers on the first ring. "Dana, how are you?"

"Much better, thanks. I got into town last night. I collected the Honda from Craig, and I'm blown away by her new look. Thank you for doing that, Agent Stokes."

"You're welcome, Dana. But even though the car looks different, please try to avoid the part of town near the QuickShop. We just raided a lab in that area, and it's a neighborhood that Ling and his associates frequent regularly."

I gulp. Any mention of the QuickShop rattles me. "I have no intention of going near that store. Sounds like you're making progress in your investigation of Ling?"

"Yes. We've raided two labs in the past week, before he was able to move them, and we've arrested ten of his associates. That's all I can say for now, but I can assure you that we've made significant strides in our investigation."

According to Shane and Dylan, Ling's operation is larger than a couple of labs. But the pressure Stokes is bringing, along with the heat from Mexico, is undoubtedly impacting Ling's cash flow, and keeping him busy.

I thank Stokes again, and hang up. He has a human side, but I still don't trust him. In his own way, he's as ruthless as Ling.

There's one other Shane problem I need to deal with: Sea Flea. Eventually, the Corolla will get towed, even in that out-of-the-way spot under the eucalyptus trees. Shane gave me the keys, but will it run after sitting this long? I'm completely at a loss about what to do with it; still, before I can come up with a plan, I need to make sure I can find it again ...

Shit, no Sea Flea. I've been up and down the streets where he left it three times. My mind races. Was it towed? Do the cops have it and not even realize what they have?

Chapter 25

A black Escalade with blacked-out windows sits in the far corner of the lot at Dylan's office building, parked diagonally and taking up nearly three spaces. Two Asian guys lean against it, smoking. Both are wearing tight black jeans and loose crewneck sweatshirts. While I'm gawking, one of them reaches behind his back and pulls out an automatic pistol. He tugs at the waist of his pants, pulls at the crotch of his too-tight jeans, and re-stows the gun behind his back. My chest heaves in and out. Even though they're at the far end of the lot and haven't focused on me, I'm frozen in fear. I melt down into the seat, and absently rub my shoulder, while my mind jumps from thought to thought. Should I make a call? To whom? The police? Stokes? Wayne?

Before I can formulate a plan, the glass door to the building's lobby swings open and a taller Asian man strides out. He's wearing black wayfarer sunglasses; his hair is stylishly cut, with a gelled top, feathered sides, and a longer, collar-length back. He too is wearing the obligatory black jeans, a black button-down shirt that's open at the neck and displaying a heavy gold chain, and a dark gray suit jacket. His dress shoes tap on the sidewalk as he crosses the lot to the Escalade. He checks his watch, and the bulky timepiece glints in the sun. As he approaches, his associates pull themselves up and stiffen, almost like they might salute. I see him mouth a word or two, not looking at them, and then he opens the SUV's back door and disappears inside. They quickly hop into the front seats.

Although I expect them to tear out of the parking lot, the luxury four-by-four rolls by at a stately pace, gleaming chrome wheels spinning, and slowly turns onto the street.

I leap out of the Honda and blast through the lobby. In moments, I slam through the door into Dylan's suite. He's in his office, pacing behind his desk. He's pale, but he isn't bloody or bruised.

"Oh god, Dylan, you're okay." I gasp, standing in the door of his office. I put my arm out to steady myself; I feel lightheaded.

"I'm fine. But given your entrance, I assume you saw my visitor...Ling." He stops pacing and clenches his fists.

"He's looking for Shane, and he threatened you?"

"You guessed it. He introduced himself as if he was at a goddamn business meeting. He was calm, almost chatty." He waves me to one of the chairs in front of his desk and sits down. "He tracked me down because one of the surf cretins told him I'd helped Shane out of previous scrapes."

I put one hand over my mouth. "I brought this on you. This is so wrong."

"Dana, he was guessing. I said I know nothing about Shane's whereabouts and that the FBI is trying to track him and will probably find him. I told him Shane's isn't my client."

"Did he believe you?"

"I think so. I sold it. Said Shane owes me ten grand for previous legal work." He runs his hands across the edge of the desk.

"That wouldn't even cover a ten percent retainer for all that you've done for him over the years." I swipe the knuckle of my index finger under my eye.

"Ling's a cool character. He sat in the chair you're sitting in now. He told me he's just a businessman and Shane made a mistake and needs to '*be a man.*' Said he hates drama, but '*business need strong leadership.*' I told him he should explore other, saner business options."

"This isn't funny, Dylan."

"Dana, I'm a criminal attorney. This isn't the first time I've been threatened and it won't be the last. I'll get Stokes to put a car over here, and I'll hire a private security detail that I've used before to watch the farm." His voice is steady, but he fidgets with a pen, twirling it through a slightly trembling hand.

I gulp down my panic. "What else did he say?"

"He might have been high. He was rambling. He said he joined a gang at ten, and he'd built his 'business' since he was fifteen, living in a slum outside Chaweng on Koh Samui. His mother did laundry eighteen hours a day; he's one of six kids. He didn't mention a father."

He rubs his chin. "He never looks at you. And when he was looking across the room I noticed that he has a wandering eye. Instead of looking at me, he kept playing with his oversize gold watch, rolling his arm and rocking it back and forth on his wrist. When I said lots of people come from hardscrabble lives and go on to achieve legitimate success, he laughed at me."

"He's proud of his business." Dylan leans back in his chair; his hands tightly grip the chair's arms. "His three brothers are day laborers and one died of an overdose, and his sister and his mother still do laundry. I asked him how he could sell drugs when his brother died from them. He didn't even get mad, just said his brother would have died anyway because '*he weak.*' Then he said, '*The fittest find a way, take what they need...this is true in the animal kingdom. This is life.*'"

My face flushes. As a judgmental teen I had these same thoughts...about Valerie.

"What else?" I lean in and wrap my arms around my stomach.

"He said, '*Be smart, if Shane come back, you tell him you cannot be friend or counselor.*' Then he stood, gave me a quick *wai*, and walked out." Wai is the Buddhist gesture of greeting or farewell, a slight bow while pressing the palms and fingers together at chest-level. A benevolent Buddhist goodbye from a violent drug dealer.

We sit in silence. I take deep breaths, trying to calm down. Still, when I speak my voice cracks.

"Sea Flea is missing. It's not where Shane parked it, I'm certain of it."

His eyes widen. "Okay...let me think. There are really only two possibilities: it's been towed or stolen."

"Oh god, Dylan, what if the cops have it?"

"Take it easy, Dana. Even if they do, these guys don't regularly communicate with the feds, and it might take them a while to process it. Was Shane's registration current?"

"Probably not. Shane's always in trouble with the DMV."

"Well, in any case, I'd bet the feds put a bulletin out on it. Let me call a friend and see if it's been impounded." I give him the license plate number, and he makes a call.

If the feds have the car, and they find the *yaa baa,* Shane could end up subpoenaed as a witness, which could get him killed. Or he could be charged as an accessory to the death. Then all our efforts to clean him up and get him out of the area will be for nothing. But right now, my fear and shame override those concerns. My friends are being threatened because of me.

Dylan sets down the receiver. "They don't have it. There's still a bulletin out on it, but neither the police nor the feds have found it."

"Okay, I guess that's good. But what do I do? Do I report it stolen?"

"Let me chew on that. For now, do nothing. We'll talk about it tonight."

*

Back at the Honda, my phone rings.

"What are you doing, beautiful?" It's Wayne's upbeat voice. I breathe out slowly, trying to sound calm.

"Just finished speaking with Dylan. How's the house hunting going?"

"I signed a lease."

I swallow hard. What does this mean? He signed a lease without me, which I think is what I said I wanted. "Wait, what?"

He's moving ahead with his life, and as usual I'm spinning. Before I can figure out what to say or ask, he barrels ahead. "I really want you to see it. Can you meet me over here in Pacifica?"

My emotions are swinging back and forth, but I want to see the place. "Yes, definitely. I'm actually down in town, so it won't take me too long to get there." He gives me the address and a brief description — it's a house up on one of Pacifica's hills.

*

As I make my way up Highway 1, tears finally come. Not because of Wayne, he did exactly what he said he would do. The confusion is all mine...and all of my own making. I grip and re-grip the steering wheel.

How can I get involved with this man when a gangster is tracking Shane and threatening my friends? No. No. No. Why can't I do what my heart wants and STOP running?

I follow his directions and make a right up a steep hill before I reach the main downtown area of Pacifica, by the fishing pier. I follow a branch to the right, "Sardine," and make another right turn onto "Mackerel," a street that ends in a cul-de-sac. All the streets in the neighborhood are named after local fish. Wayne's truck is in front of a house on the left side of the circle. It's an old craftsman-style bungalow, steel blue with white trim, with a pillared porch and a wide dormer window. On the left side of the house, I can see a paver-and-grass driveway that leads to a two-car garage and a backyard. Wayne is leaning up against his truck, waiting for me.

He tilts his head toward the house and says, "My new home sweet home."

He unlocks the front door and we step into the 1930s. The house has dark hardwood floors and wood-cased windows, but numerous windows let in tons of natural light and the interior has obviously just been painted a light cream. The original stone fireplace anchors the front room, which is separated from a dining room by wood-trimmed columns. Wayne guides me through the house. The small kitchen has been partially updated with painted cabinets, newer appliances and granite counters. I nod at the long narrow bath, with black and white tile that's probably original. Out the kitchen door, there's a wooden deck, beyond it a small lawn. Adjacent to the garage, at the back of the lot, is another small building, the size of a single-car garage. It's obviously much younger than the house.

"I've saved the best for last." Wayne leads me by the hand to the small structure. Next to its door, it has a large window facing out to the yard. Inside it has light-wood floors and built-in white shelves across one entire wall. On the other side of the room, there's a tiny kitchenette, and beside it is a half bath. He watches me explore the space.

"No pressure, but isn't this a terrific office."

"Yes." One word is all I can manage.

"Let me show you the garage." We take a paver path from the studio to the back door of the garage. It's nothing special, but it's clean, with shelves and a workbench along the back wall. It's big enough to house surfboards, bikes, etc., and still have room for one car.

I recover my voice. "How did you find this? It's pristine for a rental."

"One of the nurses on the hiring committee turned me on to a great rental agent. She just began managing this place, after the owner died and her heirs took possession. They can't agree on what to do with it; one heir wants to sell it and the other one is emotionally attached, so in the meantime they decided to rent it."

Excitement fills his voice. "I'd driven past it before my second interview, but I wasn't able to get inside until today. Once I did, I couldn't image finding anything better than this."

We walk back out into the yard. I take in the house and the office again. "I usually go for modern design, but I love the classic charm of this bungalow. I really do." But he can see that the decision is about a lot more than a great living space. I need to mull this over.

"Look, Dana, I won't deny that I chose this place partially because I can see you in it. But it's a lure, not a trap." He puts his arms around me and kisses my hair.

*

The dinner dishes are cleared and Dylan, Wayne and I huddle around the kitchen table to talk about Shane's car. But first, I have to catch Wayne up on all the details of Shane's latest mess. He wants me to trust him with the important parts of my life, good and bad. So I recap the entire drama for him:

293

Shane's relationship with Ling, his broken arm, his latest stint in rehab, Stokes pursuing him, his story about the poison *yaa baa*, the death of the addict in Palo Alto, Sea Flea and its hubcap contraband, Shane's escape out of the area. Dylan tells him about Ling's visit to his office today, and the officers now assigned to him. A security crew is already covering the bottom of the farm's driveway. Wayne tries to keep his face impassive, but I can see the shock and worry he's trying to hide.

Dylan jumps in. "I think I know what we should do about Sea Flea, but first I have two questions. Is there any chance your fingerprints are on the car?"

"Absolutely not. When I checked the car, I wore gloves."

"Okay. Second, do you think anyone saw you looking at the car that day?"

"No. That neighborhood is empty in the middle of the day."

"Good. You should call Stokes and report it stolen."

I stare hard at Dylan. "Why? How does that help Shane?"

"Either it's been stolen by a random thief or, more likely, one of Ling's crew found it and took it. If one of Ling's people has it, it's another crime, car theft. And if the drugs are still under the hubcap and the car gets recovered, there will be a stolen-vehicle report on it and Shane can say he has no idea how the drugs got there. No prosecutor could bring charges against him."

By the time he finishes describing this bit of legal strategy, Dylan looks pretty self-assured. He's analyzed the ins and outs and his plan is on sound legal footing.

There's one other part of making this plan work: I have to lie once again on Shane's behalf. I can't say anything about the *yaa baa* in the car; it's a lie by omission. And I'll need to make Stokes believe that I was just recently following up on retrieving Shane's car for him, and then discovered that it's missing. How many times have I lied on Shane's behalf over my lifetime? It makes my stomach churn, especially since we're putting this plan together in front of Wayne and he's watching me lie and manipulate the legal system for my brother.

"Okay, I'll call Stokes tomorrow." I slump in my chair, exhausted by the conversation and by the scheming.

"He'll probably need you to go to the police station and fill out an official stolen-vehicle report."

My shoulders sag, and I get up to clear the last of the dishes. I squeeze Dylan's arm and wish him a good night.

Once we're up in the loft, Wayne finally comments. "I'm starting to understand. No wonder you fear attachments, when this is where they've left you."

"Not to make an excuse, but this mess is worse than any other I've had to navigate with Shane. But yeah, working through his dramas certainly makes you lose your moral compass."

We climb into bed and lie shoulder to shoulder. I'm tense from the discussion, and nervous about the latest role I must act out for law enforcement. I have no idea what Wayne's thinking, but how could he be happy about being involved in this? I'm disgusted with all of it.

In the early light, Wayne seems to have recovered his equilibrium. He hums Beach Boys tunes as he gets dressed. Regardless of all the drama in my life, I'm so happy for him. He has a new job and a new home.

But in the shower, I stand directly under the spray and hope the rushing water drowns out my sobs. My chest heaves; I push against the shower wall, fighting an immovable object. All the tension of Anton's attack and the shame of Ling's threats to my friends batters me.

When I step out of the stall and blow my nose, Wayne stands in the bathroom doorway. The sadness on his face makes me start blubbering all over again. He gently folds a towel around me and holds me, as I try to choke down my tears. Then he walks me out into the bedroom and sits me on the bed.

"You didn't cause this. Shane did."

I gulp and grip the towel to my chest. "Shane is at the center, but I brought in Dylan and Craig...and now you."

"Dylan is a professional. If he says Ling's threats are empty, we need to trust him on that. And I believe Stokes really is dropping the hammer now. Ling will be dodging him. He won't have time to think about anyone else." He wraps his long arm around my shoulders and kisses the side of my forehead.

But my hyper energy has gone missing; I'm immobile. Wayne makes a plan and forces me into gear. We'll spend the day getting him moved in and staying out of Half Moon Bay.

*

The hours pass quickly, with Wayne moving surfboards and boxes, and me putting his kitchen together. He owns no furniture, except for a foldable futon; his ex-wife took it all in the divorce — and Sarah's cottage was furnished. But, before we left the loft, I researched several consignment furniture stores in South San Francisco, and he plans to go shopping this afternoon.

Once I've organized the kitchen, I kiss Wayne goodbye and drive down to the beach. I'm finally in motion again; I need to deal with Sea Flea. I stop at the lot at the base of the pier and call Stokes.

"Dana? Is everything okay?" Obviously he wasn't expecting to hear from me again so soon.

"Yes...well, sort of. I have a small problem." I tell him that Shane had asked me when he was in rehab to check on his car, which he'd left in a neighborhood where he has some friends. Obviously, with the shooting and me leaving town again, I was never able to do that, I explain. But just yesterday I went looking for it.

"Shane gave me very specific coordinates on where he parked it, but it's no longer there. It may have been towed or stolen."

I give him the license plate number, even though I know he already has it. Dylan has assured me that it wasn't towed, but I can't tell Stokes that. And Dylan says Stokes has an all-points-bulletin out on the Corolla. I wait for him to work through his checks...and wait to see how he'll play this.

"The car hasn't been towed, Dana. It's not on the impounded-vehicles list, which is updated every morning." Roger. What will he say about the fact that he's been looking for it for a couple of weeks?

I help him along, "So it's probably been stolen. Damn, damn, damn. It wasn't much of a car, but Shane said it was running."

"Well, you should report it stolen at the local police station, and if you like I can put a bulletin out on it?" I think to myself, "Oh, Agent Stokes, you are so predictable."

"Okay, thanks. Since Anton certainly knew what kind of car Shane drove, do you think Ling or one of his crew took it?"

"It's possible. But with a bulletin on it, if it gets driven around this area there's a good chance it will be spotted."

"I'll go fill out the report today. And you'll call me if it's recovered?"

"Of course." As the line goes dead, I chuckle. Yeah, right, Stokes. You'll call, but only after you've strip-searched poor Sea Flea down to his shock absorbers.

At the police station, the duty officer hands me a form and a clipboard. I fill it out. Thankfully, there's no lying required for this process. I'm already working on Project Shane; I might as well keep going.

I'd grabbed the boxes I'd emptied at Wayne's for my move, whenever I figure out where I'm going. I was also scheming that I could refill them with Shane's stuff. Wayne would have been livid if he knew I was even contemplating that task. But after Ling's surprise visit to Dylan's office, I'm not going near that squat and I don't want Craig taking any chances either.

I try to call him, but only connect with voice mail. I don't want to have this conversation with the virtual Craig. It's a Saturday afternoon and the ocean is glass. He should be home; he's probably working in his garage; he's probably fine.

I can't convince myself.

The Honda struggles up the hill and I yank the emergency brake so the car can cling to his steep driveway. Craig's pounding on something on his work bench at the back of the garage.

We say our hellos and then with as little emotion as possible, I tell him about Ling's visit to Dylan and his newly assigned security details. "Shane's belongings aren't even worthy of a flea market; his landlord can just toss them."

Craig looks hard at me. "I already grabbed Shane's stuff."

I stutter. "What? When?"

Yesterday evening he'd decided that he needed to re-organize his van and he'd mostly emptied it. "Drove over early. I figured the meth zombies wouldn't be out in the light of day. His busted-up shit is now under my house. You're right, it really wasn't worth collecting, but it's done."

I start to thank him, but he interrupts me, his voice gruff. "I'm done, Dana. I can't watch Shane go any lower. This is my last rescue mission."

I grab his arm. "You've been a loyal friend, the best, Craig. And I want you to walk away."

"You need to get the hell away from this too, Dana. This mess has tested us all, and it damn near got you killed. Wayne is solid. Hold on to him and move on."

This is a big speech for Craig, who's usually talks in sentence fragments. And I don't need an endorsement of Wayne, but Craig's support is the one positive in this conversation. Still, I don't say anything; Wayne and I are feeling our way. This Shane mission is pretty much over, but I still can't say I'll walk away for good, even though any sane person would. Shane is my mother's legacy; sadly, he's my inheritance.

I say nothing and just hug him goodbye, clinging for an extra few seconds.

*

"I need you. I found some great furniture, but I'm a guy; my idea of decorating is figuring out where to put the TV. Please help...please?"

How can I resist Wayne's pleading? We spend the rest of the day putting his house together. He found a great muslin-covered corner group at the consignment store, along with end tables, lamps and a dining-room set. Later, we eat takeout at his new table, and hang pictures. He's successfully recruited me to nest with him, and it's a smart move. I'm becoming vested in the bungalow.

A new king-size bed and mattress will be delivered in a couple of days. Tonight we crash on his futon. Sunday, we lounge on the deck, enjoying a fogless start to the day. Tonight, he needs to review a sixty-page document from the hospital on procedures and practices. We agree that I'll go back to Dylan's, so he can do his homework before his first day of work tomorrow.

His reverse psychology is working. The more he steps back, the more I reach for him.

I'm chewing on all of this as I make the drive back to Half Moon Bay. My other task for today is to call Terry. I dial his house and Jenna answers.

"Hey, Jenna, how are you? It's Dana."

"Oh, hi Dana." Her voice is brusque and tight.

"How are you and the kids?"

"Just fine."

That's it, two words? I keep swinging: "I'm back in town and thought I'd catch up with Terry. Is he around?"

"No, not here. You should try his cell." She offers no information on where he might be, and nothing about when he might return. She doesn't ask about my health, although Terry told her about my injuries. It's very odd.

I try one more question. "Is he at his office?"

I hear what sounds like a short guffaw, or it could be a cough. I can't be sure. She hesitates and says, "Just call his cell. Bye, Dana."

And that's it, she hangs up on me. I stare at the phone.

Chapter 26

After I recover, I dial Terry's cell. It goes immediately to voice mail, which means it's probably switched off. I leave him a brief message, saying I'm back in town and would like to connect. Should I go by his office? Terry and I have never been chummy, but I'm alarmed by Jenna's anger and unwillingness to talk. Something serious is up.

I make the drive to Terry's office. It's actually a small stucco house in a once residential area, with a detached garage behind it. The front rooms have been converted to office spaces, with desks and partitions for Terry's three-person staff. One of the bedrooms serves as Terry's office. When I arrive, the blinds are drawn tight and the place seems not just closed; it feels abandoned. Yet Terry's SUV is in the driveway.

I bang on the front door and wait. Nothing. I bang again, more forcefully, this time with the meaty side of my hand. As I'm pounding for the third time, I see the blinds move, as someone peeks around the edge. I catch only a glimpse, but I'm pretty sure it's Terry.

"Terry, I know you're in there. Answer the door."

The response from inside is muffled, but still audible. "Go away, Dana!"

"No. Let me in. Let's talk. You're freaking me out."

"I don't want to talk." He places heavy sarcasm on the word talk. His words are drawn out and slurry.

"Fine. Let me in so I can see that you're okay and I'll go away." A minute or two passes and there's no response. "Joe says he saw your car at his house the other night. Why were you there?"

I hear mumbling and swearing, and the front door swings open. Terry, normally a preppy and fastidious dresser, is a disheveled mess. His hair is pasted to his shiny scalp, dark circles ring the underside of his eyes. He's wearing a dirty gray crew-neck sweatshirt and stained khaki pants. He reeks of alcohol.

His hostility fills the space between us. "So you've seen me, GO AWAY!" He's stooped and hangs onto the doorknob to steady him.

"Terry, what's up? I called Jenna and she would barely talk to me."

"Listen, Ms. Busybody, no one is asking for your help. Just butt OUT!" Terry loves to call names, always has. He deflects questions and criticism by going on the attack.

"I probably can't help, Terry. But I can listen. Are you and Jenna fighting?"

He rolls his eyes, and loses his balance. I catch him under the arm as he goes down to one knee. He wobbles back up. "I'm fine. Let go." His breath is sour and ninety proof. Weaving his way, he stumbles to his office. I'm not invited in, but I follow anyway. He plops into his high-back leather chair, puts his feet on the desk and retrieves a half-empty bottle of Jack Daniels from behind the desk. The office was once the home's master bedroom, so there's room for the desk, a couch and a couple of armchairs. Staring straight into my eyes, he takes a long pull from the bottle. I've never seen Terry drink like this before. His face is defiant and angry.

I say nothing and just wait him out.

"Do you ever think that our family is jinxed?"

"Every family has issues, Terry."

"Right." More sarcasm pours from his voice. "Every family has suicide, drug addiction, unemployment, FBI investigations and embezzlement."

I was with him up to embezzlement. That's a new episode in the McCarren soap opera. But I'm afraid if I grill him on that he'll throw me out. I change the subject.

"Did you camp out in your car at Joe's house the other night?"

"It's a free world. SUVs are made for camping."

I wait some more. He spits. "That haughty bitch threw me out."

"You haven't been home since that night at Joe's?"

"And enjoy the company of the ice queen? The Mercedes has more warmth."

"Are you going to get another place to live? Maybe you guys just need a cooling-off period?"

He scoffs. "The bitch is plenty cool. And funds are, ah, a little tight. We're experiencing a cash-flow shortage." He says this last part in the tone of a banker making a dry financial report.

"But staying here could harm your business, Terry."

He exhales hard and cackles, a hard, metallic sound, like a car sputtering. "The business is closed, Dana; a Jenna-led reorg is underway. She's a specialist in reorgs, Ms. Human Resources Manager."

At first, I'm confused. It's Terry's business, isn't it? But then I think about Jenna's family money, Terry's desire for status, and his rapid expansion of the agency during a sputtering of the local economy. Was the agency expansion business-funded or Jenna-backed? I guess. "Jenna financed the agency's growth?"

"Her and her family's trust."

"Why is she pulling the plug?" We're getting to the sticky center of things.

"We had a small accounting discrepancy. With a little time, it could have been corrected. But no, Ms. HR has stepped in. Sheryl, my lead gal, played whistleblower and has thrown in with her."

I've met Sheryl. She's worked with Terry for a decade. She's a middle-aged woman who has grown kids. She's no power-raider, seeking to conquer and command an inconsequential insurance agency. Something tawdry must have compelled her to act. Is Terry drunk enough to confess to the specifics of the "accounting discrepancy?" I doubt there was any "we" involved. Whatever took place, it was an action taken by Terry.

I try the soft approach, complemented with a little ego stroking. "The agency seemed to be well-respected and thriving, Terry. Was there an unexpected downturn in business?"

At this question, Terry stares off into space and takes another slug from the bottle. Like many drunks, he's lost some spatial awareness, so he thuds the bottle down onto the desk and some of the brown liquid splashes up and out of the bottleneck, soaking into some papers.

He slurs. "No...yes...well, yes, we have enjoyed a good reputation, through some hard work and networking." He's warming to the topic, and the spin he can put on it. "I've been trying to capitalize on that and build the business further. But that requires investment expenses."

I raise my eyebrows, silently asking what type of expenses?

"I joined the Roundhill Golf Club, bought the Mercedes and financed a Rotary charity ball with casino-style gambling. All reasonable business-building expenses...and just a few other things." His voice fades out at the end of this last statement.

He revs up the anger again. "But Sheryl spoke to Ms. HR and she disapproved. That bitch has no business acumen; no sense of how small risks can pay rewards." Clearly, he's left out a key piece of this story. What risks? How did he finance the expenses?

I try teasing the final piece of the story out of him. "Risks can be an important part of any growing business. How did you manage these necessary promotional expenses?"

"It was just a few policies. Later, we'd be able to cancel them and adjust. And once the promotions paid off, it would have been worth the limited risk." He's alternatively smug, defiant and pleading. He's still convincing himself that what he did was nothing more than a smart business tactic.

But now, I have the full picture. He wrote phantom policies, in an agency financed by his wife, with his wife's family money and reputation on the line. He probably used the phony business to increase his line of credit, which enabled him to fund the golf membership, luxury automobile, extravagant posing. Oh Terry, so desperate to be a notable small-town business leader. And it's all crashing down. His wife has tossed him out, and undoubtedly cancelled his credit cards and lines of credit. Knowing Jenna, she's probably diligently working with Sheryl to retract the phantom policies, and make nice with the underwriter. I have no idea what she'll do with the agency in the long term, but perhaps she can salvage and sell it. For her, and the kids' sake, I hope so.

"What are you going to do?"

"I'm going to see if I can get the other gals to see things my way, and I'm going to fight her. It's my agency, Dana. Sure, her money helped grow it. But I started it. It's MINE!"

But if Jenna has already spoken to the underwriter and put the business on hold, Terry has no standing. His plan is hopeless; his threats are empty. I have no idea what he can or should do. Beg for forgiveness? Not in his current pickled state.

I try to offer the voice of reason. "Terry, you need to clear your head and sober up before you make any decisions. Let me take you out for some food, and we'll talk some more."

He rolls his head back and forth. "Nope, I'm staying right here. I'm going to review some more papers and billing. I have work to do." When he says this, it's like he's trying to convince himself, not me. Terry is one of the most stubborn people I've ever encountered in my life, and I've worked with some strident editors and pushy publishers. Arguing with him is futile.

"Where will you stay tonight?"

"I have everything I need right here." He waves his arm across the desk and nearly knocks over the whisky bottle. I suppose he can sleep it off on the office couch. And the front office area still includes a small kitchen.

"Can I bring you some takeout?"

"I can order a pizza if I get hungry. Stop trying to mother me, Dana. It's not your style or your job. Save it for Shane, the man-child."

"Fine." I'm tired of his abuse, directing his wrath at me is completely inappropriate. But that's Terry.

I get up to leave. I can't help him if he won't let me, and even if he would I'm not sure what I could do. He's going to have to sort this mess out for himself. And as part of that process he'll need to come to some kind of understanding with Jenna. I'm the last person who should give advice on relationships.

I concede the battle. "I'll call you tomorrow." He's looking at some papers and doesn't even look up, just waves me away.

As I'm driving away, I keep trying to think of something I could do to help. But what? I'm not close to Jenna, though we've been cordial in the past. Could I plead for her to go easy on Terry? Although he's my brother, I'm not sure he deserves any consideration. Writing phony policies to fund your Mercedes and golf membership? Still, Jenna has always demanded a certain lifestyle and stature. Did her high expectations contribute to the overspending, and the creative accounting that funded it? The only innocents in this drama are their kids.

I've helped Shane out of more unsavory scrapes, so I'll do what I can for Terry. But because he and I don't connect emotionally it will be harder. Terry hates to take advice from anyone, especially me. The massive chip on his shoulder extends to his place in the world and his place in our family. It manifests in him being high-handed and sometimes downright mean, as a cover for his insecurities. And yet it's sad, because I've rarely seen Terry happy. Terry has never been satisfied with his place in life, because he's always striving and manipulating, comparing his lifestyle and financial success to others...work contacts, friends, Jenna's highbrow crowd and family. His envy of others' success is palpable, and instead of respecting their hard work and wanting to equal them, he wants them to stumble and fall. It's disturbing.

I pull out of my mental fog and realize that I'm passing near the QuickShop. I'm not flashing back yet, but my hands shake. I notice how seedy this area has become, with a check-cashing franchise and dollar store fronting the edge of the hood, and dilapidated houses and apartments up the hill. Due to the recent real estate meltdown, some of the houses are boarded up, with brown yards and graffiti-sprayed walls.

Suddenly, I hear a very loud whump, and it feels as though my Honda jumps up off the roadway. Two blocks uphill from the strip mall, I see fire and smoke erupt from what I think is a house, though I can't make out much of the structure. My brain flashes back to the gunfire in the QuickShop parking lot, and I start hyperventilating. Panicked, I can't decide if I should reverse course or stomp on the gas. My foot presses down hard on the accelerator and I veer off onto the road's sloped, gravel-strewn shoulder, cutting around the slowing line of gawkers. I pass six cars before I merge back into the legal lane. Fortunately, for the mile or so ahead the road is free of traffic. I ease off the gas back to the speed limit.

Two miles further along, I'm forced to move off to the shoulder again, as a fire truck and ambulance, with sirens blaring, fly past on the other side of the highway. I'd calmed myself a bit after getting free of the traffic knot near the fire, but the sirens cause me to start shaking again. This time, the shuddering runs over my entire body and I'm breathing, but so shallowly I'm not getting any air. I travel another two miles or so and pull into a gas station, by its air and water spigots. Taking deep, slow breaths, I'm able to stop the body shakes. The rest of the drive to Dylan's is a blur, but I'm able to make it there without needing another stop to control my panic.

By the time Dylan and Maria arrive home, I'm halfway through a bottle of Zin and I'm pouring another glass. My still quivering hands cooperate enough to allow me to drain the bottle, as I fill glasses for each of them and describe what I witnessed. The local news is just about to come on, so we take our glasses into the family room to see what they have on the explosion.

It leads the news that evening. A car exploded, not a house, the news anchor reports, and two Hispanic males have been injured. Witnesses say an Asian suspect drove the car into two victims, who were standing in the driveway of a house. He ran from the scene, as the car exploded and erupted into flames. The incident commander from the fire department says they suspect a Molotov cocktail ignited it. The victims have multiple fractures and burns. Panning back from the fire commander, the camera shows the burned-out hulk of the car that was used as a battering ram and a bomb. The cameraman makes a semi-circle around the car, going from the front, down the left side and finally to a rear view.

I gasp and lean in toward the TV. Lying on the ground behind the ash-coated car chassis is a blackened but-still-identifiable PVC pipe. Sea Flea's homemade bumper. It must have been blown off the car when the gas tank explosion. As I'm still staring hard at the screen, Dylan catches on.

"Is that...?"

"Yeah, I'm certain of it."

"I'll be damned."

Maria looks from Dylan to me and back again. Marco is in his room doing homework.

Dylan explains. "That's the homemade bumper to Shane's car, or what's left of it."

I fill in the rest. "The car was stolen sometime after Shane left town. Shane had asked me to look after it, and when I tried it wasn't where he left it. I reported it stolen." Maria knows nothing about the car's role in the poison *yaa baa* story, and there's no reason to go into it.

Abruptly, Dylan starts giggling. And pretty soon he's losing it.

"What?"

"Shane. Even his car has a criminal record."

I catch his giggles and chime in. "Stokes can report it recovered...but melted. He'll be so pleased."

Dylan leans over and clinks wine classes with me. The humor is lost on Maria, but she's a good sport. She goes out to the kitchen and comes back with more wine.

"Shane loved that car. It was the most constant thing in his random life."

"Hmm. Maybe we can ask for the bumper back?" My quip sets us off on another round of bent-over laughter.

Just as we're calming down, my cellphone rings. It's Stokes.

"Hi, Dana. I assume you saw the news report on the explosion?" His voice is tight and he's back to all business for this call.

"Actually, I saw the explosion first hand."

"How? Where?" There's the hint of worry in his demanding tone.

I explain how I came to be in the area at exactly the wrong time, though I leave out any comments about Terry's situation. Dylan and Maria listen to my side of the conversation.

I want them to hear all of it, so I remain in the family room. "Was this Ling's retaliation for the stolen van?"

"The investigation is in the early stages, but yes, we think that's likely." I nod, so Dylan and Maria know that the answer to my question was yes. "But I called because I have some news related to Shane."

"Okay." I mouth to Dylan and Maria "He's calling about Sea Flea."

"The car that was used in the incident was Shane's Corolla."

"Shane's stolen car." I emphasize the word stolen.

"Well, yes, of course, though it will be difficult to tie the theft to Ling or one of his associates, since any evidence was likely destroyed in the car fire."

"Yeah, I saw it on the news. I'm pretty sure no body shop will be able to restore it." At this comment, Dylan starts giggling again.

Even humorless Stokes gives a little snort. "To close this part of the case, could you come and look at the wreckage and see if you can confirm that it was Shane's car? Our technicians will be going over it to see if any of the VIN numbers survived the fire, but a confirmation from you would be helpful."

"Yes, I can do that." Now I tell him about recognizing the PVC bumper from the news video. "I'm pretty sure it's Shane's car."

I'd described the car, including the bumper, in the stolen-vehicle report. But perhaps Stokes never read it. Tsk, tsk, sloppy investigative work, Agent Stokes. But I don't bait him.

I agree to a nine-thirty meeting and end the call. I'm beginning to wonder if Stokes is making up reasons to see me. I'm certain one of his functionaries could handle this small detail of the case.

Later in the evening, Wayne calls. I decide that he doesn't need the distraction of another Shane story before his first day of work, nor does he need to hear about another McCarren family crisis. I keep quiet about Sea Flea's fate and Terry's financial woes. He says he's made his way through the hospital's personnel manual, and he feels ready to begin his training. I wish him well and we agree to speak tomorrow after his first shift.

Maria, in her typical blunt fashion, comes right at me. "Why are you holding out on that gorgeous man, Dana? He loves you. It's obvious, and it's wonderful."

I can't argue with her on any of that. Can I begin to explain my warped psychology to a friend when I don't really understand it myself? But I owe her an answer. She just wants me to be happy. And before I can even think it out, I'm saying something I didn't really expect to verbalize. "I'm getting there, Maria. I'm trying to push my fear out of the way."

"Don't let your fears hurt your chance at happiness, Dana. You've never let fear stop you from your thrill-seeking and look at all the pleasure you get from that. You run at challenges and at life; you always have. You need to stop letting fear rule your relationships."

"I ran at marriage and look where that got me."

She frowns. "You were a kid. And you'd just lost your mother. Come on, Dana."

Forget all the time I've spent on the therapist's couch, forget the analysis of my screwed-up family and the impact it's had on my ability to make connections, Maria has just boiled this decision down to a simple equation that even an emotional dunce like me can grasp.

I turn around and hug her, my wise and emotionally fearless friend. I may be an athlete, someone people see as strong, but she is tough in a host of ways that I am not.

"And just like a swell, this opportunity has a limited life span, Dana. You can't hold off too long. Even if Wayne continues to wait you'll be hurting him and doing damage to your relationship."

She's right, but I've been in denial about the potential cost of my stalling. I've been justifying it by convincing myself that I'm being mature, not just rushing into something. Instead, I'm being cruel and a chicken.

"I'm not going to promise anything, Maria. But I've heard everything you've said and I want to respond with action and not words. And it's time I stopped being your second child."

We both laugh at this last comment, and we hug again. As I climb up to the barn loft, my thoughts are swirling. Am I ready to move in with Wayne? Shouldn't I wait until things are calmer to make this big decision? Right, when is my family situation ever calm? When is life ever predictable?

Chapter 27

A bureau receptionist leads me out behind the building where I stare at Sea Flea's burned-out hull. It's a violent end, even for a car. Stokes is supposed to join me soon, but I'm being escorted by a crime technician. He shows me a VIN number under the hood that survived the explosion and fire. They've examined the body of the car, but it looks like they haven't done anything with the wheels yet. The *yaa baa* baggy couldn't possibly have survived the fire. Still, nagging doubt is making my stomach twist.

Shane's homemade PVC bumper is lying near the car. I don't really want it back, and I don't think Shane would either. Yes, it has some humor attached to it, but in its blackened state it's a reminder of violence.

Stokes strides out the back of the offices. He asks if they've shown me the VIN number and that it's a match to Shane's Corolla.

I nod. "Do you still need me to fill out a form identifying the car?"

"We've written one up. You just need to sign it. We'll send it to the local police so they can close their stolen-vehicle case."

"Will you be able to tie the car to one of the gang members?"

"We haven't found anything yet; it doesn't look good. But we've gathered some good descriptions of the perpetrator from eye witnesses." He can't help getting a dig in. "Some witnesses actually want to help take Ling off the street, Dana."

While he's speaking, the technician has gone back to work. And as I'm watching, he pries the hubcap off the blackened back right wheel. I hold my breath...and slowly exhale. The space under the cap is empty. And from what I can see there's no melted plastic evident. Did one of Ling's men find the poison *yaa baa*? Most likely, but no one will ever know.

Stokes stares at me. I need to offer an explanation for my obvious distress. I go on the attack and play the victim. "I really don't need to see this, Agent Stokes. I've seen the horror of this drug war first hand, remember?" I start rapidly walking back toward the office door.

When he catches up to me, his tone is apologetic, but his words aren't. "We're just doing our jobs and trying to nail him, Dana. Law enforcement isn't the enemy." And now that he's taken the moral high road, he can't resist piling it on. "Have you heard from Shane? We could still use his information and possible testimony."

That's the real reason I'm here. He's still swinging, trying to get me to contact Shane and turn him into an informant. No way.

"I have no idea where he is. And even if I did, I wouldn't want him to get re-involved in this nightmare. It's not good enough that I was almost killed; you're still willing to risk my brother's life too? And he's a drug addict, Agent Stokes. If there's ever a trial, a defense attorney would question his reliability and destroy him on the stand."

We're back in Stokes' office. "Where's the form you want me to sign? I want to get out of here."

He sorts through three or four papers on his desk, and pushes a form and a pen across his desk to me. I scan it and sign it.

"Ling is busy with the Mexicans, but you still need to take precautions, Dana. Keep a low profile." Stokes calls after me as I walk to the door.

I scoff lightly at the irony. He wants my brother to get directly in Ling's sights, but he's advising me to be invisible and on-guard. "I'm finished with all of this, Agent Stokes. Don't call me again. And if you do, I'll refer you to my attorney."

As I drive away, my whole body is tense from the confrontation, and yet at the same time I feel that I may finally be able to move away from this whole sorry mess. Shane is gone; Sea Flea has been, well, cremated; and Ling is busy with his drug war. I'm out of it, and I'm going to stay out.

*

But at noon, I'm surprised by a call from Wayne, who's on his lunch break. "Dana, you're not going to believe this." His voice is tight, barely more than a whisper.

I squeeze the phone to my ear. "Tell me."

"Ling was just here, at the ER."

"What?" I'm sitting in the Harborside parking lot. I'd been checking the mushy surf (not rideable) and trying to decide how I'd spend the rest of my day. I sit forward in my seat, and peer unseeing at the rippling wind-chop churning the sea.

"He brought in his nephew, with second-degree burns on his arm."

Sea Flea. Ling's nephew must have been the driver. I recount last night's news story and my meeting with Stokes. "Wayne, how did you know it was Ling?"

"The kid, Veera, is only seventeen, so Ling had to sign admittance papers as his guardian. I recognized his full name, which you'd told me." Multiple questions pass through my brain, but my thoughts keep coming back to just one thing. Oh god, Wayne is in it now.

Wayne clears his throat; tension lowers his voice. "Should I call Stokes?"

"How did Veera say he got burned?" I'm already looking to dodge the truth, to hide and to cover. This is my journey with Shane...and now it's Wayne's.

"He said a hot pot tipped over at dinner last night, but the ER doc said it didn't look like a scalding. The burn marks are scattered spots on his arm, with deep blisters. Liquid would have rolled off and left a more uniform burn."

"Did you tell the doc who Ling is?"

"No, not yet. I'm was just observing; I wasn't the treating nurse and I had very little time with the doctor."

The conversation stalls. Wayne knows what I'm asking. Finally, in an even lower voice, he says, "You don't want me to say anything."

"If you speak up, the nurse or doctor will call the police and they'll call Stokes. And you'll become a direct witness to this drug war, Wayne. Stokes will use you; count on you for testimony down the road. And sooner or later, Ling might find out that you're not just an ER nurse...that you knew about him because of your connection to me."

His love for me, so fresh and new, comes at an ugly price — lying by omission.

He clears his throat. "I have to get back to work."

*

I beat the steering wheel after I hang up. My hands vibrate; my wrists hurt. I want to feel the pain, the punishment. Wayne, Dylan, Craig, all wrapped into this because of me. I may have saved Shane, likely just a temporary fix, but the cost sickens me. A new level of self-loathing churns through me; my temples pulse.

But I can't wallow in it; I have a new family drama to keep me busy until I start my new job. Terry.

He doesn't want my help, but he's my brother and I know him well enough to worry that this dual crisis in both his personal life and business is unhinging him. Should I call or go by his office? I decide to do both. But once again the phone rings and rings; clearly it's turned off. I just start driving over there.

When I arrive, the Mercedes isn't in the driveway. The office is shut down tight, blinds drawn. But Terry could just be hiding his car because he doesn't want to have to offer any explanations to his clients about the office closure or his expulsion from the agency. I park out front and decide to have a look around. First I check the front door. Locked. I rap firmly, two or three long series. No response. I try to peek through the blinds at the narrow window alongside the entrance, but I can't see anything but slices of gray carpet.

I stand there for a bit, trying to decide if I should just drive away or look around some more. I feel like a prowler, and I probably look like one too. My logical brain tells me to walk away. Terry doesn't want me involved. Jenna will have to give him some money to survive on — if they divorce there will be a split of assets — and they'll have to come to some agreement about him seeing his kids. All these thoughts pass through my brain, but I still can't sell it to myself. I need to make sure that Terry is handling this mess okay or at least better than yesterday.

I move to the driveway, and start up toward the detached two-car garage. It's the kind with the old one-piece, swing-up wooden door that runs nearly the width of the building. On the right side of the garage is a regular door for walk-in access, with glass in its top half. I walk up to it and hood my eyes so I can see past the glare and into the dark space. The

Mercedes is sitting there. But something is all wrong. There's a vacuum hose coming out of the car's tail pipe and running along its right side and into the rear window, which is up far enough to hold it in place. Rags fill the space left between the top of the car window and the window frame.

My brain processes all of this, but I'm so stunned that I'm frozen for a couple of seconds. I hear coughing and retching. I twist the doorknob, but it's locked. Without any conscious thought, I bend my arm and ram the glass with my elbow — it's an old door, no safety glass. It shatters and rains down onto the garage floor. I reach through the broken window and open the door. I crunch across the glass and squeeze around the back of the car, by the garage door. I quickly move up the driver's side and see Terry. He's leaning over, with the driver's cardoor open, retching onto the concrete floor. His face is ashen.

When I run up to him, he's barely conscious. His eyes are blood red and his body is shaking, and he keeps trying to vomit, but only a little watery fluid comes out. I notice that the car isn't running, but the carbon monoxide in the car and the garage is probably still very high. I run around the bumper again and punch the door-opener button. The door swings up. By now, I'm choking and coughing as well. I could dial 9-1-1 and get an ambulance, but the hospital isn't far. I sprint at full speed down the driveway and throw myself into the Honda, race it up to the garage and leave it running. I leap out and dash around the other side of the car to fling open the passenger door and recline the seat.

When I get back to him, Terry is still conscious but not coherent. I pull him out of the car and get my shoulder under his arm. I stagger, pulling his mostly limp body to the Honda, his feet drag uselessly behind him. "Terry, help me." I scream. This rouses him enough so he stumbles a little and then bends at the waist, which allows me to stuff him into the car seat. He tips over part way into the driver's seat, as I push his legs into the foot well.

In seconds, I'm burning down the highway to the hospital. Terry is twitching and dry heaving, but he's still breathing. I fly into the ER's semicircle drive, squealing the tires as I pull around in front of the over-size sliding glass doors. Fortunately, I don't have to run inside yelling. A male nurse is taking a smoking break by the door. He drops his cigarette and runs to me.

"Carbon monoxide poisoning," I scream, even though the nurse is right next to me. He turns and runs in through the automatic doors and I hear him call to other members of the ER staff. In just a few seconds, two big orderlies coming jogging out the door with a gurney. They muscle Terry onto it and strap him on.

An ER doc jogs up alongside the stretcher, as Terry is wheeled into an examination room. The doc is a thirtyish woman with a brown ponytail and big round glasses. "What's his name and tell me how you found him?" I describe the SUV and vacuum hose, and how Terry was choking and retching.

"Do you know long he was in the car with the gas coming in?"

"No."

"How do you know him?"

"He's my brother." I choke and cry as I say this.

"What kind of car? What year and model?"

Even though I register that this is a very odd question, I answer it anyway, "A Mercedes SUV, late model, but I don't know what year."

"Was he taking drugs?"

"I don't know. But he was definitely drinking heavily in the past twenty four hours."

"Is he married?"

"Yes."

"Well, if you can contact his wife that would be helpful. We'll take good care of him." At this point, one of the nurses escorts me out to the admittance desk, as I hear the doctor talking to Terry. "Terry, you're in the hospital. We need you to stay awake. Open your eyes." Her voice fades as I move down the hall.

The nurse looks hard at me and asks me how I'm feeling and how long I was in the garage. I ran in and out, I tell her.

"Did you choke or cough?"

"Yes, a little."

She strides quickly down the hall and brings back an oxygen tank and mask. She has me breathe pure oxygen for ten minutes before she allows me to do anything else. I sit in the hall, where she can monitor me from her station. My brain isn't working. I'm too stunned to move.

The nurse checks me again and gives me the okay to breathe just air. I make my way to a garden area in between two wings of the hospital. I stare at my glary phone screen; I need to call Jenna. But I'm starting to analyze and crumble. How can this be happening? I've worked for decades to keep Shane alive, to keep him from following my mother down the sucking drain, only to have Terry unravel and opt for an irreversible remedy to a temporary problem. I dissolve into choking sobs. Anguish and rage feed my breakdown. An elderly man looks over at me from the far side of the garden; empathy moves across his face but he doesn't approach.

I sit there staring through the tears at the beautiful, balmy spring day, which for Terry was clouded with self-loathing and hopelessness. In the corner of the garden, two robins come together on the ground, spinning, fluttering their wings and ramming into one another. It's not clear if they're fighting or mating...but isn't it the same thing? Jenna and Terry are tied together and right now they're destroying each other.

I can't put it off any longer. Jenna's office phone rings about six times and she picks up. "Dana, I don't want to talk." Her sharp words are loud and hostile.

"This, this is an emergency, Jenna. Terry is in Community Hospital."

"What? What's wrong?" She screeches. I pull the phone from my ear.

Should I leave out the details of how he ended up here until she can hear it in person? But I'm afraid that without the harsh truth, she may think she doesn't need to come. I give it to her straight, without too much detail. "He tried to kill himself, Jenna. He's in bad shape."

She gasps and stutters. "How? Where?"

"At his office. He tried to poison himself with carbon monoxide. He was semi-conscious when I found him. Can you come?"

"I'm on my way." She begins to cry, quietly.

Numbed, I move back inside. I tell the nurse who treated me that Terry's wife is on her way. I do my best to fill out parts of an admittance form for her, though Jenna will have to provide most of the information. Then I slump into a chair in the waiting area closest to where they're treating Terry. The ER is unusually quiet. A Latina woman in bindingly tight jeans and a peasant blouse holds a two-year-old on her lap. He's limp and flushed; his eyes are glazed. And he's quiet, which is serious for a toddler. Flu or something worse? Two chairs over from her, a Hispanic man holds his left arm, which is haphazardly wrapped at the wrist and hand in gauze.

There's a lot of blood visible under the wrapping. He wears a baseball cap and safety glasses, along with a green sweatshirt and jeans. A gardener? I guess it might have been an accident with a mower or trimmer.

Power tools make me think of Joe. Should I call him? I mull the pros and cons. He deserves to know, but I don't think I can deal with this crisis and him at the same time. Right or wrong, I decide to wait to call him until I hear Terry's prognosis from the doctor.

I start a pity party, sitting in the waiting area's hard plastic chair, staring at the linoleum floor. Another family disaster and I'm here, alone. Others in a crisis would immediately call their spouse. But I've been rejecting the man who miraculously wants to be my partner in life, who actually wants to be a part of my ruinous family. I am an idiot.

My mind moves back to Terry. Shane's decline has been long and somewhat predictable, with his increasing drug use and his lifelong battle with manic depression. But Terry's undoing was a jolt; a massive fissure caused by a couple of bad choices that he felt left his life irreparable. He was so wrapped up in his image, his financial success. Material pride is worth dying for? I have even more trouble understanding this than I do Shane's emotional demons and drug abuse.

But I shouldn't judge. Terry set out to escape our chaotic upbringing just as I did. Only he didn't run; he wanted to rise above it, prove he was born into the wrong family. And he followed all the conventional rules for success — built a business, networked with the right people, married up, drove the right car and took up the hobbies of the moneyed set. But he strove too hard and made some very bad decisions. And just that was enough to pummel him, and take it all away. Tears begin to run down my cheeks again. I've just blotted my face dry once more when Jenna rushes down the wide hospital corridor.

She sees me and comes over toward me. Guilt is causing her to physically sag in the middle; she is stooped and her eyes are pools of red. She looks up from the floor, but she can barely force herself to make eye contact. I meet her partway into the hall, and pull her into a hug. She stiffens at first, and then we cling to each other.

"I can't get my head around this, Dana...I had no clue he would do this...he was upset, sure. But he's always so commanding, so in charge. And not necessarily in a good way. And he just strives and pushes, pushes, pushes...and he got out of control. It was illegal, and I had to do something and, and...." She runs out of air. A sob catches in her throat.

"Jenna, you didn't cause this." I hug her again.

She calms down a little. "Where is he? What have you heard from the doctor?"

"Nothing yet. But you need to go to the admittance station and give them some health history on Terry and your health insurance information."

She hugs her arms to her middle and walks over to the desk. They hand her forms, a pen and a clipboard. We sit together as she works her way through the blanks and little boxes, copying information from her insurance card.

She's nearly done with the forms when the ER doctor comes and finds us.

She looks at Jenna. "Are you Mrs. McCarren?"

"Yes."

"Terry's doing okay. He's conscious and stable, and his vital signs are good." I'm listening to her and thinking, "that's the good news, here comes the bad."

"He'll need to stay in the hospital for at least a couple of days. With this kind of poisoning, we need to take steps to prevent neurological or brain damage. At the moment, he's breathing oxygen. But we'll be moving him to a hyperbaric chamber. Using the pressurized chamber, we'll be able to flush his body with oxygen and force out any residual carbon monoxide. We don't believe he inhaled too concentrated a dose. Thank goodness he has a newer-model car." She sees the confusion come across our faces and goes on to explain her comment.

It turns out that the sophisticated emissions control systems in newer-model cars greatly reduce the output of carbon monoxide, thus making it harder for people to get unintentionally or intentionally poisoned. That's why she asked me what type of car he had.

"If he had an older car, it would be much worse," she says.

Bizarre. The luxury car that pushed him to make illegal business decisions may have saved his life. Another one of life's ridiculous ironies.

"We've given him something for the pain. His head is probably pounding."

"What kind of neurological damage might he suffer?" Jenna whispers.

"Memory loss is the most common. Movement disorders and tremors can also occur. But getting a patient into a hyperbaric chamber right away has shown positive results."

"Can I see him?"

"Yes. He's pretty out of it from the effects of the gas and the pain pills, but he's awake."

"Do you want to see him alone, Jenna?" I want to give them space.

"I guess that would be best. But can you stay? I'd really like you to stay, Dana."

"I'll be here, Jenna."

She follows the doctor, and I'm left with only my whirring brain to overwhelm me. I always thought I'd be sitting in a hospital, or a morgue, after Shane either attempted suicide or succeeded. Our mother Valerie's shadow extends beyond her mental illness and the emotional damage her suicide caused us. I've read the stats — close family members of a suicide victim are three to four times more likely to commit suicide than those who have no family history of it. Still, I never thought that Terry would go down the dark tunnel and see no way out.

Time seems to suspend; I don't know if it's been ten minutes or nearly an hour when Jenna comes back. She collapses into the chair next to me, crying silently. I put my arm around her shoulders and hold her. "How's he look?"

"Okay. He just seems tired and dopey. But he was able to speak."

"What did he say?"

"That he was sorry." At this, she starts heaving, her whole body moving up and down.

"He says that when he started choking he realized he didn't want to die. He says he shut the engine off. They're moving him to the hyperbaric chamber. The doctor says he needs to spend several hours in there, probably in two sessions."

By the time he's out of the chamber, it will likely be past visiting hours. Nonetheless, I ask her about Joe. "I need to call Joe. But since Terry is stable and will be in the chamber, he probably won't come until tomorrow."

"That's fine. He needs to know. Oh, Dana, your mom and now Terry. Poor Joe. Can he take this?"

"He's incredibly tough, Jenna. He'll manage." I say this, trying to convince myself, but I wonder. Joe, always stalwart and robust to the outside world, can crumble. I've seen it, once after Valerie died and once when Shane was arrested. And that's just what I've observed. Away from the world, I'm sure he's melted down, probably doused his sorrows with a bottle. And he's getting older, more vulnerable. Plus the emotional distance between him and Terry will make this harder on him...guilt, our most insidious emotion, will batter his aged body. But Jenna doesn't need to hear any of this. She has her kids to think of.

"Do you need to pick up the kids?" It's getting toward the end of the school day.

"No, there's a carpool. And Lucinda will be there to meet them at home." Lucinda is the part-time nanny they hired, once Jenna's career took off. What do you say to your kids when you've kicked their father out of the house, and he tries to kill himself? I'm sure it won't be the truth. The ugly reality of dashed dreams and the emotional toll they take? Children shouldn't learn about that until they're older, until, sadly, the world shows it to them.

Jenna needs to see her kids and feel that there's still a normal side to her life. I encourage her to go. Terry's in the chamber; she can come back after dinner. She reluctantly agrees, we hug quickly and she's gone. She doesn't ask what I'll do.

I need to go see Joe. He shouldn't be alone when he hears this news.

Chapter 28

While I'm gathering my thoughts and getting ready to leave, the ER staff goes into high gear. Several nurses and a doctor rush down the corridor. I hear sirens blaring, getting louder as they reach the ER entrance. I stiffen and step backward.

The doors whoosh as they slide open and I see three paramedics rush a gurney down the hall toward the exam rooms. The victim's face and arms are blackened, with dark red wounds visible, and a piece of burned clothing hangs off the side of the rolling stretcher. One of the paramedics carries an IV bag. The burns are so bad it's not clear if the victim is a man or a woman, until he moans. Twenty seconds later, another cart passes, and a third. All of the victims are badly burned. The smell of burnt fabric and burnt hair wafts down the hall, as each one goes by. A minute later and I hear another ambulance pull into the ER driveway, and I think I hear other cars, tires squealing into the adjacent parking lot.

Another gurney appears, with a paramedic alongside. He tows this one more slowly. An additional escort of a uniformed police officer follows. A male victim lies on the stretcher; his ear, the hair of above it and part of his forehead are scorched. He isn't moaning and he holds himself rigid. His left hand, in a fist at his side, is handcuffed to one of the stretcher's safety bars, a gleaming watch catches the fluorescent hall light.

Instantly, I recognize Ling.

As he passes, he turns his head slightly toward me, but there's no recognition in his drifting eye. I've battled him for weeks, but he still doesn't know who I am. I intend to keep it that way. My brain swirls. Only in this tiny town, would I pass by as Sea Flea explodes and then be here and see Ling brought into the hospital.

I start moving to the door and then I jump, as a loud bang rings out. I spin back toward the sound, toward the exam rooms. Ling has rolled off the side of the gurney and spun it diagonally, knocking the officer who was alongside it into the wall and to the ground. The paramedic who was towing the stretcher has backed up, his eyes wide. Ling turns toward me and starts to run, all the while dragging the stretcher, which is oscillating back and forth across the hall. The heavy-set officer tries to get to his feet, while he fumbles with the clasp on his holster.

Ling has rolled past me and is halfway back to the ER entrance when two plainclothes FBI with I.D.'s hanging from their necks over their Kevlar vests appear just inside the entrance. They crouch in firing position, guns sighted on Ling.

"FREEZE!" one yells. "Drop to your knees. NOW!"

Ling skids to a stop. The gurney runs into the back of him. He stares over their heads at the ER doors, at freedom lost. His face is inscrutable as he lowers himself to his knees and puts his unshackled arm up. One of the FBI agents stays crouched, with his gun pointed at Ling. The other one keeps his gun trained on him as well, but steps ahead slowly and then moves behind Ling. He lunges forward, and slams Ling to the linoleum, jamming a knee in between his shoulders; the heavy gurney that's still attached to Ling tips over and clatters to the floor. The agent then twists Ling's free arm up and behind his back, until he gasps involuntarily. The other agent now runs forward and when he gets to Ling, he too drops down and puts an elbow on his turned head. Ling grunts.

The uniformed local police officer has finally made it to his feet and down the hall. He huffs and his mouth hangs open. He's finally freed his gun, but it hangs limply at his right thigh.

The agents uncuff Ling's left arm from the stretcher and cuff both his wrists behind his back. Then they yank him to his feet. They call for the paramedic to bring a wheelchair. When he does, they throw Ling into it, bending him forward and stretching his cuffed arms around the back of the chair. One of them drops to his knees and pulls two long zip ties from his vest pocket. But then Ling kicks out with his foot; he misses the agent's head and hits him in the shoulder, knocking him backward onto his butt. The officer behind the chair puts Ling into a head lock, partially choking him. "How's that feel, huh? You want some more?" He squeezes harder and Ling gasps.

Pulling back up onto his knees, the agent on the floor wraps two ties around Lings' ankles, one at a time, and pulls them tight. They then quickly spin him around and roll him toward an exam room.

At first the corridor is filled with gaping orderlies and nurses, who huddle together. But it clears quickly as they return to their rounds; one rights the tipped-over gurney and tows it away. I'm stunned in place, still standing in the waiting area. Finally I start walking toward the ER doors, and in strides Agent Stokes. Confusion moves across his face. "Dana, what are you doing here?"

"My brother, Terry, is in the hospital." I don't provide any more details. "You've just missed all the action. Ling tried to escape." I haltingly describe the melee.

He starts down the hall, but I grab his arm. I need him to say it. I need to know Ling will be caged and prosecuted.

Stokes hesitates. He wants to swat me away; he wants to go to his men.

"Tell me, Agent Stokes." My voice is low, graveled, demanding. "I was nearly killed, and I've been involved in this mess for weeks. I won't talk to any reporters."

He sharply tilts his head, reluctantly acquiescing. "Yes. We have him." Triumphant pride fills his voice; his posture is military straight. "One of his labs was bombed and he was there. Three of his gang members are dead, three are severely injured. As you probably saw, he's injured, but his wounds aren't serious."

I get in his face. "Assure me you have enough to prosecute him." I'm strung out. There's no diplomacy left in me.

"Yes. Our case is now solid, thanks to the witnesses who have cooperated." He can't resist this last dig at Shane. "After medical treatment, he'll be transferred later today to a maximum-security facility, where he'll await trial. His gang is crumbling. We're rounding up his associates. Others, that we aren't charging, will likely fade away."

"The Mexicans and their violence and pressure brought him down."

Anger washes across his face. "We were closing in on him. The Mexicans just accelerated the timetable, Dana. I have to go."

He starts moving away from me. I lift my chin. Sure, Stokes, keep convincing yourself, keep selling it. Someone is bound to believe you, just not me.

*

I walk out the ER doors. I'm glad they have Ling, but I'm extremely skeptical about the judicial process and Stokes' ability to make his case without a screw-up or some other mitigating factor. Ling is slippery. And high-profile cases like this one draw top defense attorneys. I'm not convinced that it's safe for Shane to emerge from hiding just yet.

Now I have to deliver some of the worst news of his life to my father.

*

Joe shuffles to the door in his slippers and usual uniform of a dark sweatshirt and jeans. Reading glasses rest low on his nose. My "Hi, Dad" greeting in a weak little girl voice is enough to set off his well-tuned intuition. He looks at me sidelong and invites me in. I follow him into the living room and take a seat on the worn sofa. He gathers up his newspaper from the seat of his lounger, drops into it, grabs the remote and mutes the TV.

"I don't where to start, but I have some really bad news, Dad."

He stares at me and I see him stiffen. I decide to backtrack a little.

"Remember when you saw the SUV in front of your house the other night? Well, it was Terry. He and Jenna are on the outs, and he's out of the house."

He sighs. But he doesn't ask why. "Are they trying to patch it up?" It's a hopeful question...perhaps this is the news, and the worst is already over. Just a small domestic dispute, nothing more, all couples fight.

"It's a big problem, Dad. Terry wasn't running the business properly, and Jenna has had to step in to straighten it out. They may not even be able to keep the insurance agency."

Another sigh. He pulls off his glasses. "Stupid, stupid, stupid."

332

Despite my best efforts, tears start forming in my eyes. Shock and worry register across Joe's face. He sits up a little taller, alert that some truly bad news is coming. Lady senses something too and comes over and stuffs her head under Joe's right hand.

"Oh, Dad, there's no way to say this gently, so I'm just going to blurt it. Terry was distraught about losing the business and losing his family. He was drinking heavily and staying at the office. And...he tried to kill himself this morning. He's alive and in Community Hospital. They think he will recover." I say all this in a rush so I can finish it.

He puts his hand up to his brow and covers his eyes. He coughs; his hand trembles. I choke back my emotions so I can continue.

In as clinical a tone as I can muster, I tell him about calling Jenna, and going to see Terry yesterday. I describe his drinking and his confession about the business. And I tell him about my worry and going back to his office to check on him. My throat tightens when I describe finding Terry in the garage, with the vacuum hose running from the tailpipe through the car window. I look at Joe and he seems to visibly shrink. He keeps rubbing his hand across his brow. I push on and describe driving Terry to the ER, his condition and treatment.

"Jenna came and saw him already. She needed to go check on the kids, but she's going back to the hospital later, after he gets out of the chamber."

He's silent. I get up and go to him. Leaning over the back of the lounger, I rub his shoulders. And I wait. He reaches up and across his body and squeezes my right hand. Tears slide down my face, and I bat them away with the back of my other hand.

I offer him the only hopeful crumb I have. "Dad, he told Jenna that when he started choking, he shut the engine off. In the end, he didn't want to die."

He clears his throat a couple of times. "When should I try to see him?"

"Tomorrow?" I say this as a suggestion, not an answer. "It will be late when he gets out of the chamber. And Jenna is going to stay there with him tonight."

"Good, that's good."

I move back to the sofa, curling myself up in the corner closest to my father. He starts to speak, his voice low and hesitant. "I didn't spend enough time with Terry. Valerie, Shane, they took everything. You and Terry were left to fend for yourselves. He grew up to resent me, and it made me mad, Dana. Terry judged me, and I'm his father."

He stares across the room and grips the arms of the recliner. "It was justified, but it's hard for any man. And it just pushed us further apart. By the time he was an adult, we had no real connection."

I reach over and touch his hand. "It's been the same with me, Dad. I've spent all these years trying to help Shane, keeping him going, and I spent almost no time looking after my relationship with Terry. He kept moving away from me, and I let him."

He looks at me and pushes himself up straighter in the chair, pushing to force a way forward. "He truly loves Jenna and his kids, Dana. If he can grab a hold of that, focus on that, he can right his life. I love him, but he doesn't need me, he needs them."

"Maybe not. But needs to know that you're sorry for how hurt and ignored he felt as a child."

"Yes, he does. And you do too, Dana." He stands up and pulls me up off the couch, giving me one of his bear hugs.

These few words are huge for him. With my head against his chest, I choke back my tears. I don't want him to let go of me. I feel like I'm seven years old again and getting the best hug ever from my Daddy.

He pulls back and holds me at arm's length. He gives me another firm but quick hug. "Are you going to be okay after this awful shock?"

"Eventually, yes."

"Will you see Wayne tonight?" For once, I don't feel like my father is more interested in the man in my life than me. He just wants me to be supported and loved.

"Yeah, Dad. Are you going to be okay?"

"Eventually." He shrugs slightly. "Your dad is a tough old geezer, Dana. And I'm determined to help my other son."

He walks me to the door. We lean in for one more quick hug, and I walk out.

I drive away as the day is fading to evening. A text from Wayne comes in. "Will you come visit?"

*

Traffic creeps slowly up the coast; the fog bank hovers just offshore. Seagulls circle the harbor parking lot. Like me, they're homing in on a roost for the evening.

When I arrive at the bungalow, Wayne is elbow deep in chicken and cheese for enchiladas. He hands me a beer, and I sit across the kitchen's small island as he finishes the assembly. I ask him about his first day at the hospital. I've repaired my face before I arrived, even putting on a little make-up to hide that I've been crying.

"I feel so useless, Dana. Today I was just an observer, and the place is so busy. Lori, my mentor, says I'll start actually nursing on day three. But before I jump in, they want me to see how the whole process of entry, admittance and treatment goes." He describes today's patients: an elderly man who'd fallen and may have a hip fracture, a teen with strep or mononucleosis, a drug addict with signs of hepatitis, and several others. It's overwhelming just hearing about it — I can't imagine the stress of treating these people.

But Wayne says it's like being a soldier. Nurses take orders from the ER doctors and they execute those orders. Nurses do more of patient interaction, comforting, advising, evaluating. That frees the docs up to see more people. He says it's autocratic and yet collaborative.

He's tired, as well as invigorated. He's trained for nearly three years to do this and now he's a working nurse. So far we've avoided discussing our lunch-time phone call.

We're sitting on the couch, sipping our second beers, when the conversation turns to my day. He knew about my appointment to identify Sea Flea, but he knows nothing of the rest of my traumatic Monday. Part of me needs to tell him about Terry, and yet another part is afraid to reveal yet another family drama. When will he say "Enough"?

I start by recounting Joe's suspicions that something was wrong in Terry's life. I describe my interaction with him at his office: the Jack Daniels, and the revelations about the phantom policies and Jenna's suspension of agency business.

"She threw him out of the house. It was several days ago, and it seems he's just been spiraling down since then. He made a huge mistake, and he knew it."

Wayne stares at me; he sees my distress. He picks up my right hand and sandwiches it between his two big palms. He waits. I tell him about finding Terry in the garage, the trip to the ER, Terry's prognosis and treatment, and Jenna's arrival at the hospital. Then I recount Ling's arrival at the hospital, escape attempt while dragging the gurney, and my conversation with Stokes.

"He tried to run, with officers right there?" His eyes are wide.

"Yeah, he had to try. It reminded me of Shane." I shake my head.

"But now he's finally in custody?" His eyes narrow.

"Yes, and Stokes promised me that he has enough to prosecute him." I don't say it, but Wayne clearly comprehends that this means they don't need his information about Ling bringing his nephew to the ER.

I take a deep breath and then ramble on about visiting Joe. My voice breaks and tears tumble down my face.

He wraps his arms around me. "Did Terry really did turn off the car and try to save himself?"

"I want to believe it, but he could just be saying that for Jenna."

"You'll see him tomorrow?"

"Yes. But we've never been close, Wayne. I feel helpless. I won't have a fixer role in this — it's between him and Jenna what happens now."

The oven timer dings; I pick at the meal. Without saying a word, Wayne clears the dishes into the sink and leads me to the bedroom. He makes love to me, slowly, working his hands across my face and touching every part of my body. When we start, I figure I'm too tense to let go. But he's patient, insistent. My mind shuts down, and I melt into him. I shudder and cry out and still he pulls me to him until his body gives in. Afterward, he rolls onto his back and tucks me under his arm.

"I want to be with you, Dana. You think no one would want to be part of the McCarren clan, but you're wrong. I want all of you...the fun, the drama, the professional woman..."

"The sex."

He smiles down at me. "That too. We bring out the best in each other. We'll support each other through the tough times, and we'll chase moments of pure bliss."

"And surf them?"

He smiles. "And surf them. Definitely."

Chapter 29

When Wayne leaves for work the next day, he presses a key into my palm.

"You can come and go whenever."

He kisses me. I smile and say nothing. I'm still easing into this. He knows not to push.

After he's gone, I walk out to the studio and look around. Damn if he didn't find a place with the most perfect writing space. I envision where I'd put a desk, a computer monitor, a work table. In less than a week, I'll be grinding out copy for World Business from somewhere. Why not here?

I am resolved to work on the emotional turmoil in *my* life. Dealing with Shane's problems has been a way to avoid looking at my own. I've spent time in therapy, but have I moved forward? No. Really I've been backtracking in recent years, using work and family dramas to avoid any real connections.

After all that's happened, stability and security seem like ridiculous fantasies. But that's okay. Life's road map isn't a point-to-point journey; it's a confusing zig-zag. I need to keep moving ahead, even if the route has some blind curves.

I shower and dress, stealing a surf T-shirt that swallows me from Wayne's closet. I call Dylan, as I make my way south on Highway 1.

"Hey, Dana, stayed out all night, huh, and didn't even call the parents?"

"Sorry, Dad. I figured you'd call if you were worried. I was up at Wayne's."

"Good. That's where you should be."

"Don't start. The relationship lectures are Maria's territory."

He agrees. "Oh, so true."

"Have you heard that the feds got Ling?"

"Yeah, everyone is talking about it."

"I saw him, when he was wheeled into the ER."

I stammer as I start to explain why I was there, but fortunately, I don't have to. Maria worked swing shift last night, and she ran into Jenna at the hospital's cafeteria. Because Dylan and Maria are some of my oldest and closest friends, they've met all my family members.

Dylan says that Jenna confided in Maria, but I can tell she left out details of Terry's misadventures with the fantasy insurance policies.

"I'm on my way to the hospital now."

"I'm so sorry, Dana." He exhales hard. "You didn't need another shock. How are you?"

I don't want to go into my feelings of guilt on the phone. I deflect. "I told Joe yesterday. He'll visit Terry later."

"Poor Joe. How did he take the news?"

"He's hurting. But he's determined to help Terry, and to find a way across the giant divide that's separated them." I sigh. "It sounds weird, Dylan, but I'm proud of how my Dad reacted, and what might come out of this."

"Wow, I hope this does bring them together. Terry's rejection of Joe obviously hurt him more than it did Joe."

I wag my head, as I change lanes. "You're so right. No wonder you work so well with teens, with their raging emotions."

"What are your plans after the hospital?"

"I'm open. Can I run any errands or do anything for you and Maria?"

"Let's have lunch, if that works for you. I have some gossip to share about Ling and Stokes." I can hear Dylan shuffling papers in the background.

"Really? You've piqued my curiosity. Any clues?"

"No, you'll have to wait. This is juicy, and I'm only discussing it in person."

We agree to meet at twelve thirty at a deli that's close to Dylan's office. He asks me to give his best to Terry.

At the reception desk, I get Terry's room number. They ask me to check in at the nurses' station in that wing before I visit with him. When I reach the nurses station, it's Byron, my nurse during the first part of my stay after the shooting, who's sitting at the desk, scanning a computer monitor. Despite all the patients he sees per week, he remembers me.

"Dana!" He comes around the desk and gives me a quick squeeze. "You look well. I'm pleased."

Once again, I don't have to explain my situation or why I'm here. The beauty and the curse of a small town. Maria has called the ward to check on Terry's status, and she spoke with Byron. She made the connection for him and said to expect me, and probably Joe.

"Terry is doing well, Dana. He had two treatments in the chamber yesterday, and all the carbon monoxide has been forced from his body. It's too soon to tell for sure, but I think he's going to be one of the lucky ones."

My eyebrows rise, and I'm unsure what he means. Lucky? That's not how I'd describe Terry's situation. "By lucky, I mean he may not have any lasting damage from the gas. And he's alive, in part because of your quick action." He pats me on the hand.

"Why are visitors supposed to check in with you?"

"We do that with all attempted suicides, Dana. We want to know when anyone is in the room with them. The patient can get overwhelmed, even by well-intentioned family."

What he really means is family dynamics often contribute to a suicide attempt. I mull over what to say about

Joe's upcoming visit. It could help Terry; it could be too much for him. Byron is one of those people whose inherent goodness wraps around them like a sweater — so I share with him a little bit about Joe's and Terry's history, Shane's part in it, and why Joe's visit today may be a positive, but could be potentially fraught.

"I'll keep a close eye, Dana. Thanks for telling me." He goes on to say that Jenna spent the night in Terry's room and left a little while ago. He says Terry's emotions are a raw. It's psychological internal bleeding, I think to myself.

Byron points his chin toward Terry's room. "Go on in. He's expecting you."

I rap on the hallway wall as I enter. He's sitting up. The TV is tuned to the golf channel, with the volume turned low. He's pale, and there are large dark circles under his runny eyes.

"Come on in, Dana." His voice is gravelly and nasal. I lean down and kiss him on the cheek; he squeezes my shoulder. I ease into the armchair next to the bed.

"How was the chamber?"

"I'd say like a coffin, but that's a really bad analogy." A lopsided grin spreads across his mouth.

"Sick." I attempt to smile. "How are you feeling?"

"Shaky, but okay. I'm here. You're an amazing woman, Dana. Jenna told me how you got me to the ER all by yourself. And the doctor says that your quick actions probably saved me from additional damage from the gas."

My head hangs; I shrug, as I look up at him. "I reacted the way anyone would. I love you, brother."

We both start crying, pretty much simultaneously. He grabs a tissue from his tray and holds the box out to me. "I want to tell you what happened, Dana, if you want to hear it."

"Please." I run the tissue under my eyes.

He starts by saying that he continued to down the whisky after I left his office the day before yesterday. Eventually, he passed out. And when he awoke two hours later, he started drinking again. "I was trying to just black out, but it didn't work." A while ago, when he and Jenna were fighting, she'd been given a prescription for an antidepressant, but had only taken one or two and felt she didn't need them. They were sitting in the medicine cabinet. When he stopped by the house to get clothes, after she'd kicked him out, he grabbed them. "I slammed two of those and chased them with the second bottle of Jack."

I gulp. Hell, the alcohol poisoning alone might have killed him.

He runs his hand through his hair. "That did it. I passed out for the rest of the night, until about six. When I woke up, I had the worst hangover of my life, and I was really shaky. But I didn't want any more alcohol, so I popped three more pills. Believe it or not, until then Dana I was low but I wasn't ready to check out. I swear it." He stares hard at me, willing me to believe him.

"But the pills only seemed to make me feel worse. I felt hyper and depressed at the same time, and I wanted it to STOP. The doc says that some antidepressants can actually bring on suicidal feelings. It's rare, but it happens. And I'd taken way too many of them."

He looks down; his hands clench the blanket. "I was feeling so low that I started drinking again. I don't know when I came up with the idea of gassing myself. And I don't remember rigging up the hose to the car." He stops now and chokes back some tears. I reach out and hold his hand and wait.

"When the gas started to take effect, and I was coughing and my chest hurt, I sort of came round. I remember thinking

Kathleen Doler

about my kids and Jenna, and I knew I didn't want to die. I thought about Valerie, and I knew I didn't want to do that to my kids. So I shut the engine off. Then the vomiting started and I was too weak to get out of the car. Time seemed to stop, and the first thing I remember after that is you yelling at me. Damn, you can be loud."

I grin and rub the side of my face. "Family trait. I was trying to get you into my Honda, but you were so out of it you weren't moving or bending. I screamed at you and you helped just enough for me to stuff you into the seat."

"Like I said, Dana, you saved me. You're my angel." I lean over and hug him again, as we both cry some more.

"Me, an angel? That's a stretch."

His lips turn up a slightly. But he's not done yet. The talking is helping him process the whole episode. "And the doc says that the damn Mercedes may have helped save my life because of its sophisticated emissions system. Besides, just before I shut the engine off, I saw a warning light come on. It was about to run out of gas."

I can't help it; this revelation is in fact hilarious to me. I stuff down a smile, but Terry sees it and even though he's spent his adult life trying to distance himself from our family he shares the McCarren twisted sense of humor. "Yeah, yeah, okay, I tried to gas myself with a car that was running on empty."

Byron hears us as he's passing by on his rounds. He sticks his head in the door and sees us doubled over with laughter. "Well, that's certainly music to my ears. Can I get you two anything? How's the headache, Terry?"

"I'm doing fine." Terry wipes his eyes and regains his composure.

Byron turns and walks back out into the corridor.

Terry says he and Jenna spent a couple of hours talking last night, discussing things honestly in a way that they hadn't done in years. They're moving ahead with shutting down the agency, but Jenna is insisting that Terry come home. He's supposed to be released from the hospital tomorrow.

"And I don't think it's solely because of guilt, or the fact that I'm now unemployed and a charity case, Dana. I think she really wants to try again. I love her; I did a really stupid thing, but I've always loved her. My family means everything to me." He lowers his chin and breathes deeply, controlling his emotions.

"I'm so glad, Terry." There are a million questions: What will he do for work? Can he stop living to impress? Will he have any lasting medical issues related to the gas? But all of this seems unimportant. He's alive, and he's going home.

"Joe really wants to see you. Are you up for that? If not, I'll tell him you're not ready. But he has some things he wants to say to you, Terry."

"I'm starting over, Dana. This is my second life. So yeah, I want to see him. I want to start over with him too. Will you call him for me and ask him to come for lunch? Dad has always enjoyed a free meal." This comment gets us both snickering again.

I get up to say my goodbyes. I want him to rest before Joe's visit, and I'm spent too. We hug and cling.

"Love you, brother." I whisper in his ear.

"Love you, sis."

On my way out, I ask Byron if he can arrange to have an extra lunch delivered for my Dad. He says "Absolutely." When I reach the parking lot, I phone Joe. His voice is initially guarded, but I can hear relief come into it when I say that Terry would like him to come to the hospital for lunch.

I have some time before I'm supposed to meet Dylan, so I decide to buzz up to the farm to change clothes and pack some things for Wayne's house. The alley cat is ready to start marking her territory. The fog has cleared and it's a warm humid day. The fresh smell of wet grass fills the air. Summer is approaching. Renewal is coming.

As I make my way back into town, I dial Jenna's cell.

"Hi, Dana. How did your visit go?"

I give her a short recap. "Joe will be going to the hospital for lunch."

"Wow, that's really good. Do you think they'll actually talk...about their relationship?"

"They've both said they want to." I ask her how she's doing, and if I can help her in any way.

She says she's managed to claw back the phony insurance policies. She manufactured a pretty elaborate story about a trial arrangement with an invented independent insurance sales rep, which she fed to the underwriter. If this story flies, Terry won't have a blot on his employment record that could prevent him from obtaining other work. Another family member's lie has helped cover for another McCarren. And Jenna is smarter and more inventive than me or Terry — creating phony policies is kids' stuff compared to fabricating an entire person. I'm shocked...and impressed.

"We're going to hold this family together, Dana. And I want Terry to do something he actually likes that's less stressful."

I'm murmuring "well, well, well" as I put down the phone. My family, flawed as it is, has started to come together. Shane is out there somewhere, but despite so many previous disappointments, I hope he too can fully embrace his new start...and maybe, just maybe reconnect with his brother and father. But the timing on that is dependent on how the case against Ling progresses and whether I can be assured that Stokes will no longer pursue Shane.

*

When I enter the deli, the crowd is three deep at the big glass case. It's New York-style: customers are shouting orders over the counter to gruff sandwich makers who are echoing them back. Dylan is already at the register, paying for two massive turkey sandwiches that are as thick as fists in the middle.

At a patio out back, he leans in and kisses me.

After we call a truce with the sandwiches, I start the conversation. "Ling is caught, and Sea Flea is deceased; how safe is Shane? Will Stokes make his case without trying to involve him? Can he come out of hiding?"

"Well, slow down a bit. I have some very interesting news on that front." With his sly grin, I can see that he's savoring this bit of legal gossip.

"I hope 'interesting' means positive. Come on, give it up."

"Ling is being deported. He flies tomorrow."

"What???" I stutter. "No big trial for Stokes? No headlines and press conferences? He must be furious. What happened?"

"I'm sure it's a very complicated bit of politics, but the long and the short of it is the DEA is involved, and they're giving Ling to the Thai government as a gesture of goodwill and for the promise of future cooperation on international drug investigations. Ling will be prosecuted for a long list of drug crimes in Thailand. Drug offenses in Thailand are punishable by death, Dana. And the legal system there moves much more quickly than it does here."

I swallow hard, and it's not because of the whole bird I just ate. Knowing someone is likely to get the death penalty, no matter how deserving, is sobering.

"Do you have any idea how this all came down? Was Stokes blindsided?"

"That's the best part of the story."

"Spill."

"Keep in mind this is gossip, but my sources, like yours, are pretty reliable. And they have no reason to fabricate this stuff. Turns out that Stokes might have had some real trouble making his case in court...if his interactions with the Mexican gang came to light during a trial."

I'm leaning forward, concentrating on his story.

"You're not the only one who doesn't like Stokes and doesn't trust him. His detractors are saying that he was working with the Mexicans, trading information. And they say Stokes' leaks actually helped the Mexicans attack Ling's operation."

My jaw falls open a little. I'm not surprised at Stokes' actions, not really, but still he put many innocent people at risk, including me.

Dylan sips his tea. "If that's true, and it came out at trial, the case against Ling may have become mired in all kinds of additional investigations of the FBI's actions. That's the last thing the FBI or the Justice Department would want. So they're solving the problem by shipping Ling to Thailand."

"And Stokes?"

"He's already been shipped off, as of today."

"Wow. Where?"

"My sources say Miami, which is actually a step up for someone like Stokes. It's a bigger, more important region for fighting smuggling and drug crime. He's not being punished, he's being promoted, Dana." His lips tighten and turn down.

"And justice for all."

"Kind of eases any guilt we might feel about protecting Shane, doesn't it?"

"Hmm."

As a jaded journalist, I shouldn't be surprised by any of this. And Dylan has seen enough manipulation of the legal system that he's not surprised either. But it's dirty, and we can't help noticing the stench of it.

Dylan switches topics. "How's Terry?"

I give him an abridged report. "The antidepressants paired with the alcohol did unbalance him; I need to believe that. And Jenna seems committed to trying to rebuild. I'm moved by that."

He looks directly into my eyes. "Some mates are true champions, Dana. Maria would fight for me, for us, even if I did something awful."

The lecture about finding one of those champions never comes, even though it's implied.

*

Later, I'm up at Wayne's. I've taken delivery of his bedroom furniture, and I even made up the new bed. When I'm prepping dinner, my phone rings and displays an unidentified number. I pick up, using a formal business greeting, but it's Shane.

"Hey, you surf terrorist, I was just thinking about you."

"All seeing, all knowing."

"You sound good."

"Fit, clean and ready for some dirty fun."

"Your timing is excellent. I have big news about your former employer, and it's good news for you...not so much for him."

I run through the entire story about the explosion, Ling's injury and arrest, and his impending deportation.

"So as of tomorrow, we can talk, Shane, really talk." He'll be able to tell me where he's been living.

"But how did all this happen, Dana? I thought Stokes saw Ling as a career-maker?"

I quickly relate the politics behind the deportation, and Stokes' involvement with the Mexican gang.

Shane growls, and his voice gets louder. "If I'd cooperated, I might have been killed by the Mexicans, with Stokes providing the intel. Oh yeah, that's justice."

"It's not right, it's disgusting, but it means you're in the clear, Shane. No one needs you as a witness. Tomorrow Ling will be gone."

"Yeah, and he'll likely get an injection of poison, courtesy of the Thai justice system."

We don't say it, but somehow the fact that the Thai death penalty means a lethal injection seems like poetic justice for a criminal who knowingly sold poison meth.

I add that I have more news, about Terry.

He immediately senses something bad. "Tell me."

I give him the unvarnished version, but end with the news that Jenna is committed to helping Terry recover from his bad business decisions and his emotional and physical wounds.

"Oh, damn, Dana." He clears his throat, twice, then goes on, quieter now. "Terry was just as damaged by our childhood as we were, Dana, he just covered it better. He wanted to be anything but a McCarren."

I recap my conversation with Joe, and how he and Terry are trying to reconnect.

"Wow. That's just unreal, Dana. Joe is actually talking?"

Then Shane says something unexpected. "I want to talk to Terry too. He's my brother. I want to set things right."

I'm astonished and thrilled; Shane wants to talk. No statement could convince me more that he's clean.

"That would be huge, Shane."

It's time to end the call. We agree to talk again tomorrow after I'm certain that Ling is indeed gone. I want to hear all about his living situation, his work and his recovery.

Wayne pulls into the driveway less than thirty minutes later. That evening Wayne unpacks my bag into one of the two dressers he bought, one just for my use. It's an early evening; tomorrow Wayne will start really using his nursing skills.

The next day, I'm still puttering around Wayne's house when Dylan calls.

"Ling is gone. He shipped out today on a military flight out of Travis Air Force Base." There is relief and triumph in his voice. Even though there were ugly politics behind this turn of events, it is the best outcome for Shane.

Dylan is headed to court so he has no time to chat. After we hang up, I wonder if I can call the number that Shane's burner phone left in my recent calls list. I hope it's his phone and not one he borrowed. It's early in Kauai. I take a chance and tap redial.

"He's gone!"

Shane whoops, at a volume few can match. He says he's standing on a cliff, yes in Kauai, watching a swell that isn't rideable yet but shows promise for this afternoon when the tide goes out. He's dying to tell me about his life there and quickly launches into all of it. He's working as a maintenance man for a surf buddy who runs a property management business. He even takes jobs cleaning vacation condos and homes because as a maid he gets to work at his own pace, often scheduling around tides, surf conditions. "It's good scratch, Dana." He lives in an O'hana (a Hawaiian mother-in-law apartment, a converted garage) behind a widowed postman's house in Hanalei. He says it's walking distance to the bay and affordable.

But typical of Shane, this perfect situation in paradise is now in jeopardy. "This one loud-mouth neighbor has been giving me some lip," he growls. Parking on the streets close to the bay is tight, so Shane sometimes squeezes the rusted Nissan he's buying from a waitress in front of the lava rock wall that surrounds this guy's multimillion-dollar tropical compound. "The pasty little fucker left a nasty note on my car, telling me I couldn't park there. But it's on the street! So I tossed some overripe papayas over the gate and onto his pristine driveway the other night." He huffs. "Took him all morning to clean up the mess."

I sigh. Exasperation creeps into my voice. "And you think that's going to end it?"

"Maybe not, but I'm parking legally. I'm in the right. Fuck. Him."

Shane is always right, always entitled. Ling is no longer a threat to him, so he needs another fight. His bipolar reaction to any perceived wrong is to mix it up, show the other party how right he is...with words, actions or fists. He's fighting the world and himself.

I slump. I'm no longer in a celebratory mood.

Shane changes the subject and tells me he attends AA meetings twice a week.

"I only surf with AA friends or drug-free watermen." He says that Captain Garrett emphasized the importance of "positive influences," nearly "every...single...day" of the crossing. "He was relentless, Dana."

We speak a little more about Terry, and he says again that he wants to reconnect with him. I wonder if that will actually happen, and if it could be a good thing.

But stranger things are in the offing. Saturday is my official moving day ...

Chapter 30

The late spring swell has been building for about eighteen hours, and its apex arrives on Sunday morning, perfect for weekend warriors. NOAA's offshore buoys are reporting wave heights of six to seven feet, coming from the west-southwest, with a good long interval between swells. Winds are light and predicted to be offshore later today. We cram into Wayne's truck and pile wetsuits, beach chairs, towels and a cooler of drinks and snacks in the truck-bed, topping it with three boards. Mist hangs in the cool air; happily the fog is hiding offshore.

Rolling down Highway 1, traffic is sparse. I'm squeezed into the center of the truck's bench seat, between two sets of door-wide shoulders, Wayne's and Shane's. We collected Shane at the airport Friday night and he's been staying in our guest room.

"Our." I'm still learning to say that word without a visible gulp. I moved in a week and a half ago, just after I started my new job. I've panicked once or twice, but my angst is easing.

*

Shane planned this trip as soon as he heard about Terry — it took him a few days to arrange the time off, but he was adamant about coming. Saturday, he borrowed my car and spent the morning hiking some cliff trails with Terry, walking and talking. Terry has found it surprisingly easy to open up to him. Ironically, for years Terry slammed Shane for his mistakes, but Shane doesn't pass judgment on his brother. He understands highs and lows better than most.

In the afternoon, Shane went surfing at The Hook; the swell was just starting to build. Weekends draw surfers from over the hill, so the lineup was crowded and aggressive. Shane mixed it up with a "Silicon Surfer," as he called him, who was driving a "Beamer with brand new surf racks, sure sign of a kook." He said the young guy, who'd paddled out at the same time as him, shoulder-hopped him a couple of times, until one wave where they were scrambling once again side-by-side. Shane let up at the last second, shoved the tail of the guy's board forward and caused him to "go over the falls for a true Hook-style drilling, heh, heh, heh."

When he rode in, there was a dent in the Honda's back right door where the guy had kicked it.

Later, I heard from Craig that Andy broke up the fight. Shane says he'll pay for the repair to my car. Oh, sure. With all the good that's come from this trip, I've stuffed my anger. Wayne wasn't sure how to react. He's still trying to figure out how to deal with the ups and downs of Shane, the lulls and the punishing rogue emotional waves.

Terry has been back home with Jenna and the kids since he left the hospital. They've been seeing a couples' counselor, working on their relationship and re-evaluating their work habits and goals. Striving ceaselessly may be the American way, but it can be toxic.

He's interviewed for a couple of jobs, but hasn't hit on the right fit yet. Looking at him, he seems healthy, robust. But he continues to suffer from headaches and occasional hand tremors. In time, his doc says that these physical leftovers from the carbon monoxide will fade away. His mental healing will take longer.

Terry told Shane about Anton's attempt to kidnap me, his violent death and me getting shot. I've kept the scar on my shoulder covered, but he'd asked to see it. He gently ran his fingers across the raised red skin and pulled me into a long tight hug.

"I'm so sorry, Dana. You nearly died because of me. It's fucking disgusting. How can I make amends for *that*? I never want to be that person again, a low-life whose selfish actions hurt his family and friends."

He'd told me this right after he said he'd pay for the damage to my newly dented car. He's utterly blind to the paradox.

*

At the parking lot, Shane leaps out of the truck and peers through Wayne's scratched ancient binoculars to get a closer look at the break. Deep blue skies meet shimmering steel blue water. The sound of the crashing waves fills my ears; I inhale the smell of the sea. With a swell this size, the sea mist is visible; like dust in a windstorm it says aloft in the air and changes the colors, softening them.

We watch two sets roll through, as we wriggle into our wetsuits. Two surfers have beaten us out. The surf is overhead and hollow, and that's without the predicted offshore breeze that should arrive later. We're counting on those breezes; they're a surfer's best friend — they hold up wave faces and cause them to break more slowly and peel across, making for longer and smoother rides. When the breeze kicks in, the rides could go from good to outstanding.

Shane is amped up. He's the first to shove his board under his arm and start running across the sand. His hair blows in the light breeze. When he was in the hospital, it was falling out in clumps. Now, it's shoulder length and straw colored. And his wedge-shaped torso is all toned muscle. He says that due to his flexible work schedule, he's able to surf regularly. And when there's no swell he paddles out into

Hanalei Bay on a stand-up paddle board or his landlord's one-person outrigger. Seeing him clean, fit and healthy is uplifting. He's adamant that he intends to stay this way.

By the time Wayne and I make it to the wet sand, Shane has already paddled to the take-off point. As I squat down and wrap my leash around my ankle, he strokes hard into his first wave and snaps to his feet. He drops down the steep, eight-foot face and double-pumps his bottom turn, adding an extra push to boost his climb back up to the wave's crest. At the top, he snaps a powerful, yet-flowing off-the-lip turn and glides down and out, well in front of the curl. His cutback, a deep elegant arc, brings him back to the middle of the curl. He straightens out, tucks and drags his hand, slowing his board. The wave's barrel pitches, covering him.

Wayne and I stand there mesmerized. Shane moves back and forth across the wave's face two more times, leaving deep carving tracks, before he rockets up and over the lip and gracefully drops onto his board. He immediately paddles for the next wave.

Wayne is tongue-tied at first. "Damn, he's so fluid. He dances across the water."

Shane sits up on his board and turns toward shore. He yells to us, his voice booming. "Come on, you kids, get your butts out here! The water's fine!"

We skip through the foam and start paddling.

Wayne and I raise our game, inspired by Shane's skill and enthusiasm. Taking steep drops and following them up with hard carving turns, Wayne surfs with authority. I have moments of style, followed by some spectacular wipeouts. As mere mortals, Wayne and I need several breaks. During my convalescence, I definitely lost some of my stamina. Shane surfs nearly four hours, with just one short break to inhale a sandwich. Ten other surfers join our water world, and although Shane's paddling power enables him to dominate the sets and catch twice as many waves as anyone else, his mastery awes them, and thankfully today his nonstop joking and antics keep the scene friendly and fun.

At midday, we drive back to Half Moon Bay and drop Shane at Joe's house. This afternoon he's trimming a tree in Joe's backyard. Shane says their surefire bickering about the best way to do the job is just one of the many curious forms of male bonding. Later, Terry is picking them up and the boys are going out to a sports bar for burgers.

The next day, Shane flies home, and two days later Terry joins him in the islands for a week-long getaway. Jenna encouraged him to go. "Shane can teach Terry to live life without trying to buy it." They've been stand-up paddling, hiking and attending meetings together. Terry says the AA sessions are supportive and cathartic.

Terry calls on the fifth day to recount a golfing story from the previous afternoon. Shane had scored some discount coupons for a late tee-time at one of the better golf courses.

"Shane golfed in camouflage-colored board shorts and a lime-green surf tee. That should have been a warning for the other duffers."

"Stylish. What happened?"

"His drives were so erratic some guys had to actually duck and cover. Fortunately, with Shane's booming voice, when he called "FORE!" it was audible at more than half the holes." I laugh hard and tell him that I look forward to additional travel reports.

After Terry's call, I should get back to the big feature story I need to deliver by noon tomorrow, but I'm restless and need a little more "writing process," i.e. procrastination, before I engage with the keyboard again. I turn to the boxes stacked against one wall of the studio. It's time I finish unpacking.

I spy one box that's calling me — it's the family photo filer I pulled from the loft closet, avoided opening, and just tossed into the trailer when Wayne and I loaded up my belongings for the trip north from L.A. My move into the bungalow has me looking forward, but am I strong enough to look back too?

I've been meaning to hang a picture of Wayne and me from our Baja trip that I've mounted in a tropical bamboo frame. It was taken on our casita's patio. In the background, the sun is setting in oranges and yellows over the darkening ocean. In the foreground, we're each holding up a perch we caught that day...and Wayne's finger is pointing at his, which is at least four inches longer than my puny one. Laughter is obvious on our tanned faces.

I return from the garage with nails and picture hooks. When I open the photo box, I get caught up for a half an hour sifting through pictures and albums. I select four photos and frames from the box, including one taken of Mom, grinning at the camera, while she's cooking breakfast over an electric griddle. Sunday mornings...those are some of the happiest memories of my childhood. Shane and I would slip out early on our bikes to surf or just to check the break, but if Mom was doing well we knew there'd be a huge spread waiting for us at home. The whole family would be there, and we'd linger over the food. Even Dad would hang out, reading the Sunday paper.

I don't have many conversations with Mom anymore. I think she would be pleased that her family, despite all its troubles, or perhaps because of them, has pulled back together.

I've tried to find news on Ling's trial, but so far very little has appeared on websites. That's a good thing. The news drought is protecting me from myself, forcing me to move on. Shane says he has no interest in seeing any reports on Ling. He calls him "a vortex of evil." One of Dylan's clients says the Mexicans are ramping up their smuggling and local meth production to satisfy demand from former Ling clients. Economics 101, supply and demand.

The photo of Shane captures him carving a deep turn at The Hook when the surf was hollow and overhead. In another shot, Terry is sitting and smiling at the camera; his kids, when they were very young, are perched on each of his knees. Jenna is behind him with her hands on his shoulders. For Joe, I've selected one of my favorites. It's old and faded. He's in his early thirties and strikingly fit, his muscled chest stretching tight a V-neck T-shirt. Trees and a large lawn are visible behind him; it must be a park but I don't remember where the picture was taken. At his knee is me, at about three years old with bangs and a ponytail; my knobby knees stick out of my plaid shorts. One of his hands rests on the top of my head.

I put the framed photos on the floor in a loose collage and play with the arrangement, but I keep coming back to a layout that has the photo of Wayne and me in the center, with the family photos arrayed around us. It represents how I feel today, my partner at my side, my family encircling me. It might not last. But it's enough for now.

Satisfied with the grouping, I measure and mark the wall. I place the hooks and hang the pictures; then I step back to view my handiwork. I move forward and straighten a couple of photos, and pull back again. Two of the pictures are still askew. I leave them be.

—End —

Acknowledgements

Many people helped me through my frustrations, insecurities and self-loathing to finish and publish this novel; they include Brian Grainger, Sabine Bennett, Wendy Grubow, Dan Lyons, Laura Pritchett, and Mark Sharar. And special thanks to Ken and Patty Doler for believing in me and understanding my need to tell this story.

I also want to mention just a few of the authors and books that inspired me. At the top of that list is "Damage" by Josephine Hart. Her writing is so concise and yet she can gut the reader. I was also inspired by Wally Lamb's "I Know This Much Is True" and Jeanette Walls' "The Glass Castle." And kudos to other authors who've written about the Zen of surfing, Susan Casey for "The Wave" and William Finnegan for "Barbarian Days: A Surfing Life." Also thanks to Cheryl Strayed for penning "Wild," a memoir about a woman who takes on an incredibly tough physical adventure that becomes a journey to work out her troubled past.

And here's to all the agents who gave me words of encouragement; you offered glimmers of hope that I could indeed write. To those agents who didn't respond to my queries, or rejected my manuscript with form letters, tell me I can't and I'll work incredibly hard to prove you wrong.

Author's Note: Fact and Fiction

- All the characters in "The Hook" are fictional.
- Half Moon Bay is a real place, and Mavericks is a world-renowned surf break. It is the site of a big-wave surf contest every winter.
- The Hook, Ward Creek and Harborside are fictional breaks, with fictional attributes, but they resemble some Northern California locations.
- Surf lingo is a language all its own. Surfline offers up a cheat sheet to surf-speak at http://www.surfline.com/surfology/surfology_glossary_index.cfm
- Waddell Creek is the name of a beach north of Santa Cruz and south of Half Moon Bay, and it is the site of a wave-sailing contest. The Red Triangle is the name used by many to describe the section of the ocean and coast that has a large population of great white sharks. The description of this location — "One leg of the triangle runs from Stinson Beach out to the Farallon Islands, another goes down to Año Nuevo Island, which is just northwest of Waddell, and the triangle's base runs along the shore between Waddell and Stinson" — is accurate.
- The World Economic Forum at Davos is an event held every year. The discussion of President Barack Obama's comments in advance of the 2009 conference is accurate, as is the discussion of French President Nicolas Sarkozy's keynote at the 2009 conference.
- Bob Diamond was Barclays' investment banking chief in 2009, and his comments from the World Economic Forum can be verified from several sources.

• Cape Blanco is a real point in Oregon and is accurately described; its lighthouse does operate using a second-order Fresnel lens.

• Port Townsend is a port town on the Olympic Peninsula in the state of Washington, and it is situated on the Strait of Juan de Fuca.

• The QuickShop and all other businesses described in Half Moon Bay are fictional, as are Community Hospital and Mercy Hospital.

• Rules and restrictions regarding how and when law enforcement officials may interview rehab patients were enacted in the 1970s. However, the application of these laws varies state by state.

• Meth production information in the novel is factual, though details have been purposely left out.

Despite detailed research, errors can slip through and are a fact of life. The author is solely responsible for any errors in the book and apologizes for any that may be unearthed.

CPSIA information can be obtained
at www.ICGtesting.com
Printed in the USA
BVOW03s0538300317
479737BV00001B/65/P